MR

Praise fo...

Luc...

"Lucy Monroe capture... ... ... the genre.
She pulls the readers into the story from the first
to the last page."
—Debbie Macomber

"If you are a fan of Diana Palmer's like I am,
you definitely need to give Lucy Monroe a try."
—*www.thebestreviews.com*

Louise Allen

"Well-developed characters…an appealing sensual
and emotionally rich love story."
—*Romantic Times BOOKreviews* on
The Earl's Intended Wife

"If you've a yen for an enjoyable Regency-set romance
that takes place somewhere other than London,
pick up *The Earl's Intended Wife*. Louise Allen has
a treat in store for you, and a hero and heroine
you'll take to your heart."
—*The Romance Reader*

Kim Lawrence

"Using strong emotions and vibrant characters,
Kim Lawrence pens a powerful tale."
—*www.romantictimes.com*

"This story is chock-full of passion, sensuality,
tension, love…. Katie and Niko's story lingers
well past the last page."
—*www.romantictimes.com* on *The Greek Tycoon's Wife*

ABOUT THE AUTHORS

Lucy Monroe started reading at age four. After going through the children's books at home, her mother caught her reading adult novels pilfered from the higher shelves on the bookscase. Alas, it was nine years before she got her hands on a Mills & Boon® romance her older sister had brought home. When she's not immersed in a romance novel, she enjoys travel with her family, having tea with the neighbors, gardening and visits from her numerous nieces and nephews. Lucy loves to hear from readers. You can reach her by e-mail at LucyMonroe@LucyMonroe.com or visit her Web site at www.LucyMonroe.com.

Louise Allen has been immersing herself in history, real and fictional, for as long as she can remember. Louise lives in Bedfordshire and works as a property manager, but spends as much time as possible with her husband at the cottage they are renovating on the north Norfolk coast, or traveling abroad. Please visit Louise's Web site—www.louiseallenregency.co.uk—for the latest news!

Kim Lawrence was born and raised in north Wales. She returned there when she married, and her sons were both born on Anglesey, an island off the coast. Anglesey is a little off the beaten track, but lively Dublin is only a short ferry ride away. Today they live on the farm her husband was brought up on. With small children, she thought the unsocial hours of nursing weren't attractive, so Kim tried her hand at writing. Always a keen Harlequin reader, she felt it was natural for her to write a romance novel. Now she can't imagine doing anything else.

Lucy Monroe
Louise Allen
Kim Lawrence

Hot Desert Nights

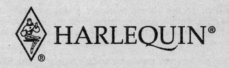 HARLEQUIN®

TORONTO • NEW YORK • LONDON
AMSTERDAM • PARIS • SYDNEY • HAMBURG
STOCKHOLM • ATHENS • TOKYO • MILAN • MADRID
PRAGUE • WARSAW • BUDAPEST • AUCKLAND

ISBN-13: 978-0-373-83721-2
ISBN-10:   0-373-83721-6

HOT DESERT NIGHTS

Copyright © 2007 by Harlequin Enterprises S.A.

The publisher acknowledges the copyright holders of the individual works as follows:

MISTRESS TO A SHEIKH
Copyright © 2007 by Lilles Slawik

DESERT RAKE
Copyright © 2007 by Melanie Hilton

BLACKMAILED BY THE SHEIKH
Copyright © 2007 by Kim Jones

CONTENTS

MISTRESS TO A SHEIKH

Lucy Monroe

CHAPTER ONE

JADE flipped shut her cellphone. "That was Therese."

Khalil looked up from the news reports he read every morning at breakfast, his sensual lips tilted up at one corner. "I gathered that from the loud squeal of delight and gasp of her name when you first answered the phone."

Amused blue eyes seared her with the intensity of his interest. It was always like that…he had a way of looking at people and making them feel as if in that moment they were the only other being in the universe besides himself. It made him a very effective diplomat. Few people ever doubted his sincerity, or the genuineness of his interest in them personally and their country's point of view.

She'd been sucked in just as easily as everyone else by his manner. At first she'd thought she was intensely special to him. Now, she realized he had a knack for making *everyone* feel that way. But not everyone could be special. And if the others weren't…*maybe she wasn't either.*

"Is something the matter?" he asked, his expression going from amused indulgence to concern in a heartbeat.

She shook her head, determined not to dwell on such depressing thoughts. She lived with him. That made her unique, which in its own way was special. Stifling a sigh at her campaign to convince herself, she looked out over Athens. The view from their balcony was an impressive one. The Acropolis in the distance, the wealthy section of the city up close—it was all too gorgeous for words, and she adored it.

She loved living in Greece, and reminded herself that Khalil had opted for Athens as a home base for her sake. It was easier for her to travel out of Athens than Zohra's smaller airport, and here they had friends and acquaintances who acceded to her existence and embraced without question her role in his life.

Unlike his family.

Letting the serenity the view always gave her wash through her, she turned her gaze back to him and smiled. "Wonderful news, actually. Therese has had her baby—or babies, rather."

"Babies?" he asked, with a sardonic lift of his dark brow, the look of concern not completely dissipated from his eyes.

She ignored it, as she ignored so much now. It was the only way to survive. "They had triplets."

"Triplets?"

"Yes. Isn't that amazing?"

"I am sure Claudio is very happy."

"He is. So is Therese. She's in shock…a daughter was born first, which makes her the heir to the throne. Apparently Therese didn't know the Isole dei Rei throne was an equal-opportunity monarchy." Jade laughed at how shocked her friend had sounded.

The diplomat's daughter turned Crown Princess

had never considered the possibility the next king would actually be a queen.

Khalil shrugged, the movement fluid and yet revealing the leashed power of his big, muscular body. Tall for his people, he got both his height and blue eyes from his Dutch grandmother. But everything else about him screamed modern-day sheikh. His black hair was cut short and worn a little spiky, his clefted chin was free of beard stubble, and his clothes suited the Western circles he spent so much time moving in.

They'd been together for almost two years, and she still got shivers just looking at him.

"It is a Western monarchy," he said, following the shrug up with words.

Jade's smile slipped at the reminder of the differences between their two worlds. He came from a long line of sheikhs, and his family's attitudes fit better with the previous century than the current one. She'd never met his parents or his siblings because she was his live-in lover, not his wife.

As far as his conservative family was concerned she did not exist, and Khalil had done nothing to change that perception. When she had first moved in with him she had argued he should. He had responded that he had no choice. He could not change centuries of belief, no matter how much he might want to.

But did he?

If she meant that much to him, why was she still his lover and not his fiancée?

"Therese has invited us *both* to the christening ceremony."

Her emphasis on the word "both" was not lost on either of them. Khalil frowned.

Jade clamped her teeth together on an apology she refused to make. She knew her comment had annoyed him and had been unnecessary. He would take for granted that he had been invited. Unlike her.

The only family members she had met—his second cousin Hakim, and Hakim's wife Catherine—were also preparing to celebrate the birth of a child, their third. Because the rest of Khalil's family had been invited to the celebration in Kadar, Jade was not expected to attend. Catherine had called to invite her and Khalil to a private dinner at the palace two nights later, but it hurt to be excluded from yet another family gathering.

"You know why you cannot attend the official celebration," he said, showing he knew exactly what she was thinking.

It was her turn to shrug. They'd had the argument enough times she knew she would never win it, so she saw no reason to even enter the fray. "Will you be able to work the trip to Isole dei Rei into your schedule?"

"When is it?"

She told him.

He consulted his PDA, bringing his calendar up at the touch of a button. "I have a diplomatic dinner in D.C. that night."

She stood up before he could say any more. "I'll call Therese back and tell her to expect only me."

"I would ask Hakim to attend the dinner on my behalf, for I am going as representative to both Zohra and Jawhar…"

"But he is enjoying the flush of new fatherhood?"

"Catherine needs him."

"Yes." She turned to go.

"Jade."

She stopped without looking back at him. "Yes?"

"Are you upset about something?"

Her body tensed. Should she tell him the truth and try one more time to get through to him? She turned, hope almost drowned by the weight of past experience. "When am I going to meet your parents?" she asked baldly.

He sighed. "I have explained. They do not understand our living together. In their world there are two kinds of women."

"Sluts and virgins."

His mouth set in a grim line. "That is a crude way of putting it."

"But accurate."

He sighed. "I am very happy living with you. You are very happy living with me. My parents have no bearing on that."

"They are part of your life…the part I'm not allowed into."

"I cannot help that."

"So you say."

"Because it is the truth. Must we continue to have this same discussion over and over again?"

"No. As far as I am concerned we don't ever need to have it again."

"Are you sure about that?"

"Quite sure."

"Good."

She nodded and turned to leave again.

"Do not forget we have an official dinner at the U.S. Embassy tonight. Perhaps you will see some old friends."

She supposed that was his olive branch…the reminder that he included her in as many areas of his life as he could.

"I won't forget." She had a full day planned, but intended to be back at the apartment in plenty of time to get ready for the dinner.

She didn't hear him move, but suddenly his hand landed on her shoulder. "Wait."

She looked up at him. "For what?"

"For this."

And she knew he meant to kiss her, but he didn't do it right away. He spent several seconds looking into her eyes, his gaze probing and claiming at the same time. "You are my woman, Jade."

She said nothing. There was nothing to say. She could not deny his words, but being his woman wasn't enough anymore. She wanted to be part of his family. She wanted to have his babies. The envy she felt toward Therese and Catherine made her ashamed, but Jade wanted more from Khalil than a consuming affair.

She wanted to matter to him…she wanted to truly belong to him. In every way, not just sexually. And she wanted him to belong to her.

The realization had been there at the edges of her consciousness for a very long time, but she'd never given definition to the nebulous feelings inside her before this. It had been enough to love him and pray one day he would learn to love her. It was only as she'd begun to suspect that would never happen that she'd realized all the other things she wanted and would never have from this man.

"You are very important to me, *aziz*."

Aziz meant beloved, but she knew she was not his

beloved. She'd used to think that him using the endearment meant he had feelings he was reticent about putting into words. She now saw it the same way she saw her mother's use of the word "darling". Jade wasn't her mother's darling. She was her mother's daughter. The two were not always mutually inclusive.

Neither was being a man's lover the same as being his beloved.

She knew Khalil was happy with her right now, that he still wanted her, but how long would that last if she told him she wanted more? Probably about five seconds...if that long. The knowledge sliced at the moorings of her heart, and she didn't know how long she could stand loving where there was no return on her emotion.

But she didn't know if she could ever walk away either.

"Are you going to kiss me?"

He smiled, predatory certainty radiating from him. "Do you want me to?"

"Maybe." Of course she wanted his kiss.

Because when he kissed her, when he touched her, she felt so connected to him that it was inconceivable they could ever be torn apart. Only deep in her battered heart she knew the inconceivable was all too close at hand.

Unaware of her dark thoughts, he laughed and covered her mouth with his own.

She was expecting a quick kiss goodbye. What she got was a total onslaught to her senses. His hands slid slowly down her arms, leaving a rush of goosebumps in their wake, and his body pressed close, surrounding her with heat that burned hotter than the Greek sun.

He teased at her lips, molding them, slanting his own against them with enticing pressure, until her own parted and he took full possession of her mouth.

She wrapped her arms around his neck and kissed him back, unashamed of the response he could draw from her so easily. This was not just sex…it was love, and the most perfect expression of it that she knew. Every time Khalil gave her his body, racking her own with pleasure, she gave him her heart.

Since the death of her grandparents, he was the only one in the world who wanted it. Her parents gave lip-service to affection, but Khalil valued her emotional generosity in ways that could be measured. Only lately she'd come to understand that was not the same as ever planning to return it.

Refusing to let the painful idea rob the moment of its pleasure, she deepened their kiss, aggressively seeking oblivion from her troubled thoughts.

He groaned, the sound both sexy and frustrated, as he pulled his mouth from hers. "I should not have started this."

"You have places you need to be. So do I."

"The Children's Hope office?" he asked, referring to the relief agency she volunteered with pretty much full-time.

"Yes. We are planning another major gala to raise funds for efforts focused on children affected by natural disasters worldwide. It's going to be huge."

"You can count on my support."

The tension inside Khalil ebbed as his beautiful lover smiled.

She brushed one hand down his chest. "I know."

He loved her affectionate nature. He had been

raised in a culture that gave a kiss of greeting and departure. Physical affection was very natural…though not between the sexes. Even married couples kept their affectionate touching behind closed doors.

Jade took it to a level that tantalized and sometimes tormented him. She was so open with her physical appreciation of him. He did not want that to change. He wanted the relationship they had to remain inviolate. If he were to introduce her to his family they would expect her to change…to be more circumspect with him.

He was in a Catch-22 situation and could see no way out. His parents would never accept his live-in lover as a guest in their home, or anywhere else they planned to be. But he wasn't willing to give up the comfort and joy of his relationship with her to gain their approval. If that were even possible—and he doubted it was.

They were very conservative, and she had two strikes against her. She was not of their people, and she was obviously no longer a virgin.

He didn't care, but they would.

He buried his fingers in her silky, straight blond hair and pressed his forehead against hers. "I don't want to leave you."

"I know that, too." To emphasize her point, she rotated her hips against his hardness.

He groaned again. "You are a tease."

"A tease never follows through. I plan to. Just later."

Images of later made his knees weak. She was so perfect for him. A physical match in every way. At five-foot-seven, she was taller than average—certainly taller than most of his countrywomen—but shorter than him. Yet they fit together perfectly, both in bed and when they were out of it, like this.

Her cat's eyes were dark and mysterious, and her lips were full and kissable. Her curves were neither too large nor small, and she matched his passion with her own so beautifully it left him breathless sometimes.

"Maybe I want you to follow through now."

"And miss your morning meeting?" she asked, but made no move to step away.

He gritted his teeth, but forced himself to let her go. He kissed her forehead, then her temple, but he didn't risk taking her lips again. He stepped back himself. "No. I can't."

She smiled wistfully. "I can't either, but I wish we could."

"So do I."

She moved into the house, but continued to face him. He knew that look. She hated leaving him as much as he hated watching her go.

"We need a vacation. Time alone." With Hakim staying close to home because of Catherine's pregnancy, it had been too long since Khalil and Jade had had time to be together, uninterrupted by his duties as diplomat.

"Apart?" she asked, her face going blank, and he realized she wasn't teasing.

Where had that insecurity come from? "*Together.* I want to be with you with no interruptions."

"Oh." She smiled softly. "That sounds nice."

"Yes, it does. How about after the christening? I could fly down to meet you in Isole dei Re and we could stay on for a few days…bask in the sun and make love until we are fully sated."

A slight frown marred her oval features. "It sounds wonderful, but we'll have to settle for the Greek sun right now, because I've got to get back the day after the christening."

"Why?"

"The gala."

"I thought the idea of you volunteering rather than getting another position with a diplomat was so that you would be free to travel with me."

"I am free to travel with you. But this is a vacation you're talking about, and I can't take one right now. Especially after the trip to Kadar and the christening being so close together."

"Get someone else to take care of your duties."

"No."

"If you were working for me, this would not be a problem."

"I don't want to work for you."

"Why, damn it?" He ground his teeth. He rarely swore, and hated cursing at her. She deserved better, but this was one bone of contention he had a hard time letting go.

"I need to be independent."

"But you are not independent. You are dependent. On me. Your job volunteering for Children's Hope does not change that."

"I don't want a job because I'm your lover. I want to earn my own place, even if I'm not paid for it."

"You were exceptionally good in your position as diplomat's aide when we met. Your former employer was very unhappy to see you go, and I have no doubts you would be equally beneficial to me on my staff."

"But others would not see it that way. They would think I had the job because I am your lover."

"Who cares?"

"I care. And I like my job with Children's Hope." She looked down at her watch and back at him. "I have to go. So do you."

"I am not finished with this discussion."

"I am." She took a step backward, as if emphasizing her point.

He followed her into the room, frustration riding him like a poorly made saddle. "And I am supposed to simply accept this?"

"Yes. My mind is made up. Whether you accept it gracefully or not, though, is up to you."

"You sound very much like my father when you say that."

"Not your mother?"

"No. She would never have argued the point to begin with."

She frowned and continued toward the door as she spoke. "I guess that's just one more way in which I'm not perfect Zohra princess material, isn't it?"

He opened his mouth to respond, but she'd turned smartly and was already out the door on the other side of the room. He wasn't about to make a spectacle for the housekeeper by yelling after Jade. He wanted to hit something, though. He grabbed his briefcase instead.

She'd been right. He could not afford to be late to this morning's meeting. But she'd been wrong about something else. They were going to revisit this idea of her working for him. It was foolish of her to be so worried about what others thought. It wouldn't take long for everyone to see that she did her job exceptionally well.

He'd accepted her need for independence for almost

two years, but he wanted to spend more time with her, and the only way to make that happen was to put her on his staff. Who knew…? If she was a member of his staff, his family might even tolerate her presence at certain functions in that capacity.

She wanted to meet his family so badly? She could bend her stubborn will and make that happen.

But something deep inside told him that it would not be quite that easy.

CHAPTER TWO

JADE stood beside Khalil, talking to a group of diplomats, businessmen and their wives in the large and very elegant reception room. Dazzling chandelier lights glittered off the jewelry on most of the women and some of the men. Twenty-first century diplomacy was not a career for the masses.

She wasn't sure it ever had been. Most diplomats she'd come into contact with either came from money or had made a chunk of it.

They entertained lavishly, talking worldwide politics while showing off designer couture and glitz that made for very interesting press shots. She'd met Khalil for the first time at one of these parties. Like most of the men in the room, his wealth had been obvious in the label and cut of his suit and the fine stitching on his handmade shoes. But that wasn't what had caught her attention.

No, she'd been starstruck from the moment she saw him because he was both gorgeous and incredibly charismatic. That impression had only improved upon acquaintance. She found him to be a man who truly cared about the condition of modern society and his country's place in the political world. He was also charming and very, very sexy.

He had asked her out that night, and then made time in his ultra-busy schedule to see her every day for the next week. They'd made love for the first time after he'd supported her in an impassioned speech about the needs and rights of children. She had moved into his apartment two weeks later.

When he had been directed to move his home base from Washington D.C. to Europe the following month, she'd agreed to give up her job and move with him. She'd enjoyed being a diplomat's aide, but she had still turned down Khalil's offer of a position in the same capacity. She'd gotten her first job because of her father's connection to another former veteran, and the next one she got she wanted to be on her own merits.

It had been Khalil's idea she pursue something in a volunteer capacity, and she'd agreed. He took care of their living expenses, and she had enough in savings to last a long time paying for her own incidentals—he insisted on buying all her clothes and the other things he considered a necessity.

She wondered if she'd made a mistake now. She liked the convenience of being able to travel with him, but she didn't like him seeing her as wholly dependent on him. Nor did she like the way he wanted to dismiss her responsibilities just because she wasn't being paid to do them.

It was a new attitude…at least she thought it was. Her position with Children's Hope rarely conflicted with his desires, and this was the first time she'd refused to take time off to go somewhere with him, but the gala was really important. It had been her idea, and so she felt responsible. It was also an idea she believed in strongly.

Khalil's hand rested gently on her shoulder. "Jade…"

Her gaze shot to his. His blue eyes searched hers as if he was trying to read her mind.

She swallowed. "Did I miss something?"

"I just asked if you planned to apply for the open position on the American delegate's staff?" the wife of another diplomat replied.

"Uh…I didn't realize there was an opening at the embassy."

"I don't think it has been made public."

Jade nodded. Most openings weren't, but she usually heard about such things anyway…through Khalil. Had he known?

"That is news to me," he offered, without her having to ask, and she believed him.

She'd never made any noises about wanting to go to work for the American Embassy, and she was sure he had no fears in that direction. However, it didn't hurt to allay any that might be sparked by the other woman's words. Nor did it hurt for Jade to affirm her feelings in the matter before rumors got started or a job offer got extended that she would have to turn down without causing offence.

For all its glitz and sophistication, the diplomatic community was very like smalltown America in that respect.

She smiled at the woman, but spoke firmly. "I'm very happy in my position with Children's Hope. And the added benefit is that it gives me more flexibility to work around Khalil's diplomatic schedule."

The other woman's gaze turned speculative. "Yes. I can imagine. But that isn't a paid position, is it?"

"No, it isn't," Khalil replied, before Jade had a chance to say anything. "But if Jade wants to work for wages, she can accept the standing invitation to join my staff."

"That would be awkward, wouldn't it? I mean, if you two were to break up she'd be in the unenviable position of looking for a new job as well as a new—" she paused, her gaze skimming over Khalil suggestively "—um…place to live."

The implication she was trying to make would be obvious to anyone with half a brain, and this group was far from stupid. That pause had been on purpose, to allow the others to fill in their own idea of what Jade would be looking for. And it was clear from the older woman's snide tone and pointed look at Khalil that her first thought had not been "place to live" but "sugar daddy", or some other equally derogatory moniker for Khalil's place in Jade's life.

Jade's smile froze on her face, but Khalil's expression lost any semblance of humor. Nevertheless, he said smoothly, "I do not make a habit of looking toward a negative future."

"But then you can afford to ignore the inevitable."

"Far from it. It is simply that the day you speak of is far off, if ever to come."

"Oh?" pressed the woman, sounding not in the least impressed by his assurances. "Are we going to be hearing wedding bells soon, then? I would not have thought your family likely to approve such a match."

Jade had no idea why the other woman was being so bitchy, except that she came from a very conservative old-money background. It might be that Jade's place in Khalil's life offended her. Not only were they not married, but Jade could never be legitimately classified as "one of them."

She bit her tongue on a sharp rejoinder. She'd faced worse than this simply because she was American and had had to keep her dignity for the sake of her former boss. She could do no less for the man she loved and their relationship.

"Jade would make an ideal partner for any diplomat. She is tactful, intelligent and has genuine concern for life beyond the borders of her own small world," Theo, a Greek businessman, spoke up.

He and Jade shared a passion for the welfare of children in war-torn countries, and served together on a charitable committee connected to Children's Hope.

"I should think they would be thrilled to welcome her into their family."

Khalil went stiff beside Jade.

"Would you?" the woman asked with a skeptical laugh. "I always believed the Greek mentality close in many important ways to the one found in Zohra or Jawhar."

"Then perhaps you do not understand either mentality as well as you thought you did," Theo said.

"That is apparent." Khalil's expression and tone mirrored icy distaste. "It is also apparent your husband did not find the treasure I enjoy in Jade. She has never offended a fellow diplomat or staff member, and she does not gossip."

The woman's eyes widened, as if she was shocked by Khalil's response. Jade was totally blindsided by it. He never let his diplomat's face slip. This woman might be married to a minor delegate, but Khalil normally reserved his harsher side for negotiations only. He was good at smoothing over any awkward social moment, and to her knowledge had always done so.

"I didn't mean to cause offense," the woman said, looking as if she was truly regretting her catty comments.

"Didn't you?"

Before she could respond, Khalil took Jade's arm and started moving away. "I believe it is time we said good-night to our host and made our way home."

She didn't even have a chance to say goodbye to anyone, much less thank Theo for his kind comments. She complained about this when they were in the car headed home.

He shifted, and the car sped up. "You wanted to talk longer to Theo?"

"I would have liked a chance to say goodbye politely."

"Perhaps you enjoyed the way he stood up for you?" There was an edge in Khalil's voice she did not understand.

"It's always nice to know that someone you admire has a high opinion of you."

"So you admire him?"

"Of course I do. He's a super-rich tycoon, but he gives time and oodles of money toward improving the lot of kids in war-affected regions."

"Whereas all I do is attempt to maintain peace between volatile countries and affect the political climate of a world torn by financial and natural disasters as well as wars."

She stared at Khalil's profile, shock coursing through her. "You're jealous!"

"Of what should I be jealous? A man you spend little time with, and always in the company of others? I do not think so. You are mine. I know it. He knows it."

"I don't know what all this chest-beating is about, but I am your lover, not your slave. I *belong* to myself."

"That is not the way I see it."

"You consider me some kind of slave?" she demanded.

"No, but you do belong to me."

"Oh, really?" she asked, her own voice going dangerously soft. She had no tolerance for male posturing, and he knew it.

"Yes, really," he said sarcastically. "And, what is more, Theo sees it that way too. He would never make a move on you while you are under my protection."

"Under your protection?"

He turned from the sidestreet into busy traffic. "You know what I mean."

"No, I don't think I do. Please clarify."

"You are mine. I have already said it."

"Your what? Your lover…your girlfriend…your *mistress*?" she asked with disbelieving emphasis.

"Yes."

"Yes, what?"

"All of those."

"You seriously see me as your mistress?"

"I see you as my woman. Are you trying to say you don't see yourself that way?"

Clever. Put the onus back on her. But then he was good at that sort of thing.

"I see myself as your lover, not your mistress," she said, refusing to be trapped in a simplified answer.

"Do you want Theo?"

"No!"

"You belong to me…to *my* bed, Jade."

"I'm more than just a convenient pillow-friend."

"Yes. You are the whole package, and you are mine."

Slightly mollified by that assurance, she said, "As you are mine…and as you belong to *my* bed."

"That is a given."

"It's an equal relationship, Khalil."

"I never meant to imply it was not."

She could believe that. Under all that sophistication beat a primitive heart that he was careful to camouflage most of the time. "So, we agree that we belong to each other…that this is a mutual relationship?"

"Yes."

"Then why are you jealous of Theo?"

"I am not jealous."

"Right."

Silence pulsed between them while he drove, and she watched him with steady regard.

He sighed. "You know me too well."

"Or not well enough."

He shot her a sidelong glance before returning his attention to the road. "Okay, so I was opening my mouth to do the diplomat thing again, and I heard him stand up for you and it made me angry. He was claiming you in a way that made me uncomfortable."

Suddenly she understood. Khalil might be a diplomat and very good at his job, but he was also a very macho man. He was pure alpha, even if he hid it behind a charismatic personality. A natural leader among men, he often held more sway than diplomats from much bigger countries.

And he hadn't liked another man taking a protective stance toward his girlfriend. It was such a guy thing she had to bite back a smile. "You stood up for me too."

"But I wouldn't have."

"And that's what really bothers you, isn't it?"

"Yes."

Theo had taken the path that Khalil now saw as the right one. And he was angry with himself because his habit of diplomacy had gotten in the way of him doing so right off, even if no one else there would have seen it that way.

"I knew you were a diplomat when I got into this relationship. I understand the limitations that role puts on you."

"Do you?" The dark interior of the car cast his angular face in shadow, and she could not tell what he was thinking.

"Yes."

"You don't understand the limitations my family puts on me."

"I don't like feeling you are ashamed of me." Which wasn't exactly how she felt, but a close approximation.

What she really didn't like was that his family was ashamed of her role in his life. That made her feel badly about that role. But she loved him, and could not imagine walking away from him. Not now, not ever.

"I am not ashamed."

"But your parents would be to meet me?" Didn't he understand that was a problem? How much that hurt her?

"They have a different way of looking at life."

"They don't want to meet your mistress?"

He grimaced. "No."

"But I'm *not* your mistress. I'm your girlfriend."

"My family does not see the distinction." He paused, negotiating traffic, but she got the sense he was thinking, weighing what he wanted to say inside his head. "Have you considered that if you were to work for me it is possible they would be open to meeting you in that capacity?"

No, she never had. "Only our relationship could not be acknowledged?"

"Naturally not."

There was nothing natural about it, but she didn't expect him to understand that. They'd been raised very differently.

"Then no, thank you."

He expelled an angry breath. "Why not? You said you wanted to meet my family. This is a way for you to do so."

"Maybe. There is no guarantee."

"Maybe," he acknowledged.

"And even if they did pseudo-welcome me, in the capacity of your employee at certain functions, I would still be excluded from family gatherings?"

"Yes."

She shuddered at the thought of that kind of life. It sounded worse to her than their current situation. It would be like living a lie in front of his family. She would hate that. "Like I said at the reception, I like my current job."

"I want to see more of you."

"If I worked for you, that doesn't necessarily mean you would see me a whole lot more. I hardly ever saw my boss in D.C."

"You would work for me in a different capacity."

"Sex on tap in the office?" she joked, not really feeling all that humorous.

He gave her a sideways glance that made her burn. "Sounds promising."

"No way."

"All right. But how does being my personal assistant sound?"

"You have a personal assistant."

"So I'd have two. Nasir would appreciate the help."

"Nasir could run the United Nations and not break out in a sweat."

"Why are you making this so difficult?"

"Why can't you accept that I don't want to work on your staff?"

"Because I want you there."

"And what you want, you get?"

"I got you, didn't I?"

"Yes, but I don't think you know what do with me."

"You're wrong about that. I know exactly what I *want* to do with you."

"Make love." Her voice was flat. She wasn't feeling entirely comfortable about this conversation.

"That is a bad thing?"

"No, but it can't be the only thing."

"You know it is not."

"Do I?"

"What are you asking me?"

"If I matter to you, why is there a big chunk of your life I'm not allowed inside?"

"You said we never had to have this conversation again."

"You brought it up." Well, technically *she* had.

She couldn't seem to help herself. But he had pursued it.

"I brought up you working for me."

"So I could meet your family in a capacity other than as your shameful mistress. Thanks, but no thanks. At least what we have now is honest, and I'd prefer to keep it that way, if you don't mind."

"I don't make a habit of lying."

"But you aren't above ignoring reality for the sake of family peace, are you?"

He did not reply. His precise, angry movements as he drove the rest of the way home in silence spoke volumes about his mood, however.

They were undressing for bed when she broke the silence. "Did you manage to adjust your schedule so you can attend the christening for Therese's babies with me?"

"I did not say that I would."

"But I knew you would try." That was one area in which he had learned equality pretty early on.

Just as she did her best to co-ordinate her schedule around his, she expected him to make efforts to be there for her on important occasions. She'd told him she planned to go alone only because she'd been irritated by the reminder that she wasn't welcomed by the people that mattered most to him, not because she had seriously expected him not to fix it.

"I did try."

"And?"

"My father does not consider the christening on a par with the political importance of the dinner in D.C."

"And?"

"And you already know that Hakim will not leave

Catherine and the new baby just yet. Nor will he ask her to travel until their child is older."

"Did you explain to your father that this was a personal issue of importance?"

He'd taken off everything but his pants, and stopped with his hands on the fastening. "That would not have been productive."

As usual, her body went haywire at the sight of his torso, the short black masculine curls covering his chest, arrowing down in an invitation she'd accepted many times before. But she could not let herself get sidetracked by her response to him. This was too important. "So, you really expect me to go alone?"

"I am sorry." His frown…the expression in his blue eyes…both said he really was. "I wish I could change it, but in this instance I cannot."

"And do you think me working for you would fix things like this?"

His jaw hardened. "No."

"I didn't think so. It would only make things more convenient for you."

"And you will not work for me because of that? Because the benefits as you see them are not completely equal?"

Soon he'd be asking her why she didn't want to spend more time with him when the answer was that she did. She wasn't going there. It was a slippery slope she was liable to lose her footing on. "I won't work for you because I make my own way."

"For nearly two years you have lived in my home, relying on my support."

"Your point is?" she asked, feeling she might shatter if he said the ugly word "mistress" again.

Her emotions were much closer to the surface than she had known. Her heart, which she'd thought was doing pretty good in this relationship, was actually aching with a pain she had been trying to stifle for months now. It wasn't working any longer, and the hurt was mushrooming inside her with nuclear force.

"My point is that *whether or not you work for me* it will not make you a kept woman. Our circumstances will not change."

"Because you see me as one already?"

"Because you are a beautiful and smart individual in your own right, and working for me will not change that."

The words were the right ones…*diplomatic* and reassuring…but they did not assuage the pain burgeoning inside her. *He saw her as his mistress.* He really did. He always had, too, but she'd never realized it. Because she'd never seen herself that way. But that was why he was so understanding about his family's attitude toward her.

He didn't respect her either. At least not enough to stand up to them on her behalf or to marry her. But men like Khalil didn't marry their mistresses, did they? The woman at the reception had gotten that right.

Now that Jade had lived with him, his family would never accept her as his bride. And he'd known that before he ever asked her to move in. It hadn't mattered to him because he didn't see her in his future either. Why had it taken her so long to see that?

"Jade?"

"What?" she asked as she headed for the bathroom, where she planned to let the tears fall in the shower.

Mistresses didn't let their lovers see them cry, did they?

"Are you all right?"

How did she answer that? Her heart was too raw for any more open and honest communication tonight. "I'm going to take a shower," she said, by way of side-stepping the issue.

His hands landed on her shoulders, and that hurt too. Not physically, but with an ache that was as visceral as any she had ever gotten from a wound. It took everything she had not to flinch. His touch had always given her comfort before, or pleasure. But right now all she felt was the need to get away.

She loved this man, but he had never seen her as anything but a temporary lover.

His thumbs caressed her neck and he spoke close to her ear. "I am truly sorry about the christening. If I could change my schedule, I would."

"Don't worry about it. It's not the end of the world." In the scheme of things it wasn't even a drop in the well of pain drowning her right then.

Warm, conciliatory lips pressed against her nape. "I also apologize for being so stupid about Theo. I know you want only me, as I want only you."

"It's okay." She just needed to get away from him. But she knew if she wrenched herself from his touch, he would follow her and demand to know what was wrong.

That was the last thing she wanted.

"You are being very accommodating." His mouth trailed a warm path down along her shoulder. "Perhaps I can convince you to be even more so?"

The shiver-producing timbre of his voice left her in

no doubt as to what he meant. She should be infuriated, or at the very least turned off by this typically male answer to how to end an argument. Only his voice skated along her nerve-endings, waking feelings that warred with the hurt. Feelings that past experience had shown her could make the hurt go away…if only for a little while.

Feelings her heart begged her not to reject. It reminded her that pleasure was a good place to hide from pain.

She'd learned that lesson when she met Khalil so soon after the death of her grandfather. Coming only two years after the loss of her grandmother, the old man's death had almost paralyzed her with grief. They'd been the two people she'd loved most in the world, and the only two who had truly loved her.

She had hidden from her overwhelming grief in the oblivion she found in Khalil's arms.

She turned to face him, seeking that same oblivion again.

CHAPTER THREE

THEIR eyes met. His were full of sensual promise and the vulnerability of honest desire. He might not see a long-term future with her, but there was no doubt that he wanted and needed her in the present.

Twining her hands around his neck, she pressed herself against him. "You might be able to convince me to share my shower."

"I am one very lucky man." His hands swept down her naked back, inciting a riot in her nerve-endings and leaving a trail of goosebumps in their wake.

"I won't argue with that."

He laughed, the sound rich and warm…like the feel of his body against hers. "You are a minx, you know that?"

"I wouldn't want you to get bored."

"Impossible."

She wished she believed that. But the very nature of their relationship gave it a sell-by date. She just didn't know what that date was. If she were honest with herself, she would admit she didn't want to know either.

"Stop it."

"What?"

"Thinking."

"But I'm not thinking." Okay, maybe she had been. But she didn't want to. Shutting off her thoughts, she brushed side to side and reveled in the zing of pleasure that went through her as her already erect nipples were abraded by the silky curls on his chest. "I just want to feel."

He swept her up into his arms. "You are so decadent."

Curling one arm around his neck, she brushed the brown disk of his nipple with her other hand. "Am I?"

"Yes."

She stilled her fingers. "Is that a complaint?"

"No. Definitely a compliment."

"Good." She went back to touching him the way she knew would drive him crazy.

He carried her into the bathroom, his muscles flexing under her fingers with their movement. He kept himself in optimum shape, with both regular exercise and weight-lifting.

"You've got the whole package, you know that?"

"Whole package?"

"Gorgeous looks, hard muscles, charm, charisma— even the whole money thing."

"You're not super-impressed with the money thing?"

"But the macho thing does wonders for me."

"The macho thing?"

She looked down at where his arms held her securely against his chest. "Definitely the macho thing."

"Ah, that macho thing." He kissed her hard, but

briefly. "It comes with the territory. All sheikhs are supremely macho beings, didn't you know?"

"Well, you definitely have that quality in spades."

"I am glad you think so."

She smiled. "I'm not thinking right now, remember?"

"Sassy."

She kissed the warm brown column of his throat, then bit it lightly, sucking gently before kissing him again. "Sassy, that's me."

"Sexy too."

"You think?"

"I know."

"That's good to hear."

"Enough talking."

She looked up at him, her eyelashes fluttering, but said not a word.

He grinned, the flash of white teeth in his tanned face sending her temperature spiking. He really did have a killer smile. Then he kissed her again, hot and demanding, right on her trembling mouth. She parted her lips for him and, like the marauder he was, he took immediate advantage.

He lowered her legs so she was standing, and he took off his pants. But he never let their lips part, and he kept their tongues dueling in a sensual rhythm that made her sway on her feet. He maintained the connection even as he leaned in to turn the shower on to the preset temperature and water pressure.

She could hear the hiss of water, but was still shocked into gasping when he maneuvered her backward and the multiple jets sprayed her body. The overhead nozzle was off, but warm droplets pulsed against her back and thighs. The massage of the water added to her excitement, and she clung to his shoulders so her knees would not give way.

He finally broke the kiss and turned her away from him, then pulled her back so her shoulders rested against his chest. Water now sprayed directly on her breasts, small jets showering her hardened nipples with caressing force. The spray from the lower nozzles hit her thighs, tantalizing sensitive skin and making her quiver with the need for his touch in her most feminine place.

"This is not exactly a position rife with the possibilities of giving mutual pleasure."

"But I must earn my place in your shower. And do not ever believe that touching you does not please me." He reached for the body-scrubbing gloves she'd bought at a small bath and beauty shop back in the States.

She'd purchased them intending to use the exfoliating texture on her legs after shaving, but he'd soon discovered much more pleasurable activities for them. His arms around her, so she could watch, he donned and then lathered the gloves with her spiced glycerin soap. Its fragrance mixed with the steam in the shower, adding to the sense of sensual intimacy he was intent on creating.

Watching him prepare to touch her, and remembering the ways he had enticed her with the gloves on previous occasions, sent her heart-rate skyrocketing.

As if he knew, he put his mouth against her ear. "You like this, don't you?"

Her body completely open to him, she let her head fall back against him in answer.

He laughed low and nipped her earlobe, making her shiver and swell with need in that secret place only he was allowed to touch. "I like it too, *aziz*. I love caressing your beautiful body in any way, but I think this is one of my favorites."

"I know…" she moaned as he began washing her shoulders with the sudsy gloves.

The contrast of the silky lather and the slightly scratchy surface of the gloves charged her senses.

Moving in small circles that sensitized each individual nerve-ending, he washed every inch of her arms, her back and her legs, before kneeling down to thoroughly wash and massage her feet.

He kissed the base of her spine and slowly, oh so slowly, brought his hands up the front of her legs, his touch so light it was barely there. She shook with longing, and he had not even touched any of the more recognized erogenous zones, avoiding even the more sensitive skin of her inner thighs.

Khalil had taught her that in the hands of her lover her entire body was an erogenous zone. Every caress increased her awareness of the sexual predator so intent on making her experience the outmost reaches of her sensuality. She had never felt so like a woman as she did when Khalil touched her with masculine intent.

And tonight that was exactly how she wanted it. She needed the physical manifestation of her own love to have a complete outlet because tears were denied her. Besides, making love was much better than giving in to a bout of tears.

Crying might be cathartic, but it changed nothing. She'd learned that too long ago to even remember exactly when she'd realized that truth. Perhaps it had been the first time her parents had left her with her grandparents in order to pursue their own dreams and ambitions. Perhaps the second... But certainly by the time she'd been enrolled in boarding school at the age of six. Papa and Nana had come to get her for Christmas break, but even *they* had been unmoved by her tears and pleas to stay with them when the new term started.

She hadn't gone to live with them semi-permanently for another full year.

Not wanting old pain to mix with the volatile brew she was trying so desperately to fight off tonight, she slammed the door on her memories.

"Please, touch me," she begged, knowing that if she did not drown out the hurt with pleasure soon it was going to drown her.

A husky growl sounded from behind her. "I am touching you, *aziz*."

"More...I need *more*."

He kissed the ultra-sensitized skin in the center of her back. "Then you shall have more."

He rubbed light circles on her belly, making her moan and gyrate her hips. Alternately kissing and licking his way up her spine, he made his way to her nape, his hands moving higher with each circular motion until his thumbs were brushing the undersides of her breasts. She shuddered as excitement coursed through her.

He bit down lightly on her nape. "You are so sexy."

"Only for you."

"Only for me." The dark satisfaction in his voice said how much he liked that.

"And you would not do this for anyone else, would you?"

"Never."

He cupped her breasts, the loofah-like gloves stimulating her nipples with their slightest movement.

She ached to have him touch her feminine core, but she was enjoying what he was doing so much she balanced on a razor-point between pleasure and torment.

"It is time to wash you intimately."

"Isn't this intimate?" she asked on a gasp, as he squeezed her breasts before pulling his hands away.

In answer, he stripped off the gloves and then cupped the damp curls hiding her heated inner moisture. "This is fully intimate. Though touching the rest of you is special and private too, *aziz*."

"Good answer..."

One finger dipped between her nether lips. "Open your legs for me, my dove."

She complied as the hot water misted around them and her world shrank to the oversized shower cubicle with its marble tiles and decadent fixtures. Nothing existed beyond this small space and the feel of his hands on her body. His fingers slid down the front, dipping into her swollen sheath.

They both groaned in pleasure at the contact.

His erection pulsed against her, and she reveled in the evidence that she affected him as strongly as he affected her. She needed that. The mutuality of their desire was an imperative in that moment. It affirmed the importance of their relationship to him in the present. And that was all that mattered...all that she would *let* matter.

She reached behind her and caressed his flanks. "I love your muscles."

"I have a muscle that would be very glad of your touch."

She huffed out a laugh. "You are so bad. That is not a muscle."

"Surely it is something very hard."

She would have laughed again, but he chose that moment to tenderly pinch one nipple, and she cried out instead.

"These are very hard also…they are delicious morsels I shall enjoy tasting very soon."

"Oh, yes…"

He didn't seem in any hurry to stop touching her and turn her around. And she couldn't even get enough breath to ask him to. She was too lost to sensation. He touched her sweetest spot and she bucked in reaction, splintering apart with unexpected pleasure on the second circle of his fingertip.

She arched into the touch, hungry for more as she rode another swell of shattering sensation. He'd taken her to this level of pleasure before, where her initial climax was merely the beginning of a journey that would leave her limp and sated. He seemed to know exactly what she needed, and he gave it to her without pause, bringing her body to one climactic peak after another.

It was only as her knees gave way and her body collapsed against his that she realized she'd been crying out so harshly her throat hurt from it. She slid downward, her legs drained of all strength. With one hand on her hip and the other cupped intimately over her, he guided her descent. Hard heat probed her body's entrance, and she took him into her as she settled against his kneeling thighs.

He filled her so completely that she felt way too sensitive to stand further stimulation, and she jerked in reaction. "I can't. It's too much," she whimpered.

Though he was rigid with tension, he did not move inside her, but soothed her instead as he reached out and turned off the water so that it did not hit her in the face. Then he touched everywhere he had before, but now with soft caresses that helped her jumping nerve-endings to cease their cataclysmic riot. Only when she sprawled, boneless, against him did he arrange her so she faced him and begin to move under her.

She wrapped her arms around his neck and let her head rest on his shoulder. He held her hips and thrust into her with short movements that caressed her inside while he kissed her neck, her shoulders and finally her lips. His tongue played with her, echoing the movements of his hard flesh, and he drew a response from her she'd believed impossible.

Incredibly, her desire began to build again, until she was moving with him in slow, sensuous parries to his pelvic thrusts. This time they climaxed together, and her tears mixed with the warm steam.

Khalil stared into the darkness of the bedroom, his body wrapped protectively around Jade's. She was fast asleep, her breathing a steady rhythm that told him she would not awake again before morning.

She'd fallen asleep right after making love. Well, not directly after. They'd had to finish their shower first, then dry off and climb into bed, but she had been oblivious to the world seconds after her head touched the pillow. She'd even gone to sleep with wet hair, and he knew how much she hated doing that. He'd dried her hair with a towel, and brushed it out, but even those ministrations had not stirred her.

It bothered him, because it had been months since she'd fallen asleep like this after their lovemaking. Admittedly, he had exhausted her, but even so it was not like her to go to sleep without at least telling him she loved him.

When they had first moved in together she had been dealing with grief over her grandfather's death, and Khalil knew she had used their lovemaking as a solace. She'd often fallen asleep immediately after back then. She'd once told him that his lovemaking was the perfect prescription for the insomnia brought on by grief. She'd said she felt warm and protected…safe…in his arms. He had liked knowing he could make her feel better, that he could comfort her in a way no one else could. But for the past several months they had always talked after making love.

And he liked it.

It wasn't what they talked about that was important, but the feeling of increased intimacy that he enjoyed so much. That time of talking was something in addition to their lovemaking that neither shared with anyone else. It was unique…special…important.

He probably should not be making such a big deal about it, but he didn't like it when Jade was unhappy, and it was obvious his family's continued intransigence regarding her place in his life hurt her. At the very least tonight he had expected her to raise the question of the christening again. He'd been looking forward to it, actually.

He enjoyed their skirmishes, the way she demanded more from him than he had ever thought he could give another person. It told him how important he was to her and reminded him how special she was to him. He should be thanking God for small favors, because he really could *not* change his schedule this time, but the fact she'd given up so easily made him feel uneasy.

It wasn't normal for her. And he was a man who liked his woman to fit her usual patterns. For all that he enjoyed traveling the world with his job, there were certain types of change he would always fight—and any change in Jade was one of them. Even if the change meant things were easier for him.

When they'd first gotten together she'd had to fly to Arizona for her father's birthday. She had wanted Khalil to come with her, but he had refused, citing a busy schedule. He had also been hesitant to meet her parents, not wanting to have Jade hurt if he and her father argued over the fact that Jade and Khalil lived together.

No big deal. He had never reorganized his schedule for his lovers—but then he'd never asked one to live with him either.

Jade had accepted his refusal to accompany her without argument. However, when she'd had Nasir make the flight arrangements she'd requested Khalil's assistant schedule an additional week in Arizona on her itinerary. When Nasir had told him, Khalil had demanded from her to know why she was going to be gone seven days longer than she had originally planned.

He would never forget the determined gleam in her lovely brown eyes when she told him she was just trying to do him a favor and free up some of his time, since his schedule was so crowded. He'd been furious, and had accused her of trying to emotionally blackmail him. She'd been unimpressed and said that if something as important as her father's birthday did not merit a reordering of Khalil's schedule then it was clear they did not hold equal importance in one another's lives. That being the case, he should be glad of a respite from her company so he could focus entirely on his job for a while.

Angrier than he had ever been in his life, he had almost left it at that. But then he'd looked into her eyes and seen the vulnerability that she made no attempt to hide. She had needed him to show her that she was as important to him as he was to her. Finally understanding that, he had been more than willing to make the sacrifice.

She had given up her job and living in her own country for him. He didn't think he could do the same for her, but thankfully she hadn't asked him to. Only to go to her father's birthday.

He had told her that if it was that important, then he would see what he could do. He hadn't made any promises, but she'd trusted him to really try, not just give lip service to doing so. It was the first time she'd told him she loved him.

He'd ended up going. And her father had not said a single word about the fact that Khalil and Jade lived together. He and Jade's mother had treated Khalil like a part of the family, and he had found himself surprisingly pleased by that turn of events. Jade wasn't especially close to her parents, but they were important to her.

Their acceptance had made his relationship with their daughter easier. He wished he could give her the same from his family, but he couldn't. Just as the way Jade lived so independently of her parents would be total anathema to anyone in his family, the fact that she lived *with him* made her an invisible person in his life as far as they were concerned.

Everyone but Hakim and Catherine, that was. They were both as welcoming to Jade as her parents were to Khalil, and for that he was most grateful to his cousin.

Which said nothing to the fact she had taken the news he could not attend the christening of the Scorsolini heir and her siblings so well. Apparently the christening for the babies of Jade's longtime friend was not as important to her as her father's birthday had been.

Either that or she had a surprise retaliatory move in store for him. This time she wouldn't be staying longer, though. She'd already made it clear she could not take that particular week off completely due to her preparations for the gala.

Three days later, Khalil looked down at the memo in his hand and sighed. Nasir had made travel arrangements for both the trip to Kadar, to celebrate the birth of Catherine and Hakim's baby, and for Khalil and Jade's trip to North America. Neither set of arrangements was going to thrill Jade, and he was still waiting for the other shoe to drop in her response to that, but the sooner he told her about them, the better.

He had been half tempted to let Nasir call her office at Children's Hope and relay the news, but Khalil had known that strategy would backfire. Instead of giving her time to cool off before he saw her, it might give her time to stew and marshal a whole set of arguments against both.

Not that she had argued with him about it or even brought either subject up over the past few days. She had been busy with plans for her gala. But he still found her easy acceptance odd and somewhat disconcerting.

She was a demanding, logical, *loving* woman, who could argue rings around most of the men in his family. But for the past few days she'd been serene and, if not loving, accepting. Too accepting. Was it the calm before the storm?

He'd been caught by sandstorms in his homeland before, and the quality of Jade's silence was much like the stillness in the desert before the fury of flying sand swept over an area.

CHAPTER FOUR

DETERMINED to face the worst, he broached the subject over dinner that night. The housekeeper had just gone, leaving dinner on the table as Khalil had instructed. He'd wanted the privacy of eating in for this confrontation…in case Jade got emotional.

The A.C. kept their ultra-modern apartment at comfortable levels, but heat prickled along his neck as he prepared to lob the first salvo. "Nasir has arranged our travel to D.C. and to Isole dei Re."

Jade took a sip of her wine and tucked a straying strand of her straight blond hair behind her ear. "Thank him for me, would you? I've been so busy with plans for the gala I haven't had time to even think about calling a travel agent."

"There would be no need. Nasir is always happy to arrange whatever you require."

She nodded, and shifted in her seat, the movement of her body irresistibly drawing his attention. She'd changed out of the suit she'd worn to the office into a clingy sea-green silk dress with spaghetti straps. It dipped at the front, revealing the shadow of her cleavage, and even though the view was hardly new to him, it was still riveting.

His body reacting predictably, he raised his gaze back to her face.

Her full, sensual lips tilted at the corners in a wry smile of acknowledgement of where his eyes had been looking, but she made no comment. "So, what are the arrangements? I assume you'll be flying in your jet to D.C.?"

Funny that she should mention the christening first, because it was after their trip to Kadar. But it was also the least worrisome of the arrangements. He certainly did not mind starting there. "Actually, we'll be flying to the States together. The jet will then take you down to Isole dei Re, because there are no direct flights to Scorsolini Island from the D.C. area."

"Are you sure you want me to take the jet? I don't mind changing planes."

He waved his hand in dismissal. "It is all arranged. The following day you will take the jet home directly to Athens. I will take a commercial flight from D.C. and should arrive shortly after you do at the airport. We will return to the apartment together."

"But you hate flying commercial."

"It is nothing."

"I really don't mind flying to Miami and then to Athens."

"That will not be necessary." She might feel totally comfortable airport hopping, but he felt better knowing she would be surrounded by his guards while she was not with him.

"Thank you."

So far, so good. She had not made even a single stinging comment about the fact she would be traveling alone to her friend's home. He chose to see that as a good sign, but had little hope their discussion would continue in such a calm manner.

Tension rippled through him. The trip to Kadar had some unforeseen complications. "Now, about the trip to my cousin's home in Kadar…"

"Yes?"

"The family is expected to stay at the palace the night before the christening. Since my uncle's birthday is so close at hand, Catherine wanted to have a dinner to celebrate that as well."

"With the celebration of the baby's birth the next day?"

"Yes."

"That sounds like something Catherine would do. She thinks about everyone."

"Yes."

"I'll be staying at a hotel, then?"

"I am not comfortable with you staying at a hotel alone."

She looked at him as if she was waiting for him to finish, so he did.

"I would prefer you to stay in Greece and join me later." He stared at her, waiting for the explosion such a thought should have elicited, but…nothing.

She simply took a bite of her food and proceeded to chew.

"It is only for two nights. You will join me at the palace for dinner with Hakim and Catherine after the celebration is over and my family has departed, as planned."

"It seems like a lot of traveling for a simple dinner. Perhaps I should give it a miss this time." She spoke in a tone laced with practical assessment and totally devoid of rancor.

"Give it a miss?" he asked faintly, feeling he'd stepped into an alternative reality, where Jade was no longer herself but this ultra-calm, understanding woman who bore no resemblance to his lover.

"You don't think that would offend them, do you?" she asked, without even a hint about how his family didn't seem to care if they offended *her.*

A week ago she would not have been able to let such an opportunity slide. Stunned by her non-reaction, he fought to gather his swirling thoughts. He'd been prepared for an all-out war and had discussed compromises with Hakim—one of which had included Khalil not attending the family parties.

Hakim had assured Khalil that he and Catherine would not be offended, but he had also suggested the time might have come for Khalil to broach the subject of introducing Jade to the family with his father. Hakim, who had lost his parents at a young age, did not understand how very conservative Khalil's father was, though. Their uncle, who had taken Hakim in when he was a child, had approved of his Western wife wholeheartedly.

Khalil's father expected him to marry closer to home, and definitely to a virgin.

Not attending the family function was a last resort, but one he had nevertheless considered. He hated hurting Jade, and had decided that in this instance he was willing to make the sacrifice. Even if it drew his family's wrath. But Jade was making it clear that she expected nothing like that from him.

He forced himself to answer her question in an even tone. "I think Catherine might be hurt, yes."

"Then I suppose I'd better go. Will we be spending the night?"

"I thought that since you are not coming for the first two nights, as we had originally planned, we could stay on for a couple of days afterward."

She thought about that in silence for several seconds. "I think I can make that work."

It amazed him how much information she could store in her mind. He knew she had just gone through her entire schedule for the week in question and had reordered things so she could be absent the latter half of the week rather than the beginning.

"You know, my memory is good, but you rival Nasir for your ability to recall a schedule."

"That's why I was such a good aide."

"And you wonder why I am so keen to have you on my staff."

"I don't wonder." She smiled, her eyes glowing with confidence. "I know I'm good at my job."

"But you won't do it for me?"

"Who would do what I do for Children's Hope?"

"That is a good question. I cannot imagine the organization being happy with you leaving."

"They offered me a paid position again."

"What did you say?" Once he would have taken her refusal for granted, but lately things were different.

"I told them they were better off hiring another staff member since I was willing to do my job without monetary compensation."

"You are right."

"I often am."

"And so modest."

She gave him a cheeky grin just like she used to,

and he dismissed his feelings of unease as being sparked by too much imagination.

The flight to Kadar from Athens was short, and a bit lonely—but Jade did not let herself dwell on that reality.

Her new motto was to live in the moment and not spend time regretting what could not be changed. She'd only spent two nights away from Khalil, but it felt like much longer. Which would make their coming together that much sweeter, she told herself.

It wasn't as if this was the first time he'd left her behind to attend some family function in Jawhar or Zohra. She should be used to his absences. But after the first couple, he had always contrived somehow to take her. They could be together in the hours he wasn't with his family, and she had seen much of his homeland on those trips.

She'd been busy while she had remained behind in Athens. Not only had she had the charity gala to plan, but she had plenty of other ongoing projects with Children's Hope to keep track of. The board hadn't just offered her a job, they'd offered her the directorship when the current director moved on in a month's time. But she didn't want that kind of responsibility.

She loved what she did for the organization, but in the same way she'd realized that she never wanted to be a diplomat she knew she didn't want all the political responsibilities that came along with being director of a worldwide charitable organization. She wasn't sure she wouldn't like a lesser position, though. But that could wait.

She had plenty of contacts and possibilities for when

her relationship with Khalil ended. Incredible that it had taken her so long to realize the relationship *would* one day end. It wasn't as if the catty diplomat's wife had been the first person to make such allusions about Jade's future, but it was the first time she'd really taken them seriously.

Khalil could take the credit for opening her eyes completely. It was realizing that he saw Jade as a mistress and not simply his girlfriend/lover that had ripped her blinders off. Had he always felt that way? He must have, to have moved her in and made her an "untouchable" as far as his family was concerned. But Jade certainly hadn't seen it.

Now it glared at her like a glowing neon beacon, casting its sickly green light over their relationship. She'd considered walking away, but the damage to her heart had already been done. She loved him. Leaving *now* wasn't going to hurt any less than losing him *later.* And it would carry with it the regrets and "if only" thoughts that came with a decision that had an alternative course of action her heart cried out for.

By living in the present and not dwelling on the future she was determined to enjoy as much as she could from their relationship and let the future take care of itself. It was how she'd always handled the too-brief visits from her parents, or her time spent living apart from them as a child.

It had worked then and it would work now. However, she wasn't giving him one more centimeter of her heart. That part of the stupidity was over. Luckily for her she'd also learned the skill of protecting her emotions. She would have employed it earlier with him if she hadn't been so vulnerable to begin with from her grandparents' deaths.

Better late than never, though, right?

Khalil waited for her on the hot tarmac as she climbed down the steps from the jet's door. Dressed in full desert garb, and flanked on both sides by bodyguards who looked a whole lot less intrusive in their stance in his homeland, he looked like the sexy sheikh of every woman's fantasy. His *guttrah* framed his face, making it look leaner and more primitive.

And his robes did nothing to diminish the masculine aura that surrounded him like a living shield. He was all the man—sheikh, or not sheikh—that she could ever want. And for now he was hers, and hers alone.

She smiled at him, knowing she would have to wait until they were inside the limo before he would take her in his arms. She stopped a respectable distance from him, when all she wanted to do was throw her arms around him and hold on tight. "Is the baby gorgeous?"

"What? No greeting?"

"Hello, Khalil. You are looking well." She teased him with the formal greeting of his people. "Now…what does the baby look like?"

He laughed, and started leading the way to the car. "You saw the pictures Catherine sent in e-mail."

"But that was a week ago. I'm sure Baby Hadya's changed a lot already."

Khalil shook his head. "What is it with women and babies? My mother has already decided Hadya is going to be tiny, like her Bedouin great-grandmother."

"She must have similar features?"

"She's a baby…her features are minuscule. How can they be similar to an adult's?"

"Are you saying you saw nothing of Hakim or Catherine in her?"

Khalil shrugged. "He swears she has his eyes."

"And you don't agree?" They were at the car now, and he helped her into the back of a stretch limo with tinted windows. The partition between the front and the back was closed, as was its privacy cover.

"Who am I to gainsay him?" Khalil settled onto the seat, leaving a good foot between them.

"I'm sure you will be no different when you become a father."

"No doubt. But thankfully that day is far into the future."

She said nothing to that, considering that it had to do with a topic she was determined not to dwell on.

The chauffeur closed the door, sealing them in.

With lightning speed Khalil closed the gap between them and pulled her into his lap. "I have missed you, *aziz*," he breathed against her lips.

"Have you?"

He pulled back to look into her face as the car started moving. "Are you saying you did not miss me?"

She bit back a smile. "I was awfully busy."

"Our bed was not too large with only yourself to fill it?"

"I sprawled, and no one stole the covers."

He growled at her teasing and kissed her senseless— which, when all was said and done, was a very nice reward and no incentive not to tease again in the future.

When he finally lifted his head she snuggled into his arms, seeking the warmth she felt only when he held her.

"So you did miss me?" he said with satisfaction.

"Maybe. A little."

He sighed. "You notice I am not too proud to admit I missed you *very much*?"

"I know that you hope to seduce me into your bed and are smart enough to realize that not to have missed me would do your cause grave disservice."

"It is true I have every intention of seducing you, but my admission is not part of it."

"Well, you would say that, wouldn't you?" she drawled.

He made a sound of exasperation. "Stop teasing me, woman."

She nuzzled his neck, inhaling his masculine scent, her body almost shaking from the relief of finally being close to him again. "I thought you liked it when I teased you."

"There is teasing and there is *teasing*."

"And *this* kind of teasing is off-limits?" she asked, between tiny baby kisses to his throat.

"Kissing me is never off-limits, but telling me you did not miss me when I could barely sleep for your absence is not allowed."

"I'll remember that."

"See that you do. And you could greet me with a little more effusiveness after an almost three-day absence as well."

"Oh, you mean if I'd thrown myself in your arms and lip-locked you in front of the pilot and chauffeur you would have been okay with that?" But she knew that wasn't what he meant.

He had wanted her to tell him how much she missed him as soon as she got off the plane, instead of asking about the baby. She knew how his mind worked, but she liked catching him off guard. It kept life interesting, and he rose to the bait so well sometimes.

He tensed against her.

"Do the limits of behavior in my homeland chafe you?"

She raised her head so she could kiss the corner of his mouth, and then smiled reassuringly. "Don't worry about it. We aren't here often enough for it to matter."

She left unsaid the fact that his family did not acknowledge her was far worse than having to control the urge to kiss him. It had all been said before, and it would not be said again...not by her, anyway.

"What if we were to be here more often? Do you think the differences in our cultures would bother you too much?"

"That's not likely to happen, so why worry about it?"

"But if it were."

It was her turn to tense. "Are they wanting you to move your base again?"

"No."

"Then it's nothing worth considering."

"Is that your way of saying it would?"

"Why are you pushing so hard on this?"

"Why refuse to answer?"

"Because I don't have an answer. It's not something I've ever thought about." She'd always instinctively known that if he got called back to Zohra, even if she went with him, she would see less of him than she did in Greece. There would be too many activities and functions at which she would not be welcome.

Not one to dwell on unpleasant realities, she had simply never considered the prospect of living among his people.

"Never?"

"Not like you mean, no. I've lived all over the world for brief periods of time. You know that. I'm very adaptable, okay?"

"All right."

"It's a short ride to your cousin's palace. Why are you wasting it talking when you could be kissing me?"

"I do not know. But I will rectify the omission immediately."

And he did.

Catherine's welcome was effusive. She hugged Jade and kissed her on both cheeks in welcome, before insisting Jade hold the baby right away.

"You do not know what an honor she does you." Hakim's tone was filled with droll humor, but he looked at his wife with tender love that made Jade's heart contract. "After the family visit, and so many others holding our precious new daughter, my beautiful wife swore no one else was going to hold Hadya for at least a week. She has even refused the nanny's services repeatedly today."

"As if you are any better," Catherine chided, her blue gaze mocking. "I caught you in the nursery at two this morning, just staring."

Hakim shrugged. "It was time for her two a.m. feed."

"So you planned to wake her up for it? Is that it?"

"No, of course not."

Catherine's smile said she doubted his strength of

will, and Jade laughed. "Well, I think you both deserve to be as besotted with this darling creature as you like. She's gorgeous."

The baby was so tiny, and right now she was sleeping, but the warm burden felt terribly right in Jade's arms and she had to blink back tears.

"Yes, just like her brothers…she is perfection," Hakim said complacently.

Catherine shook her head. Her reddish-blond hair was pulled into a ponytail that swayed with the movement. "But you knew I did not mean Jade when I said no one else would be holding her."

Hakim winked at Jade, his serious sheikh's demeanor in abeyance, as it so often was around his wife and children. "Naturally not."

"I wish you had been here for the celebration," Catherine said on a sigh.

Khalil tensed, and Hakim frowned, but Jade merely gazed down adoringly at the gorgeous baby in her arms. "It was a family celebration, and I'm not family, but I'm here now."

Catherine opened her mouth, and then shut it again at a significant look from Hakim. She frowned at him and then smiled at Jade. "Yes, you are here now."

"She's so tiny," Jade said, and then laughed. "I'm sure everyone says that."

"Even parents of several children. It's as if we all forget how small a baby can be."

"Well, I've never had one, but I can certainly see the appeal." Hadya's tiny bow mouth puckered in her sleep and Jade's heart caught again, this time with a feeling of longing so strong that she had to stifle an involuntary gasp.

"There's something about holding a baby that makes you want your own, isn't there? I felt that way when my sister had her children. I was far too young when my nephew was born to be a mom myself, of course, but I remember an inexplicable and rather hopeless desire to hold one of my own."

"I know exactly how you felt." And she did…both the unexplained longing and the hopelessness of that longing.

As long as she remained with Khalil Jade knew she would never have the opportunity to be a mom—but then leaving him wouldn't make it any better. She couldn't help feeling it would be a long, long time— if ever—before she let another man into her heart.

"Khalil said you are here for three days. I'm so glad. We've got so much to catch up on."

"Considering how frequently you call and e-mail each other, that is hard to believe," Hakim said with a dry laugh.

"It's not the same," Catherine and Jade said at the same time, and then laughed.

"No, it isn't." Khalil surprised Jade by agreeing, an odd expression in his azure eyes.

Did he mean he had missed her in some special way the last couple of days?

They had certainly talked enough on the phone, and he had e-mailed as well. Early in the morning, usually before she woke, or late at night when she was supposed to be sleeping. He hadn't used the computer's instant message service because he'd called when he had a break from his family. Apparently, the calls hadn't been enough.

But then, considering her role in his life, that should

come as no surprise. She'd never gone in for phone sex, and she was sure he was feeling pretty deprived. He had a strong libido that required frequent outlet.

She didn't mind. She wanted him too…all the time, and with a ferocity that had frankly scared her at first. Until she had admitted her love for him. Then she had seen it as part and parcel off the consuming emotion. Sometimes when they were making love she could tell herself he felt the same.

But she wasn't going to indulge in that kind of fantasizing anymore, she reminded herself.

Catherine's two small sons chose that moment to come hurtling into the room. They insisted on pointing out details they were sure Jade had missed about the baby, and then attacked their papa and Khalil. They started a tickling match that brought a huge smile to Jade's lips.

"You really enjoy children, don't you?" Catherine asked.

"Yes."

"When are you and Khalil going to start a family?"

The question shocked Jade, and at first she didn't know how to respond. But then she remembered that Catherine had always had a different view of the world. She saw things as possible that others thought impossible, and, as much as Jade usually admired her for it, right now that optimism was hurting.

"You're such a good couple, and I'm still not sure I understand why you couldn't be here for the celebration."

"It was for family."

"But—"

"I'm not family, and children aren't something Khalil and I are joint-venturing on."

"But you would both make such great parents."

"Not together."

"I'm sorry. I didn't mean to offend you."

"You haven't. Believe me. I accept my role in his life, and it's not as the mother of his children."

Catherine sighed, her eyes filled with more understanding than Jade had thought she could have. "It hurts to be wanted for what feels like the wrong reasons, doesn't it?"

Jade wondered where Catherine had learned that lesson. She shrugged. "It's better than life alone."

"What is better than life alone?" Khalil asked, one small boy hanging like a sack of grain from his arm.

CHAPTER FIVE

JADE grinned at the child. "Why, life with an arrogant sheikh, of course."

"You have complaints?" Hakim asked Catherine, his tone implying he was certain of a firmly negative answer.

"Only when you race camels."

"Oh, I want to go to another camel race," their oldest intoned, from his spot high on his father's shoulder.

Catherine made a comical look of horror and everyone laughed.

The rest of the day was like that—all very feel-good, family warmth. Jade loved it, and was glad she'd agreed to stay for the extra couple of days. But she had to check her e-mail and return calls about the gala that night before dinner, so she excused herself and did so.

Khalil came in just as she was hanging up on her last call-back. "Everything okay?"

"Just fine. The caterers are donating the food, so that leaves only having to pay for the labor, and the hotel is giving us a deal on the ballroom."

"You certainly know how to get things done," he said, with patent approval.

She grinned. "That's why I get paid the big bucks."

He surprised her by frowning instead of smiling. "Does it bother you not to have a paying position?"

"No. I like my life."

"A month ago you would have said you loved it."

She rolled her eyes, refusing to rise to the bait. "You know what I mean."

"I know that I am glad you are here now." He moved forward and took her into his arms. "I missed you, *aziz*."

"So you said."

"But I am still waiting to hear the words pass your beautiful lips."

"That would be telling."

"So, tell me."

She kissed him instead.

They were on time for dinner…barely.

The children had all been fed and put to bed earlier, and the two couples talked business as well as family. For Hakim and Khalil "business" meant discussing the condition of the world at large. But Catherine wanted details on the upcoming gala, and even made noises about perhaps bringing the family to Athens so they could attend.

"It's a short flight, and Hadya's a perfectly healthy baby."

"I'd love it if you two could come."

Catherine smiled, and then proceeded to chat family gossip, just as if Jade *was* a part of the connected clans from Jawhar and Zohra. They went star-gazing in the observatory after dinner, and Jade loved looking at the stars and listening to Catherine's tidbits of astronomy fact.

Late that night, Jade was curled into Khalil's body after making love. She was on the verge of sleep, her eyes slitted to see the same stars through their open balcony windows.

Khalil's hand brushed a lazy pattern on her bare back. "Do you want children?"

"Why do you ask?" she asked around a yawn.

"Catherine made several pointed remarks about how good a mother you would make."

"Hmm..." Jade snuggled in closer, refusing to let the fact he'd brought up the topic feed the tiny tendrils of hope that remained moored to her heart by the thinnest of threads. "I suppose, someday."

"But not now?"

"My current circumstances are hardly conducive to parenthood." With that, she slipped into sleep.

She'd done it again. Khalil sighed. He'd wanted to talk about this whole children idea with Jade, but she had gone to sleep again.

He'd overheard her tell Catherine that she wanted a baby of her own, but she'd never said anything like that to him. She'd never brought up children at all and, considering her own childhood, he had not been surprised. Only now he felt as if she was hiding part of herself from him—not deceiving him, but simply not sharing that side of her nature with him. As if she thought he would not be interested. But who would have more interest in her desire to be a mother than her lover?

He knew she wouldn't try to trap him into fatherhood. She was too careful about birth control. She took the pill, but insisted he use condoms as well, since no single form of birth control was one hundred percent effective. She'd been the result of an accidental pregnancy, she'd told him once, and was determined her child would never wear such a label.

He didn't always remember the condoms—like the other day in the shower—but she made sure he never got so lax he stopped using them altogether. He had never seen her almost fanatical determination to avoid an unplanned pregnancy as anything but a product of her own growing-up years, often neglected by her parents.

But now he wondered for the first time if she was so adamant about not getting pregnant *by him* rather than not getting pregnant at all. By her own admission she wanted to be a mother. Her actions said she did not want *him* to be the father of her children.

Angry panic he did not understand assailed him. His arms involuntarily contracted around her into a more possessive hold, and she made a noise of dissent in her sleep. He forced himself to loosen his hold, but his heart was beating much too fast and he felt an inexplicable emptiness inside.

But why should he be so agitated? He had always considered parenthood a far-off prospect. Just like marriage. He and Jade were lovers…they were partners…but they never discussed the distant future. Frankly, he had always been too content in the present to do so. It had been enough for him to feel that she belonged wholly to him.

He'd never considered marriage with her. He had not considered it, period, but if he had he could not imagine feeling more committed to her. She was his, and for good or ill he was hers. He accepted it. But did she?

If she wanted to be a mother, but did not consider *him* in the role of father, that meant she did not see him in her future.

He'd never put a label on their relationship, which was why her talk of *girlfriends* versus *lovers* versus *mistresses* had caught him so off-guard. She was simply his woman, as he was her man. But if he *had* put a label on their connection, it would have had permanence inherent in it.

Just as he had never contemplated the future in any detail, he had never contemplated letting her go, and he wasn't about to begin doing so now.

However, in her recent behavior, and her unwillingness to discuss her desire for children, he sensed a sell-by date stamped on their time together. He hated the feeling, and if she thought he was going to tolerate it she was fooling herself.

She'd made many jokes about being with an arrogant sheikh, but she had not yet tapped into the deepest layer of his nature. Like his ancestors before him, he was a possessive man for those people and things he held dear. She could just take a big black marker and scratch out that sell-by date she had fixed somewhere in her head, because he was not about to let her go.

She belonged to him, and it would always be so.

The next day they took a procession of ATVs out into the desert to visit Hakim's Bedouin relatives. The drive through the desert in the early hours of dawn was breathtakingly beautiful. The sun painted the sand with golden rays, and what looked like a huge expanse of nothingness was actually alive with desert blooms, interesting rock formations and unexpected life when she watched closely out the window of the slowly moving vehicle.

Lizards darted in the sand, and she even saw a hawk high in the sky come swooping down on its prey.

Once they'd arrived at the encampment, and stepped out of the air-conditioned vehicles, Jade stood for several seconds soaking in the heat of the dry air. It felt good against her skin, and she closed her eyes to soak in the sounds and smells of the desert encampment. Voices sounded from the tents, mixing with those of the tribe who had come to greet the caravan.

She could smell the lingering scent of incense on the clothes of their welcoming party, and she opened her eyes, worried she'd be caught daydreaming when introductions were made. Hakim's grandfather was a charming, elderly man who had the vibrancy and presence of someone half his age. His dark eyes seemed to see into her very being, and Jade found herself wondering what he had seen.

Once their group was led into the encampment she was immediately fascinated by the Bedouin people and their nomadic way of life. The tents were obviously movable dwellings, and yet the clotheslines hanging with freshly laundered robes and blankets, and the fire pits, as well as the other comforts of camp life, gave their surroundings a permanent feel.

Despite the fact that it had to be moved from encampment to encampment, the tent of Hakim's grandfather was huge and as opulent as any palace. Rich silks covered the walls in the large central room used for entertaining, and the spicy incense that lingered on their clothes permeated the room as well.

The Sheikh had settled against a plethora of brightly colored pillows, and the rest of the family took their places around them. Jade and Khalil sat close together, but not touching.

"This is all too like an Arabian Nights fantasy for words," she leaned close to say to him, as Hakim and Catherine showed off the newest member of their family to others.

Khalil sat with his knees up and his arms wrapped around them. "It is an amazing way of life."

"Do you have Bedouin relatives?"

"No. Unlike Hakim's, my mother's family has no colorful relatives such as these. But were we to look back far enough I am sure I could come up with a connection. Would that please you?"

"Since I could not meet them, I don't suppose it matters, does it?" She regretted the words as soon as she had said them.

She should not have said that about his family. She was determined to focus on the positives in their relationship and ignore the negatives…as long as she could. When she couldn't…well, then their relationship would be over.

Khalil frowned, his gorgeous blue eyes hardening with an unidentifiable emotion.

"Will you be participating in the camel races?" she asked hurriedly, changing the subject before he could answer her ill-conceived comment.

"I prefer a horse when riding."

She smiled. "Catherine stresses out when Hakim races. I'm glad I won't have to."

"I am glad I will not be causing you undue distress as well, but it is a part of my cousin's heritage he cannot ignore."

"Yes, I'm sure. Do you know he's already made noises about teaching his sons to ride a camel?"

"Does this *stress out* Catherine as well?" Khalil asked, with some amusement.

Jade grimaced. "Yes, but she tries to understand the need. She's a really unique and understanding person."

"Are you saying you would not behave similarly?" he asked with that same dark look she did not understand.

"Oh, I'd try to be supportive, but I'd probably bite my nails off worrying."

"Which makes you unique as well."

"I suppose."

"You are definitely special to me."

She smiled vaguely, knowing he did not mean the words the way she needed him to mean them, and refusing to fool herself into thinking that he did. "And you are special to me."

"Of course I am. You have never had another lover."

Her gaze skittered to the others, and she was glad to see they were all still busy cooing over the baby and chatting with Hadya's older brothers.

She frowned at Khalil and said under her breath, *"Don't talk like that."*

He shook his head, his sensual lips quirking. "You have a very conservative nature in some ways, and yet you come from a culture far more open about such things than my own."

"We've already established I'm a bit different."

"Yes, but in a very nice way, *aziz*."

"I wish you wouldn't call me that."

"Why?"

"It's so Hollywood…like calling everyone darling. My mom does that, but it doesn't mean anything to her, and *aziz* doesn't mean anything to you."

He frowned. "I assure you that it does."

She gritted her teeth, angry with herself for raising the issue now. What was the matter with her today? She'd already decided how she was going to handle their relationship, and this was not part of the plan. Besides, the whole endearment thing wasn't something he was likely to understand anyway. In addition, this was probably the worst possible venue to attempt a discussion on the topic.

She needed to get herself together before she caused a scene she did not even want to get into.

She shrugged, forcing a slight smile. "If you say so."

"I say so." He sounded so serious.

Only where a couple of weeks ago she would have taken that to mean he did love her, but just hadn't gotten to the point of being able to say it, she now knew he meant something else.

He cared for her. She was sure of it. But that wasn't the same thing as loving her…as wanting to spend the rest of his life with her or wanting her to have his babies. She wondered if he had any idea how much he had hurt her when he'd asked if she wanted children. It had been like him asking what she planned to do after they broke up.

Her eyes settled on the three children garnering so much family attention and her lips curved in a genuine smile. They were so precious, and it was really wonderful to see so many family members show love and concern for them.

For most of her growing up she'd had her grandparents on her dad's side, but that was all. Her mother's parents were still alive. However, they'd never been close. They weren't particularly close with her mother either, but then…neither was she. Her parents had chosen their path, and it did not include making time or any real space in their lives for their "oops baby" daughter.

She supposed she should be grateful that her mother had given birth to her at all, and she was. However, she planned to give her own children—if she had any—a lot more than just the gift of birth. She was never going to allow her child, or children, to feel like an unwanted part of her life.

Or anyone else's.

Which was why she was so fanatical about birth control. Khalil could not want their baby. Not when someday he would marry a woman his parents would approve of. No child deserved to grow up knowing they were not wanted, even if they were loved.

Jade's parents *did* love her…in their own fashion. But that love did not extend to the kind of sacrifice a parent would normally make for a child. She had always known that she was a complication in their lives they would rather not have had.

That hadn't changed when she'd become an adult, though they had tried to develop a closer relationship with her since her grandmother's death. She'd taken it hard, and her grandfather had made sure her parents had known it.

Since her dad had retired from the military and started a flight school in Arizona, it had been a lot easier for her parents to make the effort. And she'd cooperated as much as she could. She needed them, even if a part of her could not trust them to really love her as she needed to be loved…as her grandparents had loved her.

Yet when Khalil had asked her to move to Greece with him there had been no contest. If her parents had wanted to spend more time with her on a more consistent basis they would have retired to the East Coast at least. But they hadn't. And she knew that she came low on their list of priorities.

Putting her relationship with Khalil ahead of her relationship with them had been a "no-brainer"…even if it had hurt a little.

Losing Khalil, on the other hand, would hurt a lot—and that was not something she was willing to dwell on. She wasn't going to rob her present of joy because her future held certain pain.

She unobtrusively brushed his thigh before folding her hands demurely in her lap.

He sucked in a breath and his eyes promised retribution.

She couldn't wait.

The camel races later were every bit as thrilling—or frightening, as the case may be—as Catherine had assured Jade they would be. The Bedouin men competed with a ferocity of purpose that drew her into the race in spite of herself, and she found herself cheering loudly for Hakim. When he and his brother-in-law came in a close second and first, to almost tie, everyone cheered…even the families of the losing racers.

Jade turned to Khalil, her eyes shining. "That was incredible. It really is terrifying, though… I'm glad you don't race."

"And I had only this moment been reconsidering my stance on riding camels. Your admiration for the riders is obvious."

Jade laughed, the sound mixing with the other joyous noises around her. "They are amazing…they're so intense."

"I am intense about other things, my dove…or had you not noticed?"

She shook her head at him. Had he always had this insecure streak where other men were concerned and she just hadn't noticed it?

"So, you think I lack intensity?"

She gaped. He really was full of unfounded doubts. "Don't be silly. I didn't mean that. I was shaking my head at you for even wondering. Your driven nature is one of the first things that drew me to you."

She'd felt safe expressing her own deeply buried passions because his were so intense.

"What else did you find to appreciate in me?"

"I'll tell you later tonight," she promised with a wink.

But he did not smile. "You need so long to think about it?"

"I prefer privacy to discuss it," she whispered, with a tinge of exasperation.

"Surely it is not only my prowess in the bedroom that recommends itself to you?"

She gasped, but kept quiet, knowing that amidst these people an argument would be seen as even more outrageous than his words. "Khalil!"

She could only hope that in the hubbub around them no one had heard…or understood, since he'd said it in English.

"What has my cousin done now?" Hakim asked from behind her.

She turned and gave him a wide smile. "Congratulations on winning."

"Second place is not winning."

"You two were neck and neck."

Hakim shrugged. "But still there is only one winner. Perhaps next time it will be me."

His sister laughed. "*You and Ahmed*. Will the rivalry never stop?"

"Not until our sons are old enough to race one another." A deep voice belonging to a tall Bedouin sounded from behind her left shoulder.

Ahmed had joined their group, having made it through the throng of well-wishers.

"That is a long way off," Catherine said with conviction, and everyone laughed.

They had dinner that night out under the stars. Multiple campfires set an orange-golden glow over the camp, casting mysterious shadows between the tents. Jade sat between Catherine and Khalil, eating from a plate piled high with Middle Eastern delicacies. Her mouth watered, but she wasn't eating very much.

She was too busy enjoying her surroundings. She loved listening to the cadence of voices around her. She understood enough Arabic to get the gist of the stories, but it would not have mattered if she didn't. She just loved the sound of the language, and the way the voices mixed in a musical rhythm.

The smell of campfires and spicy food mixed with the still but cooling desert air in a pleasing aroma, giving her a sense of being in an entirely different world. She'd experienced many different cultures on her visits to her parents' different homes as her father's assignments had changed, but none had entranced her as fully as the culture she'd found in Khalil's homeland.

Catherine had once told Jade that Hakim had actually kidnapped his wife to this desert paradise when she hadn't been sure of the viability of their marriage. Seeing the two together now, it was hard to believe it had ever been in question. But she did not doubt her friend's words.

She, more than most women, knew both the pleasure and pitfalls of loving a sheikh of the proud family.

"Do you not like the food?" Khalil asked.

"It's delicious." She took a bite and moaned in enjoyment. "I've just been soaking it all in."

"You enjoy the desert."

He'd made it a statement, but she answered anyway. "Very much."

"One day we will have to make a longer trip."

"That would be nice."

"There are places like this in Zohra. Places so magical that when you are somewhere else in the world you cannot believe they exist."

"That sounds wonderful." She bit back the comment that she was not likely ever to see them. "But I am content to enjoy this magical place right now."

"I also. But I am very glad Catherine does not wish to stay overnight with the baby just yet."

"Why?"

"Hakim's grandfather would insist on you sleeping in the harem."

Away from him. She wouldn't like that, but she teased, "That could be fun…more of the Arabian Nights fantasy experience."

"That is not an experience you need, *aziz*."

Feeling secure in his physical need for her, at least, she laughed and went back to her dinner.

CHAPTER SIX

THEY flew back to Athens the next day.

As they settled into their daily routine Khalil felt a constraint between them, but it was not something he could put his finger on. In fact in many ways their relationship was smoother than it had ever been.

Jade wasn't short-tempered. Quite the opposite. She was more even-tempered than she'd ever been in the past. She did not complain when he had to work late, nor did she bring up her lack of a relationship with his family again. Not even through innuendo. He could not deny that he enjoyed the increased sense of harmony with her, and if that had been all it was he would not have questioned it. However, it was not.

In addition to showing little concern for the extra hours he had to spend away from her, she did not call him at odd times during the day any longer. She did not demand equal time with his work or his family or anything else. She was affectionate, but she was not loving, and he discovered there was a vast difference between the two.

He could not remember the last time she had told him she loved him, even in the heat of passion. He thought he'd never put much energy into contemplating the future, but he realized that had not actually been the case when she stopped referring to the future at all. Strange that he should only now realize that a deep part of his psyche had always assumed her presence in his life.

Which meant only one thing…marriage. He'd never considered it, but now he knew it was the only possible long-term solution for them. Two months ago he would have assumed she would be more than willing to fall in with such plans. Now…he was not so sure. It was not a comfortable feeling.

Just the day before he had overheard her on the phone with her parents making plans to visit them in a couple of months. Yet she'd said nothing about her upcoming trip to him. When he asked about it, she told him it was planned for the time he usually went to Zohra, for annual diplomatic talks and time with his family. She explained that she understood there was no choice about him accompanying her and left it at that.

How could he argue with such reasonable assumptions? The answer was that he could not. But they still bothered him. If she had not responded so passionately in bed, he would have thought she had grown apathetic toward him. And sometimes he caught her looking at him with an expression of longing he did not understand.

The times he'd asked her about it, she'd said it was nothing. And she'd been so serene he'd felt a fool trying to press the point. He'd found himself calling her "my dove" rather than "*aziz*", because she tensed up or frowned when he used the latter. He did not understand why and, again, he had asked her about it.

She'd told him he was imagining things, and he could not be sure he was not. He was not a callow youth—a boy who needed constant affirmation of his importance in his lover's eyes—was he? He refused to exhibit such a level of insecurity by pressing a point he was not even sure *was* a point.

But it bothered him.

Jade could not believe the change the last year had wrought in her dear friend Therese, Crown Princess of Isole dei Re. The quiet, dark-haired beauty positively glowed, and it wasn't only with the blush of new motherhood. No—the woman knew she was loved, and it showed.

The rest of the world knew it, too. Prince Claudio made no secret of his adoration for his wife. Not only did he show his affection without even a hint of the cool sophistication men in his position usually hid behind, but he said the words…in easy hearing of others. And Therese just ate it up.

Jade could not have been happier for her friend.

"The babies are gorgeous," she said with a grin, as Therese cooed over one of the frilly bassinets that lined the wall of the oversized royal nursery.

"Yes, they are."

"Trust you and Claudio to wait years and then over-populate the nursery all in one go."

Therese laughed, her soft eyes filled with warm humor and a joy that lit her face from the inside out. "I'll be honest…I'm more than a little glad to be a princess in this instance. I have more help than I know what to do with, and that's a great improvement over trying to cope with three babies at once on my own."

"I have a feeling you and His Royal Highness would have handled it regardless of your circumstances."

"He would not be offended if you called him Claudio, you know."

Jade shrugged. "I met him as a diplomat's aide. He was the most royal of all the royalty I'd ever come into contact with."

"What you're saying is that he intimidated the heck out of you?" Therese said with a laugh.

"Yes. It's hard to overcome first impressions."

"He intimidated me, too."

"But you ended up married to him, so he couldn't have awed you too badly."

"You ended up with Sheikh Khalil, and don't tell me he's any less overwhelming than Claudio."

"I ended up the man's lover, not his wife, and he's a second son…not heir to the throne." But Therese was right…Khalil was as *royal* as any ruling sheikh she'd met during her time as a diplomat's aide.

Therese adjusted the blankets around her infant daughter. "Take away the trappings and a man is still a man. Just look at King Vincente."

The King was not someone Jade had ever considered as having a softer side the few times she'd met him after Therese's marriage to Prince Claudio. It just went to show that even the mighty could fall. "He and Flavia are one of the sweetest couples I've ever seen."

"It took them long enough to find each other again." Therese had moved on to the bassinet of her son, and stood gazing adoringly down at him. "And you know what is funny? The only one who really saw the reconciliation coming is my sister-in-law, Danette. She saw the writing on the wall the first time Flavia spoke to her about the King. You can be too close to a situation to see its true parameters sometimes."

Jade felt there might be a message for her in Therese's words, but she didn't dwell on it. She was not going to spend time with her friend obsessing over her relationship with Khalil.

Jade moved on to the third bassinet and did some gazing of her own. The babies really were beautiful. "Some people take longer than others to get it right."

"How long are you going to take?" Therese looked up and asked, with a teasing but very direct glint in her brown eyes.

"What do you mean?"

"I mean when are you and Khalil going to make it official?"

"Make what official?"

"Your relationship. I'm talking about getting married. Don't you think it's about time?"

"We've only been together two years."

"And you'll be together fifty more. Isn't it time you both faced that and proclaimed it to the rest of the world?"

Unexpected tears burned Jade's eyes, and she turned her body so Therese wouldn't see them. "I don't think so." She could do nothing about the husky tone of her voice.

"Are you two having problems?" Therese asked with concern.

"Nothing new." She sighed. Only her awareness of the problem was new. The reality had always been there. "He's not going to marry me, Therese. It was never a possibility."

"Of course it is. He loves you." Therese had come to stand beside her, and spoke in earnest tones that caught her second son's attention.

He blinked up at the two women with his father's eyes.

"You're wrong. He doesn't love me." It was a difficult thing to admit out loud, but she trusted Therese more than any other friend she had in the world.

The Crown Princess would never betray Jade's confidences.

Therese laid her hand on Jade's arm. "Listen to one who knows—with men like that, things are rarely as they seem. He may not have said the words, but the man's besotted. It's obvious. Believe me."

"So besotted that he made me his live-in lover fully aware that doing so would make me permanently unacceptable as a future mate in the eyes of his family? Even if they would be willing to look outside their own culture for a wife for him, it definitely would not be toward a woman they consider little more than a hussy."

"No," Therese gasped. "You don't really believe that."

"I do, because it's the truth—and you know it. You're a diplomat's daughter, for goodness' sake." It was how they'd met. Jade spun away from the bassinet and the beautiful happiness that the baby represented, because right then it was just too painful to see. "You know the score in that regard in countries like Zohra."

So did she. But somehow, for two years, she'd never put two and two together.

"But Khalil loves you. I know he does."

"Khalil loves his family. He wants me, but desire doesn't last forever."

Surprisingly, Therese smiled, her eyes filled with secret knowledge. "I think you are going to end up surprised on that score."

Jade was able to return the smile, but she shook her head. "You always were an optimist."

"So are you…at least you used to be. Where is that optimism now?"

"I woke up to reality."

"To what you think is reality."

"Therese—"

"Just do not give up on him, or yourself. Promise me you won't do that."

Jade stared at her friend. She'd never seen Therese so passionate about advice. She was usually a better diplomat than the official delegates.

"I'm not going to walk away tomorrow, if that's what you're worried about."

"Give him a chance to make things right before walking away at all."

"What if he doesn't want to?"

"What if he does?"

The Crown Prince came in at that moment, and Jade and Therese did not have another chance for a private chat before it was time for Jade to leave. But she could not put her friend's comments out of her mind.

Therese had found her happy ending, and naturally she wanted the same for her friends. But she'd been speaking the truth when she'd said she was a woman who should know. Jade was probably the only person in the world who had known of Therese's unhappiness in her marriage. She'd known rejection and pain too intimately in her own life not to recognize it in someone else.

Prince Claudio had come around…would Khalil?

Jade had little hope, but she could not dismiss the possibility entirely. And, even though she hadn't said the words, she felt as if she'd made a promise to Therese…one she had to keep even if it meant risking more rejection.

True to his word, Khalil's flight landed shortly after hers, and they were able to return to the apartment together.

The minute they closed the door of their home behind them, he spun her into his arms and gave her a scorching kiss.

"I missed you, *aziz*," he husked against her lips.

"It was only overnight," she said, on a laugh she didn't really feel because she'd missed him too. So much.

"It was thirty-two hours."

"You counted the hours we were apart?" she asked in shock.

His startling blue gaze bored into hers. "You did not?"

"Um…no."

"You did not miss me?" he demanded, no evidence of humor in his voice at all.

Now was not the time to tease. She could see that. Wrapping her arms around his neck, she pressed her body against his. "I missed you."

"A little?" he asked, that unexpected insecurity in ascendance again.

"A lot. More than I have words to say," she admitted generously.

Hadn't he been equally generous already? He'd

made no bones about the fact that he had not enjoyed his time away from her. And it was probably bad of her, but she was glad their separations were so hard on him. It meant he cared.

Or that he didn't enjoy going without sex, a cynical voice taunted in her mind.

Well, she hadn't liked going without their lovemaking either. So even if that was the case, it made them two peas in a pod. She was no more a sex object than he was. To prove it, she kissed him with all the pent-up passion being without him had elicited.

He made a very primitive noise low in his throat and kissed her back, breaking her lips open with his mouth. The uncontrolled sensual aggression excited her as nothing else could have. It wasn't often her sophisticated lover let his need override his insistence on making sure she was with him every step of the way.

She was, anyway.

She found that bottling up her love inside her made her physical need for him even stronger. It was as if her body had to have some way of expressing the love she refused to give voice to any longer.

His hands ran roughly down her back to cup her bottom, and her senses sparked in a conflagration of need that made her heart beat so hard and so fast she could hear the blood rushing in her ears. He lifted her up and she wrapped her legs around his hips, uncaring that her dress had hiked up. She only cared about the feel of him against her bare thighs.

He was moving, but she couldn't stop herself kissing him for long enough to look where he was taking her. All she knew was that each step made his hard body rub against the apex of her thighs. Instantly sensitive, she felt as if the barriers of their clothes were not there.

But they weren't naked, and she wanted to be. Desperately. She wanted to feel smooth skin against hair-roughened masculine contours. She wanted to touch and be touched, and she wanted it all five minutes ago. She hadn't been prepared for this level of response to him, but Therese's words had started something deep inside her…a need for primitive proof of a love she was logically convinced did not exist.

Did it?

Her thoughts splintered as he laid her down on the bed and came down over her. Instead of settling against her, he started undressing them. First his shirt went, then her dress. He kept their lips connected until the last moment, only breaking the kiss long enough to get the fabric over her head. Then he shoved his trousers and briefs down his legs in one impatient move, kicking them off with a sound of relief echoed in her own heart.

He unclipped her bra, pausing to slowly peel the lace away from her burgeoning breasts, using it to roughly tease her achingly rigid nipples before sliding it off her arms. She moaned, arching up toward him, frustrated by the barrier that still existed to their intimacy.

But she could not make her hands unclamp from the silky thickness of his hair in order to remove her own underwear. His hands ran over her semi-nudity with a possessive intent that had a message she could not decipher in her current state. He broke his mouth from hers to kiss his way down her writhing body. He made love to her with his mouth in a frenzy, nipping at her flesh and then soothing it with his tongue. Then doing it all over again.

He spent a long time on her stomach and, though they had been lovers for almost two years, she had never known how erogenous touching her there could be. She was wild by the time he finally hooked his fingers into the waistband of the last bit of silk covering her feminine secrets.

"Please, Khalil, I need you," she groaned, lifting her hips so he could pull the silk off.

"Just as I need you, *aziz*. In this we are well matched." He tugged her panties off with jerky movements and she kicked them free, spreading her thighs invitingly immediately after.

They both shuddered with pleasure as he lowered himself over her into full body contact. The heat of his body against hers felt so good. She groaned and arched her pelvis in demand for total connection.

With unerring accuracy, he speared her humid depths in a single powerful thrust. She cried out against his lips as his body penetrated hers to the very core. He was big, and usually careful not to go too deep, but sometimes that was exactly what she needed. This was one of those times, and she managed to unclamp her hands from his head to grab his butt and hold him just that deep.

The possession was complete and fully mutual.

In this moment he belonged wholly to her, as she belonged to him. His family had no hold on him, her parents had no claim on her…not here, in this bed that had only ever known Jade and Khalil as a couple. This was their world, and she reveled in it with every fiber of her being.

But her hold on him was no match for the passion raging through his limbs, and he set up a rhythm that was fierce and untamed. She matched him thrust for thrust, twisting her hips under him to increase the friction against her sweetest spot. Every movement was incredible pleasure…and exquisite torture. She built toward release faster than she ever had before, but then she hovered on the brink with mind-shattering intensity.

Her whole body strained toward the culmination, but it was just out of reach. He said sexy, enticing things in Arabic, pushing her closer and closer to the cataclysmic moment of pleasure. But she did not go over.

She could barely breathe, and her heart felt as if it was trying to beat out of her chest, and still she shimmered with bliss on the edge of the abyss.

Khalil looked down at her, his eyes dark with desire and feral in their concentration. "Come for me, my dove. Give me the gift of your pleasure."

It felt beyond good, more than wonderful…better than anything she'd yet known in his arms. But at the same time the pleasure was becoming unbearable. She needed the final culmination so badly her throat thickened with tears of frustration. "I want to," she choked. "But I can't."

He smiled wickedly, seemingly unmoved by her desperation…by her tears. "Oh…you can, *aziz*. Believe me." He pushed deeply into her, hitting a spot that increased the agonizing pleasure tenfold. Then, instead of withdrawing, he rotated his hips to caress her clitoris.

Only then did he withdraw almost completely,

teasing her with his blunt-tipped hardness at her very sensitive entrance. She moaned. He repeated the sensual thrust and twist combination twice more and her body detonated. She bowed under him, lifting them both off the bed as muscular contractions so strong they made her entire body convulse shook her.

She screamed, her throat raw with the strength of it, and he gave a powerful shout as his big body shuddered over hers.

He rode out his own climax, bringing her another one almost immediately and then forcing aftershocks from her still-contracting muscles until he finally collapsed on top of her, his breathing every bit as ragged as her own.

They lay in total silence but for their gasping breaths for several minutes.

Then he turned his head toward hers and kissed the shell of her ear. "That was amazing, Jade. You are truly the lover of my dreams."

She would have liked to be the partner of his dreams, but she would settle for this. For now. "I feel the same."

"Yes…you said so. Very loudly there at the end."

She blushed, remembering some of the things she had screamed. But then she reminded herself what he had said as well, and she smiled against his neck. "You weren't very quiet yourself."

"No."

She felt there was something he wanted to say, but he remained silent. That was odd…for him. He rarely practiced the art of avoidance with her.

"Is something wrong?" She could not imagine what it could be after what they had just shared, but still she felt an inexplicable need to ask.

He lifted up and looked down into her face, his own set in serious lines. "You said a lot of wonderful things…but you did not say you loved me."

"Oh."

"You *never* say you love me anymore."

He'd noticed. She should have expected that. He was a very observant guy about most things. "Does that bother you?"

"Yes."

"I don't understand why," she said with blunt honesty. Surely her love was *her* cross to bear, and of little real interest to him.

"Tell me what you mean by that."

"Since you don't love me, I don't see why it should bother you that I don't say the words to you."

"Are you sure I do not love you?" he asked, his expression giving away none of his own thoughts.

"Absolutely sure." And this conversation was draining away all the feelings of wellbeing their making love had given her. "Do we have to get into this right now?"

"Why are you so certain I do not love you?"

"The fact that you have to ask says it all, doesn't it?" she asked, her goodwill dissipating by the second.

"I do not follow that reasoning."

"Look…if you loved me you would have said so by now, wouldn't you?" Was some small part of her hoping he would argue her assumption? "After all, we've been together a while."

"Perhaps I am not good at the words."

The man who knew the right words to avoid war and other global political disasters? She didn't buy that for a second. "It doesn't matter, Khalil."

"It does not?"

"No."

"Why?" He went very tense above her. "Because you have stopped loving me?"

"That isn't something I want to discuss." She frowned and pushed against his chest. "In fact, what I'd really like to do right now is take a bath."

Maybe that would help her relax again. Besides, her muscles felt as if she'd just come off a marathon exercise binge and her body was slick with sweat.

He looked down at her, his expression turned blatantly predatory. "That sounds like a good idea, my dove. I'm very good at washing your beautiful body."

He gave her no chance to protest as he withdrew, rolled to his feet and lifted her in one swift movement.

They were already halfway to the *en-suite* bathroom when she got the wherewithal to say, "I can bathe myself."

"But why should you have to when you have me here so willing to do it for you?" Then his lips sealed hers, and prevented any further protest she might have made.

If their lovemaking on the bed had been wild and wanton, their time in the bath was a lesson in gentle pleasure. By the time he took her back to bed she was feeling replete and very good, with no thoughts of their earlier conversation allowed to disturb her blissful daze.

CHAPTER SEVEN

As THE gala drew nearer, Jade's days grew increasingly hectic. The fundraiser seemed to take on a life of its own as the guest list of the rich and powerful grew daily. She had the connections she'd made through the diplomatic community to thank for that, as well as Khalil's efforts on Children's Hope's behalf. He'd been wonderful.

He'd encouraged several foreign dignitaries to attend, and he'd also purchased tickets for an entire table which he planned to populate with his personal friends and even some family members. Hakim and Catherine were coming, but so was the King of Jawhar, which required an entirely different level of security for the event.

Jade sighed as she looked at her full schedule for the next few days.

"What was that all about?" Khalil asked, before taking a sip of the aromatic Greek coffee they had every morning with their breakfast.

She grimaced, their peaceful surroundings on the balcony doing nothing to calm her fractured thoughts. "I've got back-to-back meetings all day today, and over the weekend."

"I have a luncheon with the American delegates on Saturday." He reached out and touched her hand, the caress light but comforting. "If you can't make it, I'm sure everyone will understand."

She'd forgotten about that—probably because it wasn't written in red in her schedule, like all the last-minute meetings for the gala. She rubbed her temples and then smiled, grateful for his understanding. "I'm glad you won't be needing my services. That will help a lot."

His hand fell away and he went very still, staring at her. "What did you just say?"

"I said that it's going to work out well for me if I don't have to try and squeeze one more event into my already packed schedule."

"No," he said, in the measured tone he usually reserved for extremely delicate negotiations. "You said that you were glad I was not going to be needing your *services*."

"Well…yes…" She looked at him with a puzzled frown.

What was the matter?

"What services precisely are we talking about, here?"

"The whole companion for luncheon thing." He wasn't tracking very well this morning. "Maybe you need more coffee."

"What *companion thing*?" he asked carefully.

"What do you mean, what companion thing? I am your companion—ergo the companion thing."

"You are my woman."

"Is there a difference?"

"Yes, I think there is. *Companions* charge for their services."

"Oh, that kind of companion." She laughed, finally understanding. "I didn't mean *that*, though it is sort of fitting."

"In what way is it fitting?" he asked, in a voice that said he did not get the joke at all.

"Well, we've got the bed thing going on too…" She let her voice trail off when his eyes narrowed with unmistakable anger.

"The *bed thing*?"

"Do you have to repeat everything I say? I was only kidding. I don't understand why you're getting so upset."

"Because you are implying you are my whore."

"I am not. Ladies of the evening get paid nightly. I have it on good authority." She didn't know why she was still teasing him, why she felt the need to push…except there was a small part of her that wanted him to acknowledge her limited role in his life. Even if it was just in jest.

Why that should be, she didn't know. Maybe she was the one who needed coffee. She wasn't sure she was thinking straight. She didn't want to undermine what was left of their relationship.

"Mistress, then." He said the word distastefully, apparently forgetting or merely ignoring the fact that he'd been content to apply the label during a previous conversation.

"That's what I am. You said so," she reminded him.

"You are my lover."

"Fine. Can we drop this now?"

"How are you my mistress?" he demanded, showing zero inclination to drop anything.

And suddenly she wasn't teasing anymore

either…if she ever really had been. She also felt no more capable of dropping the subject than he seemed to be. Now was not the time. She did not want to ruin their rapport. They were good together and she didn't want that to end.

But none of those things could make her bite back the words that needed to be said…had needed to be said since that first devastating discussion when the word "mistress" had been used.

"You support me, but we aren't married. We aren't even engaged. In fact, our entire relationship is based on sex…not love. When it's over, you'll no doubt send me on my way with some extravagant gift and an oh-so-cool goodbye. That makes me your mistress by anyone's definition."

"The independent woman who moved in with me almost two years ago would never have allowed herself to be referred to that way, or dismissed that easily."

"Maybe I'm not her anymore. Not that I expect you would have noticed the change. It's most apparent out of the bedroom."

He winced. "I had noticed a change."

She didn't believe him. "Right."

"This is truly how your see our relationship?"

"Yes."

Something feral moved in his eyes. "And will you move on to another wealthy benefactor?"

The question was like a knife slicing straight into her heart. "No."

Some of the tension seemed to drain from him. "So, you are making this exception for me?" he asked, almost gently.

"You have always been the exception."

"Why?"

"That isn't something I want to deal with right now."

"Maybe I do."

She jumped up from her chair, her nerves at breaking point. She wasn't even sure how they'd gotten to this point...how this conversation had blown up out of nowhere. "Maybe you'd better start thinking about unique parting gifts, because I've given you all I can afford to. One more chunk and there won't be anything left of my heart when we say goodbye."

"And if I tell you I never want to say goodbye?"

Was he saying that? And, if he did, could it matter?

"A man who has not once in two years told me he loves me? Not likely."

"But if I *was* saying it?" he demanded, ignoring her comment about love.

She wished she could dismiss his lack of words as easily. "I would say that was a nice sentiment, but not very realistic."

Suddenly he stood too, and moved to tower over her, his blue eyes saying impossible things. "I refuse to contemplate a future without you in it."

"I'm not cut out to be a real mistress, Khalil. I couldn't stand by while you married another woman and remain a part of your life."

"I would never ask you to," he gritted out.

"But—"

"The only woman I would consider marrying is you."

He hadn't just said that. He couldn't have. They'd never discussed marriage, and she now realized there was a very good reason why. "It's impossible."

"I assure you it is not."

"But your family will never accept me…not now that I've lived openly with you." Her heart hurt as if someone was squeezing it with a vice. "They think I'm the last word in Jezebels for the modern era."

He actually laughed, the insensitive jerk. "They think no such thing."

"They refuse to meet me because I'm your lover."

"They will meet you as my wife." His arrogant assurance was breathtaking.

"You're not serious. You can't be."

His hands landed on her shoulders, their warm strength a painful reminder of what she had to lose when one or both of them agreed to part. "I am very serious, *aziz*. You were wrong when you said I did not love you. I do."

She shook her head. "You can't."

"But I do."

"You've never said."

"A terrible oversight, but not the result of a lack of feeling." He said it so fervently, with such aching emotion.

She stared into his eyes, reading things there that she'd refused to see before…because of their circumstances. But there was too much truth in his gaze to be ignored.

"It's too late," she said painfully. "The die was cast in our relationship the day I moved in with you."

"You did not believe that then."

"But I realize it now."

"Unrealize it, then, for it is not truth. I will never let you go, my dove. Never."

"You'll have to. Your family will not accept me, and you won't dismiss your duty to them."

"Do *you* want our relationship to end?"

"No!"

"Then it will not. For I do not want it to end either."

"It's impossible."

"Stop saying that…do you not know that with faith all things are possible?"

"You can't have thought this through."

"I have."

"No," she whispered, terrified to believe. She wanted it too much.

"You are my woman; I will never allow that to change."

She shook her head, and only as tears splashed from her cheeks did she realize she was crying. "Your family—"

"Will love you as I do."

"You can't love me. You never said so…not in almost two years."

Burnished red scored his cheekbones. "I did not feel the need to."

She didn't believe him. He was talking off the top of his head. But she didn't know how to make him stop. He sounded so serious. "Please, Khalil, don't say stuff like this. Not right now. I feel like I'm holding myself together with bailing wire at the moment…there's just too much going on. You need to think about this stuff, and we'll talk about it later. After the gala."

He sighed. "You do not trust me."

It was true. She didn't. But saying so would hurt too much…maybe for both of them. So she said nothing.

"I have made mistakes, but I will rectify them."

"You can't."

He just smiled, and then he kissed her until her tears stopped and her body went boneless against his.

"I will never let you go," he said again.

She sighed and snuggled into him. Her parents had let her go, and she didn't believe that he wouldn't do the same. Eventually. But it soothed some very ragged edges in her heart to know he didn't want to.

He gently pressed her back into her chair, then bullied her into finishing her breakfast. She did her best to forget they'd had such a shattering conversation.

Over the next week he was as supportive as any woman could wish for. He put his assistant at her full disposal for the final days before the gala, and with Nasir's help she got all the last-minute preparations made.

But, no matter how busy she was, she couldn't forget their breakfast conversation. Khalil wouldn't let her. He didn't browbeat her into talking about it, but now he told her he loved her. Not only when they were making love either, but all the time. He said it when they talked on the phone, he said it when they were alone together in the apartment, and when she was at his office going over final details with Nasir.

She was beginning to believe him. How could she help it? But even if he did love her that didn't mean they could get married and live happily ever after. His family would never approve of the match, and for a man like Khalil, a sheikh in his family, to disappoint his parents would be an intolerable smirch on his pristine honor.

He insisted on acting as if he was courting her too.

He managed to make each day special with something. Whether it was eating out at her favorite restaurant, or dozens of scarlet roses to fill her office, or a beautiful new silk negligee lying on the pillow when she went in to get ready for bed... He reminded her each day that she was indeed his *aziz*, his beloved.

Before her big revelation she'd believed she was that important to him. She was starting to believe it again...maybe even starting to trust him...though her doubts refused to be completely banished.

It all felt strange, but really, really wonderful too, and no matter what the future might hold she would never forget this very special time.

"Are you sure you want to do it this way?" Hakim asked Khalil, his expression somber.

He, Catherine and the children had flown in for the charity gala that morning. Catherine was resting at the hotel with the baby. Jade planned to bring her to the apartment on her way home from Children's Hope. The boys were playing on the balcony with their nanny, while Hakim and Khalil were talking in the living room.

Khalil leaned forward, his certainty stamped on his features. "Yes."

"It could backfire."

Khalil knew that. He also knew he had few other options, and none of them palatable. "We must trust in Providence that it will not."

"That is going to take a lot of faith."

"I must have enough for both myself and Jade. She is firmly stuck in pessimism where our future is concerned. I must prove it will not be as she expects."

"It would have been a great deal easier on you if you had married her to begin with."

"I acted the fool, and now I must rectify my mistake."

"I hope this works."

"If it does not, I have a back-up plan—but it is not one I wish to employ except as a last resort."

"I understand."

Khalil had no doubt Hakim did. The other man was very much like him, and their minds thought in similar paths. He too would have seen the potential for a civil ceremony in Greece followed by getting Jade pregnant as soon as possible. His parents would never reject their grandchild, but he wanted more for Jade than grudging acceptance into his family.

He also wanted more for his relationship with his parents than the coldness that would result from him marrying without their approval. He had been raised to know his duty and to do it. It was an ingrained part of his nature that he did not think his Western contemporaries could understand…not even Jade. But he had a duty to her as well.

She was his wife already as far as his heart was concerned, and he would do whatever it took for her to take her rightful place by his side.

"You are not above taking risks when the situation warrants it," Khalil reminded his cousin.

"As long as your risky behavior is backed up by love, there is always a chance for success."

"Mine is."

CHAPTER EIGHT

THE gala was everything Jade had hoped it would be. Not only had participants been happy to buy tickets, but they had donated money with an open-handed generosity that made her choke with tears as she announced the amount that would be dedicated to the new children-at-risk relief project.

Khalil smile at her from their table near the front dais. She grinned back, but lost sight of him quickly as several associates from Children's Hope came up to congratulate her, as well as many of the guests. She finally made it back to her table to find Khalil speaking to his uncle.

"This is somewhat irregular. Are you sure it is the course you wish me to take?" the King of Jawhar asked, piquing her curiosity.

She could not see Khalil's face, but his tone was rock-solid. "I am certain of my course."

"Then I will do my part."

"I am grateful."

The King nodded his head, accepting his nephew's gratitude with regal aplomb.

Khalil turned to face her as if he had some kind of

sixth sense for her presence. "Hello, my dove. You have had amazing success tonight, have you not?"

"Oh, yes." Still feeling a little shy, she smiled at the King. "I wanted to thank you again personally for your donation to our cause. It was incredibly generous."

He'd given an amount five times greater than any of the other attendees, but his generosity had started when he'd first arrived.

Khalil had introduced her as his girlfriend, and the older man had not so much as blinked before taking her hand and telling her his nephew had obvious good taste. He'd gone on to say that he had heard many good things about her from his foster son/nephew Hakim, and looked forward to getting to know her better.

The King bowed his head to her. "My country is fortunate to be so richly blessed. It is a small thing to share that good fortune with those who are not."

Her eyes blurred with tears again. "Your attitude is truly commendable."

Khalil took her hand and squeezed it. "She takes her position with Children's Hope very seriously."

"Which is commendable in itself, Miss Madison."

She shook her head. "It's nothing. I'm only a volunteer."

"Who takes her position as seriously as any paid staff member, my nephew has told me."

She blushed, not sure if the King thought she should put Khalil ahead of her efforts at the relief organization, or if he was complimenting her. She thought it was probably the latter, but she was feeling disoriented by his ready acceptance and couldn't be sure.

Khalil's parents refused even to meet her, and here his uncle was, treating her as if she was someone special.

He smiled, his dark eyes warm with approval. "You will make a blessed addition to our family."

The words hit Jade like a wrecking ball, and all the air whooshed out of her lungs while her heart ran wild. She turned to Khalil. "What...?"

He smiled when she could get nothing else past lips stiff with shock. "My uncle knows of my plans and approves them."

She turned back to the King. "Thank you," she croaked, and then took a stabilizing breath. "Your support means more than I can say, but I'm afraid the King of Zohra will not be so accommodating."

"My sister's husband labors under a misapprehension about your role in his son's life. I will be at peace only when that has been rectified."

"*You* will be?" she asked, not understanding.

"You are great friends with my daughter-in-law, are you not? She has claimed your bond to be much like that of sisters."

Jade shot a quick glance to Catherine, who was smiling secretively. "I have never had a sister, but I cannot imagine having a better one than her if I did."

"Though she has one sister already, and another by marriage, she assures me she feels the same bond with you."

Catherine nodded vehemently from behind the Sheikh.

Emotion choked Jade again, and she blinked back tears. Since the death of her grandparents she had missed close family ties. She felt as if Catherine were offering her the world. "I am honored."

The King crossed his arms over his chest. "This pleases me. You realize, do you not, that if you are the sister of my daughter-by-marriage, then that makes you *my* relative?"

Jade's mouth fell open and she gasped at the claim. "Um…" She just stared at him, shocked he should say such a thing. "I honestly don't know what to say."

"It is enough if you are content to acknowledge the connection. Are you?"

Khalil went stiff beside her. "I think we should discuss this later…at the apartment."

Was he afraid she would offend his uncle by rejecting the claim? She wasn't about to. She didn't mind being counted as part of the generous King's family, and said so.

The King gave a regal nod. "Then it is done."

That sounded ominous. "*What* is done?"

"Your place in my family is established. I therefore have a responsibility to look out for you as I would any other single female relative."

"You do?"

"Yes."

"But I didn't expect… You don't have to do anything… I'm not sure…"

"Be at peace, *aziz*. My uncle *and I* only have your best interests at heart."

She was getting dizzy with confusion. None of this made any sense to her. "What does that mean?"

"It means that I would like you to return to Jawhar with me," the King replied. "Khalil believes that since the gala is over you might have the free time to do so. I hope he is correct, for that would be the best course of action."

"I do have free time." Time she had looked forward to spending with Khalil. "But I don't know…" She stared up at Khalil helplessly. "Why do I need to go to Jawhar? I don't understand."

"It is necessary, my dove. But not something you should fear."

"Indeed not." The King smiled reassuringly. "Khalil is welcome to accompany you, but your relationship will of necessity be altered slightly."

"Altered? How?"

"Further details of this nature should be discussed in the privacy of my suite." The King's tone brooked no argument, and she was not about to give him one.

She still had duties to perform, but she spent the final hour of the gala in a total daze. All she knew was that she was now considered a member of the King's family, and because of that he wanted her to return to his suite with him and have a discussion…about her relationship with Khalil. She'd got that much out of the odd conversation, but not much else.

It worried her. She couldn't help it. But Khalil didn't seem upset by the turn of events. He had acted startled at first, but then he had nodded his head, as if approving the inexplicable. He'd told her to trust him, to believe they had her best interests at heart.

She clung to those thoughts as she climbed into the heavily guarded limousine. She sat beside Catherine, while the King and Hakim took the seat opposite in the spacious interior. Rather than sitting with his family, Khalil took the empty spot on the other side of Jade. He laced his fingers through hers and held her hand tightly.

The King looked at their clasped hands and frowned. "Your forwardness with my ward is unseemly."

"Your ward?" How had she gone from being *like* a sister to his niece-slash-daughter-by-marriage to being his ward? Wasn't she too old to be *anyone's* ward?

"You are under my protection now."

"Because you said I was part of your family?" she whispered in shock.

"And you agreed to it."

"Well, yes, but…"

"My nephew has compromised your innocence."

Heat climbed into her cheeks while Catherine patted her knee, her expression one of commiseration. "It's horribly embarrassing, and pretty much archaic, but the whole virginity thing is a big deal for this family."

"But I'm not a—"

"You were when we met, my dove, and that is all that matters," Khalil interrupted.

"You told them that?" she asked, aghast.

Catherine sighed from beside her. "You might as well get used to it. Stuff like this isn't as private for them as it is for us."

"It was necessary to impart the information to my uncle," Khalil said soothingly, but Jade was far from feeling soothed.

"Though in truth, even had you not been innocent, I would still have taken exception to the lack of honor my nephew has shown toward you."

"Lack of honor?" She'd thought he was on *their* side.

She realized she'd whispered the anguished words aloud when the King's eyes softened. "Indeed I am. But things are done a certain way in our world, and we must abide by those standards—for they have served our people for thousands of years."

"But…" Were they going to demand she and Khalil stop seeing each other? Her heart contracted at the thought. And if that was what they meant by her traveling to Jawhar, then she wasn't stepping foot outside of Greece.

"Trust me, Jade, all will be well." Khalil kissed her temple, earning another ferocious glare from his uncle, which he was apparently much more adept at ignoring than she was. "Believe me, *aziz.*"

"You wish to marry my nephew, do you not?"

"Isn't that between him and me?"

"Not in our culture."

It certainly seemed as if lots of stuff in their culture wasn't as private as she was used to. "I see."

"Well?" Khalil prompted. "Do you wish to marry me and get started on those babies you told Catherine you wanted?"

"Do you think me answering this will get you out of a proper proposal?"

He laughed softly. "No, but this circumstance will make it possible for me to do so with full family support."

She couldn't believe that.

"We hope," Hakim added.

"Don't be a pessimist," Catherine chided. "Khalil's plan is brilliant, and it's bound to work."

"Khalil's plan?" Jade asked.

"It is *my* will that you place yourself in my hands." The King's stress on the word *my* was not lost on any in the interior of the car, and everyone went silent. "Will you do that, Miss Madison?"

"If I'm your ward, shouldn't you call me Jade, Your Highness?"

"And you will call me Honored Uncle."

"Thank you." She took a deep breath and let it out.

She didn't understand what was going on, but Khalil had said she would have to trust him. That was hard for her, but she did love him, and after the past week and all the reminders of the way he had treated her for the past two years she really did believe he loved her too. Enough. It must be enough, or he would not have approached his uncle to help him.

"I do trust Khalil, and if he says you can help us to be together then I believe it. And I do want to be with him."

She didn't say she wanted to marry him and have his babies, because those were words that should be spoken between two people in private, but she was sure the King got her message.

"I do say it, Jade," Khalil said with an emotional undertone in his voice. "I am honored by your trust."

"Then you will accompany me to Jawhar?" the King asked her.

"Yes."

"Khalil will come, but when you are there you will not live as a married couple because you are not married."

Jade swallowed back her fear of being separated from the man she loved. He had said this would be for her benefit, and she believed him. "All right."

The King nodded and turned his steely eyes on Khalil. "And you will make a trip to the United States to speak to Jade's father, as you should have done two years ago."

"Yes, Honored Uncle."

The King sat back in his seat, his expression complacent. "All will be well."

That "all" included flying out early the next morning on the King's private jet to Jawhar. Catherine and Hakim accompanied them, and for that Jade was eternally grateful. Because it had been decided—sometime last night, after she'd gone to bed alone—that Khalil would make the trip to visit her father immediately.

Jade had a lot of experience of being abandoned, and she had to fight old feelings hard so she would not give in to fears that had no place in their relationship.

She was given an opulent suite of rooms in the part of the huge palace compound reserved for the single women of the family. Catherine brought the children to visit Jade soon after arrival, and they spent the day together while the King and Hakim discussed matters of state.

Khalil called before she went to bed that night.

"I have spoken to your father."

"About what?" she asked, fairly certain she knew, but wanting confirmation.

"I have asked him for permission to court you."

"Shouldn't that have been done a week ago?" she teased, thinking of the wonderful days leading up to the gala, during which he had cherished her in every way possible.

There was a pause at the other end of the line and then a sigh. "As my uncle said, it should have happened two years ago, but I am stubborn."

"Stubborn?"

"I knew I wanted you for my own, but since I was not considering marriage I did not consider it with you. I moved you into my home and I was content."

She hugged the phone close to her ear, wishing he was there. "I was content too."

"But you were not certain of our future."

"Actually, I've never made a habit of thinking too far into the future."

"Nor have I…and my present with you has been all that I could wish."

"It was that way for me too."

"But then it changed? Tell me how, *aziz*."

She bit her lip, and knew that she had to be honest with him. He'd more than earned that right. "It started that night when we went to the diplomatic dinner, a few weeks ago."

"That bloody woman!"

"Yes, well, something she said got me thinking. And then you said I was your mistress."

"I didn't."

"You did."

"I have only ever thought of you as my woman."

"I believe you. But thinking you saw me differently, and waking up to the way your family felt about me, made me realize they would never accept me as a candidate for your wife. I know how important family is to you, and doing what you consider your duty. I felt like a real idiot for never considering how impossible our relationship was, but I couldn't help thinking you had to know before you'd ever moved me in. That made me think you'd gotten together with me believing that someday we would definitely break up. It hurt."

"I am sorry." He was silent again, this time for

several seconds. "The truth is, I was too arrogant to consider such a possibility. But believe me when I tell you, *aziz*, that I never considered a future without you in it. Not from the first time I touched you."

Her throat clogged with emotion and she couldn't speak.

"I love you, Jade. I have from the moment I saw you, and I will until I give up my last breath."

"I love you too, Khalil, so much."

"Your father gave his permission."

"I'm not surprised."

"But I think you will be surprised by the events to come."

"Tell me."

"It is better if I do not."

"Why?"

"Because I can only guess at my uncle's actions, not predict them with a certainty. We will wait and see what he has planned."

"I miss you."

"Finally you say it without being cajoled."

"I always miss you when we are apart."

"And I miss you. I will be at the palace tomorrow."

"Will I see you?"

"You talk as if you are in a prison."

"It feels a little like it. It's a gorgeous prison, but the women's compound is so separate from the rest of the palace, and I have this awful suspicion that if I tried to leave someone would stop me."

"Only for your own protection."

"But they *would* stop me?" she asked, a little fear she could not help winding its way around her heart. Things were so different here.

"Yes. You must not let that frighten you."

"Too late."

"I would never let you be harmed."

She sighed, believing him. "I know… It's just so different."

"Yes, but you and I…*we are the same*. You are my woman and I am your man. Nothing can or will change that."

"You're sure?"

"Absolutely certain."

"I love you, Khalil," she said again, repeating the words inside her heart like a talisman.

The next twenty-four hours were nerve-racking. Catherine visited again, and so did other women of Hakim and Khalil's family. They were all very nice, but none of them breathed a word about what was to come. Not even Catherine.

Jade was only able to see Khalil for the dinner hour, and in the company of a dozen other people. They could not even hold hands, for they were not allowed within two feet of each other.

"My sister and her husband will arrive at the palace tomorrow," the King announced from his spot of honor.

Tension gripped Jade and squeezed her heart. She'd never met Khalil's parents, and she did not want to do so under a cloud, but she didn't know how it could be otherwise.

"I am very pleased to hear this," Khalil said, showing no signs of disquiet at the prospect.

"Will I be meeting them?" Jade asked, with trepidation she could not quite hide.

"If I deem it in your best interests, yes," the King said with inoffensive arrogance. "My esteemed brother-in-law is not unaware of the details of his son's life outside his country."

Was that supposed to make her feel better? She'd never doubted it, but it was that very awareness that made her so unacceptable to the King of Zohra.

"You have nothing to fear in his and my sister's arrival. Had they refused to come, then the situation would not have looked so bright. It is wise to remember that, like any good father and king, he wants only what is best for his son and his country. Luckily for you both, he has my advice based on grave experience with Hakim to guide him."

Since Hakim had married a Western woman, that sounded hopeful, but Jade knew that the family had actually *wanted* the marriage to begin with. Still…she was trying to remember the positive attitude Therese had reminded her she'd used to possess.

In that vein, she called her friend that night, to tell her about the recent baffling events.

"I told you Khalil would not let you go."

"But I don't understand what is going on, and no one will enlighten me."

"It's obvious that Khalil has hatched some plan to get his family's approval for his marriage to you."

"With his uncle's help?"

"Yes."

"It has something to do with the King claiming me as part of his family."

"That is actually extremely clever. It gives you a lot more cache with the King of Zohra than if Khalil was presenting you as his American live-in girlfriend."

"I figured that out. My time as a diplomat's aide wasn't entirely wasted. But I'm still not sure exactly what they are going to do."

"I imagine it is still not entirely settled. You know…things could get rocky. You are going to have to have faith in Khalil's love for you."

"I know."

"I am glad you figured that out."

"It's not easy."

"Believe me…I know. My parents warped my outlook and, frankly, I know yours did yours too…but we have as much hope of happiness and being loved soul-deep for who we are as anyone else."

"I guess you know what you are talking about."

"I guess I do."

They both laughed.

"I'm glad I was wrong," Jade admitted.

"Me too. You deserve happiness. Just make sure you invite us to the wedding."

"I promise."

CHAPTER NINE

CATHERINE did not come to see her the next day, but
shortly after breakfast Jade was called in to an
audience with the king.

He was seated at a long table in a room decorated
with the rich colors and textures of the Byzantine
empire. Another man, who looked like an older version
of Khalil, was seated at the other end of the table in a
matching ornate chair. Everyone else sat in less osten-
tatious chairs along the sides of the table. The Crown
Prince of Jawhar, whom she had met at dinner the night
before, sat to the left of his father, while Hakim sat to
his right. A man she did not recognize, but who also
bore a striking resemblance to the man she loved, sat to
the right of the man she guessed to be the King of Zohra.
Khalil sat to his left, and her own father sat on *his* left.

The protocol was obvious, and a little intimidating.

The King of Jawhar stood, and the rest of the men
at the table followed suit. "Jade, please come and stand
beside me," the King commanded.

She did so, keeping her gaze set firmly ahead, but
her heart was beating so fast it was all she could do
not to tremble.

"I have brought my sister's esteemed husband and King of his people to my home to discuss a grievous insult his son has levied against my family."

Jade couldn't help it, her gaze shot to Khalil. But he looked completely impassive. Not in the least offended by the insult.

She looked at his father, and if she hadn't believed it would be impossible under the circumstances, she would have thought that his eyes, so like Khalil's, gleamed with latent humor. Though his face showed no sign of emotion.

"For the sake of clarity in our negotiations, I would like you to tell this room by what term you address me."

"You are my Honored Uncle," she replied, working to keep her voice steady.

"Do you accede that I have as much right to speak on your behalf as your own father?"

"Yes."

"And you agree with this?" the King asked her father.

"I do."

Jade sent him a grateful glance which he intercepted with a short nod.

"That is all. I believe Catherine awaits you with my grandchildren in the room beyond. You may join her until you are summoned to return."

She didn't know what she was supposed to return for, but she hoped it was to hear what in the world was going on.

"Thank you, Honored Uncle."

Khalil was incredibly proud of Jade as she walked from the room, her carriage erect, her fears hidden from everyone in the room but him. He knew her too well. He wished he could take a moment to comfort her, but he knew that it was crucial he maintain control of his emotions at this juncture.

"You have heard that Hakim and Catherine appealed to me on Jade Madison's behalf because of Catherine's sisterly love for the other woman. You have now heard by her own lips that Jade Madison has accepted her place in my family and that her father has granted my right to speak on her behalf."

"I have heard," Khalil's father replied formally.

"You are aware that for the last two years Jade has lived with your son as a wife lives with her husband and yet they are not married."

"I am aware."

"I am not pleased about this."

"Nor am I."

Khalil's uncle nodded gravely. "Your son accepted the gift of her innocence but did not honor it with marriage. This is not acceptable to me."

"It was a gift."

"But a woman who endows a man with such a precious blessing by rights may expect due respect in return."

"This is true."

"Your son has shamed his name and my family."

The words were not easy ones to take without argument. However, Khalil would accept more than a little humbling of his pride if it meant Jade was given her rightful place in his family and accepted in that place without prejudice.

"There is only one remedy sufficient to redress this wrong."

His father nodded solemnly. "Marriage."

"I would not accept a grudging marriage as redress."

"I am fully willing," Khalil spoke up.

"But is your father willing to receive Jade as his own daughter, to protect her with all the power of his name and his family?"

"She is a woman worthy of my respect and the acceptance of my family," Khalil's father replied, shocking him. "Your sister, my esteemed wife, and our other sons and daughters are eager to meet Khalil's intended."

Khalil stared at his father. He had hoped for acceptance; he had never dreamed his father would be so accommodating.

The older man smiled. "Catherine does not have the reticence of our people, and she has been singing your beloved's praises since the day she met her. She has your mother convinced that no other woman could make you happy."

"Then this—"

"Is a bridge for which I am grateful. You could not bring an unknown woman you had lived with into our family without offending our honored traditions, but now that she has been taken under your uncle's protection I am content to accede to his demand for redress of the wrong. All will be well."

"So, this was your plan all along…to get your uncle to tell your father that you were some sort of dirty dog and had to marry me to save the family name?" Jade asked with shock.

She would never have guessed Khalil would

humble his pride for her in such a way. She'd never felt so loved in all her life.

They were talking on the phone again, because she wasn't allowed to be alone with him until the wedding. Though he had not proposed properly yet.

"Yes, it was my plan, and by the grace of God it worked."

"What would we have done if it hadn't?" she asked, a shiver of reactive fear slipping down her spine.

"I would have asked you to wed me without their approval and then give me a child. My parents would never have rejected their own flesh and blood... But such a course of action would have been difficult for you. It might have been years before you felt the full acceptance of my family, regardless of what lip-service they gave to doing so for the sake of our child."

"So you humbled yourself instead?"

"It is only right. It is my job to protect you, *aziz*. Always."

"Even with your pride?"

"With my very life."

"I love you so much... I wish you were here with me."

"Soon."

"Your mother and sisters are very sweet."

"Catherine has told them how wonderful you are."

"And you?"

"I spoke so glowingly of you when I was finally free to do so that my eldest brother finally told me to shut up."

"He did not."

"Well, not in those words, but close enough."

She laughed, more happy than she had ever been. "So, what about my proposal?"

"My uncle has agreed to a private dinner on the balcony off his office, provided we leave the door open."

Despite knowing that they were being chaperoned quite stringently, it was very romantic.

Dressed in full royal desert garb, Khalil went down on bended knee and took her hands in his. "I will love you into eternity. Will you do me the honor of becoming my wife and the mother of my children?"

"Yes." Then she started to cry.

He kissed her, and it very nearly got out of hand, but the King's assistant was there, clearing his throat discreetly and asking if he could share the happy news with the rest of the family.

The wedding was a huge event. Her honored uncle, the King of Jawhar, insisted on hosting it, and dignitaries came from around the world to celebrate with Khalil and Jade. Therese and her royal husband were there, along with the triplets. As were other friends she had made during her time as a diplomat's aide.

There were hundreds of guests from both sides of Khalil's family, but none more precious to Jade than Catherine…her honorary sister and matron of honor. Therese also stood up with Jade, as well as Khalil's sisters.

The party went late into the night, until Khalil simply lifted her in his arms and carried her off, explaining it was a Western tradition.

Her father and mother had come too, and Jade was glad. She hoped that they would be more involved grandparents than they had been parents, but wouldn't be worried if they weren't. Khalil's family would surround their children with love, just as they had surrounded her.

She couldn't believe she'd known him almost two years without meeting his mother and sisters, but the women had certainly made up for that purposeful oversight by spending as much time with her as possible leading up to the wedding.

She had never been so filled with joy and peace, and told him so as he laid her down on their marriage bed.

"I too am happier than any man has ever been before me."

She just laughed at his exaggeration. But she wasn't laughing ten minutes later, when he had her out of her clothes. She moaned and cried out, but Khalil cursed and stopped touching her when he leaned over and opened the drawer beside the bed.

"What's wrong?" she asked.

"The condoms—they are gone."

"I had them removed." It had taken a full conspiracy with Catherine and the wife of the King's eldest son to see to it, but, as her grandfather had always used to say, "Where there is a will, there is a way."

"You had them removed?" he asked, his arrogant assurance cracked by confusion.

"You aren't the only one with sneaky plans up your sleeve."

"What are your plans?"

"I stopped taking the pill the day after I came to Jawhar."

"You want a baby with me? Now?"

"Very much. It was part of the bargain, remember? Marriage and being the mother of your children."

"*Aziz*, I can think of no greater gift."

Their lovemaking had a quality to it that had never been there before, because for the first time they truly knew that they belonged to each other...in sickness and in health, for richer or poorer...until death they would not be parted.

"I love you, Khalil," she cried out upon completion, as she'd used to.

"And I love you, *aziz*." He shuddered above her, his big body bowed with pleasure. "Into eternity!"

And she knew that he would. Finally, the part of her heart that had grieved the loneliness of her life was totally filled, and it would never be empty again.

For Stacy and JudyF in thanks for the cards
and messages just when I needed them and for
working so hard to help me find the perfect
inspiration for each of my heroes.
You are both very dear to me.
Hugs,
Lucy

DESERT RAKE

Louise Allen

CHAPTER ONE

The Hertfordshire countryside. January 1817

'TURKEY? You want to go to Turkey? Have you taken leave of your senses? A titled lady, a widow, travelling alone? Outrageous! I absolutely forbid it.' Sir Hubert Morvall fixed his stepmother with what he no doubt believed was a look of firm authority, suitable to the head of the household.

'I fail to see how you can stop me, Hubert.' Caroline, Lady Morvall, returned the glower with a smile of sweet reasonableness which she knew was bound to inflame him further. Try as she might to love her stepson, she had never found him anything but a humourless, self-absorbed bore, who seemed indecently pleased to have stepped into his father's shoes and become fifth Baron Morvall.

At her side, her pregnant daughter-in-law produced a faint cluck of distress. 'But you are not out of mourning yet, Caroline Mama,' Clara whispered, her small hands fluttering above her swelling figure, ignoring Caroline's tightened lips at the form of address.

Why a woman scarcely two years younger than herself insisted on calling her *Mama* she had no idea—unless it was Hubert's influence. It made her feel ancient.

'Tomorrow is the anniversary of dear Sir William's death,' Clara persisted, dropping her voice to a reverential whisper.

'And the day I intend putting off my blacks and packing my bags,' Caroline responded briskly. Her husband would have hated this mawkish sentimentality. She could think of no better way to honour the memory of darling William than by making the journey he had read and dreamed about and which he had planned in such minute detail for years; she could almost hear his whisper of approval in the stuffy room now.

The death of his first wife and then the restrictions put on travel by the long war with France had first postponed the journey. Later, his second marriage had made the Baron reluctant to expose his young wife to the rigours of such an expedition. Finally they had decided to go—just when he was struck down totally unexpectedly.

'I have it all organised,' Caroline added, pushing away the bad memories and cheerfully heaping fuel on the flames of Hubert's wrath. He reminded her of the turkey cock at the Home Farm, gobbling with indignation, his incipient double chin quivering. 'I have hired an experienced courier whom I shall meet in London on Tuesday. We sail on Saturday.'

For an awful moment Caroline feared Hubert was about to succumb to a heart stroke, like the one that had carried her husband off at the age of fifty-six, then the puce colour faded a little to crimson, and she breathed again. 'You have been planning all this behind my back. To do such a thing at your age is outrageous!'

'Hubert, I am twenty-six. You are twenty-seven. I fail to see what my age has to do with it. Or what you have to say in the matter, come to that. As you well know, I am legally and financially independent of you, and may do as I wish. I most certainly do not have to make you privy to my plans or my correspondence. I am simply informing you now for Clara's convenience.' She turned to the younger woman. 'I am sorry not to have confided my plans before now, but I knew we would find ourselves having this discussion, and I could not bear weeks of Hubert's opposition.'

Clara took her hand and whispered, 'But Sir Hubert is head of the family now. We must obey him.'

Caroline, as so often, marvelled at Clara's sheeplike obedience to Hubert's pompous demands. It was hardly that she loved him—or at least if she did physical passion did not enter into it. Only the other day, when Caroline had sympathised with her morning sickness, she had confided that the discomforts of pregnancy were amply compensated for by an absence of what she referred to coyly as *marital demands*.

Caroline had enjoyed a short but extremely happy marriage to Hubert's father. Sir William had proved to be a man of abundant physical energy, a huge appetite for life and an undoubted talent for making love to his young wife. Caroline was well aware that he had acquired his ability to please her from years of extramarital adventures, and could only be grateful for it. She had to conclude, looking from Hubert to Clara, that amatory skills, and the desire to acquire them, were not inherited traits.

She missed William's enthusiastically noisy company greatly, but she also pined for his lovemaking. Twenty-six was far too young to learn to be celibate, she concluded with an inward sigh. Although how one went about solving that without finding oneself tied to another husband, one whom she was certain not to like so much as the first, was a puzzle.

'What are you smiling about, Caroline?' Hubert snapped. 'This is not a laughing matter.'

'Nor are your manners,' she rejoined coolly. 'I was just thinking how very unlike your dear papa you are, Hubert. Must I remind you again that I do not have to have your permission to do anything?'

'Papa must have been besotted to leave you so much money without the slightest provision for control or guidance. You will end up like that dreadful Stanhope woman,' he scolded, pacing in front of the fire, which was smoking sullenly.

'Living in a Lebanese palace with a succession of virile young lovers, do you mean?' she teased. 'That is what the gossip says about Lady Hester, I believe. It does not sound such a bad situation to be in. Certainly more amusing than another dreary Season at Almack's.'

Could I take a lover? Would I dare? It would answer the risk of finding oneself permanently tied to a man. It was a scandalous thought—although she suspected William, were he able to advise her now, would be quite encouraging. Her pleasure had always been his first consideration, and he had had little regard for the conventions. But how did a respectable widow set about finding a lover without finding a scandal at the same time?

This intriguing train of thought was cut short by Hubert. 'How dare you mention such a thing in front of Clara?'

'Clara is a married woman. I hardly think she is going to be corrupted by mention of subjects which are common knowledge.' Clara was like all the married women of Caroline's circle, regarding sensual matters as shocking, and apparently considering that respectable women could take no possible pleasure in them. Clara Morvall would certainly not be titillated or tempted by the prospect of a lover.

Caroline got to her feet and gathered up the book she had been reading—*Travels Through Ancient Anatolia* by Andrew Fenton—her notebooks and her reticule. 'My mind is quite made up, Hubert. I am leaving tomorrow.'

The rain spattered against the window as she turned to leave her fuming stepson, and she drew her sombre black shawl defensively around her shoulders. It seemed a year had gone by when she had hardly glimpsed the sun or felt true human warmth; now she was determined never to feel cold again.

The Sea of Marmara: five months later

Caroline leaned on the rail of the ship and narrowed her eyes against the sun-dazzle on the waves. Over there was Asia. *Asia.* She could hardly believe that she was here at last. The long sea voyage, the excitements of calling at Naples and Malta, the discomforts, all faded into unreality as the shore that was her destination drew closer.

She turned a little, away from the Asian side, straining to make some sense of the jumble of minarets, spires and domes that crowded the skyline of the city ahead. Which mosque was the Blue Mosque? Where was the Sultan's harem located? Where was the Golden Horn? The other passengers, apparently familiar with this amazing scene, were all below, packing or gathered round piles of belongings further back near the hatches. Her courier was somewhere below too, and there was no one to ask which building was which.

Before her, inching closer through the haze, was Constantinople, an exotic city of Muslims and Christians and Jews, all worshipping and trading and existing in a city large enough to swallow the population of Essex. It could not be real. It must be a dream, a mirage.

The warm wind picked up a little, shifted and brought with it the scents of spices and woodsmoke, fish and more than a hint of drains, and the dream vanished, replaced by exotic reality. Caroline found herself sighing, as though a weight had been lifted from her shoulders—one she had hardly been aware of carrying.

She truly was here at last. A strange shiver passed through her: part fear, part excitement, wholly—and strangely—sensual. This was not a place to be alone. This was not a place for buttoned-up English restraint and respectability. This was a city for all the senses. Faintly, the sound of music from some unfamiliar high-pitched flute drifted across the water.

The breeze ruffled her thin skirts around her legs, caressed her unveiled face like the touch of soft hands, warm fingers stroking languidly down her limbs, teasing and soothing. Involuntarily her own fingers tightened on the rail as her breasts became heavy with the memory of skilled kisses and, stirring from long months of celibacy, the achingly familiar, intimate pulse of desire began to throb.

In a sensual daydream Caroline was scarcely aware of the tip of her tongue running over the fullness of her lower lip, of the soft flush rising in her cheeks. *I wish I had a lover.* The thought whispered through her mind. *A tall, handsome, charismatic man.*

It is incredible how powerful the imagination is, she thought hazily. It was conjuring him up even as she dreamed. Her heavy-lidded gaze, which had fallen to the deck as she mused, travelled up a pair of long, well-muscled legs to narrow hips and a flat belly. Her fantasy was even obliging by responding to her in a way that the cut of his snug-fitting trousers made quite outstandingly clear.

Caroline felt the pulse in her throat beat harder and let her eyes drift up, away from that disturbing piece of imagination, up to a white shirt exposed by a carelessly open coat, up to broad shoulders, a firm chin and a mouth that was curved in a slow smile of lazily erotic recognition of her needs. *Oh yes.*

With a little sigh Caroline met the grey eyes. The grey eyes fringed with black lashes. The very amused, very *real* grey eyes, belonging to the very real, completely non-imaginary man who was leaning against the rail six feet in front of her.

Oh my God... Caroline could feel the blush flooding her face and stared round wildly for some sort of salvation. A tidal wave, a pirate attack, a raiding party of Circassian slavers. Nothing. And the man was straightening up and coming towards her.

She was the most beautiful, most desirable, most erotic thing he had seen in a very long time. And, given years spent in one of the most exciting and cosmopolitan cities in the world, that was saying something. Drew kept very still, willing the tall blonde to hold the trance she was locked in. He did not flatter himself for a moment that he was the object of her heated—very heated—thoughts. If she could see him at all through that haze of desire, then her imagination had taken over and was superimposing some other man on his form.

But, even so, it was a thoroughly arousing experience to be on the receiving end of all that carnal longing, and Drew felt more than a twinge of envy for the lucky man who would benefit from it.

He was aware of the very physical effect she was having on him, and tried, without any success at all, to control it by making himself focus on those wide, mistily unfocused blue-grey eyes. They were wandering up his body like a caress, and the soft lips were parted, with the tip of her tongue just touching the fullness of the lower one. He tried to ignore the enticing swell of her breasts and the long, slender legs outlined as the breeze whipped her muslin skirts tight against them.

Hopeless. Sooner or later he was going to have to break this spell, or they were both going to faint from the sheer strain of it. Despite the potential embarrassment of appearing in public in a state that could only be described as seriously over-excited, and an increasing feeling of jealousy of this woman's lover, Drew's sense of humour was beginning to get the better of him. He knew that, despite his best efforts to remain both still and expressionless, his mouth was curving into a smile.

That delicious gaze moved to his mouth, hesitated. There was an answering curve of her own full lips that nearly had him moaning aloud, then the grey-blue eyes met his and he caught the precise moment that she came to herself, snapped out of her daydream and realised she was staring lasciviously at a real flesh-and-blood man—and a complete stranger.

How would she react? She was experienced; there was no doubt of that. Whatever had been going through her mind it had not been the romantic day-dreams of a virginal young lady. He found himself hoping against hope that this delicious girl was not going to turn out to be a hardened woman of pleasure, and was rewarded by the wide-eyed shock in her eyes and the furious blush which stained her face.

She was exquisitely confused, her eyes darting round in search of escape or rescue. Drew got his face under control, straightened up and strolled over to close the narrow gap between them.

He was going to speak to her. Caroline's hands closed together in an agonising grip, as though the pain might punish her for her wanton thoughts, and as a reward this man would vanish. It did not work. He kept coming.

He lifted the wide-brimmed straw hat he was wearing to reveal black hair and a tanned face. He was still smiling that devastating smile, half gentle mockery, half unblushing recognition that she was a woman and he was a man and that there could be consequences of that fact.

'Sir—' Her voice quavered and she shut her lips tightly before she could add squeaking like an idiot to her tally of embarrassments.

'Madam,' he rejoined gravely, replacing his hat. Even shadowed, the grey eyes sparkled with emotions she did not dare contemplate. 'Might I make a suggestion?' His voice was deep, easy, like warm honey running over her skin, with beneath it the hint of strength he was keeping tightly under control. His accent told her he was English—and yet something about him had convinced her he was not. She gave herself a little inward shake. What on earth did it matter *what* nationality he was?

'Mmm?' she managed. *Oh, heavens, what is he going to say? Is he going to proposition me? He hardly needs to, does he? I must have been looking at him as though I wanted to tear his clothes off. I do want to tear his clothes off, here and now. Shameless... I wished for this, and now I do not know what to do...*

'If you move to the rail on the other side you will get the best view of the city. We are approaching the Sarayburnu, the Seraglio Point. You can see the Topkapi Sarayi clearly now. This is your first visit to Constantinople?'

What? 'Mmm! I mean...yes. Thank you...'

'Enjoy,' the tall man said, with a smile that seemed to touch her mouth. He raised his hat again and strolled off across the deck, to where a man in robes stood guard over a trunk and a pile of portmanteaux.

Enjoy, indeed! Caroline made her shaking legs take

her to the spot he had indicated. Mercifully, she found herself screened from the rest of the main deck by a stack of casks. *He did not mean* Enjoy the sights *or* Enjoy the food *or even* Enjoy the shopping. *He meant* Enjoy doing what you were dreaming about. *I wish I could! He must think I have a lover on board, or a husband, or I am travelling to meet one or the other. Could that possibly have been any more embarrassing and awful?*

Well, yes it could, she realised ruefully as the hectic colour began to ebb from her face and her thoughts became a little more coherent. He could have come across and made a very crude proposition—or even a tactfully worded one, come to that—and she would not have had the slightest justification for resenting it.

CHAPTER TWO

'LADY MORVALL?' The voice at her elbow made her jump.

'Yes, Mr Lomax?' It was her courier. Caroline smiled upon the rotund figure with something like affection. Certainly with relief. No one could ever find themselves incorporating Mr Lomax into an improper fantasy, bless him. He was a head shorter than she, with a shiny bald pate under his straw hat, a *pince-nez* perched on the end of his nose and a little pot belly.

He was also an experienced and knowledgeable courier and had shepherded her and Gascoyne, her maid and dresser, all the way from England with impeccable organisation and without the hint of an unpleasant incident. Unfortunately, he could not be expected to save her from the consequences of her own torrid imagination.

'I must apologise for having been away so long, Lady Morvall, but the canvas cover of your larger travelling trunk had been torn in the hold and I have had to stand over the ship's sail-maker to make sure he repaired it properly. Gascoyne has everything packed, and our luggage is over there.'

Caroline followed his pointing finger and located the maid, waiting watchfully by a pile of familiar baggage—right next to where *That Man's* robed attendant was standing. Hastily she turned back.

'Please point out the major buildings, Mr Lomax. I do not wish to go and stand in the crowd before I need to.' *That Man's* directions had been enough for her to orientate herself, given all the reading she had done, but she wanted an excuse to stay apart. Her heart-rate was slowly returning to normal, and she had no intention of raising it again.

'Of course, my lady. The large mosque on the left is the Blue Mosque, in the centre is Aya Sofya mosque, which was built as a Christian church, and all the rest of the buildings as far as the point are the Topkapi Sarayi—the Sultan's palace. Very soon we will sail into the mouth of the Golden Horn.'

'So that will be Seraglio Point, where courtesans who offended would be tied up in silken sacks and thrown into the water?' She pointed to where the stranger had indicated.

'Er…yes.' Mr Lomax did not seem comfortable discussing courtesans. 'And not only such…er… ladies. Constantinople is still at heart a violent city in many ways; it is essential that you take the advice of the staff at the Embassy and do not go out without your escort.'

Caroline nodded with a meekness that would have stunned Sir Hubert. But defying her stepson's pompous demands for respectability was one thing; taking advice from an expert in an alien city was simply common sense. Besides anything else, to travel outside Constantinople she would need a *firman*, the equivalent of a passport, showing the Sultan's permission to go freely about the countryside, and to secure that she must behave with impeccable regard to all the conventions.

They remained at the rail as the ship swung into the Golden Horn and slowly glided into dock on the opposite bank to the old city. Above them loomed the hill where the quarters of Galata and Pera housed the Westerners and their embassies.

'I think we should get back to our luggage,' Mr Lomax pronounced. 'If you would just care to take my arm, Lady Morvall, then there will be less risk of you being jostled in the crowd.'

Jostling was the least of her anxieties. Wishing her smart bonnet possessed a veil, Caroline kept her eyes down, only risking raising them as she negotiated the gangplank to the dockside. There, in front of her, a clear head over most of the jostling throng of porters and passengers, was an instantly recognisable pair of broad shoulders and a rakishly tilted broad-brimmed hat. Then she was down on the firm ground and he had gone.

She did not realise she had sighed aloud until Mr Lomax looked at her with some concern. 'Are you quite well, my lady? Perhaps you are feeling a little unsteady after so much time at sea? I have sent a porter for a carriage; it will not be long coming.'

'No, no, I am quite well, Mr Lomax. I was merely reflecting on my first Turkish…encounter.' And hopefully all the rest would consist of colourful sightseeing and interesting exploration. It had, at least, taught her the foolishness of dreaming about taking a lover. *I simply do not have the courage for that sort of thing,*

*and it is as well to discover it now. Imagine what I
would have done if he had made me a proposition!*

The British Embassy was a handsome double-fronted
residence, with overhanging enclosed balconies and
great double gates through which the carriage bearing
Caroline's party swung, followed by the carts with
their luggage.

Feeling slightly dazed by the crush of the streets, the
babble of different tongues, the colour and endless
details that had her head swivelling from one side to the
other until she was dizzy, Caroline was only too glad
to allow Mr Lomax to take control. She was going to
have to learn to manage affairs herself soon, she knew,
for she had only hired him as far as Constantinople, and
he would return as soon as he acquired a new client to
escort.

'Lady Morvall—welcome.' The thin, scholarly man
who hastened down the steps of the inner courtyard
held out his hand and shook hers with enthusiasm
when she extended it. 'Terrick Hamilton, ma'am, I
am the Foreign Languages Secretary to the Ambassador, who sends his most sincere apologies for not
being here to greet you in person. Unfortunately there
is a tricky matter with some English and Russian
traders on the Black Sea coast, and Sir Robert has
found it necessary to deal with it in person. Do come
in, ma'am.'

He snapped his fingers at a number of men who
were waiting in the shadows. Caroline studied the
turbans—no two seemed exactly the same—and noted
the baggy trousers beneath the knee-length tunics that
most of them wore; they would form the first subject

for her Constantinople sketchbook, she resolved. The men began to unload the trunks.

'*Dikkat! Yavafl!*' Mr Hamilton called as one or two bags were dropped.

Caroline tucked the words away in her mind: *careful* and *slow*. She had seen them written down; now she tried to pay attention to pronunciation, determined to learn the language as much as possible. She would need guides and a dragoman, but the more she understood of what was going on around her, the less vulnerable she would be.

Established at last in her room, with only Gascoyne for company, Caroline cast off her bonnet and light pelisse and flopped down on the bed. 'Phew! Gascoyne, do sit down and rest a while. The housekeeper says she will send up some refreshments and warm water shortly. How good it is to be in the quiet and to have nothing moving about!'

'Indeed it is, my lady.' Gascoyne, who had been with her only since William had died, and was outwardly the most conventional and starched-up of dressers, had amazed Caroline by offering to come with her on her journey. She had expressed a desire to visit what she described sweepingly as *foreign parts*, but, much to Caroline's secret amusement, insisted on maintaining herself and her mistress in a state which would pass muster in Bond Street.

Suggestions that bonnets might be replaced with sunhats, that corsets need not be laced quite so tight, and that the weather was hot enough to dispense with the lightest of pelisses outside, were met with a disapproving sniff. 'You are an English lady, my lady,' Gascoyne would pronounce. 'And I know what is due to one of my ladies, whatever heathen customs might prevail.'

Caroline had given up explaining that Italy and Malta were far from *heathen*, and knew she faced an impossible task in convincing the dresser that Constantinople might be different from what they were used to, but its inhabitants were God-fearing, each in their own way, and that it could be considered as sophisticated and highly developed as London. More so in some ways, if what she had read about the baths was true. Caroline was looking forward to trying out a *hammam*.

With a characteristic sniff Gascoyne shed her gloves, bonnet and pelisse, placed them neatly on one chair and sat, bolt upright, on the edge of another. Even that appeared to strike her as frivolous idleness, for she drew a portmanteau towards her and began lifting out underwear and sorting it onto the camphor wood chest next to the chair.

'What happens now, my lady, if I may be so bold as to enquire?'

'We rest here at the Embassy, and one of the secretaries will send a request to the Sublime Porte—the palace—for us to be granted a *firman* which will allow us to travel. Then I can find a suitable dragoman and porters, and buy pack animals, horses and supplies. Then we set out for Anatolia.'

'Where's that, my lady?' Gascoyne frowned at a minute mark on a camisole and placed it to one side. 'I thought we were arrived, now we're in Turkey.'

'It is part of Turkey—the land to the east.' Caroline rolled over onto her stomach and propped her chin on her hands. 'It is unchanged for centuries, and there are many beautiful natural features and fascinating archaeological treasures that are hardly known about. This book—' She pulled over her bulging reticule and dug out the volume she had been carrying around since leaving England. 'This book tells all about what has been discovered so far. It is by the best-known explorer of the area—Mr Fenton. He writes so compellingly.'

Gascoyne looked down her long nose at the proffered volume. 'I'm sure I wouldn't understand it, my lady. It doesn't sound very suitable for English ladies either. How many carriage dresses do you think I should pack? And what about evening wear? Full dress, or only demi?'

'Neither!' Caroline rolled off the bed and straightened her gown at the sound of a knock on the door. 'Come in. Oh, thank you; will you also send bathwater to my dresser's room, please?'

The housekeeper bowed, and supervised the setting out of a cold collation, while menservants struggled in with a bathtub and ewers of hot water. Disappointingly it seemed that the Embassy did not have its own *hammam*.

'No evening gowns, my lady?'

'No. I shall take two gowns, and otherwise all those riding habits I had made.' Caroline bit her lip as a thought struck her. 'Provided I can find a lady's side-saddle out here. If I cannot, then I shall just have to resort to breeches and a long coat over. It can't be so difficult to ride astride, can it? Men do it all the time.'

'Astride? In breeches? But, my lady, that is enough to ruin your reputation!'

'Amongst whom?' Caroline enquired tartly. 'Anatolian shepherds?'

'But are we not taking a travelling carriage? I cannot ride on *any* sort of saddle,' Gascoyne wailed.

'I will hire a small carriage for you and the luggage,' Caroline promised, firmly trampling down the thought that roads to run a carriage over might not exist. The idea of Gascoyne on a camel was irresistible, if cruel, but she kept it to herself. Time enough to worry about that if the problem arose. 'Now, shall we have our baths before we eat?'

Gascoyne, despite an initial protest that she should stay and attend on her ladyship before taking her own bath, was surprisingly easy to persuade—presumably too shaken by the awful revelations about their mode of transport to protest about anything else. She went off, after unlacing Caroline's corsets and abjuring her to lock the door behind her.

Caroline sank into the cool water with a sigh of relief and lay back, idly twiddling her feet over the edge. It was a nice big tub, with a high back and deep sides. William and she had used to have a lot of fun in baths. He would sneak in and pounce with a soapy sponge when she least expected it, or pour in far too much scented oil and then rub it in all over her until she was as sleek as a wet seal and twice as slippery.

And then, when they were both thoroughly wet and laughing, he would tumble her out onto the piles of linen towels and they would make love…

'Stop it!' Caroline sat up abruptly, slopping water over the sides onto the highly polished wood. *For goodness' sake, I have got to stop thinking about that! I have just made a complete fool of myself with a man, and proved I haven't the temperament to even think about taking a lover. And I certainly don't want to get*

married again: I would never find anyone as sweet as
William, and I would probably end up with an insen-
sitive lump like Hubert. So I had better learn to stop
thinking about sex once and for all.

Which was an extremely sensible resolution, of
course, if only one knew how to carry it out. And if
only the memory of a mobile, sensual mouth and a pair
of mocking grey eyes did not intrude every time one
closed one's own lids.

Two days' rest in the Embassy served to restore the
tone of Caroline's mind somewhat. She had not
ventured out yet, taking Mr Hamilton's advice to adjust
to the air and food, to rest, and decide what equipment
she needed to purchase for her onward journey.

'You will be visiting Bursa, I expect,' he said con-
fidently. 'That is a relatively easy journey by land. If
you wish to explore further along the coast, then I
suggest hiring a boat.'

'I am sure it is fascinating,' Caroline replied
politely. 'And I will visit there at some stage. But my
purpose in coming is chiefly to go into Anatolia.'

'Anatolia? But very few westerners ever do that. It
is wild and quite unchanged for centuries.'

'Exactly—that is why I want to see it.' She could see
he was anxious, and added, 'Will I have a problem
getting a *firman* for that area? Is it restricted in some
way?'

'I do not think so—but it is so unusual, especially
for a lady.'

'I did not come all this way to do the usual thing,'
Caroline said briskly. 'Now, what must I do to get my
firman?'

'I have sent a note to the official at the Sublime Porte who deals with such things. I expect an answer within a few days.'

Caroline told herself that she should not expect an instant response, and requested the loan of an interpreter who could show her around the city while she was waiting. Mr Lomax had departed even more promptly than he had expected, in the service of a returning diplomat rendered temporarily lame as a result of an injury.

She had been promised a guide for the afternoon, and had retreated to the sitting room placed at her disposal to con her notebooks for those sights she wished to visit first, when the Secretary reappeared, an expression of mixed alarm and satisfaction on his face.

'The most extraordinary thing, Lady Morvall. A message from the Topkapi Sarayi: the Sultan will receive you personally in audience.'

'The *Sultan*? But I did not ask for an audience! How has he even heard of me?'

'Possibly officials dealing with your application for a *firman* were intrigued by the fact that a titled English lady is asking for such a thing. Lady Hester Stanhope caused no little stir, you know—she still does, for all that she is now in Syria.'

'Well, I am no Lady Hester.'

'Indeed not, I am glad to say,' Mr Hamilton pronounced, reminding her forcefully of Hubert for a moment.

'I presume declining is out of the question?'

'Most certainly. I beg you would do nothing so deleterious to British interests, ma'am. This is a great honour.'

'But what should I wear? How should I behave?'

'Dress and behave as though you were summoned to a daytime audience with the Prince Regent, Lady Morvall.'

'Should I wear a veil?'

'No—His Majesty will want to meet an English lady in her native habit, as it were. His Majesty the Sultan Mahmud has a French mother, you know. She is a great influence upon him.'

'His father married a Frenchwoman? I had no idea.'

Mr Hamilton coughed discreetly. 'Not...er...*married* as such. Aimée Dubucq de Rivery, the Queen Mother, was captured by slavers and sold into the harem. She is the cousin of the late Empress Josephine.'

'My goodness.' Caroline was virtually speechless. It was like a sensational novel. But this was real. 'When must I go?'

'Tomorrow, after morning prayer. I will send a guide with you who can then take you on a tour of the old city, if you wish. Or you can return here if the visit has wearied you.'

'Thank you.' Just getting through an audience in a palace where the Queen Mother was a captured French slave was as far ahead as she could think. 'I must go and tell my maid, and decide what we are to wear.'

'Your maid is not included, Lady Morvall. To take her would imply a lack of faith in the protection His Majesty is able to extend to a visitor.'

'Oh.' One could only hope that in 1817 keeping female visitors was not considered an acceptable way of filling vacancies in the harem. 'Well, I had better choose a gown and practise my court curtsey, Mr Hamilton.'

CHAPTER THREE

BUMPING down the hill to the dockside, taking the Embassy *caique* to the far shore and then climbing into the Embassy's best coach, which had been sent over the night before, Caroline tried to recall if she had felt this nervous before being presented at court in London. She rather thought not.

There had been the towering and hideously expensive ostrich plumes in her *coiffure* to manage, and the long-outdated hooped skirts to worry about, so, really, making her curtsey and dealing with the Prince Regent's rather broad compliments had seemed a positive anticlimax.

Now she had neither hoops nor feathers to distract her—simply her very best half-dress gown and a bonnet which she could remove to display an elaborate *coiffure* suitable for Charlton House in the afternoon, if not the Topkapi Palace in the morning. She had been far too nervous to eat any breakfast, or do more than sip distractedly at a cup of coffee. If she made a poor impression, and the *firman* was refused, she would have made this journey for nothing, and her gesture towards William's memory and his dream would end unfulfilled.

Opposite her sat the translator and guide the Secretary had given her, introducing him simply as Ismael. He was tight-lipped with nerves, obviously wondering what he had done to deserve having to guide a mad Englishwoman to the very steps of the Sultan's throne.

'We arrive, my lady,' he said, twitching the lowered blinds back for a moment. 'As part of the Ambassador's household we may drive through the gate into the first court: it is a great honour.'

Caroline removed her bonnet and patted her hair into place. The carriage stopped, the door was opened and the steps let down. Hardly knowing what to expect, she stepped down into a large courtyard, bustling with people. All were men; she felt as conspicuous as if she was wearing a placard.

'The Court of the Janissaries,' Ismael whispered. 'See?' She followed the direction of his gaze and saw the groups of tall men in belted robes, their strange headdresses falling in long flaps of cloth behind. She noted the swords pushed through their belts and averted her eyes.

An official, his head swathed in a white turban of infinitely intricate folds, approached, spoke to Ismael and gestured for them to follow, barely sparing her a glance. It occurred to Caroline that, although she was the only woman in the courtyard, anyone could be behind the myriad of shuttered windows, watching.

'The Ortakapi—now we enter the Second Court.'

Caroline tried to move with dignity across the seemingly endless space, managing her skirts, attempting not to start in surprise as a gazelle bounded out from behind a bed of roses, chased by a scolding peacock.

'The Gate of Felicity and the Third Court.' Ismael seemed steadier now he was working. 'The Audience Chamber is before us.'

Caroline knew she should be making mental notes, that she should fix all this in her memory so that she could write it up as soon as she got back to the Embassy, but it was rapidly becoming a blur. The Prince Regent would faint with excitement at what she was seeing: the Pavilion at Brighton was a pale shadow of this confident sophistication.

They moved through a great portal, heavy brocade curtains were opened, and she was in a lofty square chamber, every surface decorated in marbles, vivid blue tile, ornate carving. And in the centre at the back stood a wide golden throne, half-chair, half-bed, covered in massed cushions.

An attendant in a sweeping fur-trimmed caftan thundered some announcement she could not understand. On the throne the man sitting cross-legged lifted his head from the document he was perusing, and at her side Ismael fell to his knees and prostrated himself.

Control, Caroline murmured, sinking as slowly as her shaky knees would allow into a deep curtsey. She held it for a long moment, then rose again, took six steps forward, sank again, rose and took a final six steps, sinking into the deepest curtsey yet, holding it until her thigh muscles screamed. She rose to stand before the Sultan.

The man regarding her with piercing black eyes was broad-shouldered in his purple brocade robes, black-bearded, and gave the impression of holding himself in stillness by sheer will-power. He was younger than she had expected, handsome. And he

exuded a kind of virile, ruthless power that did not
have to be expressed to be perfectly understood.

He spoke, a rich rumble of words, and the man
standing to his side translated. 'His Majesty the Sultan
Mahmud, Commander of the Faithful, Lord of the
Golden Horn, bids you welcome.'

'I am deeply honoured by His Majesty's gracious
condescension in receiving me.'

'His Majesty wishes to know what brings you to
Constantinople.'

'I desire to visit his beautiful city and his great
lands, and to learn from what I see, should His Majesty
be so gracious as to grant me a *firman*.'

The jet-black eyes regarded her steadily, then
Mahmud spoke again.

'Where is your husband?' the translator asked.

'I am a widow, Majesty.'

'Of what years?'

'Twenty-six years, Majesty.'

Silence. She forced herself to stand without fidget-
ing, her eyes modestly lowered. The Sultan raised a
hand and a man stepped out of the shadows behind the
throne. Caroline glanced up, and for a moment almost
lost her composure. Then she realised she must be
mistaken. She did not know him, although this man
was black-haired, tall and broad-shouldered. He
moved with a grace that reminded her of a big cat—
and of a fantasy who had proved to be only too real.

But this was no Englishman: this man wore robes—
yet another variation of the Ottoman court dress she
saw all around her. His tall frame was clad in a silver-
grey brocade robe, trimmed with black fur and worn
over full black trousers; he was bareheaded and his

black hair fell loose to his shoulders. It was not—of course it was not—the man from the ship.

He was stooping respectfully next to the Sultan, answering some question. Perhaps he was the official who had been dealing with her application? With a low bow he withdrew back into the shadows, and Caroline forced her attention back to the Sultan.

'What man protects you?' the interpreter asked, making her jump. He must have assumed she failed to understand him. 'You have no husband; who then has you in his protection?'

'No one!' *Idiot, he does not mean a lover. He means a bodyguard.* 'I mean, I shall hire such guides and escort as I require when I travel, Your Majesty.'

'What garment is it that you wear now?'

'It is described as a half-dress gown, Majesty. I thought it proper to dress as I would for an audience with my own sovereign.'

'You do not then dress in men's clothes, as your countrywoman does?'

'Lady Hester, Your Majesty? No. I do not.' Was that a bad thing, or good? Was she appearing dangerously inexperienced, or reassuringly respectable?

'His Majesty graciously grants you your *firman*. May you travel safely, if the Prophet wills it.'

Yes! I have my firman—*now all I need to do is to get out of here.* 'Your Majesty is most gracious.' Caroline curtseyed, backed away, curtseyed again and finally found herself outside the door, Ismael mopping his brow at her side.

'Oh, my goodness, what a relief that is over.' Her hands were trembling, she realised. 'Do you think we could sit down for a moment?'

'No, my lady, we must go back to the carriage by the most direct way.' A slight movement of his head towards a turbaned figure with the inevitable curving sword waiting behind them underlined the point. Ismael began to walk, pausing only as a man with a black panther on a chain crossed their path. The beast's green eyes swivelled to examine Caroline. She held her breath, then it responded to a tug on its jewelled collar and padded on.

'On the right side of the Court is the harem,' Ismael hissed. 'Do not stare directly, my lady.'

'It is so big.' Caroline glanced at the rambling range of buildings. 'How many women are there within it?'

'Two hundred, perhaps.'

Two hundred. A whole village of women who would spend their entire lives shut up here, their sole purpose to service the whims and desires of the man whose presence I have just left. And if they do not please, do not conform, then presumably they are disposed of. She shivered, chilled by the opulence of the prison around her.

The click of the carriage door shutting behind them, and the rumble of wheels as it passed through the gate into the outside world, made her sigh with relief.

'My lady wishes to visit one of the great mosques? Or to view the Hippodrome? Or perhaps my lady is tired and wishes to return to the Embassy?'

Her head was spinning: it must be relief and excitement. 'No—none of those things. What I want to do, Ismael, is to be completely frivolous.' He frowned, internally translating and obviously failing to understand her. 'I wish to go shopping.'

'To the Grand Bazaar, my lady?' He looked more

cheerful. This was a comprehensible desire. 'Or the small one?'

'To the Grand Bazaar,' she said recklessly. There was absolutely nothing like shopping to relax one.

Now where was she going? The black-haired man in the grey brocade robes stood in the outer gateway, a head taller, even without a turban, than the men around him. He had come as soon as the Sultan had graciously dismissed him, striding through the Second Court, scattering peacocks and quail as he did so.

He snapped his fingers, and the boy who had been dogging his steps ran forward and spoke to the gate-keepers. 'Her guide told the driver to go to the Kapali Carsi, my lord.'

'What is the fool thinking of to take her there?' the tall man demanded rhetorically, receiving only a comical shrug of incomprehension from the lad. 'She is tired, hot, nervous and completely unused to the place. She did not look as though she had had enough to drink.' He frowned, then appeared to reach a decision. 'Get me my horse, Abdul.'

As the boy sprinted away he shrugged off the heavy robe to reveal a lighter, knee-length tunic over the full trousers beneath it. He rolled his shoulders in relief at having the weight removed, then threw it up across the horse's withers when Abdul returned, leading a bay Arab gelding.

'Here—up behind me.' He swung Abdul up one-handed. If he had to search through the Bazaar for her then he would need the boy to hold his horse.

To ride through the crowds packing the maze of streets leading to the Bazaar was difficult enough even with an escort; for a lone horseman in a hurry it was a matter of skill and aggression, and he would have been dead within minutes if any of the curses directed at his back had struck home.

By good fortune the carriage had stopped at the nearest entrance, but it was empty, the driver leaning against the shafts, exchanging noisy gossip with a melon-seller.

'Where has the lady gone?'

'To look at the silks, Lord. I know not which merchants Ismael will take her to.' The man eyed the rider's horse and clothing uneasily, knowing he should not discuss an Embassy guest, but intimidated by the thought that this man had come from the Topkapi Sarayi.

'Wait here, Abdul.' The tall man swung down from the saddle and strode into the broad thoroughfare through the Bazaar. In the alcoves on either side stall-holders hovered beside their wares, calling out to attract interest. None ventured to catch the attention of the robed man, striding through with only a cursory glance for fruit, vegetables, spices and piles of carpets.

It was cool, despite the crowds, and pools of light fell on the tiled floor from the half-moon clerestory high above. The man reached a crossroads, seized a pillar with one hand and swung up to stand on the corner of a pottery-seller's stall. Nothing down there, nothing there...perhaps her guide had taken her into one of the rooms behind the stalls? At least then she would be offered refreshment. But it was likely to be only the fiercely strong coffee which she would not be used to.

He swung out further and caught a glimpse of

bobbing plumes and the outrageous poke of an almond-green bonnet at the far end of the smallest passage. It could only be her—unless there was more than one Englishwoman with a taste for French milli-nery loose in Constantinople.

The lady did not appear to realise she was in need of rescue, but that was most certainly what she was about to experience—whether she liked it or not.

'Goodness, it is very crowded in here, Ismael. I had not realised.' Caroline felt her head was spinning, but then, with the tension of her reception by the Sultan, the frisson of horror from her first sight of a harem and her relief at being out of the place, it was no wonder.

And, of course, Gascoyne had laced her with all the severity needed to ensure a good fit for the elaborate gown she was wearing. Really, it was *very* hot. Perhaps when they found a good merchant's shop she would be able to sit a little.

'Here, my lady.' Ismael indicated a wide stall, groaning under a rainbow of colours and a bewilder-ing range of weaves and textures. 'This is the very best place to look.'

'Oh, how lovely!' Caroline stepped forward, en-tranced, hardly noticing the jostling in the wonder of the shimmering material. 'The colours are entrancing, so rich…' Indeed, they seemed to shimmer and move in the shafts of sunlight penetrating from above. She took another step and the ground beneath her moved, the colours of the silks whirled. *What is happening?* The sounds of the Bazaar began to fade; the colours lost their brilliance. She was falling. Caroline stretched out a hand to try and find support and met only air, and then there was darkness.

She came to herself not on the hard floor of the Bazaar, but lying on something firm, yet yielding. The noises of the great market had vanished, leaving only the sound of trickling water close at hand, the soft purr of doves on a roof, and the faint cry of a muezzin calling from a distant minaret.

She must have fainted. Poor Ismael, having to cope with that! Still, she was back in the Embassy now. Caroline lay, letting the light breeze play over her still body, enjoying the scent of jasmine it brought. With returning consciousness came the recollection of quiet voices, of soft hands undressing her, of cool water on her face and hands and a glass held to her lips.

The heat was less too—or perhaps it was just the blissful sensation of not wearing her stays and feeling the breeze drift gently over the thin silk covering her limbs. *Thin silk? I do not own anything in thin silk.*

Caroline's eyes flew open and she found she was looking at an entirely unfamiliar ceiling, its ornate arches springing from gorgeously tiled walls of white and blues and greens. She was lying on a wide upholstered platform, spread with rugs and scattered with heaps of silken tasselled cushions.

Looking down the length of her body, she realised she was dressed in wide trousers, caught in at the ankle by narrow bands. She was wearing a long-sleeved bodice, which hugged her figure but left her midriff exposed, and over it all the filmiest of tunics; buttoned at the front and slit at the sides.

She was not in the Embassy; she was in a harem.

She had been kidnapped. Caroline lay frozen, trying to control her breathing. The room was quiet, yet she sensed she was not alone. If she sat up, what—who— would she see?

CHAPTER FOUR

SLOWLY she raised herself on her elbows and found her instinct had not betrayed her. Three deep-set windows faced the long divan she was lying on. Each had a window seat, and in the central one a man was sitting reading, his back against one wall, his feet up on the seat, a book propped on the natural easel of his knees.

Something must have alerted him, although she had moved with stealth, for he turned his head and smiled. 'You are awake at last. How do you feel?'

Caroline scrambled into a sitting position as he placed his book on the floor and swung his legs down to stand up. 'You! It *was* you in the audience hall with the Sultan—I thought I recognised you, and then I told myself I was imagining it.' His hair was still loose on his shoulders, black, with the sheen of a raven's wing: it gave him an exotic look—with his tanned skin the Sultan had hardly been darker. She had not consciously noticed when they'd first met that it had been tied back, rather than cropped short, but that, she realised now, was what had confused her, made her think he was not English.

'Well, on board the ship you did not appear to be

in any state to commit my face to memory.' She felt
the blood staining her own face at the thought of just
how she had been staring. 'I think I should introduce
myself, for I have the advantage of you.'

*That is most certainly true—in every sense of the
word.* He moved closer and her eyes flickered over his
clothing. He wore loose black trousers caught at the
ankles with a band of silver brocade, and over them a
tunic of black silk, subtly shot with silver, reaching to
mid-thigh, slashed at the sides and at the neck. The
fabric was so fine she could see the shadow of dark
hair through it, the points where his nipples pressed
against it. It was outrageously exciting.

'Lady Morvall, I am Drew Fenton. They will vouch
for me at the Embassy, where I am well-known to
the staff.' She must still have been staring at him, for
he smiled and continued, 'I am the younger son of
Viscount Wellingham.'

'Yes, I know you are—if, that is, you are the
Andrew Fenton who wrote *Travels Through Ancient
Anatolia*. I have a copy in my luggage.' This was ridiculous. She was in this exotic room with a man who
seemed to have stepped straight out of a tale of the
Arabian Nights, and he was introducing himself as
though they were at Almack's. And this was the man
whose writings had formed the greater part of her
reading matter for months.

'I am flattered that you know my work.' Drew came
and sat next to her on the wide platform of the divan.
He was just within touching distance, close enough for
her to smell the faint spiciness that drifted from his
garments: cedarwood, perhaps.

'It was one of my main sources while I was preparing for this journey. My husband had your book in his library, and all of your articles for the Royal Society. We read them together.'

'So you did not plan to come alone?'

'No. William died eighteen months ago; it had been a dream of his to travel to the Ottoman empire.'

'And so this is a pious gesture to his memory?' He sounded dry.

'No. It is not—not entirely. I wanted to come too, very much. And it is certainly better than sitting at home with my pompous stepson and his wife, learning to be a respectable widow.' That prompted a flash of amused warmth in his eyes that was decidedly unsettling. Caroline hastily changed the subject. 'How did I come to be here? Where am I?'

'You are in my home. You fainted in the Kapali Carsi, do you recall?'

'I can remember feeling dizzy. It was very hot.'

'And what had you had to drink today? Not very much, I think. And dressed like that, trussed up in those ridiculous corsets and all those layers of cloth.' He ignored Caroline's gasp of outrage at his shocking mention of her stays and pressed on. 'I could see at the audience that you looked pale, and so, as soon as His Majesty released me, I followed you—in case you were foolish enough not to return at once to the Embassy.'

Tight-lipped at the reproof, Caroline inclined her head. 'Thank you, Mr Fenton, but I fail to understand why you were there, or why you did not simply assist my escort to take me back to the Embassy.'

'You are here because you collapsed virtually on the doorstep of my trading *khan*, and I thought it best to make you comfortable and get some liquid into you as soon as possible. We then brought you on to my house. Your very unobservant escort has taken a message to the Embassy. I have promised to return you tomorrow, if you feel up to it.'

'And that will reassure them, will it?' she enquired tartly. 'The knowledge that I am alone and unchaperoned in the house of a strange man?'

'I am known to both the Ambassador and, as you observed, to the Sultan, who is kind enough to consult me occasionally on matters concerning foreign travellers in his lands. He wished to be reassured that he was not letting in another Lady Hester Stanhope to cause a stir, and, at the same time, that you could look after yourself.' The dark grey eyes lingered on her flushed face.

'Do you wish me to call a chaperon for you? Are you uncomfortable being alone with me?'

'What chaperon?' Caroline enquired cautiously.

'One of the women of my household. One of the ones who undressed you—which I imagine you are itching to ask about, but cannot quite find the right words.'

That was an uncomfortably accurate observation. Caroline dealt with it by attacking. '*One* of the women of your household? You mean your harem?'

That produced a crack of laughter that had her tightening her lips in irritation. 'No, I do not mean that. I do not keep a harem. True, you are in the *selamlik*, the men's quarters, and not, as you should be, in the *haremlik*, but that does not imply that the women's quarters are full of my concubines. Or slaves, for that matter, if that is worrying you. The women of this household are paid servants—maids, housekeepers, cooks—all the same roles as your servants at home.'

'I see,' Caroline said stiffly, feeling gauche and unsophisticated. 'And the...the lady of the house does not object to my presence?'

'You mean my mistress?' Drew settled back onto the divan against a sumptuous pile of cushions, drawing his feet up. It felt indecently as though they were lying side by side on a bed.

'Yes.' She refused to allow him to embarrass her. 'I assume you are not married?'

'As it happens, I am not. Nor, at present, do I have a mistress.' There was a silence as he watched her. Caroline was reminded forcibly of the black panther in the courtyard. Or of the Sultan. This man had the same aura of utterly relaxed power. 'You might say that there is a vacancy in that department.'

He has a vacancy for a mistress and he is telling me? Is this an offer of employment? The arrogant devil! He has been living in the East too long.

'I am sorry.' The soft, deep voice cut through her indignant thoughts. 'I am forgetting your health. Please drink something: you are becoming flushed again.' Drew leaned across her and lifted a glass from a side table she had not noticed. 'It is spring water, with a little orange juice and honey to give you strength.' He held the glass to her lips until she took it from him and drained it defiantly.

'I can manage, thank you.'

'Of course.'

He leaned back, and Caroline found she could breathe again. The drink was certainly refreshing.

'What was I saying? Oh, yes—that I have no mistress at present, therefore no hostess for my house.'

'How very trying for you,' Caroline observed crisply.

'Yes, indeed.' He lay back and stretched like the big cat she had been comparing him to. 'Prolonged celibacy *is* very trying, is it not?'

'I really could not say.'

'How very dashing of you! I conclude, therefore, that the ending of your marriage was not the cause of any great regret, and that you have been suitably comforted ever since?'

'Yes, it *was* a matter of great regret! And you misconstrue me—no doubt deliberately. I loved my husband very much. Naturally a lady does not dwell on…on *carnal* matters, so the question of finding celibacy trying really does not occur,' she finished, hot-faced and indignant.

'My dear Lady Morvall! Doing it rather too brown, if I may say so. Forgive me for mentioning it, but if you were not thinking about *carnal matters* on the first occasion we met, just what were you dwelling upon? A delicious new hat? The prospect of unlimited Turkish sweetmeats?'

'Oh! I refuse to answer you, Mr Fenton. No lady would.'

'I think that what you were contemplating was this.' Drew leaned back towards her, placed one hand on the rugs at the far side and effectively caged her in with his body, although only his arm brushing against her side actually touched her.

Caroline drew in her breath sharply, as though he had burned her, and Drew took her lips with his. Shock and outrage held her still for a moment. Then she tensed herself to resist him and found her treacherous body simply would not obey her. His mouth angled over hers, firm but gentle, cajoling a response, not demanding. His tongue ran along the join of her lips, teasing, then insistent, and she opened to let her own touch his.

It was so strange to kiss another man. He tasted different, he smelled different from what she was used to, and as she reached up to encircle his shoulders with her arms she discovered just how very different his body was.

William had been a big, powerful man in his prime, and even at fifty-six had been strong, able to ride all day if the need was there. But time had softened his big frame, laying fat over the muscle, loosening the skin. He had remained masculine and tough, but by the time they had married Caroline found him endearingly cuddly.

But this man was hard. No one could ever call *him* cuddly, any more than the black panther was anything other than smooth velvet pelt over killing muscles and tendons.

Muscle bulked sleekly wherever she touched. He held up his weight away from her body on his arms, without the slightest apparent effort, and the silk slid under her flattened palms over smooth, taut, warm skin.

Drew played with her tongue-tip, duelling lazily with his own until she began to stir restlessly beneath him, then plunging into the moist warmth of her mouth, thrusting with unambiguous purpose. Caroline could hear herself shamelessly whimpering as he ravished her mouth, opening to him without inhibition, revelling in the sensation of abandoning herself mindlessly to passion.

How long he kissed her she had no idea. Time

ceased to have any meaning. But her body was counting, registering every passing second of arousal, until its demanding ache became almost more than she could bear.

She was dimly aware of arching upwards, trying to meet the body held so tantalisingly away from hers. Her fingers dug into his shoulders, trying to pull him down, as her whimpers became moans and her moans became sobbing gasps.

Then Drew left her mouth, bent his head and took her right nipple in his mouth through the thin silk of her tunic and bodice, sucking it into his mouth ruthlessly as she cried out, nipping the hard peaking tip in his teeth.

It sent her over the edge, broke her into fragments, tumbled her into a spiral of sensation that left her finally, trembling and gasping, in his arms.

Caroline came to herself to find she was held against Drew's chest as he lay back on the cushions, his arms encircling his shoulders.

'You might not be cuddly, but you are very comfortable,' Caroline murmured. She had to keep it light: to say what she felt, what she thought, was beyond her.

'Cuddly?' With her ear pressed against his chest his voice was a deep and faintly affronted rumble. 'You just wanted *cuddling*?'

'No.' She laughed. It was that or cry. She could not imagine how she was going to look him in the face after disintegrating in his arms like that. 'William, my husband, was cuddly. He was the only other man I have ever…ever been with.' As soon as the words were out of her mouth it occurred to Caroline that comparing a man to another, moments after he had made love to you, was tactless, to put it mildly.

'A plump young man?' The deep rumble sounded amused now, thank goodness.

'William was fifty-six.'

'Oh.'

'He was a lovely man.' Indignant at the implied disparagement, Caroline pushed herself up so she could look Drew in the face. He looked politely interested—if one did not look at his mouth, which seemed swollen from that endless kiss. 'He *liked* women. He thought it was very important to please me in bed; I did not realise until I talked to other wives how uncommon that is.'

'Do respectable women discuss such things?'

'Of course we do.' Caroline was amused, grateful for the distraction from her body which, far from being sated by its recent release, was beginning to quiver with new demands. 'Very discreetly, of course, and only married women. But most of them who talk about it do not appear to find it at all pleasurable. In fact my daughter-in-law—my stepson's wife—positively welcomes morning sickness, because when she is pregnant Hubert does not *bother* her, as she puts it.'

'Hubert does not have his father's skills, I collect?' Drew settled back against the cushions, holding her so he could watch her face.

'Not, apparently, in bed, and to my knowledge of less intimate matters not in any other field either. How dear William produced such a humourless bore I cannot surmise—unless he gets it from his mother.'

'Well, let us hope that his wife is naturally of a chilly disposition and does not suffer, as you would, from such deprivation.'

'Yes, of course.' Caroline felt awkward and tongue-tied. What could she talk about to a man with whom she had just been so intimate?

Drew solved the problem for her with disconcerting frankness. 'So, on the ship, you were daydreaming about making love?'

'Mmm. Yes.' She could not meet his eyes, but dropping her gaze only left her looking at that sensual mouth. She looked lower. His chin was firm, square, and just becoming hazed with stubble. Lower, the column of his throat, brown like his face, was strapped with muscle. A visible pulse beat against the long tendons. She let her eyes stray further, down into the shadowed vee of his tunic. How would the skin there feel?

'Almost eighteen months of virtuous abstinence must be hard for a woman used to a satisfying love-life,' Drew observed. She would have thought it a disinterested observation if his fingertips had not been trailing across her shoulders to the nape of her neck.

'Yes. You must think me very wanton to have behaved as I did just now, but I am grateful…' She shivered sensuously against the light caress and tried, unsuccessfully, to hide her reaction.

'Again?' She met the grey eyes, read the knowledge and the gentleness in them, and felt something inside dissolve into hot, quivering yearning. 'I would very much like to know you, absolutely and completely,' he continued. 'But I rather think that there is still so much neglected need that we would not be able to prolong the moment, enjoy it as we should. I think I should pay your very lovely body more attention first, Caroline.'

CHAPTER FIVE

'I…' WHAT could she say? She had dreamed about
finding a lover, someone she could like, and here was
this positively gorgeous man, whom she already knew
from his writings, who seemed to want to assuage
every desperate need her body had. Either she was
dreaming or this was reality. And in either case she was
not so foolish that she would throw it away. 'Please,'
she said simply, tipping her face up for Drew's kiss.

But it appeared that kissing was not his immediate
priority. 'You are wearing too many clothes,' he said,
tugging the filmy tunic over her head and bending to
attack the tiny pearls fastening the front of the tight
bodice. Her breasts felt so full and heavy she was
amazed that the buttons were holding.

'Ah,' he sighed as he released their weight into his
palms. 'How lovely—and how white.'

'You should undress too,' Caroline demanded,
trying to regain some control, only to bite back a gasp
of desire as Drew's thumbs began to circle her nipples.
'I want to touch you.'

She was fascinated by his body, so strangely hard,
yet so flexible, so smooth. He stripped off his own

tunic, then caught her wrists as she reached out to touch
his chest. Each muscle was so clearly defined against
the tanned skin, even under the dusting of dark hair that
arrowed down and then darkened at the waistband of
his trousers.

'Wait,' he said huskily, gathering both wrists in his
right hand and pinning them down above her head.
'Don't be greedy.'

*Greedy? How can I not be greedy when he is doing
that? Or—oh my God!—that?* 'Drew,' she gasped as
he relentlessly nipped and sucked at one nipple while
toying gently with the other with his free hand.

'Yes?' He looked up, his eyes sparkling wickedly.

'Don't…just don't stop.'

'I have absolutely no intention of stopping.' He
reached down for the tapes that tied the wide trousers
at her waist. 'But I do intend moving about a little.'
The flat of his hand slipped under the loosened
waistband, down to the tangle of blonde curls at the
apex of her thighs. His fingers lingered, tantalisingly, then he insinuated one long finger into the
moist aching folds.

It was shameful how hot, how wet she was for him,
how his touch drove everything out of her head but the
need for more touches, more kisses. Caroline arched
up, pushing herself into the palm of his hand, and he
pressed down in response, almost sending her over the
edge again.

Desperately she held on, determined not to reveal
her weakness and longing by giving way so quickly.
But it seemed he knew exactly where to touch her to
send her wild. For long minutes he held her on the
brink, writhing under his caresses until she was panting

in desperation, then he let his weight come down on her and began to kiss her, while his wickedly knowing fingers never stopped.

She could feel the length and girth of his erection branding her thigh hotly through the two fragile layers of silk they wore. Her imagination baulked at the thought of accommodating him, and the frisson of fear was all that was needed to shatter her tenuous hold on control. This time she knew she screamed. She heard her own voice in the midst of the sensual explosion that rocked her and shook her and finally cast her up, heated and gasping, on Drew's broad chest.

'Oh…' was all she could manage. She felt him bend his head and kiss her brow where the hair was sticking, damp with sweat. She rather suspected that he was smiling, but she did not care; she knew she was beaming like an idiot.

Caroline let her hand run over his chest, savouring the contrast between hot, damp skin and the friction of the curling hair. Her fingertips curled down to caress the skin just below his armpit. 'That is so soft,' she wondered aloud.

'Your skin is very soft there too.' He caressed in his turn. 'Very, very soft.'

'Yes, but you are a man.'

'True,' he agreed with a chuckle. 'And I think we have just demonstrated very clearly that you are a woman. Are you hungry?'

She twisted round until she could rest her forearm on his chest and study his face. 'Well…' The cleft of his upper lip was quite pronounced, the curve of the lower one full, sensuous, without being in any way feminine. She wanted to bite it.

'Not for that, my little wanton. For food. When did you last eat?

'I don't know.' That was back in some other world. 'Breakfast—but I was too nervous to eat. Last night at dinner, I suppose.'

'Then we must dine. But first a visit to the *hammam*.'

'You have your own baths? I was so disappointed that the Embassy has western baths. I was going to ask about visiting a public women's *hammam*.'

Drew uncoiled his length from the divan and stood up, pulling his tunic over his head. Caroline watched the flex and movement of his muscles greedily, dropping her own gaze hastily as he turned and handed her the thin over-tunic. 'No point in doing up all those buttons again,' he observed laconically, clapping his hands sharply.

Almost on the sound the door opened, and two young women stepped into the room. *They must have been standing right outside: they must have heard me cry out!* Caroline could feel the heat washing up over her throat and cheeks.

'Drew, *pasha*?' It was the elder of the two, wearing a striped tunic of fine cotton over a white shift and baggy white trousers, tight at the ankle.

'Harika, Caroline *hanim* wishes to bathe. Will you and Sahiba assist her, please?'

He added something in Turkish which made the girl smile, but she merely said, 'Of course, Drew *pasha*. Would you come with us, Caroline *hanim*? The bathing rooms are prepared.'

Caroline managed a smile and tried to remember the right phrase for *thank you*. For some reason her brain seemed to be completely scrambled. Harika held out a hand to help her to her feet. 'Please, Caroline *hanim*, I would like to practise my English. Sahiba, too, speaks a little.'

'Harika is the *kalfa* of this house—the senior maid,' Drew explained. 'We will eat when we have bathed.'

We? Surely he will not bathe with me? But Drew did not follow as the two girls led her away, gently touching her arms to steer her through the maze of corridors.

'I have never been to a *hammam* before,' she ventured.

'No? I am sure you will enjoy it. Drew *pasha* has everything of the best for the bathhouse here. May I ask, is it true that in the West people bathe in tubs of still water, sitting in it?'

'Why, yes.' The girls' noses wrinkled in distaste. 'It is different here?'

'But of course.' Sahiba pushed open ornately carved doors and ushered Caroline through a tiled antechamber and into a square room with tiled platforms around the walls and copper pipes spouting lightly steaming water into stone basins. The room was shadowed and mysterious, with light flooding in through saucer-sized holes in the domed ceiling to make shining spots on the floor.

Her attendants pressed Caroline to sit down and began to bustle about, collecting sheets of white linen, piles of towels, cakes of soap and jars and bottles. Harika surveyed the array, nodded in satisfaction, and announced, 'Now Caroline, *hanim*, first we undress you.'

Naked except for a swathing linen sheet, Caroline

was led to a slatted wooden stool in front of one of the gurgling basins. 'Now we wash you three times all over,' Harika continued, ignoring Caroline's modest squeak of protest as she began to work up a lather on her arms. 'Sahiba will wash your hair, then soak it in almond oil, then egg yolk, then wash it again and rinse it with rose-water.'

It seemed to take hours. After the embarrassment of the first all-over wash, Caroline surrendered to the inevitable, even as Harika slipped a bag of coarsely woven cloth onto her hand and began to rub vigorously all over Caroline's body. Finally, after a final dousing with clean water from the tiny brass bowls the girls wielded, Caroline's feet were placed into high wooden pattens and she was guided, tottering slightly, to lie down on soft towels spread on the platform. Perhaps now they would let her rest?

Sahiba seized one wrist and guided it over Caroline's head. Caroline resisted, then stopped with a shriek as cool oil was dribbled over her skin. Up went her other arm, more oil.

'What are you *doing*?' Caroline demanded. 'Stop it!'

Harika whipped back the linen sheet and started applying the oil all over her.

'Please do not struggle, Caroline *hanim*. I need to be careful that I cover you completely with this first oil.'

'*First* one?' Caroline gave a little squeak as Harika began to massage it into her legs.

'There are three oils,' Sahiba explained. 'To soften the skin, to perfume the skin and to make the skin more sensitive.'

More sensitive? Much more sensitive and I'll scream if I'm touched! But there was no escape—not without deeply offending the two girls. Caroline surrendered years of English repression and gave in to the sensation of being utterly pampered, utterly relaxed.

At last Sahiba combed through Caroline's damp hair. 'Now you come to the cool room and rest, and your hair dries,' she announced.

Teetering on her high pattens, and once more wrapped in a sheet, Caroline let herself be led through into another room, with a fountain in the centre and a deep divan against the wall. A hookah stood on the floor, and a stack of hard cushions beside the divan was topped off with a great copper platter of fruit and a pitcher of sherbet.

'Now you must rest a little,' Harika encouraged her. 'I will go to the kitchens and make sure that all is as it should be for your meal.'

The girls vanished in a cloud of almond oil and rosewater and head veils, leaving Caroline limp on the divan. What would Hubert say if he could see her now? The thought provoked a gurgle of laughter.

'What amuses you?' It was Drew, leaning against one of the pillars, with only the briefest of towels around his slim hips.

'I was wondering what Hubert would make of this,' she admitted. 'I think he would be shocked to his core.'

'Poor Hubert. What a dull life he must lead.' Drew padded across to the divan and sat down. The skimpy towel shot up his thighs. Caroline gazed fixedly at the hookah. 'Dinner will be about ten minutes.' She could feel his gaze, burning through the thin linen. 'Or another hour. Are you very hungry?'

'Not *very*,' she admitted, biting her lip as the thrilling tension shot through her again. *I must be insatiable*, she thought dizzily. One climax and an affectionate embrace was what she had expected to make up a satisfactory evening's lovemaking. This was not at all the same thing: her body was demanding more the more she had.

Drew flicked back the top edges of her sheet and ran his fingertip down her oiled, perfumed skin. Caroline stretched like a cat.

'Delicious,' Drew murmured. 'Let me see.'

Before she could protest he tossed back the sheet and ran one hand over the swell of her belly to the plump curve of her mons. 'Goodness!' This frank study of her body was scandalous. 'Stop it!'

But Drew did not seem to find it scandalous as he leaned forward and delicately ran his tongue over the soft lips, then in, to feather the intricate folds with deadly expertise. Caroline gasped and fell back, only to find herself gripping his damp black hair as he drove her to madness not once, but twice.

'And now, I think, it is my turn.' His weight over her on the firm divan imprisoned her, even though he took the brunt of it on his elbows. Caroline could feel the insistent nudge of his erection at the place between her legs that was already quiveringly sensitive from his mouth.

She opened her eyes and stared up into the dark grey ones above her, intent on her face.

'Am I too heavy for you?' She shook her head mutely. 'You are shivering: do I frighten you?'

'Yes.' She nodded. 'But don't stop. I couldn't bear it if you stopped.'

Without moving his upper body at all Drew began to rock his pelvis gently against hers, pushing and retreating until the feel of him no longer alarmed her and she began to relax beneath him. Imperceptibly the rocking became gentle thrusting, and without conscious decision Caroline began to move with him, gasping with delight as her body yielded, then moulded to the heat possessing her.

Through a haze of mounting ecstasy she wondered how he could be so hard, so strong, so male, and yet be so tender. And then she found she did not want him to be tender any longer. She curled her legs around him, gripping with her ankles around the slim hips and digging in her heels. 'Drew—please—more, deeper…oh, yes!'

He seemed to understand what her incoherent pleas meant, taking her hard and fast while she cried out in astonished pleasure that she could match him in this, that her passion was as intense, her strength in this hot, sweaty struggle equal to his.

Nothing in the world existed but the feel of his skin under her grasping hands, the scent of him, sweat and arousal and clean, oiled skin, the heat of him filling her and the knowledge that she was giving him back pleasure for pleasure as she looked up into his intent, focused face, every emotion save desire stripped away by the intensity of what they were experiencing.

He bent his head suddenly, took her mouth, thrust with his tongue as his body surged within her, and with a shock that had her arching up away from the cushions against his bowed body the world split apart. It had already before that day, so many times she had lost count, but this was different. For Drew was part of her, and even as she lost touch with everything else she was utterly aware of his body, his breathing, his eyes locked with hers as he withdrew from her with a groan, convulsed, hung rigid above her for a moment, then collapsed onto her, utterly still.

CHAPTER SIX

DREW lay there, so relaxed he did not think he could lift a finger. Beneath him Caroline's soft, lithe body fitted against his as tightly as if moulded to it by some master sculptor. As though someone had stripped away a layer of his skin, he could feel every tiny flutter of her pulse and of her breathing. The scent of her perfumed skin mingled in his nostrils with the musk of their passion.

Gradually his brain began to reassemble itself from whatever parts of the galaxy it had splintered into. 'Am I squashing you?' he asked, his eyes still closed, his cheek against her hair.

'Yes,' she said consideringly, her breath tickling his jaw. 'But I like it.'

'That is a good thing. I do not think I could move.'

She wriggled against him, then, apparently satisfied, tightened her arms again and fell silent. Drew made himself think about what he was feeling— because he could not understand it. He had followed this woman from the Sarayi because he was concerned for her, and because she had aroused both his body and his interest when he'd seen her on the ship.

He had made love to her because she was, quite simply, lovely, and because she wanted him. And then he had found he could not stop. And it was not only because he had wanted physical gratification for himself, he realised. He could have taken her at once and satisfied both of them—and that would have been that. But instead he had wanted to make love to her for her pleasure, and for his too, watching her react to his caresses, over and over again.

She was so sensual, so responsive—and she could become a drug, an obsession. And that he could not afford. Not since Mara. With her he had found himself in love, and he had fooled himself that he could take a woman into the wilds of Anatolia with him. That he could protect her. And so he had—against enemies he could fight with a sword or a pistol, or by his knowledge of the wilds. But he could not protect a fragile girl against fever, miles from any doctor, and she had died, and his capacity to love with her.

Since then his mistresses had been women of the world—exotic creatures who were more than happy to lounge at home, waiting for him to return, making only the lightest pretence that this was anything but a mutually beneficial business transaction. His emotions need not be engaged: it was much safer that way.

But this woman was neither a bird of paradise to be bought, nor an innocent and wide-eyed girl who adored him uncritically. Caroline was a widow, independent, intelligent and courageous.

He remembered the way she had stood her ground as he approached her on the ship, even though she had been dying of mortification and any other woman would have fled in hysterics. In the audience chamber she had curtseyed before the Sultan with as much poise as though she were in the familiar ballroom of Clarence House, and the sovereign in front of her the jovial and indulgent Regent, yet the hem of her skirts had trembled with her nerves.

'I think my feet have gone to sleep.' The breathy whisper in his ear made him open his eyes and raise himself enough to look down into her flushed face, soft with the aftermath of his lovemaking.

'I'm sorry.' He rolled to one side and caught her into the crook of his arm. 'That was—'

'Very nice?' she finished primly, her eyes twinkling with amusement. 'I do not think I have the vocabulary.'

'Neither do I,' he admitted. 'But, yes, it was very nice.' He found himself held by her shy smile. She was not quite sure what to say next, and, he realised with a glow of pleasure, she was feeling comfortable enough with him not to be embarrassed by that.

'It is difficult to make conversation in this position, isn't it?' he offered. 'Should we have dinner?'

'Please. I know I should not say so, but I am *famished.*'

'Must be the exercise,' Drew said slyly, helping her to her feet. He slung the towel, now considerably the worse for wear, round his waist again. 'Just clap your hands when you are ready, and they will bring you your clothes.'

Your clothes did not, apparently, mean her own clothes, but instead a sweeping caftan of soft shades of blue, shot through with gold thread and heavily embroidered at the slit neckline, and kid slippers, embossed with gilt and with curling toes.

Harika and Sahiba brushed out her hair so it fell in a curling mass to her shoulders, and then caught it up in twists of deep blue silk.

'You are very beautiful,' Harika pronounced solemnly. 'You will look good by Drew *pasha's* side. He is so dark; you are so fair.'

She held up a mirror and Caroline gasped. That was not her. She was pretty enough, she had always believed. Not so lovely that she had acquired the reputation of an *Incomparable* when she was just out, but well enough, if one liked blondes who were not particularly fashionable.

William had always insisted she was a beauty. But William, bless him, had doted on her, and had failed to see the slightest flaw, even on the dreadful day when she had acquired a pimple on the end of her nose just before the Duchess of Beaufort's ball.

There was no sign of a pimple now. Her skin, lightly kissed into pale honey by the sun, was smooth. Her hair shone, rivalling the gold in her caftan. Her mouth was full and red and swollen from kissing. Her eyes, which she had always considered a regrettable greyish shade, had become azure with reflections of the blue she was wearing.

And the exotic garment which had seemed so loose as it had gone on, actually clung over her breasts, outlining them, before sweeping down to hint teasingly at the curves below.

'I do not look *too* bad,' she said carefully, a lifetime of schooling in modesty and restraint shaken in the face of what the mirror showed her. It seemed indecent to be wearing so little. The caftan covered her from shoulders to toes, yet under it she was naked save for the finest linen shift. *And Drew knows exactly what I am wearing*, she thought with a delicious frisson of erotic danger.

He stood up as she was shown into the room where their meal had been set, uncoiling himself from the cushions with a grace that took her breath. Then she saw his expression and forgot to breathe entirely.

'Caroline.'

'Drew,' she managed, before she suffocated. 'I am sorry, I must have kept you waiting, but the maids seem to want to polish me all over!'

She said it as a joke, to lighten the atmosphere, and saw his eyes glaze over with what could only be desire.

'Lucky you,' he said as he settled her amongst the cushions in front of the wide, low table heaped with platters. If she had not grown to know him so well in the past few hours she would have missed the hitch in his breathing as he composed himself. 'My masseur's idea of sending me out in a fit condition to eat dinner involves scrubbing me all over with a horsehair brush, then beating the living daylights out of all the muscles he can find, and digging for those he cannot.'

Resolutely stamping on the mental picture of Drew's naked, hard-muscled body, Caroline accepted a tall glass of pale golden liquid and sipped it cautiously. Apples and honey and gentle spices all rolled over her tongue, chilled from the ice the pitcher had been sitting in.

'You keep to the custom of the country and do not drink alcohol?' she asked.

'Yes, although I drink it when I dine at the Embassy. I have not converted. It is just that I do not choose to give offence to my household, and when I am travelling it is pointless to expect to find wine. Easier to become accustomed to abstaining.'

'And you are travelling again soon? Or are you writing?' Caroline took one of the tiny stuffed pastries from the tray in front of her and bit into it. It was filled with a delicately balanced mix of minced, spiced meat and fruit. She savoured it, then took another. 'These are delicious.'

He nodded in acknowledgement of her opinion and took one when she offered the platter. 'I am planning a trip into Cappadoccia to look for the ancient rock-cut villages that are rumoured to line the Ihlara Valley. The whole area sounds spectacular, but no Western travellers have ever reported back on it. Before I go I want to finish an article for the Royal Society on Aya Sofia, and I have some business to complete before I can leave the *khan* for my manager to run.'

'You will be away long?' There were skewers of some pale meat—chicken, perhaps, or kid—glossy with a golden sauce. Her mouth watering, Caroline lifted one and began to nibble on it.

'Six months, possibly a little more.' His eyes were on her mouth as she nipped at the savoury morsels, his gaze hooded.

'And what do you trade in from your *khan*?' She knew about those, the fortified storehouses and trading rooms built around courtyards large enough to encompass a camel train. They studded the city, forming hubs where the wealth of the empire poured into Constantinople and flowed out again, bringing gold in return.

'Silks—like everyone. Embroidered cloths from Anatolia. Amber, uncut gemstones—anything I see that I think may have a market here or in Europe. I was coming back from a trip to Rome to talk to my agent there when we met.'

Caroline found her gaze straying round the room, taking in the ornate carving, the richness of the tiles, the sumptuous silks and brocades.

'You are wondering if that pays for this house and for my travelling?'

She blushed. 'I…yes. I do apologise—so ill-bred of me.'

'To imply that a gentleman depends on trade?' He was laughing at her, not unkindly.

'Yes,' she agreed bluntly. 'Such a stupid attitude people have—as though breeding miraculously conveys wealth on you! I used to despise people who sneered at the nabobs who came back to English Society having made a fortune entirely by their own hard work, when the people doing the sneering were often up to their ears in debt to unfortunate tradespeople.'

Drew filled his glass and sat, twirling the long stem absently between his fingers. 'I was always determined to travel and to write. My father had other plans for me as the second son—I was destined for a glorious military career, in his eyes. When I pointed out that I am very bad at taking orders, a fact of which he was only too aware, he announced that I would join the diplomatic service instead. He expected me to be pleased with this decision as it would, he pointed out, involve travel and hob-nobbing with foreigners.

'My carefully rehearsed explanation of where I wanted to go and why I was interested in archaeological research and the study of other cultures lasted about ten minutes. We then got down to one of our usual blazing rows, which ended with him disinheriting me and throwing me out of the house.'

'Could he do that?' Caroline asked, appalled.

'As I'm the younger son and nothing is entailed on me, yes.' Drew grimaced. 'I won't pretend it was not unpleasant. If my mother had still been alive I would have apologised and tried to get back on terms with him for her sake. But she was not, and so I turned up on my godfather's doorstep, full of righteous indignation, and scared to death by what I had done. Not that I would have admitted that for the world.'

He leaned across to pass her a dish of meatballs. 'Try these—and some of that salad, with the flat bread. My godfather told me that my father was a damned fool and that I took after him—and then gave me five hundred pounds and told me to go away and earn my own living. I did.'

'And are you still estranged from your family?' Caroline realised she had lost count of the number of delicious little meatballs she had popped into her mouth, and guiltily applied herself to the salad.

'Not from my brother and his family. I sent his wife a bride-gift of some very handsome silks, with the mark of my trading house prominent on the packaging to annoy Father, and Giles and I write quite regularly. We see each other too, on the occasions I get back to England. He tells me he is taking care of what should have been my inheritance, with a view to giving it back when our esteemed father finally departs, which is decent of him.'

'Yes,' Caroline agreed. 'It would be dreadful to be cut off from all your family and from your English ties.

I expect your brother is thinking of your own sons and making sure they have an English inheritance.'

She had spoken warmly, thinking of her own brothers and their loyalty to each other and to her, and she was not prepared for the shuttered look that came over Drew's face. She had blundered, drawn into an unwarranted comment on his personal affairs, and bit her lip in mortification. 'I am sorry. I have no right to comment.'

Drew smiled at her, the restraint gone. 'No, I confided in you—you have every right to respond. It is good to have someone with whom to speak of such matters. I live a full life, but sometimes a lonely one.' He gave himself a little shake and grinned. 'Lord, how self-centred I sound! I will have you feeling sorry for me in a minute—although of course that may have benefits, if you are moved to console me.'

Caroline sent him a sidelong glance from beneath her lashes. 'I think we have established that you have absolutely no need to rely on any feelings of pity on my part to bring me to your bed.' She sighed. 'Which is a very lowering and mortifying thought.'

'It is?' Drew put down the skewer of grilled fruit he was biting into and regarded her. 'Why?'

'Because…well, obviously because it is shocking…not respectable, not— Stop laughing at me!'

Still laughing, he bent over the corner of the table and kissed her lightly, his lips tasting of sugared fruit. 'You are unattached. You are adult. No one knows, no one is going to be hurt by what we are doing.'

'Everyone at the Embassy knows I am here.' Her tongue ran round her lips, licking off the juice; his eyes grew smoky as he watched her, and she felt the throb of the pulse between her legs start into life again.

'And they believe I am sleeping at my *khan*. I mentioned it the other night, when I was dining at the Embassy—I have a valuable shipment of Baltic amber there. I reminded the Secretary of that conversation when he came in answer to my message, all the while carefully assuring him that I had ample security at this house.'

'You lied to him?'

'Certainly not. I simply commented on rumours still persisting that a gang of thieves was after amber. He made the connection himself.' He watched her, his lids hooded. 'You are an independent woman. All that matters is that we are discreet. Now, try this honey cake.'

'I am full,' she protested, eying the golden nut-encrusted confection. 'Well, perhaps just a little…'

'I will lick the honey off,' Drew offered, spooning a slice onto a plate for her. 'Eat it with your fingers—get really sticky,' he teased hopefully.

Defiantly Caroline seized a fork and began to eat in tiny, ladylike morsels, carefully keeping the dripping sweetness away from both her chin and her fingers.

'Spoilsport.' He watched her as she ate, bringing the colour up into her cheeks. How was he able to wreak such havoc on her feelings, on her respectability, on all her reserve, in the course of barely a day? Never mind what Drew said, it *was* mortifying that she had no self-control as far as he was concerned.

As long as it was just him. It was an awful thought—but what if she would have been this wanton with *any* man she had found herself alone with? What if, at heart, she was abandoned and a loose woman?

'Now what are you brooding about?' he asked, and she realised she was sitting with the fork suspended in mid-air.

'Oh! Just something in your book. I have been rereading the section on Alinda, and I do not understand how you can conclude the carvings are as old as you say they are.'

'By comparison with those elsewhere, which have been dated by their association with known Greek work,' he explained.

If he was surprised by her abrupt question he did not show it. He rinsed his fingers in a bowl of warm water which had slices of lemon floating in it, picked up a linen square to dry his hands on, and leaned back, apparently content to answer her questions.

'So that is how all antiquities are dated?' She had got honey on her fingers after all. Absently Caroline sucked it off and put down her plate. 'I had wondered about that. Is it the same for Egyptian objects as well?'

'You are taking me out of my depth with ancient Egypt.' She did not believe that for a minute. 'But, yes, it is the same. Often we cannot put a definite date on something, only say it is before this or after that.'

They talked on while the shadows grew long across the floor and the sounds of the muezzins calling evening prayer drifted across the city. Flocks of pigeons wheeled across the sky, making for their roosts, and the street sounds, penetrating faintly through the high walls and the heavily planted garden, changed their rhythm from day to night.

Maids came in and lit lamps, cleared the table, brought coffee for them both and a hookah for Drew. He toyed with it rather than smoked it, mesmerising her with his long fingers on the carved mouthpiece as they talked. Occasionally he would draw on it, filling the room with a bubbling sound as smoke escaped through the water to scent the air with another layer of exotic sensation.

Caroline longed to try it, but resisted asking. She would end up coughing and spluttering, and she did not want anything to break the spell in the room.

Night-scented flowers perfumed the air, mingling with the Turkish tobacco and making her head spin pleasantly. The air was balmy, no longer hot, and Drew's voice was easy to lose herself in. She was warm, well fed, her limbs massaged and oiled into silken sleekness, her body loved into sensual relaxation. She thought hazily that if she could purr, she would.

CHAPTER SEVEN

DREW leant to put down his coffee cup, then stretched. God, he felt good. And there was an entire night ahead of them. Hours of darkness to explore this fascinating woman until he knew her completely. Hours to sate himself with her so that the uncomfortable feelings she evoked in him were quashed and he could safely view her as just another lover.

Caroline was a good listener. She had curled up in the nest of cushions, following what he said, answering him with more questions—questions which revealed the depth of her reading and the extent of her understanding. She obviously had access to a wide library and the intelligence to read it with discrimination. Oh, for a male companion with that level of interest—someone to share the adventure of exploration and discovery with.

But now there was another voyage of discovery to continue. He rose from the divan and went across to her, ready to pull her to her feet, carry her to his bed.

He was greeted by a very soft snore, a little wiffling noise as she snuggled down against a bolster embroidered with tulips and lilies in shades of scarlet and green. Drew stood with arms crossed, watching her, a smile curving his lips. So much for fantasies of a night of erotic delight! He should know better than to encourage a woman to sample every dish on the table if he wanted her to stay awake. Gently inching her into his arms to avoid rousing her, he lifted Caroline out of the cushions and carried her to his bedchamber.

The maids had left the sheets drawn back. He stood her on her feet, murmuring in her ear. 'Just like that for a moment, darling. Just hang on to me.'

Obedient, even though only half-awake, she clung to him while he slipped the caftan over her head, hesitated at the sight of the shift, and then left it. It was one thing to glory in her naked beauty while she was a willing participant, but to strip her while she was unaware felt like voyeurism.

He pulled off his own clothes and lay down beside her, pulling one sheet over them, as much to shut off the sight of her slender body and the outline of her long legs than for any need for warmth.

Beside him, completely relaxed on the piled mattresses, Caroline slept while he lay, watching the shadows on the ceiling and trying to formulate a plan to better fortify the *khan* against jewel thieves. It was the least erotic thing he could think of, but it did not seem to be working. This could be a long night.

There was someone breathing in her bedroom. Caroline lay listening to the unmistakably male sound while the fogs of sleep cleared and she remembered where she was. *Drew.* She was with Drew, and apparently in his bed. She tried to remember what had happened last night, but all she could recall was eating far too much and then listening to Drew talk, asking all the questions that had been filling her notebooks. And then the colours in the room had begun to fade, his voice had become a deep, soporific murmur—and she must have gone to sleep.

And then what? Caroline opened one eye and raised her head so she could look down the length of her body. She was modestly clad in the linen shift she had worn under the caftan last night. With a sigh of relief she lay back, then smiled at herself. What nonsense—she had spent the previous day in a quite scandalously intimate manner with a man she had hardly known, and here she was worrying about being naked in his bed. *Idiot.*

Oh, but I feel so good! She almost spoke the words out loud. She could have gone to the window and shouted them, they clamoured so loudly in her head. She felt as though every muscle and sinew was velvet, that her skin was a hundred times more sensitive than it had ever been, and her body ached softly, pleasantly, in every intimate, hidden place.

Drew was asleep. She recognised the sound of a man deeply unconscious without having to look and see. She lay there, putting off the moment when she turned to see him much as a child might prolong the delicious anticipation of a sweet by leaving it in its bag for a few seconds longer.

When Caroline turned carefully to her right she found Drew was naked, stretched out on his back, his arms flung above his head, the long-fingered hands lax on the pillows. The sheet was crumpled at the foot of the bed, twisted round one of his feet. A restless sleeper, she concluded, turning back to her scrutiny.

The way he was lying stretched his ribcage out, so she could admire every defined muscle. She lay, propped up on her elbow, and studied the length of his dark lashes, fanned on his cheekbones, the way his hair, loose, fell across the pillow. She resisted the temptation to brush one lock back from his forehead.

If he did not shave, his beard would be as dark and thick as the Sultan's, she realised, studying the stubble, wondering how it would feel under her palm. The hair on his chest was as dark, curling and crisp. Caroline stretched out a hand and brushed it lightly. He did not stir. What would happen if she touched a nipple? Would it react as it did when he was awake?

She tried, with one fingertip. It did, hardening instantly to her touch. She snatched back her hand and touched the other one, with the same result. Catching her under-lip in her teeth she let her flattened palm drift down over the dark hair to his navel. And stopped.

He had been lying completely relaxed. *All* of him had been relaxed—including the very impressive member that had given her so much pleasure yesterday. Now it was stirring. Caroline glanced guiltily at Drew's face, but his lids did not flicker, his breathing was as deep as before. She let her hand rest on the flat stomach, then spread her fingers. There was no mistaking it. Even profoundly asleep, he was aroused by her touch.

It is nothing to be flattered about, she told herself. *He doesn't know who is caressing him.* But the urge to touch would not go away. She let her fingers glide downwards, into the denser curls, brushing the head of his erection that was growing more…erect…every moment.

Any minute now he would wake up, take control, and she, Caroline Morvall, would no longer be scandalously caressing a man, taking the initiative in this wanton manner. She had never done so with William, she realised. She had always been the one made love to. From the hissed confidences and gossip of the other matrons she gathered that some women—loose women—did that sort of thing. But naturally well-bred wives did not.

It was so hot. She let the back of her hand rest against the length of it and found the skin softer than she had realised. The urge to stroke was a positively physical force and she gave in to it, let her fingertips graze downwards from tip to root, then up again. Drew sighed, turned his head on the pillow, and she froze, then relaxed as regular breathing resumed.

What she wanted to do, she realised with fascinated horror, was to kiss him—*there*. Some men liked it, apparently: Mrs Bartholomew had shocked and titillated the entire group of matrons by confiding that her daughter had been utterly traumatised by her husband's demand that she do such a thing. It was, the ladies had agreed, the sort of perverted outrage that a man might demand of a whore, but never of a wife.

Why not? Caroline wondered. *It would not be shocking if I kissed the rest of him.* More than kissing was involved, she had gathered from the whispers and murmured outrage. Although that sounded very…daring. It might wake him up—although stroking him as she was doing now had not, so far. What if she did it wrong? *Unless I actually bit him, I don't see how I can,* she decided, inching down the bed.

She leaned over and touched her lips to the hard, thrusting curve, then licked cautiously. Musk, spice, man—the scent she had come to know as simply *Drew*. It felt good, the skin velvet under her caress. She lapped upwards, summoned all her courage, and took him in her mouth.

It was not what she had expected to feel at all. She felt powerful, aroused, shaken by a desire that lanced through her. Caroline straightened up, shifted to straddle his legs, threw her hair back over her shoulders and bent to repeat the caress.

This feels right, she realised. *He kisses* me *this intimately. It must be right.* Instinctively she used tongue and lips, lost to the outside world now, focussed utterly on learning this new art. Her hands were pressed either side of his narrow flanks, and she felt it as his body began to respond, thrusting to meet her. Her tentative movements became more assured as she followed his, then, just as she thought she had got the rhythm exactly, Drew climaxed.

With a gasp, she sat back. Had she meant to go that far? She did not know. All she knew was that she was powerfully aroused, and far too shocked at herself to wake him. For he was still asleep, although he had moaned aloud, and there was a flush of blood across his breastbone and on his cheeks.

'I love you,' she whispered, then froze at the sound of her own voice. *No, I love William. I don't know this man...*

Yes, you do, another voice inside her head told her. *You have read his writings, you have been inside his mind, you have talked with him, you have made love with him. You know he is brave and intelligent, and that he makes you laugh with him and sob with passion in his arms. And William has gone.*

But... Caroline got down from the bed, jarring her heels as she discovered that they had been sleeping on a heap of five mattresses. *The Princess and the pea,* she thought wildly as she fled from the bedchamber and through the first door she came to. *I wouldn't have noticed if there was a pound and a half of peas under those mattresses.*

She was in Drew's study. An English writing table stood in the window, a pile of manuscript paper weighted down with a fragment of marble on one side. The fragment was a hand, the slender fingers curving protectively over the paper. She could see they were covered in writing, but she did not want to pry.

There were books everywhere—some she recognised from William's library, many that were new to her. And everywhere there were maps: pinned to the walls, weighted down on the divan by more books, rolled and stacked in corners.

The one pinned up next to the desk must be his next expedition, she decided, calming her breathing by making herself focus. She studied it, trying to place the location, but although she could read one or two names in what seemed an uncharted mass, she could not place it. One location was marked by a large cross. *Ihlara,* she read. That must be the site. Pinned to the map were notes, most of them crumpled: some quotes from other works, some lists, some questions. *Byzantine, certainly. Hittite?* one read. Another scribble ran across the bottom of a quote about desert hermits: *All monasteries? Surely not?*

Caroline stood and read the notes, trying to make

sense of them and find the place-names on the map. *I want to see it. A new site, one never studied scientifically, never mapped out. What an opportunity. He will let me come with him. He knows I understand. He knows I am truly interested...*

There was a movement behind her and she swung round to see Drew, a robe around his shoulders, regarding her steadily. 'I had a dream,' he remarked.

Drew had woken, shaking. Never, not even after the longest period of sexual abstinence he could recall, had he had a dream like that. And he had passed the previous day doing virtually nothing but making love: frustrated he was not. So what had prompted that? It had been so vibrantly real it was hard to believe it was his imagination. *And what an imagination,* he congratulated himself wryly. Caroline's lips, her tongue... *Oh, Lord, did I wake her up?* The embarrassment of that had had him gritting his teeth and opening one eye.

She had gone. Drew had sat up with a groan, intending to bury his head in his hands—and had found he was looking at one long blonde hair, draped elegantly across his loins. And at either side of his thighs the indentation of two knees in the yielding mattress.

It had not been a dream. He'd flopped back onto the pillows, shaken. And what did that mean? Did it make any difference? No, it didn't. Although it gave him some wonderfully stimulating ideas for the morning.

But where was Caroline? He'd swung his legs off the bed, tugged on loose trousers and found a robe, dragging it round him without bothering to find the cord and tie it. She was in the first room he tried—his study. He stood in the open doorway, watching her as she studied the map, her head on one side, the glorious mass of her hair hanging down and the sun streaming through the window, silhouetting her naked figure with graphic accuracy through the fine linen shift.

He must have made some noise, for she turned, the colour flooding up under her skin to stain her from breastbone to hairline.

'I had a dream,' he remarked, trying to control the urge to take two long strides across the room and take her there and then on the desk, crushing his paper for the Royal Society under their hot bodies.

'Oh.' She put her hands to her burning cheeks. 'But it wasn't…'

'I know.' He held up the long hair. 'You should check for evidence.'

'I am so sorry.' She held his eyes with what seemed to be grim determination. He was puzzled, and tried not to show it. 'I should never have…not while you were asleep… I just couldn't help myself.'

'There is no need to apologise,' Drew said warmly. 'Just do it again while I am conscious.'

'But I don't expect I did it right.' She was twisting her hands in her shift now. 'I've never done that before. I don't expect I would please you if you were aware of what I was doing.'

Drew realised he was staring at her blankly, and made himself cross the room to her side. 'What do you mean?'

'I thought it would be obvious,' Caroline said, embarrassment making her voice sharp. 'I have never touched a man like that before. I know it is very shocking and forward, and you probably think I am positively abandoned, only I wanted to touch you. And then…I couldn't resist.'

She is more sheltered, more innocent than I thought. This is a woman who has been cosseted by a middle-aged lover, and now she has dived in over her head. And it is all my damned fault.

'I wanted to please you—and myself. You are very beautiful,' she admitted, with a frankness that took what little breath he had away. He tried to pull himself together, to ignore the fact that she was quivering with nerves and that he wanted to take her into his arms.

'Caroline, you are making me out to be something I am not. You do not know me.'

'Yes, I do. I have read what you have written and I have talked with you. I know how you make love, and I know that you are kind to foolish women who embarrass themselves on ships. I know you are a gentleman.'

Ouch. Yes, I am a gentleman, and it is about time I remember it and take her back to the Embassy before she starts to feel for me what I very much fear I am feeling for her.

She turned away, more at ease now she had unburdened herself of that confession, apparently completely unaware of the effect she was having on him. 'Is this your new expedition?'

Drew glanced at the map. 'Yes.'

'Then take me with you.' She turned from the map, laying her palms flat against his chest. 'Take me to Cappadoccia.'

The clear morning light seemed to shimmer. The clear blue eyes, smooth, faintly blushing skin and clean, luxuriant hair of the woman in front of him blurred and became the thin, fever-flushed face of Mara, her unfocussed black eyes fixed imploringly on him, her lank, sweat-soaked hair falling over his arm as he supported her, tried to make her drink, take what medicines he had.

'Drew?'

Mara had begged him too—begged him to make her better. But he had not.

'No.' He snapped out the word like a blow. 'No. Absolutely not!'

CHAPTER EIGHT

'Absolutely not!' That was not just a refusal: there was anger in his voice, and something else she did not understand. Shocked, Caroline stepped backwards, coming up hard against the sharp edge of the desk. He was turning her down? Just like that? After what had just passed between them?

'Why not?' she asked, forcing herself to speak in a calm, reasonable voice, as if he had refused to take her for a drive in the park rather than spurned her and everything she was offering him of herself.

'It is not safe. I cannot look after you, and you would be a damned nuisance.' Drew stalked off to the other end of the study and began to roll up maps with the air of a man who would rather be wringing necks. 'This is not some jaunt a few miles along the coast to look at pretty Roman ruins. There is desert and steppe and tribes who have hardly seen a Western face before. I have no clear idea of where I am going, or what to expect when I get there. I will have more than enough to contend with without bear-leading a tourist.'

'A *tourist*?' Caroline demanded indignantly. It was still not real. He would relent in a minute. All she had to do was explain properly and he would understand. 'I am not a tourist! I am a traveller. I have crossed Europe to get here, I have read everything I could lay my hands on, I intend hiring only the best guides and dragomen—'

'My great-aunt who is eighty could have got this far with a competent courier. But you have stepped into a different world now, Lady Morvall. You are a young woman. You are a young, *single* woman.' His words had the dispassionate hurtfulness of hammer-blows, and pain began to break through the shield of practicality she had thrown up. A dim realisation that it was going to hurt much more, very soon, began to penetrate her confusion.

'You have absolutely no idea about the East except what you have read in books, and you are so far out of your depth that if you looked down you would realise that you will drown the moment you are out of reach of the Embassy.'

'I had a successful audience with the Sultan,' she began hotly. Losing her temper was better than breaking down and crying with the hurt of it, she told herself fiercely.

'You had a successful audience because I—fool that I am—told him that you would be safe enough, and could be influenced to go only to those coastal resorts that are much frequented by Europeans. I was wrong. Whatever made me think that you are safe out? You haven't even the sense to eat and drink adequately to cope with a hot climate. You fainted in the Bazaar and I had to rescue you. You talk about taking off for Cappadoccia and you haven't a clue where it is.'

'Yes, I have! It is in Anatolia.' She read from his uncompromising expression that this was inadequate. Panic that he really meant it made her babble. 'Central Anatolia. To the south. Oh, for goodness' sake, don't look at me like that! What are maps for?' She marched up and prodded him in the chest with one finger. 'I told you—I will hire guides.'

'How do you know who to trust?' Drew leaned one shoulder against the wall and regarded her from under hooded lids, his voice ominously calm.

'I will take advice from the Embassy.' She was pleading now. Where had her pride gone? Caroline fought for it—fought to turn this scene from a rejected woman begging to her lover into one in which a fellow traveller had made a reasonable request which he had rejected unreasonably. She had to persuade him… He couldn't leave her, not now.

'Indeed? There are very few men in Constantinople who know the route, who are trustworthy and who would be prepared to go with European travellers. And I am hiring them.'

'If I go with you, then I won't need to hire one, will I?' she pointed out, feigning sweet, acid reason, and she saw his eyes narrow even more. 'I will pay my share, if that is what is worrying you.'

'No, it is not what is worrying me. What is worrying me—other than the nuisance of having my expedition cluttered up by a gaggle of women—is going into virtually uncharted wilderness with a very valuable object which might as well have a large sign on it saying *Steal Me*.'

Caroline pushed away the insulting reference to gaggles of women. He was hitting out at her, as she was at him. 'What valuable object?'

Drew reached out and picked up the mass of her blonde hair, letting it run through his fingers. 'Why, you, my dear. You had your little frisson of titillating horror over the Sultan and his harem, you were shocked to think I might keep one—but many men do, and the women in them are slaves, captured, sold and bought. And guess which ones fetch the most money? The European blondes.'

'You are just trying to frighten me,' she said, forcing the quaver out of her voice with an effort.

'But of course,' Drew said lazily, then swung round with a speed that left her gasping, caught her wrists above her head, hard in one hand, and pushed her back against the wall, his body trapping hers. Through the thin shift she could feel his hard thighs, the heat of his bare chest. His breath was in her face; his eyes held hers. 'Who knows where you are?'

'The Embassy. Ismael.' Only pride stopped her begging to be freed, and pride was all that was keeping her together now. Her body was quivering, and she realised, despising herself, that she did not know whether it was from fear or desire.

'And who told the Embassy?'

'You…you did.'

Drew only grinned, wolfishly.

'And, if you didn't, Ismael would have told them what happened.'

'He is for hire. I pay well. I am Drew *pasha*,' he said with breathtaking arrogance.

'I don't believe you.' *The endless shuttered windows of the royal harem, the grilles over the windows, two hundred women shut up to service the lusts and whims of one man…*

'I might not want to be bothered with you on a journey,' but it is very tempting to keep you here until I return.' His mouth came down, feathered lightly over her lips. The ease with which he was holding her still was positively insulting. Caroline raised one knee sharply. Drew chuckled, simply leaning his weight against her so that her legs were trapped, and proceeded to plunder her mouth with leisurely thoroughness.

Now she was in no doubt about how she was feeling. She was furious. That he was finding the experience arousing was patently obvious. From the evidence of the sensational novels she had beguiled her journey with, most women finding themselves in the arms of a handsome ravisher in exotic circumstances would too. Caroline had a fleeting thought of writing to the publishers of the Minerva Press and complaining—when she got out of this—and bit his lip.

It worked admirably. Drew let her go, rubbing the back of one hand across his mouth. 'You, my dear Lady Morvall, are more trouble than you are worth.'

Caroline slapped him. To her fury it did not even rock him back on his heels. 'I would not travel with you to the end of the street if you asked me!' *Yes, I would. I would. Just one word...*

'Excellent,' he remarked. 'We are entirely in accord, then. You go back to the Embassy, spend a week or two learning tourist Turkish, hire a dragoman who knows all about Bursa, go and see the sites and buy some expensive silk to take home.'

She stared at him, the hot anger gradually ebbing away and leaving her cold. This was not Drew—not the real Drew. For some reason he wanted to get rid of her. But only since she had said she wanted to travel with him. What had she said that could account for this blatant attempt to make her fear and dislike him?

The inimical grey eyes stared back at her, willing her to give in and admit she could not cope, that she was afraid. Fear. That was the other emotion in his eyes when he looked at her. But fear of what? Fear that she might be getting too close? Fear that she might be falling in love with him?

And of course she was. She had. How could she not? And she had fallen in love with a man who could, apparently, cope with anything except clinging, lovesick females.

'I shall do just that,' she said frostily, dragging the rags of her pride around her like a cloak for her breaking heart. 'I wish you well in your expedition and I look forward to reading about it eventually. I am sure, unencumbered by *a gaggle of females*, it will be a great success.'

She walked to the door, so close that the hem of her shift flicked the brocade of his robe. She was damned if she was going to let him see how he affected her. If he put out his hand now, if he said anything… 'I envy you your freedom, Mr Fenton, and I envy you the sights you will see. But I am sorry for you as well. Independence is admirable, but are you quite sure you know what you are running away from?'

He said nothing, made no move to stop her. In the passageway she clapped her hands sharply and the two maids materialised as though by magic.

'*Günaydin,*' she said crisply. It felt as though her mind was working on two levels—one of them confused and weeping, the other cold and focused.

'Good morning, Caroline *hanim*,' they chorused.

'I must go back to the Embassy now. Please can you fetch my clothes and arrange for a carriage?'

Sahiba glanced towards the half-open door of the study.

'Drew *pasha* does not wish to be disturbed,' Caroline announced loudly. The door shut with a snap that was a more than adequate answer.

So that was the end of a quite extraordinary episode. Now all she had to do was put it behind her, forget the fact that she had fallen in love, and decide what to do next. *How easy, how simple,* she thought wildly.

If she listened to Drew she should confine herself to the well-trodden tourist paths and behave like a respectable English lady abroad. If she listened to the small, cringing ball of hurt pride and fear that was inhabiting the pit of her stomach she should turn tail and flee back to England. And if she listened to her heart she would open that door, walk back in there and tell him she loved him. And have her love thrown back in her face. Caroline knew, deep inside, that she could not face that rejection a second time.

And what does my head say? she wondered as she followed the girls down the passageway and into a room where her own clothes were laid out, brushed and immaculate.

'Caroline *hanim*?' Harika asked, watching her with concerned brown eyes.

'What? Oh, I am sorry. I was thinking.' *Think, plan, survive. You did it when William died. Have courage. You can live without love.* She pressed the back of her hand against her mouth and successfully stifled the sob that threatened to escape. 'Please—I must leave now.'

* * *

'Lady Morvall!' Mr Hamilton almost ran down the steps into the courtyard as her carriage drew in. 'Thank goodness. I was just about to send the doctor and a carriage, despite what Mr Fenton said.'

'Good morning, Mr Hamilton.' Caroline allowed herself to be helped down, stumbling slightly. It was extraordinary how quickly one became accustomed to loose garments and an absence of stays. She felt as though she was trussed up like a parcel now. The fact that her mind seemed disconnected from her limbs did not help, either. 'And just what did Mr Fenton say?'

'That you should be allowed to rest for at least twenty-four hours and that his household would take care of you. He assured us that it was nothing more than heat exhaustion and lack of sustenance…' He put one hand under her elbow and ushered her inside. 'I will send for Dr Remaud. He is attached to the French Embassy, but we find him excellent.'

Caroline suppressed a wry smile that so soon after the end of the war the old enemies were cheerfully co-operating. 'No, there is no need of that. Mr Fenton's staff were most attentive, and I feel much better now.'

'Did you see much of Mr Fenton?' the Secretary enquired, with an air of making only casual conversation.

I had my eyes closed much of the time… 'I had the opportunity to thank him,' Caroline said mendaciously. 'I believe he told you he was staying at his *khan.*' *He deceives so easily. Am I just another gullible fool? But he was so tender, so passionate, so…*

'Yes, of course.' Mr Hamilton sounded reassured. 'I was a little concerned that the Ambassador might feel I should have sent your woman over, but I felt it would demonstrate an insulting anxiety about Mr Fenton's intentions. And, after all, he is very well known to us here.' He smiled. 'Still, I am relieved to know my instincts were correct.'

Of course they were, Mr Hamilton, Caroline thought bleakly. *Mr Fenton was the perfect host. He gave me food, water and relief for my most pressing desires. And all he took in return was my heart.*

'Oh, excuse me, *madame.*' A tall man in Western dress stopped abruptly at the foot of the stairs, just before they collided.

'Ah, yes. Lady Morvall, may I introduce Herr Dettmer? Herr Dettmer is the swordmaster who is training His Excellency's sons while they are here. He has just called to discover when the Ambassador and the young men will be returning.'

'My Lady!' The German clicked his heels and bowed.

Caroline bowed in return. *What a very large, calm, competent-looking man,* she mused. 'Do you teach horsemanship as well as swordplay, Herr Dettmer?'

'Myself, no, *madame*, but my cousin Friedrich does.'

'Indeed. Mr Hamilton, I wonder if you would be so good as to send my maid to me here?'

The Secretary hurried off, leaving Caroline alone with the German. 'There is something I may assist you with, *madame*?' Yes, she had been correct. He was perceptive.

'Indeed there is, Herr Dettmer. Tell me, do you and your cousin have any room in your no doubt busy schedules to take another pupil who will require intensive tuition in both horsemanship and self-defence?'

'But, yes, *madame*. And who is the young gentleman who requires tuition?'

Gascoyne appeared before she could answer him. 'My lady! Are you all right?'

'Yes, I am fine, Gascoyne. Now, I need you to find me a good local tailor. Mr Hamilton, I require a teacher of Turkish. And, Herr Dettmer—*I* am your student.'

Caroline looked round at their astounded faces and smiled, despite the cramping misery inside. *So, he thinks I am not safe out and that I will simply be a liability, does he? Well, Drew Fenton, it is time I showed you, myself and everyone else that I am not reliant on a man to manage my life. I thought I needed love to be whole, and I was right—so right. But it seems I can live with part of me missing, and I am not going to sacrifice everything else because of it.*

Cappadoccia: late September 1817

Caroline laughed out loud for sheer joy, dug her heels into the flanks of the grey Arab and gave him his head. The wide grey-green plain stretched to the horizon, broken here and there by low hills and patches of scrub. The air was warm, with just the faintest hint, now that the sun was beginning to set, that autumn was on its way.

Dust and the aroma of crushed herbs rose from beneath the pounding hooves, the long, sleeveless coat she wore over her tunic and breeches flew behind her like a banner, and the short tails of her turban snapped in the wind.

But even as she gave herself up to the exhilaration she was scanning the horizon as she had been taught, marking distance in her head, watching the ground ahead. *Time to go back.*

She tightened the reins, speaking to the stallion, and it slowed, swinging in response to her signals to canter in a wide arc before heading back to where her party were setting up camp.

'You lovely thing, Cloud,' she crooned, running one hand down the muscled neck. 'You beautiful creature.'

He was stolen, of course. Caroline had guessed it a week ago, when they had ridden into a small town to find a crowded horse market in full swing. She had welcomed the opportunity, wanting to purchase a second animal capable of taking the solid side-saddle with a footboard that Gascoyne insisted on using, sitting as though in an armchair, refusing to turn to the front, but suffering herself to be led wherever Caroline chose to take them.

Finding a suitably strong and patient pack animal had taken time, and then Caroline, congratulating herself on her bargaining powers, had rounded a corner and fallen instantly in love.

The Arab was almost white, its mane and tail black and its beautifully rounded hindquarters covered in dark dapples, as though someone had spilled black coins over the white coat. He had the high arched powerful neck and deep chest of a stallion, but true to his breed he was fine-boned, built for elegance and speed.

He was a horse fit for a prince, but no prince had ridden him lately: the pale coat had been dirty and un-brushed, and there had been blood at the corners of his mouth, where a careless hand had jabbed at the bit.

'Rashid.' She had seized the arm of the tall Turk who managed her bodyguard of five armed men. 'Go and bargain for that horse for me. I will never be able to appear indifferent about it; the dealer will see me coming a league off.'

'How much, my lady?'

'Whatever it takes,' she said. 'I want that horse.'

He had been too cheap—suspiciously cheap. So cheap that she and the men had spent two hours back in camp checking him over, convinced there was some hidden illness or injury, some drastic fault in temperament or pace.

'He has been stolen, I suppose,' she observed eventually to Rashid, who was standing in his customary pose, feet apart, one hand resting on the hilt of his evil-looking dagger. They had been unable to find a single fault, and now the lad who helped with the horses was grooming him, his face split in a great grin at the pleasure of having such a lovely creature in his care.

'Yes, my lady. But what can you do? If you did not buy it, someone else would. How can we find the owner?'

Now, as the stallion she had named Cloud slowed to an easy lope under the pressure of one hand, she raised the other to wave to Gascoyne, who was standing talking to Ismael, waiting while one of the men winched up a bucket from the well.

They had found a good place to camp. There was a spinney of trees, an ancient well, and an area of flat ground in the shelter of a scrub-covered knoll. From the signs of old fires it was a popular spot.

'That is a fine animal,' the interpreter observed. Out here he was a different man from the nervous guide of Constantinople. Caroline had brought him to continue her Turkish lessons and to interpret where she could not yet manage, and he had settled happily into their nomadic life.

'The water will be warm soon.' Her dresser nodded towards the steaming cauldron. 'There was plenty of wood for the fire.'

Caroline stood for a moment, looking round at the rapidly assembling camp, feeling a kick of pride at the sight. She had begun cautiously enough, by following Drew's scornful advice and going to Bursa, and then, once she'd felt confident away from the Embassy, she had taken a ship along the coast to Xanthos. There she had made a determined effort to live as the local people—albeit, thanks to the efforts of Gascoyne and Ismael, at the standard of a rich merchant.

Gascoyne had finally yielded to the realities of camp life, given up on stays and bonnets and had adopted her own version of Turkish dress which suited her well. Caroline had spoken to the local agents, and, after much thought, had employed Rashid and his men. They had proved an excellent choice. She took the precaution of paying them well and taking their leader's advice. He in return responded with respect and loyalty which had already paid off, most dramatically when they had been attacked by bandits, but over and over again as the men dealt with the difficulties of everyday life out in the wilds.

Her entourage was impressive now. Besides herself and Gascoyne, Ismael, Rashid and his men, the horse-master and his boy, there was a cook and a maid, his skinny daughter.

Tents were going up in a circle around the fire, the big one for her set slightly apart, Gascoyne's by its side. The dresser snored with the unstoppable energy of a steam engine, and Caroline refused point-blank to sleep in the same tent with her. The whole team was working with the easy efficiency of long practice, and Caroline realised that, in truth, it was not so very different from running a big household in England.

This was not easy, but she could do it. Learning the language had been key, and the clothes helped, making her appear less vulnerable and allowing her the physical freedom to ride and to stride about with the men, not having to follow meekly in their wake. Honesty, open-handedness, a refusal to be taken advantage of—all those characteristics won her respect when they stopped. And the knowledge that thanks to Herr Dettmer she could take down an antelope with a rifle— or a bandit with a pistol—gave her an assurance that she knew showed.

'I will write up my notes while I wait for the water,' she told Gascoyne, snagging a folding chair from the hands of the man who had just unloaded it from the pack horses and setting it up in front of her tent. 'I made sketches of those strange rock formations this morning, but I want to pinpoint them better, and to note the colours and the scale of them.'

The chest of notebooks and maps was already standing in the tent. It was the first thing unpacked wherever they stopped. One day, when she was back in Constantinople, Caroline intended to write a book about her travels, and it would be every bit as good as Mr Andrew Fenton's. She was determined upon it.

She took a small knife out of the top of her boot as she sat, and began to whittle the point on her pencil into perfect sharpness, focussing on the small task until the ache inside subsided again. *I will not think about him*, she swore, as she did a dozen times a day. It seemed to be the one thing she consistently failed at. *Where are you, Drew?* Was he somewhere close? Or miles away in this vast country?

Her own eventual destination was Ihlara. Not, she assured herself, because that was Drew's objective, or because he had refused to take her there, but because it sounded interesting. Naturally she would not steal his thunder by writing much about it, she told herself piously. It had been his idea first; it was only fair to defer on that point. She was not, for goodness' sake, a vindictive woman…

The point of the pencil broke and she realised she was digging it into the paper like a stiletto. If she was honest, she was thinking about him far too much. At first she had thought that it would be his lovemaking that she'd miss—for she was far too angry with the man himself, surely, to pine for his company? But it seemed that being in love meant you loved the whole man, even if he was infuriating, rude, patronising, mysterious… The pencil broke again. *Damn Drew Fenton!*

CHAPTER NINE

DREW slid under the low sweeping branches of a
prickly shrub on the top of the low rise behind the
tents. A small telescope lay under his hand, but he did
not dare use it. This vantage point was the best there
was, but he was looking directly into the low sun, and
the guards who were patrolling the perimeter of the
camp would catch the glint of reflected light off the
lens.

Not that he needed the aid of the telescope to
identify his stallion: there was not another piece of
horseflesh like that for a hundred miles around. He
would take his oath on it.

The stripling taking his ease in front of the big tent
directly in front of him certainly knew what he was
about, acquiring that horse, and he had men about him
to carry out his dirty work. Drew raised his head
cautiously and counted, trying not to wince as the
movement disturbed the heavy bruises across his back
and shoulders.

Five of them, controlled by that big man in the dark
red turban. They looked professional, easy yet alert,
as two of them walked a random round of the perime-

ter, rifles in the crook of their arms. The others were setting up their tents, fetching water, stopping to exchange words with the chef.

A man and a boy were setting up horse lines, but the Arab—*his* Arab—was getting special attention, he was glad to see.

Drew was hurting, hungry, and as mad as hell. He had been returning from the valleys around Ihlara, his saddlebags bulging with notes, his sketchbooks filled. By some providence he had left the train of camels and the embroidered hangings he had bought in the rock villages in the *khan* of his old friend Aslan, back in Aksaray. But Aslan had told him about reports of a ruin that had been exposed by a sandstorm three leagues away, and it had seemed too intriguing to leave.

Aslan had not been able to give him a guide from his own men, but the six travellers who had brought news of the sandstorm and the mysterious site had offered to show him the way. With Hasim, his constant companion, scarred, grizzled and grumbling dire predictions about going off on wild goose chases with unknown guides who asked suspiciously little for their services, they had ridden hard and fast.

The ruins had been there all right. And Hasim's worries, for once, had been right too. As they had dismounted in front of the shattered portico of a temple the men had struck. Hasim had taken a bullet in the shoulder. Drew had been hit by a ricochet, cutting a groove through his scalp and knocking him unconscious.

When he'd come to the men had gone, leaving them bleeding on the sand. Their horses, weapons, money and water had been taken and, possibly in bitter disappointment that they were not carrying more of value, the thieves had administered a savage kicking as a parting gesture.

It had taken two days to walk back the nine or so miles to the village. Aslan's household had taken them in, tended their wounds, and traded one of the camels and some of the textiles for new horses, supplies and money.

But Hasim was too weak yet to travel, so Drew, who found his temper inexplicably shorter these past few months, had set out alone once he was sure his friend was recovering, bent on retrieving his stallion and meting out some justice.

He had picked up the fresh tracks of this group that afternoon and followed them, hoping for news of some kind. He had been rewarded by the galling sight of that elegant youth riding his horse as though he were part of it.

The sensible thing to do, of course, would be to ride into the camp and to negotiate for the horse. But, damn it, it was *his* horse, and he was not at all sure that the six hard-looking men who were obviously the lordling's bodyguards were not also the men who stole it in the first place.

No, a quiet word with the young man when the camp was asleep would be more productive. Drew drank from the water flask at his side and settled down as comfortably as possible under his bush.

It was a beautiful night. The cloudless sky was the colour of darkest purple; the stars were brilliant. It was also bitterly cold. Caroline dragged herself away from her seat by the embers of the fire. Gascoyne had long since retired, and the rhythm of her snores merged into the background noises of low voices, horses stamping, the cook clattering away the last of the cooking pots and the call of some night bird.

Rashid came to speak to her as she stood up. 'I have posted two men, Caroline *hanim*. And I have ridden around, one league out—no one else is near; it will be a quiet night.'

'Thank you. Goodnight, Rashid.'

Caroline undressed sleepily, donning a pair of light linen trousers and a plain shirt. Ever since the night she had been awoken by the sounds of a large herd of cattle stampeding through their camp and had found herself outside, clad only in a bedsheet, she had made sure she would not be caught like that again.

When she blew the lamp out the tent became dark. The faintest glow from the fire penetrated its walls. She snuggled down into the comfort of the thin mattress and pulled the quilted covers over her shoulders. There was time for only the most fleeting thoughts of Drew before she was asleep.

A hand over the mouth and the prick of a knife-blade at the throat was guaranteed to wake the heaviest sleeper. Caroline came to herself with no intervening seconds of sleepy befuddlement. Someone was in the tent, kneeling behind her bed. She rolled her eyes back without moving her head—the message of that knife-point was quite clear—but all she could make out was a slight thickening of the darkness.

On the other hand she was not dead yet. If the intruder was bent on murder he could have cut her throat while she slept. She made herself relax cautiously and think. Behind her, all she could hear was the man's breathing: it was disconcertingly even and controlled. If she had stolen into someone's tent in the middle of the night she was pretty sure her breathing would have been all over the place. A professional, then.

The knife moved, but the hand remained, hard over her mouth, effectively pinning her into the pillows as the man moved round to kneel alongside her to her left. Not murder, then. Was he intent on rape?

Her heart began to thud and she swallowed hard. A revolting thought, but not, she told herself sturdily, the end of the world. She was not going to get herself killed resisting, she resolved, trying not to shake. What was he doing? What was he waiting for? Reinforcements? They could hardly stay like this until morning.

As she thought it, she saw the shadow stoop over her and breath tickled her ear. 'Silence.' The hoarse whisper was in Turkish. The knife-point pricked her neck again.

Cautiously Caroline nodded her head, and the pressure on her mouth lifted. 'Sit.' She sat, shifting slightly as she did so, to loosen the covers over her legs. Slowly she raised one hand and pushed back the short tumbled curls from her face. Her hair had been a sacrifice to practicalities; now she was grateful not to be impeded by its weight.

The bandit did not seem alarmed by the movement, so she shifted position again as she lowered her arm, and let her hand slide under her pillow. Her fingers closed thankfully round the hilt of her knife. She had thought Rashid melodramatic when he had insisted she sleep with it; now she could only be grateful.

'What do you want?' she whispered. Her eyes were becoming used to the gloom now. She could just make out his silhouette against the walls of the tent. *Oh hell, he is big...*

'My horse.' The answering whisper held anger and barely controlled patience. 'The grey Arab.' There was no local accent to his Turkish. If she had not known better she would have thought him an educated man.

'It is mine,' she hissed back. 'I bought it.' She let her left hand drift across the quilt until she could grasp the right top corner, while she kept her knife hand out to the side, clear. Slowly she drew her legs up, ready to push.

'How much?' There was a sneer in the low voice now. She named the price, honestly, and the man gave a snort of unamused laughter. 'You must have known it was stolen.'

She was damned if she was going to admit it. If he had walked into her camp, made a claim on the horse, perhaps demonstrated the truth of it by his knowledge of the animal, then, yes, reluctantly she would have had to agree to part with it. But she was most certainly not going to submit to *this* treatment.

'No, I did not,' she lied vehemently. As she did so she swept the quilt up and into his face, rolling away from the knife onto her knees on the far side of the mattress.

She opened her mouth to scream and the man's weight hit her squarely, bearing her to the ground, and the scream emerged as a pained whoop of breath.

Hell, but he's fast. Grimly ignoring the pain in his bruised back and shoulders, Drew rolled over and over, locked with the lithe figure which seemed as active as an eel in his grip. Mercifully the tent seemed clear of obstructions, or they would have attracted the notice of the guards by now. He just had to stop him shouting for help until he had knocked some sense into him, the thieving, lying brat.

Instinct made him flinch to one side, and a knife-point thudded into the rug that covered the grass. *How did I miss that he had a knife? I'm getting old...* Drew lunged for the weapon, ripped it out of the ground and threw it across the tent. Sharp teeth fixed on his wrist. Swearing under his breath in gutter Turkish, he hit out with the pommel of his own knife and was rewarded by a yelp of pain and his wrist being freed.

'I do not want to kill you, you fool,' he snarled, tossing his own knife away in the direction of the other. It was too dark to see properly; he could end up knifed as easily as his opponent in these conditions. With both hands free, he set about subduing the youth.

Short, soft curls brushed his reaching hand. He took hold and shook, and was rewarded by a rapidly raised knee in his groin. He rolled away, cursing, just in time to save his testicles, taking a handful of hair with him. His opponent gave a short sob of pain. *Damn it, but the boy's young—seventeen?* He should stop this fight, he knew, but how did he extract himself without calling down six heavily armed men on his head?

The youth wriggled, rolled over and managed to get to his feet, heading for the door flap. Drew could hear his rasping breath and realised he had not enough air in his lungs to shout. But once he was through that flap all hell would break loose.

He surged to his feet and threw himself full-length on his opponent, bringing him crashing down on the rugs. It shook Drew, and he was on top. Under him he could feel the youth, frantically trying to get a deep breath. He knelt either side of the slim writhing hips and leaned forward, grabbed both wrists and slammed them down above the boy's head. It brought him down on his chest, face to face—if they had been able to see each other—with the struggling figure.

Beneath him the youth went still, the only sound his laboured breathing. 'Bloody fool,' Drew gasped in English, his Turkish knocked out of him. 'I only want to talk to you.' There was a soft gasp that brought the hairs on the back of his neck to prickling attention. His body, now he was no longer tensed to fight, began sending him messages about exactly what he was lying on—and it was not a man.

The hips might be slender, but they were also sweetly curved. Crushed to his chest were contours no man had, and the skin of the wrists he was clasping was soft, the bones fine. And the scent in his nostrils, a light grace note above their sweat and the smell of crushed grass, was white jasmine oil.

'Don't scream,' he said, low-voiced, as reassuringly as he knew how.

'Drew?' The voice in the dark was the voice in his dreams. He shook his head, half-certain he was hallucinating. The wound in his head… 'Drew?' she said again. 'You are squashing me, you lout.'

That, at least, answered that. The Caroline in his dreams did not address him as *You lout*. That Caroline murmured words of love.

'Caroline?'

'Get off,' she demanded between gritted teeth. 'Are you deaf?'

Slowly he released her hands and rolled off her. For a long minute they lay, side by side on the crumpled rug, in silence. Then Caroline got stiffly to her feet, scuffed round by the doorway, apparently for shoes, and ducked out into the open air.

Drew got to his feet but stayed where he was, waiting for the inevitable outcry, the arrival of her guards, the manhandling. She'd had no reason to wish him well even before this. Now she had every right to give her men their heads. She was talking to someone outside, but there was no disturbance. Obviously the men were well trained. He heard returning footsteps, saw the glow of a light, and braced himself.

'Yes, a friend of mine, Rashid,' Caroline said patiently, wondering just what a mess she looked in the flickering light of the fire. 'I was expecting him, but not yet,' she lied.

'And he sneaks into your tent at night?' the bodyguard demanded.

'Yes,' she said bluntly. There was no way of dealing with this without shocking Rashid. She might as well get on with it. 'He was my lover.' Both thick dark brows shot up. 'Send Kati with some food and something to drink, please.'

'You want that I should have a bed made up for him in my tent?'

'Er… no. He can stay in mine.' His eyebrows came together into a frown. 'Rashid, I am employing you to guard my safety, not my morals. And I should point out that he got into my tent without any of you noticing. What if he had been a robber?'

That was enough to silence him. He shot her a mortified look. 'Yes, Caroline *hanim*, I will do as you ask.'

She scooped warm water from the cauldron into a pot, and picked up a lantern from beside the fire, touching a smouldering stick to the wick. There was no sound from her tent. Drew had made no move to open the flap and come out. If it were not for the bruises she could feel smarting all over her body she might almost believe this was a strange dream. Taking a deep breath, she walked back to the tent. What—who—did she want to find inside?

CHAPTER TEN

THE light flared up as Caroline ducked through the flap, chasing the shadows back. The tall man standing in the centre of the space wore dull clothing that seemed to absorb the light, and his face was in shadows. She walked round, setting light to the wick in each lantern until the whole tent was illuminated and she could see his face at last.

His hair was half out of the thong he had tied it back with, his long fur-trimmed jacket was discarded at the side of the bed, where he must have ripped it off when they'd begun to struggle, and his shirt was open to the waist of the breeches he wore. His feet were bare, and one side of his face was darkened by a vicious bruise.

'I did not do that, surely?' Caroline was at his side without thinking, her palm lifted to brush gently against the damaged cheek. There was a cut in his eyebrow, and now she was close she could see there was a barely healed wound in his scalp. 'What has happened?'

He seemed to be having trouble with his voice. Drew cleared his throat. 'The men who stole my horse. They shot both my companion and myself, stole our animals, our money, our water.'

'No wonder you are angry,' she said inadequately. Somehow—foolishly, when it had been obvious he'd had no idea who was in the tent—she had thought his anger and his passion were for her.

Caroline let her hand drop abruptly, lest he misinterpret the gesture, and went to find her medicine chest. 'Sit down. There is a folding chair over there.' As he turned she saw blood on his shirt. 'And take off your shirt. Your back is bleeding.'

She fought back the instinct to fuss over him, hold him. It was as well to recall on exactly what terms they had parted, and not let those dreams come chasing back to weaken her.

His back was a mess, although none of the cuts was deep. Caroline made herself focus on the job in hand and tried not to think about how much it must hurt. 'These would be healing well if you had not been so stupid tonight,' she said tartly, pouring a particularly strong lotion onto a cloth and dabbing at the worst cut in the small of his back.

'Bloody hell!' he snarled as the fiery liquid bit.

'Sit still.' She placed one hand firmly on his shoulder. 'I do know what I am doing.'

'You do, don't you?' he said, after a moment.

'Is that an apology? You may put your shirt back now.'

'It is an acknowledgement that you *now* appear to know what you are doing.'

'Thank you. I am, I believe, perfectly capable of taking advice, and of researching a subject thoroughly. I am capable of learning. You note, for example, that this party contains only three women. A gaggle, as it was pointed out to me, would be unmanageable.' She soaked a cloth in a little of the lotion and applied it to her own scalp, hissing in pain as it found the patch where he had pulled out her hair.

'I do not think I specified what amounts to a gaggle.' Drew stood up and came to take the cloth from her, pressing it gently on the sore patch. 'Did I do that?'

'Yes.'

'Then I apologise for it.' His palm brushed softly through the shorn curls. 'This is charming.'

'I had it cut for practicality,' she snapped, moving away from him abruptly. 'I did not do it to appeal to men. Certainly not to you.' Having him so close was weakening her. She wanted to sway into his arms, raise her face to his for his kiss. And then what would happen? He might make love to her, but he had already proved she could not trust him.

Drew made a move as though to close the distance between them again, and stopped as little Kati, the maid, ducked through the flap, her hands full with a tray.

'Put it there, please,' Caroline said in Turkish, and without thinking continued in the same tongue to Drew. 'Is there anything else you would like?'

'*Yok. There is not.* Who taught you your Turkish? Your accent is good,' he added in English.

'Ismael. He travels with us as interpreter.'

'And who taught you to ride astride and to fight?' Drew poured two beakers from the tall jug and held one out to her. Their fingers brushed as she took it and her eyes flew up to meet his. The shadows in the corners seemed to close in, then she shook her head and the tent was bright again.

'Two German cousins who teach the Ambassador's sons to fence, shoot, and ride. Their tuition in hand-to-hand combat in tents was limited, however.'

'I'm glad to hear it. You obviously have a natural aptitude. It was like trying to subdue a conger eel.'

Caroline fidgeted around, realised what she was doing, and sat down on the end of her mattress, her legs curled up. 'I thought I was being attacked by a murderer or a rapist.'

'Hell!' She was glad to see Drew's expression was suitably horrified. 'I had no idea you were a woman, for heaven's sake.'

'I realise that now. At the time, what did you expect I was thinking?'

'No wonder you were such a handful. If I had realised you were fighting to escape a fate worse than death…'

'My first thought was murder and robbery, and then I thought about…about rape.' She pushed away the memory of the fear; just thinking about it turned her insides to water. 'I thought I would survive somehow, and at least I would have been alive to castrate you later.'

'You had a damn good go at that, if you recall,' he said, in a surprisingly amiable tone, although his eyes were still bleak with the reflection of her feelings.

'Did I…did I hurt you?' she asked anxiously, then realised who she was talking to. 'Not that you didn't deserve it.'

'It was merely agonising. I will live to love another day.' His smile was sending goose-pimples up and down her spine. 'Or possibly tonight.'

'Do not flatter yourself,' Caroline snapped. 'I have no desire to find myself in bed with you again—not now I know what you think of women.'

'And that is?' He was demolishing a chicken leg with fierce bites.

'Poor, inadequate creatures who are simply a burden to the men around them when they are not serving their natural function of being decorative sexual objects.'

'Did I say that?' He was plastering chickpea paste onto flatbread—apparently a far more riveting occupation than looking at her while she was speaking.

'You said, *"I might not want to be bothered with you on a journey, but it is very tempting to keep you here until I return"*,' she mimicked savagely.

'Do you recall everything I say so accurately?' *Yes. The flatbread was disappearing rapidly. Goodness knew when he had last eaten. Oh, my God, he looks so battered...*

'Only the insults. I like to keep score. And I should remind you that I have the horse and you have the bruises.' Rewarded by his grimace of acknowledgment of the hit, she got up and went to the door. 'Kati—more food, please!'

'Thank you.'

'The food is for me. I find being woken up in the early hours and then fighting for my life quite stimulating to the appetite. Thank you, Kati. Please can you make up a bed over there?'

With a wide-eyed stare at Drew, the little maid hastened to lay out a spare bedroll and find a pillow.

'You are letting me sleep in here?'

Caroline picked up a chicken leg for the look of it, and nudged the rest of the food in Drew's direction. 'I have no intention of leaving you to steal my horse while we are asleep.'

'*My* horse.'

'We will see about that.' Caroline got up, deposited the tray beside the new bed and began to blow out lights, leaving one small one beside Drew. 'I suggest you get some rest. Goodnight.'

She climbed into bed, turned her back on him and tried to sleep. Then found she had to lie there while he systematically demolished the rest of the food. She should be gratified, she knew, that he was eating properly. And she should also be very relieved that he was not making any further attempt to flirt or to cozen his way into her bed. It was just infuriating that, having braced herself to repel an advance, he did not care enough to make one.

Finally she heard him moving around, blowing out the light, settling into the bedding. Was the bed soft enough with his bruised back? She worried for a good five minutes before telling herself that it was all his fault. He was a big, tough man, and he could look after himself.

Cautiously Caroline turned over until she was facing him. But all she could see was a dark mound of bedding. She reached out a hand, inching it across the rugs until her arm was at full stretch, towards Drew. It was strangely comforting as she drifted off to sleep.

Drew settled himself on his side, the softness of the thin mattress and the warmth of the quilt bliss after the past few nights. Food, warmth, comfort—all were threatening to send him to sleep. The closeness of Caroline, which should have made sleep impossible, was mysteriously soothing. To have found her was a miracle. To be on the receiving end of her temper was…stimulating. *Will she forgive me?* The question fretted at the edges of his exhaustion-fuddled brain and he reached out a hand, edging it across the rug towards where she lay, finding an obscure comfort in it even though he could not touch her.

'*Aiee!* Rape! Rashid—come at once! Oh, my lady!'

Caroline sat up as though jabbed by a bayonet to find herself confronted by an outraged dresser. Her hand, she realised, was clasped in Drew's. He was sitting up too, his hair tumbled about his face. They stared wildly at each other, and freed themselves as though from red-hot iron.

'Gascoyne, stop that noise this minute and go outside, before all the bodyguards burst in here!'

With another shriek Gascoyne vanished. From the raised voices she was presumably arguing with Rashid about the man in her mistress's tent. 'I'm sorry about that,' Caroline said stiffly.

'No, I am. I should have thought last night of how it would look.' Drew got up, cautiously flexing his shoulders.

She wanted to ask how he was feeling, but found the words would not come.

'I'll go and wash.' He scooped up his outer clothing and went outside.

I wish it had been how it looked, she thought wistfully, rolling out of bed as the dresser came back. 'Mr Fenton is injured,' she said repressively, before Gascoyne could open her mouth.

'Yes, my lady. Rashid told me. Rashid knows Mr Fenton by sight, my lady.'

'Does he?' Caroline flattered herself that she

sounded suitably indifferent. As, of course, she should
be. After breakfast they would settle the matter of the
horse—she knew perfectly well that she was going to
give it back—and he would be on his way again.
Which left her with the satisfaction of knowing she had
proved to the great Drew *pasha* that she could manage
an expedition as well as anyone, and the realisation
that the intervening weeks had done nothing to cure
her of loving him.

No one appeared to notice her silence at breakfast.
Rashid was deep in conversation with Drew in a flow
of idiomatic Turkish which left her floundering.

As soon as Kati began clearing platters she stood
up. 'Let us resolve the matter of the stallion.'

Rashid walked along with them, apparently unaware of the tension crackling in the air.

'Cloud!' she called as they approached the horse
lines, and the grey raised his head.

'Cloud?' Drew said at the same moment, and the
horse reared back, snapped the halter rope, and trotted
over to nuzzle the front of Drew's shirt. 'Conclusive, I
think,' he observed, rubbing his hands over the arching
neck.

'It would appear so,' Caroline conceded between
gritted teeth. 'You called him Cloud too?'

'Hardly very original of us, was it?' He grinned, then
swung up bareback onto the stallion, the broken halter
rope in one hand. 'Come on, boy, let's see how you are
moving.'

She stood, her eyes narrowed against the early sun,
watching the man and horse cantering in easy circles.
Apparently satisfied his horse was sound, Drew gave
him his head away from the camp.

'Beautiful,' Rashid observed.

'Um? Oh, yes,' she agreed fervently.

'The horse, I meant,' the bodyguard added dryly.

'Rashid! Are you *teasing* me?'

'Certainly not, Caroline *hanim*. Drew *pasha* I know of by reputation. He is a good man.'

'Yes.'

'So why are you not with him any longer?'

'Rashid, I—' She wanted to snub him, to reprove him for daring to trespass into such intimate matters, but the look of understanding on his face gave her pause. 'He thinks women unsuited to travel. He told me I could not go with him, and he was not…kind when he told me.'

'Ah.' The big Turk frowned thoughtfully. 'He would feel like that, of course, after what happened before.'

'What? Rashid, if you are going to talk in riddles I am going to be very angry.'

'He took his mistress with him, deep into the country, and she fell ill and died. They say he loved her. I do not know, but they also say he changed after that—became harder.'

The horse and rider were coming back, growing out of the dust cloud they had created. *Of course. It was fear in his eyes when he refused to take me with him. Fear and the memory of that loss and pain. Fear for me.*

'Let me try bareback,' she said brightly, as Cloud came to a snorting halt in front of them.

Herr Dettmer had tried to have her ride bareback when he was teaching her, on the grounds that it would help her balance. She had fallen off every time.

Drew threw a leg over Cloud's withers and slid to

the ground. 'Very well,' he agreed, surprising her, and cupped his hands to give her a leg up.

Cloud's paces were smoother than those of the raking gelding that she had learned to ride astride on, and she managed quite creditably at a walk. She was not going to risk the jarring rhythms of a trot, and dug in her heels, knowing he would go into a canter at once.

But even that was smooth. It was going to be harder to fall off and look natural than she'd imagined. Then Cloud solved the problem by swerving slightly to avoid a rock, and Caroline found herself sliding over his shoulder to hit the dusty ground with a thump.

Slightly winded, she lay there while Cloud nuzzled her anxiously. The sound of two pairs of running feet warned her, and she closed her eyes, moaning faintly. *Careful—don't overdo it.*

'Caroline *hamin*!' That was Rashid. *Not* according to plan.

'Get out of my way.'

That was Drew. She braced herself for her body-guard's reaction to being so curtly ordered away from her, but he appeared to yield without a murmur. Hands were running gently down her legs, her arms.

'Does anything hurt?'

She let her eyelids flutter open. 'No, I just feel so…shaky.' She felt genuinely shaken when he bent and lifted her without any assistance from Rashid. It was shameful how wonderful it felt to be held like this, to surrender to a strong man. Possibly the Minerva Press had it right after all.

CHAPTER ELEVEN

IT SEEMED the entire camp was crowding into the tent after them. 'Make them all go away,' she whispered. 'I just need to rest.'

Drew cleared the tent with brutal efficiency. When she was certain they were alone Caroline opened her eyes and looked directly at him as he knelt beside her bed. The anxiety in his eyes caught at her.

'I am all right—truly, Drew.' She lifted a hand and touched the back of it against his bruised cheek. 'Now, tell me, truthfully, why would you not take me with you when I asked back in Constantinople?'

If he was startled by her question he hid it well. But the shutters came down in his expressive grey eyes, guarding his feelings. 'I told you why.'

'You did not tell me why you felt that way. You did not tell me why it made you afraid.'

'Afraid? Yes, I was afraid. I had not realised I was so transparent.' Drew got to his feet. 'Has Rashid been talking?'

'Yes. Drew, accidents happen.'

'I took Mara into harm. I thought I could protect her and I could not. Not against fever.'

'No one dies of fever in the city?'

'Of course they do,' he said impatiently.

'You do not know what would have become of her if you had left her behind. Neither did she. Do you not think that perhaps she had the right to make the choice of where she wanted to be?'

'That is easy for you to say,' he flung at her. 'You do not have the burden of losing someone you love on your conscience.'

That brought her to her feet to confront him. 'Yes, I do. I did—until I had the time and space, out here, to think it through. I loved William. I could have influenced him to drink less, to eat less, to live less recklessly, less fully. When he died of a heart stroke they all said it was the fault of his young wife, that I had encouraged him to live as though he was half his age. I believed them.' She curled her fingers around Drew's arm and he did not resist her. 'But he had a right to live as he liked; who was I to make him old before his time? And who were you to tell a young girl how to love?'

The look in his eyes brought tears to hers. 'Oh, for goodness' sake—look at us, maudlin over lost loves. Would they thank us for it?'

'No. No, I do not think they would.' Drew raised his hands to pull her towards him. 'And I do not think they would thank us for using the memory of them to cut off the possibility of new love.'

Something deep inside, something that had not dared to hope, even when he had lifted her in his arms, fluttered into life. *Love*, he had said. 'Drew, it broke my heart when you were so brutal. I knew, I suppose, that there was something more than a rejection of me behind it, but it hurt so much.'

He pulled her into his arms and held her against his chest. Under the thin linens they wore she could feel his heat, his breathing, the strength of him.

'I meant to hurt you,' he said at last, his voice muffled in her curls. 'I was beginning to feel things for you that I could not dismiss lightly. I knew I had plunged you in over your head into an environment that was quite beyond your experience. I was afraid that you were starting to feel what I was feeling, and I dared not risk it. Dared not risk you. So I tried to frighten you.'

'You did not succeed,' she said, finding that if she pushed the opening of his shirt aside with her nose she could kiss the bare skin there. She felt his whole body tense as her lips moved. She lifted her mouth enough to speak again. 'You made me very angry, though, once I could think about it.'

'A bad move.' She could tell from his voice that he was smiling. 'Don't stop.'

She licked, her tongue flicking over salty skin. 'You should have told me how you felt.' His hands were cupping her buttocks now, holding her against him. She had no doubt whatsoever what he was feeling now, on a purely physical plane. But was that all it was? Could she settle for that?

'Caroline, this morning I was going to tell you I loved you, that I would take you back to Constantinople, cherish you, protect you.'

'You do?' Her heart was thudding so hard it was difficult to hear. *He loves me. He loves me.* Then she heard his words again in her head. 'You *were* going to tell me? What has changed? Drew, please, do not play games with me now.'

'Nothing has changed, my love, except that perhaps I need to learn to do rather less protecting.' He put one hand under her chin and urged her to look up. She could not doubt that he loved her. She had dreamed of seeing that look in those grey eyes; it seemed dreams could come true.

'I find I like it—being protected,' she said demurely, the sheer joy of it beginning to bubble inside her. 'And I think it was very brave of me to fall off a horse to demonstrate just how much I want to be in your arms.'

'You fell off deliberately?' Drew demanded, a smile beginning to transform the tension in his face. It seemed he had not dared believe it either. 'To show me that you are prepared to let me protect you?'

'Mmm.' Caroline nodded. 'I may be learning to take control of things, but it is still very difficult for a woman to tell a man she loves him and wants to marry him if he doesn't say it first. I couldn't risk you riding off into the sunset with nothing being said.'

'You love me?' He sounded incredulous. 'You want to marry me?'

'I have told you,' she said in affectionate exasperation. 'Drew, darling, for a very intelligent man you are being remarkably dense. I behaved with shocking abandon in your arms, I begged you to take me with you on your travels, I kept you in my tent when you had scared me half to death and nearly knifed me—how many more clues did you need?

'As for me, I should have guessed right from the start. I had been thinking about taking a lover months before I met you, but I never would have done—not until you. It was a fantasy, and when I met you it became reality. Only I did not want a lover who would satisfy me for a while. I wanted a man to love—who would love me for ever. And then I knew I had to be with you. Even though it was not until the morning that I realised I loved you.'

'In that case,' Drew said, gathering her very firmly into his arms, 'I accept your proposal.'

'Mine? *You* proposed!'

'I said nothing at all about marriage. Of course, if you feel you need to make an honest man of me…'

He got no further. Caroline pulled his head down and kissed him, hard, with all the pent-up longing of the weeks they had been apart.

Somehow or another they found themselves on the bed. She had no recollection of getting there, nor of where her clothes had gone. Drew's were tearing off under her hands.

'The door,' he said, breathlessly.

'If Rashid is not out there guarding it, I am dismissing him,' she managed to gasp, before she found herself crushed under Drew's body, his hands tangling in her hair, his knee urging hers apart. 'Drew, love me. Love me completely…'

'I intend to.' He broke off with a gasp as he entered her. 'Caroline, how do you feel about children?'

'Positively,' she managed to say. Conversation, under the circumstances, was not easy. 'Yours… anyway…Drew!'

'Good,' was all he said, before he began to thrust. She kept her eyes open, locked with his, as the heat surged through her body, the power, the tenderness, the love. She felt her body surrounding him, loving him, responding, until she cried out, arching under him as he came, shuddering, still part of her. All of her.

'I love you,' he murmured against her neck as they lay, entangled, heedless of the heat of the closed tent and the sweat glazing their bodies. 'It is like finding another piece of my life, one I did not even know was missing. I feel whole now, complete.'

'I know. I feel the same. When you made me leave you, I felt it like part of me being ripped away. Now it has healed.' She took his earlobe in her teeth gently, and nibbled. 'I want to show you how much I love you, over and over again. Only this is the only bit I can reach.'

'Thank goodness,' he said, so convincingly that for a moment she believed him. 'I would remind you that I am in a fragile condition. You have exhausted me. I think the Sultan has the right idea: I will spend the day reclining on a couch and you can wait upon me. Cooling sherbets might help. Perhaps you could fan me?'

'Yes, Drew *pasha*,' Caroline said meekly. *We will see about that*, she thought, smiling as she felt his lips curve against her neck. 'I will see what I can think of to make you feel better.'

BLACKMAILED BY THE SHEIKH

Kim Lawrence

CHAPTER ONE

THERE were two men in the private sitting room just off the Intensive Care Unit in the Swiss clinic. The older one watched as the younger man received the news he had delivered in total silence. Nothing beyond the ripple of muscles in his brown throat as he swallowed convulsively revealed he had even registered the information.

'A *note*?' he said finally.

The older man nodded and, unlike most men, didn't drop his gaze before the laser-like scrutiny of eyes that had been compared on more than one occasion to the blazing blue of the desert sky.

'Hamid read it out over the phone,' he explained inclining his head respectfully as the other man approached. 'I copied it down.'

He paused as the paper was taken from his hand and scrutinised.

The younger man screwed up the paper between his long, tapering fingers with a vicious deliberation that belied his outwardly calm demeanour.

'At least it is not a kidnap, sir.'

Karim, in the act of walking towards the window,

stopped dead, causing his flowing traditional robes to swirl around him. Nostrils flared, he sucked in air and bit back the scathing retort that hovered on his tongue, contenting himself with a silkily sarcastic, 'Yes, it was extremely thoughtful of my sister to leave a note.'

Though it was not his habit to lash out at those who could not respond in kind, given the pressure of the moment he might have yielded to temptation and vented his anger and frustration had the person standing beside him been anyone else but Rashid. The deep respect and affection he felt for the man who had been his bodyguard since childhood made such a response impossible.

In some ways Karim was closer to him than he was to his own father who, in his youthful eyes, had been a distant, glittering figure more akin to some mythical hero of legend than a parent. It was hard to reconcile the lingering image in his head of that enigmatic and charismatic figure with the frail, elderly man whose lined, paper-dry hand he had touched moments before. A sadly shrunken figure whose life was being maintained by machines.

He inhaled and ruthlessly pushed aside the images and emotions that crowded his mind, threatening to impede his ability to think clearly. Karim had taught himself not to waste energy over situations that he could not control—fortunately they were few—but his father's heart surgery was one such. On this occasion he had to place his trust in the medical skill of those who now cared for Tair Al-Ahmad. That and his father's indomitable will, which he knew could not be underestimated.

In the situation threatening his father he might have

to relinquish control, but Karim was not similarly impotent when it came to his sister. Her future depended on him making the right decisions and making them fast.

Karim nodded. 'You're right—we have to be thankful that this is not a kidnap.' His blood ran cold at the thought of his sister being in the hands of those who would use her as a political pawn, those who would not hesitate to harm her. 'If she comes to any harm I will—'

'I am sure she will not.'

At the soothing intervention Karim's long lashes swept upwards from the razor-sharp angle of his cheekbones, revealing the cerulean glitter of his heavy-lidded eyes. In the modern world, the threat of kidnap was an unpleasant reality that many people like his family had to live with. It was always a balance to maintain security while avoiding the trap of living in a state of constant anxiety.

The problem, it would seem, was that his sister did not have *enough* anxiety.

He had every intention of personally raising her anxiety levels when he got hold of her.

'Yes, we will work on that assumption,' he agreed. 'What I don't understand,' he continued, 'is how a schoolgirl could slip away from a security team of— how many?'

More worrying than how this had happened was the threat that if this information leaked his sister could be in real danger. His jaw hardened. It wasn't going to.

Both men stopped speaking as the door opened and a young woman in a nurse's uniform poked her head into the room. She stared with wide eyes at the two tall men in flowing robes, one with a jagged scar down his left cheek, the other possibly the most incredibly handsome man she had ever seen.

'*Pardon, messieurs…*' she mumbled, before hastily retreating.

The door closed, and the two men continued speaking, switching unconsciously from the language the young nurse had used. Both were fluent in many languages, as Zafsid was a multilingual country.

'I believe there were eight, sir. Not including the two who have been working undercover as a janitor and a gardener.'

'*Eight!*' Karim ejaculated, throwing up his hands and muttering under his breath as he commenced pacing the room, reminding the older man of a caged panther.

'The Princess is a very…resourceful young lady.'

'The Princess is…' Drawing a deep breath, Karim made a visible effort to contain his feelings on the subject as he dragged a chair from under the window and sank with innate grace into it. Elbows set on the mahogany arms, he rested his chin on his long, sensitive steepled fingers. The golden-toned unlined skin of his high, intelligent forehead creased as he turned his not inconsiderable intellect to the problem before him.

'My father will be conscious in twenty-four hours.' His eyes brushed the other man's face briefly as he gave an almost careless shrug. 'I will get Suzan back by then.'

'Of course.' Nothing in Rashid's manner suggested that he doubted the younger man's ability to fulfil this ambition.

'And after that…' He stopped and grimaced. After that the real problems started. Short of locking the runaway Princess in her room—a ploy which would no doubt have won the approval of the small but vocal few who frowned on his family's modernising ways— he wasn't sure how he was going to stop her repeating this stunt, or something equally reckless.

Her behaviour over the last months did not suggest he could rely on her better judgement—a quality which had *not* been very much in evidence when she had attended an unapproved party some weeks back. An innocent enough event—except the party in question had ended with the police being summoned when the parents of the day pupil throwing it had arrived home to find their lovely home trashed by drunken revellers.

Along with the report from his own security team, who had assured him that they had been poised to intervene if the Princess had been in any actual danger, moral or physical, there had been a letter from the headmistress. In it she'd asked for a contribution towards the cost of the damages, which, she explained, she was asking from the parents of all the pupils involved.

The extra information that the fortuitous presence at the party of one of the school's teachers, Miss Smith, meant that the police were not pursuing the matter further had not offered him the comfort it had obviously been meant to. The sight of that woman's name on paper was never going to offer him comfort. It was the same *Miss Prudence Smith*, with her opinion that backpacking around Australia was a mind-broadening experience, who had turned Suzan's last vacation into a running battle of alternating tears and tantrums.

What had a teacher been doing at the illicit party to begin with? No one had explained this to his satisfaction. The affair had only confirmed his opinion that the woman in question did not maintain an appropriate distance from her pupils. It was her job to maintain discipline—not to become friendly with her charges, and *definitely* not to encourage young girls like his sister to plan backpacking trips around Australia.

A fact he had explained in the note he had sent to Miss Prudence Smith.

Karim felt that under the circumstances he had expressed his feelings with admirable restraint. But the letter he had received in response had had very little to do with restraint! Silkily polite it might have been, but the message between the lines had fairly leapt out at Karim, namely: *you're a total idiot who doesn't know what he's talking about.*

In particular, a passage laced with heavy irony in which she had assured him that she was extremely grateful for his advice on the discipline of young girls, had moved him to pick up his pen to respond in kind. With some regret he had ripped up his rebuttal, recognising it was beneath his dignity to enter into a tit-for-tat correspondence with this person. And, as Suzan only had another few months left at school, he had reluctantly decided to let the matter drop.

Now he realised that this decision had been a mistake. Given her genius for interference, he had no doubt he would find the hand of Miss Smith behind this present situation.

'They are good men, but they made a fatal mistake. They underestimated her.'

This quiet observation caused Karim to lift his

head. His deep-set, startling electric-blue eyes held an ironic gleam as he gave a self-condemnatory sigh and admitted reluctantly, 'Not just them.' He ran a frustrated hand through his glossy dark hair and rose to his feet in one lithe, fluid motion. 'You do realise, Rashid, that if I had not interceded on her behalf she would never have gone to that damned school in the first place?'

Recalling the conversation that had taken place on her sixteenth birthday, he now realised—wasn't hindsight a marvellous thing?—that his sweet little sister had known exactly which buttons to push to get her own way. She had plugged into the guilt he felt because he had always recognised the inequality of their treatment, and just in case that had not been enough she had employed shameless flattery.

She had produced a glossy brochure and pressed it into his hand.

'I just want to be treated like an ordinary school-girl—just for two years, Karim. I could just be Susan Armand and people would believe it. I'm not like you—I don't look like I'm someone. No guards following me around, Karim... I know how much you hated that when you went to school... Father respects your opinion...he would agree if you asked him...'

It hadn't actually been as easy as Suzan had made it sound, but Karim had eventually persuaded their father to permit Suzan to attend the English boarding school, where only a select few were privy to her true identity. The security issue had been resolved by buying a suitable property close to the school and staffing it with a team of security staff, and placing others in undercover positions at the school.

Nothing had happened to make Karim regret his decision until the end of Suzan's first year at the English school. She'd come home for her summer break barely recognisable as the shy, modest little sister he knew. He should, he knew now, have responded to the warning signs, but he had not… Well, he was going to make good that omission now.

'I will need…' He glanced down at his robes with a frown. He would need to change.

Rashid cleared his throat. 'I took the liberty, sir, of alerting your pilot. The jet is on standby and there is a car waiting. Though, if I may suggest, sir…?'

'Suggest away, Rashid.'

'There is no actual need for you to fly to England. I'm sure that if you brief them the security staff will be able—'

'I know they could manage the situation perfectly well without me,' Karim cut in, fixing his brooding regard on the distant mountain peaks. 'But allow me the conceit, Rashid, of thinking that I'm needed.' His lips twisted into a frustrated grimace as his glance swept the room. 'I'm definitely not needed here. All I can do is pace and wait. I need to *do* something or I will…'

'Drive the staff here insane with your constant questioning of their medical expertise? Yes, I think you should go.'

The two men's eyes met, and a slow smile relaxed the austere contours of the Crown Prince's classically sculpted features. 'I think you find me painfully predictable, Rashid?'

Rashid shook his head. 'Your ability to do the unexpected, sir, is what makes you such a dangerous adversary. That and your ruthlessness.'

A spasm of shock crossed Karim's face. 'You consider me ruthless, Rashid?' The idea did not please him.

The older man paused, considering his response carefully. 'It is no bad thing that when you make up your mind about something you are...focused.'

'You are suddenly very diplomatic, Rashid.'

Though a grin split the older man's craggy face, his eyes were serious as he admitted, 'I would not like you for an enemy, sir. When you decide something is right you do not let sentiment get in your way.'

'Sentiment will not get Suzan back.'

Rashid could not conceal his curiosity. 'Back from where? How will you know where to start looking for the Princess?'

'I know *who* to look for.' His eyes narrowed. 'Unless I am very much mistaken Miss Prudence Smith is behind this. Find her, and we will find out where Suzan is.'

Rashid looked confused. 'But who is *Miss Smith*? Have I met her?'

'No, and neither have I. But I have heard a great deal about her.'

Even before the party incident and the backpacking debacle—which had firmly established him as the evil enemy in his sister's eyes—throughout the previous year if he'd said something with which his once adoring little sister disagreed, her retort had inevitably been preceded by, *'Well, Miss Smith says...'*

Karim knew a lot more than he'd ever wanted to about the irresponsible teacher's views on subjects as diverse as the innate superiority of females to sex outside marriage... Virginity, his rebellious sister had announced, was an outdated concept.

Oh, yes, Karim thought grimly. He knew enough about Miss Prudence Smith to know that they disagreed on almost every subject of consequence.

CHAPTER TWO

IT WAS not Karim's intention to draw attention to his presence in England.

Anonymity in mind, he had requested a vehicle not likely to draw any second glances, and had waited until dusk was falling before driving twenty miles from the private airfield where his pilot and plane remained, awaiting his instructions.

Now, rather than alert his prey by taking the road to the cottage, he vaulted over a fence and took a rather more direct route across open farmland.

A gentle jogging pace brought him to his intended destination in a matter of minutes. At least they had been able to supply him with the woman's address. When he had requested the file on Prudence Smith— as a matter of course his father had had an in-depth dossier made on all the staff who might be likely to come into contact with his daughter—nobody had been able to track it down. This incompetence was an irritation, but he doubted the file would have told him anything he didn't know already.

The cottage she lived in was situated on the edge of the school's grounds. When he arrived it was in darkness. When his imperative ringing of the doorbell brought no response he banged a hand on it in frustration. The door immediately swung inwards in silent invitation.

Karim walked without hesitation into the hallway, which was little more than a vestibule. Before he had time to consider his next action he heard the unmistakable sound of creaking floorboards overhead. Head tilted in a listening attitude, he paused. Someone was home. The suspicion was confirmed the next moment, when he heard the sound of breaking glass.

His expression hard and set—did this woman really think she could hide from him?—he bounded up the steep, narrow staircase. In the upper hallway there were two doors; the first when he opened it revealed a bathroom, the second a bedroom.

'I know that you're here, so—' Before he had finished speaking a large black cat darted between his legs and out through the door. The animal and the smashed remains of white pottery on the floor beneath the dormer window offered the most obvious explanation for the noise he had heard.

The wretched woman was not here, but *he* was. In a pragmatic frame of mind he decided that he might discover something that would give him some clue to Suzan's whereabouts.

Walking first to the window, to draw the curtains against prying eyes, he then switched on a light. He paused and looked around the cramped room, wondering about the person who slept here. It was dominated by a massive metal-framed bed, which took up half the available space. The patchwork quilt that covered it was almost obscured by the piles of freshly laundered clothes which were presumably waiting to be put away. There were more clothes and sundry items on the floor and tumbling out of the open drawer of a wooden chest. One side of the speckled mirror was covered in snapshots and postcards, which he afforded a cursory glance.

Some people might find the colourful chaos charming. Karim, who valued order and organisation in his life, did not. The only thing he found pleasant in the room was the faint perfume that hung in the air. He inhaled, his brow furrowing as he attempted and failed to identify the elusive scent.

Head bent to avoid a low beam, he moved forward, but despite his caution he almost tripped over a stray shoe. Releasing a low curse in his native tongue, he ducked his head to avoid a second low beam and put his hand on the bed to steady himself. When he removed it there was an item from the pile of fresh laundry snagged in the clasp of his watch-strap. Karim removed the offending item and held it up: a skimpy pair of silky leopard-print knickers, edged in shocking pink lace.

Prue switched off the engine and reached into the back seat for the bag of groceries she had picked up on the way home. Humming softly to herself, she pushed open the creaky gate and walked up the path towards her back door, her bare legs brushing against the night-scented flowers she had planted and causing a rich perfume to fill the warm night air.

She gave a sigh of pleasure and inhaled deeply. She had the entire summer ahead of her, and even if her finances didn't stretch to a holiday she was going to make the best of every precious moment of freedom. And if Ian managed to tear himself away from his studies for a few days it would be even better. Still humming happily, she inserted her key in the lock.

Pausing in the kitchen only to place the melting ice-cream in the freezer compartment, she took the stairs two at a time, a cold shower high on her wish-list. The headmistress, who encouraged staff and pupils at the exclusive girls' boarding school where Prue was head of English to take an active part in the life of the community, had volunteered Prue for yet another village fund-raiser.

Unlike many of the other staff, who had the long summer break variously earmarked for walking in the Pyrenees, white water rafting in Canada or simply soaking up the sun on some Mediterranean beach, Prue was staying at home. She didn't want Ian to leave university weighed down with student debt, so all her spare cash went on helping him out.

Karim paused in the act of skimming through the contents of a drawer in the bedside table as the sound of a car engine got closer. A smile of satisfaction tugged the corners of his mobile, sensually sculpted lips upwards as he discovered something useful—a passport. Straightening up, he flicked it open. The smile faded from his face as he saw the photographic image inside.

His brows lifted as he was obliged to ditch his preconceived mental image of a bitter, middle-aged spinster who lived her life vicariously through her students. The big eyes that looked back at him were set in a face that belonged to a female who looked barely out of her teens—her expression was sombre, but just below the surface there was a smile, struggling to escape.

I want to see that smile.

Frowning at the maverick thought, and almost immediately dismissing it from his mind, Karim shook his head. The furrow above his masterful nose deepened as he continued to study the soft features. There had to be some mistake, he decided, his indignation growing as he noticed the way pale and wispy tendrils of hair sprang from a brow which was as smooth as alabaster.

Surely parents would not pay the sort of fees that this school demanded to have their precious daughters taught by someone who didn't look old enough to drive, let alone be head of an English department? Though if a mouth that invited a man to think about kisses was a qualification for a position of responsibility…that would be another matter, he decided, as his glance lingered on the full, lush outline of her lips.

He was still looking at the photo when he heard the creak of the stairs. Head tilted to one side, he listened as the creaks got louder—as did the slightly off-key humming of an unidentifiable tune. Sliding the passport into the pocket of his slim-fitting black trousers, he switched off the lamp he had turned on when he closed the drapes. Crossing the room as if he had every right to be there, he settled himself into a wicker chair which, like most other pieces of furniture in the room, had seen better days, and waited.

Pushing open the bedroom door with a sigh, Prue lifted the tendrils of hair that had escaped the loose knot she had confined it in from her neck. The breeze that blew in through the open window caused the heavy curtains she had inherited from the previous tenant to flutter.

She noted the closed curtains with a slight frown. She could have sworn she had left them open. Kicking off her sandals and rubbing first one and then the other aching foot, Prue began to peel off her clothes without bothering to switch on the light. She had stripped down to her bra and pants when a deep voice emerged from the shadows.

'Where is she?'

Prue, in the act of shaking back the hair she had just released from its ineffectual knot on her head, let out a startled shriek and stepped backwards. She hardly registered the pain as her thigh made contact with the sharp corner of an open drawer in the heavy Victorian chest of drawers.

There's someone in the room.

She heard the voice again in her head and thought, *Someone male.*

Do not panic.

She recognised this as great advice but, like most great advice, totally impossible to follow. Surely a certain degree of panic was permitted under the circumstances?

Prue's thoughts raced, fuelled by a massive surge of adrenaline. There was a man... Who was he, and why was he in her bedroom? She almost immediately dismissed the *who* from her thoughts. The intruder's identity was not immediately important. None of the possible reasons her fertile imagination supplied for there being a strange man lying in wait for her in her bedroom made her feel any farther away from dissolving into gibbering panic.

The thought of the invisible man's eyes on her body made her skin crawl. If he hadn't spoken when he had she would have been stark naked by now, and feeling—if that were possible—even more vulnerable and exposed. Straining to see in the dimness, her eyes raked the area from which the voice had emerged. Her pounding heart tried to climb out of her throat as she located the long, lean and infinitely sinister outline of a figure that appeared to be sprawled in the chair beneath the window.

Prue was reaching for the shirt she had dropped onto the bed when the intruder snapped curtly, 'I am not a patient man, Miss Smith.'

Clutching the shirt to her chest, Prue began to edge backwards towards the door.

My God, he knows my name. Up until now she'd been assuming that this was some sort of crime of opportunity. If you took that out of the equation, what was left was infinitely more sinister.

Her imagination went into overdrive.

Did she have a stalker? Had someone been standing outside in the dark watching her, waiting to make his move?

Didn't that make her the victim who got killed off in the first reel of the film?

Prue started to shake her head. This wasn't a film, and she wasn't a bit-part actress. Nobody was writing her lines. She needed to reassert some control here.

Oh, sure—that should be easy. What was she going to do? Threaten him with detention if he refused to leave?

Ignoring the sarcastic voice in her head, she lifted her chin. 'Who are you, and what are you doing—?'

A voice like ice cut dismissively across her. 'That is not important. Just answer my question.'

She ran her tongue across dry lips. There was the bitter, metallic taste of fear in her mouth, and her throat was so dry it took her several attempts before she managed to speak.

'What question?' Questions she had plenty of. It was answers Prue was struggling with.

'You are trying my patience. Where is she?'

She? Could this be a case of mistaken identity? But he knew her name. This sort of thing only happened in films, not in Greater Budstow—where the last serious crime had probably been someone stealing a prize-winning marrow.

'I've no idea what you're talking about,' she rebutted, fighting her way into the shirt, her hands shaking so hard she didn't even attempt to button it. To her immense relief he made no attempt to prevent her. 'I've nothing worth stealing, you know.'

'This is something I have noticed.' Despite the fact that his eyes had adjusted well to the darkness, the features he had seen in the passport photo remained a pale blur. But he now knew that she was of a diminutive stature—certainly a good head shorter than his sister, who was five ten.

A stray sliver of light shining through a chink in the curtains reached across the room to touch the top of her head, giving the illusion of a halo. Karim reminded himself that there was nothing even vaguely angelic about this woman, but even so he had to subdue a spasm of disquiet. He might not be able to see her expression, but the quiver in her unusually husky voice and her body language were eloquent. She was terrified, and he despised men who intimidated women. He quashed his chivalrous instincts, reminding himself of his reason for being here. A little fear might even work to his advantage.

Prue filed away the distinctive foreign inflection for later reference, for when she gave the police a statement. Of course that was presupposing she got to speak to the police. She could be talking to a homicidal maniac who had no intention of allowing her to speak to anyone ever again. She could soon be nothing more than a crime statistic.

Prue bit her trembling lip. She was getting out of here in one piece—she *had* to. She was the only family Ian had. The thought of her brother left alone in the world brought a gleam of resolve to her eyes. She reminded herself not to think like a victim or she'd become a victim—*think like someone who is going to get out of here.*

'When you were looking, I suppose.' She shuddered, fully appreciating for the first time why people whose houses had been robbed said they felt defiled by the intrusion. 'My God, how do you sleep nights?'

'I could ask you the same question.'

Prue shook her head in the darkness. She was obviously dealing with someone unstable—nothing else could explain that bitter retort. Her previous thought came back to her. 'Have you been stalking me?'

'You are clearly delusional.'

Prue bit back a sharp retort. Tact and diplomacy were called for, admittedly not her most obvious talents…

CHAPTER THREE

'WHAT perfume are you using?'

'I'm not... I don't wear perfume.' Hovering by now on the brink of total blind panic, she heard the voice in her head sensibly encouraging her to change the subject. 'I've got a few pounds in my purse,' she volunteered, pulling the sides of her shirt together and clinging to them until her knuckles turned white.

'I do not want your loose change.'

It was the contemptuous sneer in his deep voice that made something snap inside her. Forgetting all about discretion being the better part of valour, impetuous words tumbled from her lips before she could check them.

'So, if you don't want money I can only presume that this is the only way you get to see women take off their clothes, you slimy, inadequate, perverted little voyeur!'

Dark bands of colour appeared along the jutting angles of Karim's high cheekbones. The truth was, he was not proud of the fact he had delayed revealing his presence. It had certainly not been his intention.

He had known women for whom striptease was an

art form, but there had been nothing remotely seductive or intentionally titillating about the way this woman had revealed her feminine curves. This made his inability to drag his eyes away from her all the more bizarre. Perhaps, he pondered, it was the perfume she denied wearing. But of course she had to be. The moment she had walked into her room the scent that had earlier intrigued him had intensified.

There was a moment of total silence that dragged on, during which Prue had ample time to wish she had kept her tongue under control. There was simply no point in antagonising the man when she had no idea what he was capable of.

The lamp flicked on, and she was suddenly wondering if there was anything the man sitting about four feet from her was *incapable* of!

The breath snagged in her throat as her eyes widened to their fullest extent. He was the most incredible-looking male she had ever seen or even dreamt existed outside a fantasy.

Beneath the fear and loathing she felt as she looked at him, Prue was aware of feelings stirring inside her at some primitive level—feelings she was ashamed to acknowledge.

Fingers steepled, his long legs stretched out in front of him as he sat back in the chair, his attitude was laconic, his brooding, unblinking cerulean eyes trained on her face.

Dressed in black from head to toe, his skin glowed a rich vibrant gold against the sombre colour. The waving hair that sprang from his broad brow had a blue-black sheen, and it was collar-length—or it would have been had he been wearing a collar. His features—

a wide, overtly sexual mouth, straight aquiline nose and slashing cheekbones—just stopped short of being classically perfect.

As he rose to his feet in one fluid motion she was too awed to feel the appropriate degree of fear for her situation. His dark head grazed the low exposed beam. He had to be close to six four, but there was nothing about his lean, athletically muscular body that brought the word *gangly* to mind. Power, strength and innate grace were appellations that more readily sprang to mind.

Towering over her, he regarded her with utter disdain, his electric-blue gaze lingering on the heaving upper slopes of her breasts. 'You will tell me where my sister is.'

The heat rushed to Prue's cheeks as she gathered her straying wits. So this man had more undiluted sexual charisma in his little finger than any normal man had in his entire body? It didn't make him any less dangerous. On the contrary, even if he hadn't been a total raving loon, it made him all the more dangerous. A man who looked like him would leave a trail of broken hearts and shattered dreams in his wake.

She took a deep breath before lifting her chin. She was damned if she'd let him see how scared she was. He was just the sort of pathetic creep who was likely to get a kick out of seeing his victims scared—*and I'm not a victim*, she reminded herself.

The door was her only route of escape, and he was closer to it than she was. If she made a dash for it he would cut her off. She had to get nearer to it before he realised what she was doing.

'My boyfriend will be here any minute. He's big and…and…he plays rugby.'

One dark winged brow lifted. 'What position?'

Prue, taken aback by the response, frowned as she continued to edge towards the door, resisting the temptation to break into a run. 'What?'

'What position does he play in?'

'Position?' Clearly she was dealing with someone who was not quite right in the head—she just hoped he was a lunatic of the relatively harmless variety. Though everything about him told her was the opposite of harmless. 'How should I know?'

While he was talking he wasn't doing anything else, like grabbing her, and she was so close now that she could smell the warm male scent of his body, see the mesh of fine lines fanning out from the corners of his eyes.

Without warning her stomach took a lurching dive. Alarmed by this development, Prue swept her eyelashes downward until they lay against her heated cheeks. Looking up at him through the concealing mesh, she tilted her chin to a belligerent angle and said, with as much confidence as she could muster in the circumstances, 'Look, I should warn you that I know judo.'

'Now, I call that really sporting of you to warn me.'

The mocking drawl made her feel like a mouse being toyed with by a large, sleek and malevolent cat. Clearly the man didn't believe a word she was saying, and she for one had had enough of being diplomatic.

Forgetting her intention of humouring him, she announced with venomous sincerity. 'Yes, I am terrified.' Her lashes lifted, revealing the glitter of loathing in her golden eyes. 'I'm sure that makes you feel like a big man,' she sneered in disgust.

A gleam of reluctant admiration entered Karim's eyes. Whatever else Miss Prudence Smith was, she was not a coward.

'And, for the record, I really, *really* hope they send you to jail for a long time.' Her eyes flickered sideways as she tried to judge if she was close enough to make it to the door before he did.

'It would not be a good idea.'

Guilty colour ran up under her fair skin. 'What do you mean?'

He took a menacing step towards her. 'I am speaking of whatever escape plan you are feverishly hatching.'

He needn't have worried. She couldn't run because her feet were practically nailed to the ground with fear. 'If you touch me I'll scream.' She might even scream if he didn't. Her shredded nerves were just about at breaking point.

'Look,' he said, sounding bored, 'can we cut out the dramatics?' He unhooked a towelling robe that had been draped over the chair he had just vacated and tossed it to her.

'Dramatics…' she echoed incredulously. 'I come home to find some lunatic in my bedroom…' She grunted, struggling to pull the loose robe over her shirt.

'Tell me where my sister is.'

Prudence was willing to tell him anything he wanted to hear if it meant getting this beautiful, dangerous crazy man out of her house. The problem was, she wasn't sure *what* he wanted to hear.

'Your *sister*…?' she probed, playing for time. The door was still a possibility, and while he stayed where he was there was an outside chance of escaping if she chose her moment well.

Leaking patience from every perfect pore, Karim folded his arms across his chest and fixed her with a narrow-eyed, cold stare. No doubt she was accustomed to her big innocent eyes getting her out of tight spots. 'My patience is not infinite.'

More like non-existent. This man had a combustible quality which, even if he had been sane—and he clearly wasn't—would have made him a person to avoid. 'Does she have a name?' It seemed sensible to humour him.

'Suzan Al-Ahmad.'

'Suzan...? I don't know any—' She stopped as a possibility struck her, and her sharpened glance skimmed the perfect contours of his strong-boned face. But she failed to detect any family likeness beyond basic colouring between her devastatingly handsome intruder and the sweet, bright girl who until recently had been her student.

'You don't mean Susan Armand, do you?'

Prue took the slight, impatient inclination of his dark head as assent.

'Susan is your sister? Goodness, but she's—'

'Missing.'

'I was going to say normal. But...*missing*?' She stopped as his words sank in. 'Susan is *missing*?' Dismay spread across her face as she asked, 'Missing as in lost, or...?'

'A nice act, Miss Smith, but your sincerity is wasted on me. I know full well that you have been instrumental in my sister's disappearance. Did she confide her true identity to you? It may have amused you to encourage, or possibly orchestrate this.' He had not yet made up his mind as to the depth of her involvement. When he did he would make sure that the punishment fitted the crime. 'But believe me when I say you will rue the day you ever interfered with my family.'

Prue stared at him. He was obviously mad. '*Me?* Why on earth would I...? Look, this is utterly ridiculous—you're talking as though I'm part of some conspiracy, and actually...well, actually,' she added, realising that she only had his word that he was even related to Susan, 'she never mentioned a brother to me.'

'You doubt my word?'

She laughed in reaction to the stark incredulity in his voice. The sound caused almost visible sparks to fly from his blue eyes.

'She did, however, mention *you* to me.' His contemptuous glance slid over her curves before returning to her face in time to observe a long curling strand of blonde hair fall across her cheek.

Prue, whose colour was heightened by his scrutiny, clenched her teeth and cinched tight the belt on the robe around her waist, unaware that the action caused the neckline to gape, revealing the smooth upper slope of her breasts and a portion of their lacy covering. She didn't think she wanted to know what Susan could have said to this vile man to make him look at her with such disdain.

'Suzan considers you her role model.'

'*She does?*' Shock chased across Prue's face, and she shook her head in a slow but emphatic negative gesture.

He pulled the leopard-pink pants from his pocket.

'I just hope my sister has not decided to adopt your taste in underwear. Or, for that matter, morality.'

The colour flew to her cheeks at the same moment as she threw caution to the winds. 'Pardon me if I don't feel inclined to meekly accept lectures on *my* morality from a man who has broken into my home, rifled through my belongings and has my knickers in his pocket!' Breathing hard as she fought to contain the fury that consumed her, she reached across and snatched the offending item that dangled tauntingly from his finger.

There was a moment's total silence. 'You will not speak to me in that manner.'

Her eyes were drawn to the dark bands of colour delineating the chiselled angle of his cheekbones and the thin white line that framed his lips—lips that suggested their owner was capable of great cruelty and great passion.

She wasn't sure which discovery made her feel more uncomfortable.

'Have you never heard of free speech?'

'For the duration of this conversation I think you should consider it as a luxury and not a right.'

She planted her hands on her hips, unknowingly exacerbating the gaping situation. 'What are you going to do? Gag me?'

'I will do far worse than that if you don't tell me what I need to know. And please,' he begged, 'don't waste your time with any more displays of ingenuous shock or suggest that you are oblivious to the worship of your students. I have no doubt that you find it very pleasant to have young people hanging on your every word. It is,' he observed darkly, 'a power which can very easily be abused. You feed these young women seditious nonsense, encourage them to reject the values of their families, to experiment sexually—'

This last outrageous accusation enabled Prue, who had up to this point been listening with her mouth open, to find her voice. 'Now, hang on there. I teach my students to appreciate and enjoy literature. And,' she admitted with a rueful grimace—they did after all live in the real world, 'to get good exam results. But I do not encourage them to have sex!'

Her voice went dangerously high on the last word. The man was mad. If anything, she was the target of some good-natured teasing from her sixth-formers, who found their teacher's lack of a boyfriend amusing.

'Or attend drunken parties with them?'

'Parties? What? Oh, Sara's… I was hardly attending. I just heard about it, and I wanted to check things weren't getting out of hand. It was just a bit of innocent fun, and it wasn't *drunken*. At least the girls weren't, but the boys with motorbikes from the town, who gate-crashed, were a bit…' Actually, what they had been was frankly terrifying. Not that Prue had made the mistake of letting them see how intimidated she felt when she had given them their marching orders.

'You knew about this party and you made no attempt to stop it.'

Prue, who wished she had done just that the moment she had walked in and found the leather-clad gatecrashers, blushed under his withering contempt. 'Admittedly it was a bad call,' she conceded. 'But I did help the police.' Her eyes widened. 'My God, was it *you* who wrote that incredibly patronising and rude letter? I thought you were Susan's father.'

'Lucky for you, I am not. I am no one's father. And as for *rude*…' He lifted a sardonic brow. 'Suzan admires your amazing intellect. On the evidence so far, I'm less than impressed.' One corner of his mouth curled contemptuously as his heavy-lidded eyes slid down her body. 'Though,' he admitted, in a throaty drawl that made Prue's stomach muscles flutter, 'your body is better than I had anticipated.' He sucked in a deep breath then, and as he released it allowed his appreciative glance to drop once more. 'A *lot* better. If you ever feel like a change of direction you could always get a job as a centrefold model.'

Angry colour high in Prue's cheeks, she squared her jaw. 'You'd know more about that than me,' she choked, eyeing him with loathing. 'I can see now why Susan didn't mention you. If you were my brother I'd try and pretend you didn't exist either.'

'If I were your brother I would keep you behind locked doors,' he responded, eyes narrowed. But he doubted that would keep the men out. What amazed him was that he had found no evidence of male occupation in the bedroom. It made no sense that a woman with a body that invited sin would not have some man in her clutches.

'I've never been to Paris, but I suspect that that sort of thing does not go down too well with French women.'

'I do not live in Paris.'

He did, as it happened, keep an apartment there—though he couldn't recall the last time he'd visited it. Karim had not added his voice to that of the medical professionals, who had suggested forcibly that the King cut back on his workload, as he had known that getting his father to take it easy was not an option. Rather, he had very subtly taken on an increasing number of duties which the King would normally have dealt with in the hope of taking some of the pressure off, and as a consequence his days of flitting around the world's pleasure spots had ended.

'I am not French.'

'But Susan—'

He cut off her protest with an imperious wave of one beautifully shaped brown hand. 'Suzan is not French either. We are of the Royal House of Zafsid, though our grandmother was French.'

Not just mad—the man was delusional. And maybe he wasn't the only one, she reflected, tearing her eyes from the long tapering brown fingers that inexplicably fascinated her.

'That's very interesting.'

At least this removed any doubts she'd had that she was dealing with anything less than a total crackpot. Though you had to hand it to the man, she thought. He did have the regal arrogance off to perfection.

Karim, who had never in his life had his status doubted, did not quite know how to react to the fact that this bolshy blonde was obviously humouring him.

'I suppose that makes you a sheikh, or something?'

CHAPTER FOUR

'IT MAKES me close to losing my patience,' he retorted, regarding her with simmering dislike. Though explaining himself did not come easily to Karim, he recognised that under the circumstances he had little option but to make some concession. 'It is not common knowledge,' he began stiffly, 'but our father—'

'Is a sheikh too?' she placatingly finished for him.

'King, actually.'

The matter-of-fact revelation drew a nervous laugh from Prue's throat, which she hurriedly changed to a cough. 'A tickle in my throat.' She risked a quick sideways glance to gauge the distance to the door. 'Did your father come with you?'

Another inch and she would be able to reach the door before he could stop her. Her plan after that was a little vague, but she reasoned that anything would be preferable to staying in this room with him.

'Our father is in Switzerland at the moment. He had emergency heart surgery yesterday. When he wakes up tomorrow morning Suzan will be by his bedside where, but for your interference, she should be now.

Now, you will—' He released a grunt of sheer irritation as she bolted for the door, and shot out his hand.

Prue, finding herself pulled backwards against the solid wall of his chest, let out a shrill cry of frustration as he restrained her. The total lack of effort this took on his part suggested that the steely strength he projected was no illusion.

Her feet several inches off the ground, she continued to flail wildly. It was one thing to look at him from a distance; it was quite another to be plastered so close to him that her spine was pressed up tight against him. She had gone beyond fear. Actually, fear might have been healthier than the tight knot of something that approached excitement in the pit of her stomach.

She began to struggle even harder, her nostrils filling with the scent of his body as she gasped for air, adding to her desperation.

'Stop, you little idiot,' Karim commanded, grunting in pain as one of her wild kicks made contact with his shin.

'Put me down,' she panted. 'This instant, you big bully.'

'When you are calm.' Even as he contained her struggles Karim was conscious of the softness of her body, and the scent that continued to tantalise him. For someone so soft she packed quite a punch.

'I *am* calm!' she shrieked.

'Then I would not like to see you when you lose control. Now, listen to me.'

'Do I have a choice?' Relieved to find her feet back on the ground, she stopped fighting. 'Breathing would be good, if you don't mind, and I'm rather fond of my ribs.'

Before she had a chance to welcome the fact that the arm wrapped around her middle like a steel band had loosened, she found herself turned around. One heavy hand came to rest on her shoulder, the other cupped her chin. Their eyes collided and Prue felt the fight drain from her.

'These are the rules.'

Prue opened her mouth and found a finger laid against it. Her captor shook his dark head. 'You will listen, I will talk, and then you will tell me what I want to know. My name is Karim Al-Ahmad. I am the eldest son of Tair Al-Ahmad, who has been the ruler of Zafsid for the past forty years. My sister Suzan has spent the last two years incognito, attending a very exclusive girls' school. The only people aware of Suzan's true identity are the headmistress, the head of governors and of course Samir and Malik.'

'Who are Samir and Malik?'

Karim frowned at the interruption, his dark brows drawing into a straight line. 'The junior gardener and the janitor,' he supplied, and watched her golden eyes widen. 'You will find they will not be returning after the summer break.'

It couldn't be true, could it? As if sheikhs wandered around the Home Counties, breaking into houses and terrorising the occupants—and even if they did, they would never look like him.

'You expect me to buy into your fantasy?' she challenged.

'You want proof of my identity?'

Prue watched him unclip the metal-banded, expensive looking watch from his wrist, and touched her face where his fingers had rested.

'Read the inscription on the back. It was a present from my mother when I was sixteen.'

Prue looked at the watch he held out towards her. After a moment she sighed and shook her head. 'No, I believe you.' And she did. Sometimes the truth was more bizarre than any fantasy you could dream up, and this was one of those occasions. 'So something has happened to Susan…sorry,' she said, correcting herself with a rueful smile, 'Suzan.'

'And this is news to you?'

Prue stuck out her chin and refused to respond to the jibe. 'Yes, it is,' she said, planting her hands on her hips.

Her action again emphasised the womanly curves of her body, and made Karim think about the way her pale skin had gleamed in the darkened room.

'Does she know about your father—I mean, the King, being ill?'

'Rashid was going to break the news to her when he came to collect her, but it didn't quite work out as planned.'

'I don't know who Rashid is—and,' she added, holding up her hand, 'I really don't want to. I'll accept—and I so can't believe I'm saying this—that you're a prince or a sheikh, or something.'

'Both, actually.'

'God, it would certainly explain your off-the-scale arrogance.'

'I am not arrogant.'

She ignored his quick denial. 'But the fact is I'm not one of your subjects or slaves or whatever, and though I'd love to help I've not the faintest idea where Sus…Suzan is.'

'You do.'

His total conviction was incredibly frustrating.

'Think,' he commanded, standing over her like some dark angel bent on retribution. 'My sister knew nobody outside the school. She could not have wandered off without any help—more specifically, *your* help.'

'Why would I help her do that?'

'The same reason I imagine you encouraged her to backpack around Australia.'

'I didn't *encourage*, I just said it was something I wish I had been able to do. If you must know,' she snapped, 'I felt quite envious of the girls planning it.' At their age she had been faced with the responsibility of bringing up her brother.

He brushed aside her protest. 'Suzan's note indicated that she was going somewhere, meeting someone.' His eyes narrowed on her face. 'You have thought of something, haven't you? Tell me.'

Prue shook her head, and the steely fingers curled around her upper arm tightened, causing her to wince. 'It's nothing,' she protested, rubbing the area his fingers had fallen away from.

'Let me be the judge of that.'

Relieved that his laser-sharp gaze had moved from her face to the area of her arm she was rubbing, Prue shook her head again. 'I'm telling you, it's nothing.' Even she could hear the edge of uncertainty in her voice.

'You are shielding someone.' His steely blue gaze zeroed in once more on her face. 'Who?'

When Prue's eyes slid from his, she knew that she looked as guilty as hell.

'Your lover?'

A rosy flush flowed over her pale skin. 'Of course not.'

What was it with this man? He seemed totally obsessed with her non-existent love-life.

Familiar as he was with this young woman's modern attitude to sex, he found the indignation sparkling in her eyes a little perverse. 'Then who?'

'Ian—my brother—came to visit one weekend,' she admitted, unable to wrench her fascinated gaze from the muscle that was clenching and unclenching in his sexily hollow cheek. 'Susan met him. They seemed to get on well.'

'You engineered an assignation between your brother and my sister?'

A hissing sound of aggravation escaped her clenched teeth. 'No, I did not.' His ability to twist everything she said was really beginning to get under her skin. 'Dear God, a man and a woman can exchange a few words without it automatically being something sordid or sexual.'

At least when the man was her brother they could...but with this man? She shot a covert peek at him through the upward sweep of her lashes and felt her stomach muscles quiver. She was forced to acknowledge that the same rules did not apply to Karim Al-Ahmad. His sexuality was such an integral part of the man that it would be hard to overlook or ignore; it would be easy to allow yourself to be distracted by it.

Wasn't that exactly what she was in danger of doing now?

His eyes dropped to the heaving contours of her bosom, and the expression on his lean face when his eyes lifted was one of studied insolence. 'You really can't be that naïve.'

'It was an innocent, casual meeting,' she insisted. 'My brother was staying and Susan—'

'Suzan,' he enunciated, between gritted teeth.

'Fine—Suzan,' she faithfully repeated, 'came by to return a book.'

'You left them alone?'

'I've not the faintest idea. But if it's your sister's virtue you're bothered about, don't be. My brother is not that sort of boy.'

'All males are *that sort of boy*, given the opportunity. How old is this brother of yours?'

'Twenty.'

'Twenty!' he exclaimed. 'Twenty is not a boy, it is a man.'

'I'm sure you'd had a shed-load of conquests at that age, but my brother is...' Loyalty stopped her saying a *geek*. 'He's more interested in books.'

'You are his sister; you would believe that. Though I have to say you behave more like his mother.'

'I suppose I've been that too, for the last few years.'

'Your parents?'

'Dead.'

'And where is your brother now?'

She laughed. 'Sure, and have you barge in, scaring the life out of him.' Ian would definitely not know how to handle a man like this.

And you do?

'Did I make it sound as if that was a suggestion...? My error.' He bared his white teeth in a wolfish smile. 'It was not.'

There was no trace of a smile, wolfish or otherwise,

as he said, in a voice as hard as granite, 'You will tell me where your brother is, or you will regret it.'

'Just what do you think you can you do to me?'

'I'm assuming that if you lost your job you would also lose the home, such as it is, that goes with it. I think it might also be hard for you to secure another post without references.'

She met his eyes and knew immediately it was no empty threat. He was more than capable of carrying it out.

'Promise me that you won't hurt him.'

'What?'

'You heard what I said. Unless you promise me you won't lay a finger on Ian, my lips are sealed.'

His frustrated simmering glance slid from her to the watch on his wrist. 'If I had more time…'

'Well, you don't.'

'You have my word,' he conceded, reluctance written in every line of his taut features. 'So tell me where he is.'

Prue did so, adding, 'There was nothing even vaguely romantic between them, I'd swear to it. She was just interested in learning about the university and—'

'Get some clothes on.'

'*What?*'

'Get dressed. You are coming with me.'

All that undiluted testosterone was giving her a headache here in this room, but in the even more claus-trophobic confines of a car—it simply didn't bear thinking about. 'That really isn't going to happen,' she squeaked, shaking her head.

'I only have your word that your directions are

correct. I could easily arrive and find that they have never heard of your brother. Or,' he added, forestalling her protest, 'he is there, and you will ring him the moment I leave.'

Prue felt the blush climb up her neck until her face was bathed in guilty heat, but she refused to lower her gaze in the face of his horribly knowing smile.

'In which case I will find the birds have flown. So, you see, you *are* coming with me. One way or another, you are coming with me. And, if it is any comfort, you would not be my first choice of travelling companion, either.'

With anyone else she might have suspected that sinister *one way or another* was just for effect, to panic her into capitulation. But Prue was getting the distinct impression that this man was not into empty threats.

When she had dreamt of meeting a man who meant exactly what he said, this wasn't what she'd had in mind. That authenticity had been more to do with straightforward sincerity and no hidden agenda—not threats, coercion and intimidation.

She narrowed her eyes and gave him an unfriendly glare. The man of her dreams would not have looked like this one, either. She never had been into dark and brooding outside of the pages of a Gothic romance.

'So I suggest that, given that time is a factor here, you get dressed, or…'

'Let me guess—you'll dress me yourself?'

'I was going to say or you'll come like that. But either works for me, so long as we're on the road within the next four minutes.' Amusement tugged at the corners of his sensual lips.

'Not three or five?'

'You're wasting time.'

'Do you really think I'm going to get dressed with you standing there?'

His brows lifted. 'That's a truly charming display of false modesty.'

There was nothing false about it. The idea of exposing her body to his scrutiny for a second time made Prue's blood run cold.

'It's a little too late in the day to be convincingly prudish, and I'm not letting you out of my sight for a second until my sister is safe.'

'There is nothing prudish about feeling uncomfortable taking off your clothes in front of a total stranger.' Presumably he was basing his apparently unflattering opinion of her morals on a pair of knickers.

'I will try and control my baser instincts,' he promised.

At that moment Prue would have given a good deal to wipe that smirk off his smug, superior face. 'You're hateful.'

'You're wasting time.'

Keeping her back to him, she stiffly selected a pair of pale linen trousers and a white tee shirt from the pile of fresh laundry stacked on her bed. Pulling the trousers on before she slipped off her robe, she maintained a frigid silence.

It wasn't easy to pretend someone wasn't there when you couldn't rid yourself of the childish idea that they were scoring you out of ten.

It took about ten seconds for her to slip off the shirt and pull on the clean tee shirt.

Freeing her hair from the neck of her top, she turned back to him. 'You do realise that this is kidnapping? That's a very serious offence.'

Karim watched her pale tresses settle around her shoulders before he met her challenging glare. 'No— kidnapping is when you travel in the trunk of the car. I'm letting you sit up front.'

'You have no idea,' she choked, 'how lucky I feel.' The bitter comment drew a laugh from his throat.

CHAPTER FIVE

'DO YOU have to drive so fast?' They had been in the outside lane for the past ten miles.

'I am not exceeding the speed limit.'

'Well, it feels like it,' she grunted.

'Would you like to drive?'

'I'd feel a lot safer.'

'I would not,' he retorted.

'Are women in your country even allowed to drive?'

'Alas, not all progress is for the better.'

Prue took her mobile from her bag. 'I might be wrong—she might not be there. Maybe we should ring ahead and check?'

Karim slanted her a sideways look of derision. 'Do I look stupid?'

No, but he did look like the total and complete barbarian he was. A man of the harsh desert, capable of anything.

'No wonder Sus…Suzan ran away, if there are any more at home like you.' She slid a sneaky sideways look at his profile. Her last suggestion seemed fairly unlikely. She doubted there was another man on the planet like the one seated beside her.

'If anything happens to her I will hold you personally responsible.'

'That's totally unfair,' Prue protested. 'I already feel guilty enough as it is, and for no good reason. She might not even be with Ian. What if she isn't? What are you going to do then?'

Karim's jaw tightened. 'For your sake I hope she is there.'

The brush of his hooded eyes sent a shudder of apprehension down Prue's spine. 'How much farther is it?'

'Take the next exit.'

The porter recognised Prue immediately and greeted her by name, informing her that her brother was in and probably working through the night, as usual, before telling her to go right on up. To Karim he gave a respectful nod. Prue was beginning to suspect that there were very few people who would question Karim Al-Ahmad's right to be anywhere, and even fewer who would not adopt a respectful manner in his presence.

'Number?' Karim barked, taking the lead as they approached the stone staircase. He no longer bothered to hide the urgency in his manner.

'Twenty-two. His room is on the top floor,' she warned—not that she expected a few flights of stairs to tax this man. Whatever else he was, he was obviously at the peak of physical fitness.

Averting her eyes from the taut outline of his behind, she put all her effort into matching the pace he set as he ran up the steps. She reached the top several vital seconds behind him, panting as though she had just run up several flights of steps—which she had. He, on the other hand, was not even breathing hard as he pushed open the door without knocking.

'Wait,' she panted without any real belief that he would listen.

Despite his earlier promise, Prue had no doubt at all that if he discovered his sister in a compromising position Karim Al-Ahmad would be unable to keep his word. And, although she was sure there had been no spark of attraction between the young couple, this was the sort of situation where she could be excused a few doubts.

She threw herself through the door, yelling, 'Leave him alone, you big bully!'

On the other side of the study bedroom, Karim, one hand on her brother's collar, was standing over his sister, who was curled up in a sleeping bag that had been arranged on a camp bed in one corner of the crowded room. From her sleepy, confused expression and tousled hair she had been asleep when her brother barged in.

The only light in the room illuminated a whiteboard which covered most of one wall. From the marker still in Ian's hand she assumed that he had been adding to the lists of what was indecipherable gibberish to her when Karim had unceremoniously walked in.

'You will tell me what has happened here.' Karim addressed the demand to her alarmed-looking brother. 'You will answer me. This assignation is—'

'*Assignation?* Look, I think you've got the wrong idea here.'

'Oh, for goodness' sake—there *is* no assignation,

Karim. Nothing *happened*. Not the way you mean, anyhow. And Ian didn't invite me, or anything. He just let me have the use of his floor for a couple of nights.' Suzan got to her feet and aimed a defiant look at her glowering brother. 'I'm meeting Clare and Amber and we're off to Australia—and you can't stop me.'

The last comment was noticeably lacking in confidence.

'You don't think so?' Karim said, and then continued to speak, but in Arabic. Whatever he said made the colour drain from his sister's face.

'*Papa!*' she cried, in a voice that would have made a man whose heart wasn't made of steel melt—unlike this one.

Prue could bear it no longer.

'Let my brother go.'

Karim turned. His expression as he looked at her was similar to the one she imagined he would adopt when dealing with a troublesome gnat. Prue's temper stepped up another few notches.

'Teenage boys and girls… My,' she drawled admiringly, 'aren't you the big man? I bet you make puppies cower.'

'I will get to you presently. In the meantime, be silent.'

'Miss Smith, what are you doing here?'

Prue, her eyes blazing, barely registered the teenage Princess's interruption. 'What am I meant to do? Tremble with anticipation?' She had been told to shut up before, but never with such crushing contempt.

Accustomed to snapping his fingers and having people rush to respond, it had obviously not even crossed his mind that she would not do as she was bade.

'My God—you really are the rudest and most unpleasant man I have ever met. Can't you see how upset she is?' she demanded, turning her attention to her tearful ex-student. 'Susan, I'm so sorry, but—'

Karim gritted his teeth and said something in Arabic as he glared at Prue.

'Suzan, you will wait here. You too,' he said, shifting his attention momentarily towards Ian, who looked relieved to be released and held up his hands in a peaceable gesture. Grabbing Prue's arm, Karim propelled her back into the hallway and closed the door behind them.

'How dare you?'

'I dare a great many things, Miss Smith, as you will learn if you do not close your mouth and listen.' A mouth that was distracting even when she wasn't screaming abuse… He looked at the full pouting outline through the dark mesh of his lashes.

'And how are you going to—'

'Like that,' he said a moment later, as he lifted his lips from her own. Breathing a lot harder than he had after running up several flights of stairs, he ran a hand down his jaw. A man who prided himself on being master of his emotions, Karim could not quite believe this lapse in control.

He knew, however, who to blame for it.

Prudence Smith, her big eyes wide and dazed, had her hand over her mouth. She was staring at him as though he were all her nightmares made flesh.

'You b…barbarian,' she stuttered fighting to regain some control of her breathing.

'Yes, and I suggest you don't forget it—unless you wish to experience first hand some more of my brand of barbarity?' His blazing blue gaze slid to the trembling outline of her full lips, and for a weak moment he found himself half wishing that she would do something to excuse a second lapse in control.

The threat drove every vestige of colour from Prue's face. 'Touch me again and I'll—'

'React very much as you did that time and kiss me back, I shouldn't wonder.'

She tried to treat his taunt with the scorn it deserved. Not so easy when only seconds before a thrill of illicit excitement had blitzed through her body, rendering her a weak, compliant puppet. And on top of that the nerves in her stomach were still jittery when she looked at his mouth.

Then don't look!

It was sound advice that Prue had every intention of following.

If ever a situation called for leaving well alone this was it. But Prue felt she had to defend herself.

'I did *not* kiss you back!'

Even as he angled a dark satirical brow in response, the hazy memory of moaning into his mouth while she grabbed a handful of his shirt surfaced in Prue's head. A wave of shame washed over her. She was utterly appalled to have responded at any level to a kiss that had been intended only to establish mastery—never mind with the sort of wanton and totally uncharacteristic abandon she had displayed.

'I'm sure many women would be flattered to be interviewed for your harem, but I happen not to be one of them.'

'I don't have a vacancy at the moment.'

Her teeth clenched, she smiled—wishing she could

think of some cutting response that would deflate his massive ego. 'Thanks for letting me down lightly.'

Against all the odds her retort drew a laugh from him—an attractive, uninhibited sound.

'You are such an ass! Are there no depths to which you won't go? You just made your sister cry, and I—'

'No, for once you will listen. My sister wept because she recognises that her actions could have had serious consequences. She has not lost all sight of what is appropriate behaviour for someone in her privileged position.'

'Not having a life of her own does not seem very privileged to me. Neither does having a brother who thinks he is the moral arbiter of—'

'I do not *think*. I am. And Suzan has satisfied me that nothing untoward has happened between her and your brother.'

Prue gave a sigh of relief. 'I told you. So that's it?'

'However, I am not satisfied that she will not pull a stunt like this again. While my father is recuperating I will not have the time to go running after an errant sister. Because of this I have decided to take steps to make sure that she does not escape again.'

'Do those steps involve a high tower and chains?'

'Only as a last resort,' he came back smoothly. 'No, my plans, Miss Smith, involve you.'

Baffled but wary, Prue shook her head. 'I don't know what you mean.' She wasn't totally sure she wanted to know.

'I *mean*, Miss Smith, that you will return to Zafsid with us. It will be your task to make sure that there is no repeat of this episode. You planted this idea in my sister's head, and you appear to be one of the few people she listens to.'

'In the alternative universe you live in, am I supposed to say that's a brilliant idea and why didn't I think of that?' She loosed a laugh that was borderline hysterical. 'You know, first impressions are sometimes right. I thought when I first saw you that you were insane. Now I *know* you are. Myself, I blame the inbreeding.'

Her steely-eyed tormentor didn't respond to the taunt except to warn her, 'When we are in my country you will have to watch your tongue. You have an unfortunate habit of voicing opinions that would be considered treason there.'

'Which seems a pretty good reason for me to *not* go to your country.' A country where his word presumably was law—now, *that* was scary thought. 'You know, I'm starting to think I did you an injustice—you *do* have a sense of humour. Will you stop smiling at me in that smug I-know-something-you-don't way?'

'Abduction, especially of a foreign royal, is a serious charge.'

Her frown deepened, causing her feathery brows to draw together above her slightly tip-tilted nose. 'What are you talking about?'

'My sister tells me that your brother is one of the most amazing minds of his generation—a genius, no less. And even if she is exaggerating—'

'She isn't,' Prue cut in. Her brother might be vague and impractical, but academically he was widely accepted by those who came into contact with him as one of the most gifted scientists of his generation. His gifts had already opened doors, and universities were fighting to offer him funding for his future research doctorate.

'So he has a glittering career ahead of him. It would be hard to enjoy that career if he were languishing in a prison cell. The idea of all that talent with no outlet would no doubt be frustrating for a genius—though I believe the library facilities in this country's prisons are excellent.'

'My God, are you threatening to accuse Ian of abducting Suzan?' she asked incredulously. 'But that's preposterous—you have to be joking. Nobody in their right mind would believe that Ian's capable of abducting anyone. The police would laugh in your face.' Even as she made the claim she realised that nobody had ever laughed in this man's face.

'I think you will find that the authorities would take such an accusation very seriously.'

'Suzan won't go along with that. She would never…'

'You think not?'

Prue moistened her dry lips with the tip of her tongue and struggled to sustain her air of defiant confidence. Underneath she was seriously worried. Would the younger girl really be able to withstand the pressure this man would bring to bear? After the past couple of hours she had spent in his company she seriously doubted it. He was like a human hurricane, blasting everything that did not bend to his will.

'You're saying that if I don't come with you you'll ruin Ian. But that,' she protested, 'is wicked. It's blackmail!'

'A harsh word, but in this instance perhaps not unjustified,' he conceded. 'You look at me as though I am sentencing you to a few months' sojourn in a rat-infested cellar. I think you should try to be more pragmatic. Think of this as a holiday.'

'A *holiday*.' Prue stared at him. The man was certifiably insane. 'Are you trying to be funny?'

'Where is your spirit of adventure?'

'My what?'

'Many people would envy you, being able to see a new culture first-hand and to enjoy surroundings more comfortable than what you are accustomed to.'

'Suzan ran *away* from her luxurious surroundings,' she pointed out.

His broad shoulders lifted in an expressive shrug. 'Children rebel. It is what they do.'

'Suzan isn't a child.'

'No, this is true. My mother was married with a child at Suzan's age.' The recollection of his mother, who had finally died after a long battle against cancer three years earlier, brought a shadow to his face.

'Oh, my God—you're not going to force her into some sort of arranged marriage?'

Karim, who had all his adult life been an advocate against the practice of arranged marriages, looked into her outraged face and found himself saying, 'My parents had an arranged marriage; they were very happy.' There seemed little point in mentioning that a marriage between his father and the daughter of a very influential family had had to be *un*-arranged before that of his parents could be arranged. Even thirty-five years after the event the insult had not been forgiven.

'That's a bit like saying my grandfather started smoking when he was six and he lived until he was ninety. Sometimes people get lucky against all the odds.'

'Arranged marriages often work very well—better than so-called love matches.'

'Your wife might disagree.'

'I am not married.'

'I thought that you'd have an heir and several spares by this point. Isn't that pretty much the only use you have?'

It was in the stunned, simmering silence that followed her provocative words that the door opened and Suzan poked her head out.

'Is everything all right?'

Karim inhaled deeply and produced a smile for his sister. 'It is fine. Everything is arranged. I have agreed that Miss Smith may accompany us home.'

Suzan let out a squeal of delight and flung herself into her brother's arms. 'Oh, you're the best brother. Thank you, Karim, thank you.'

Above her dark head Karim smiled at Prudence.

Lips compressed, her head held at a defiant angle, Prue stalked past him into her brother's room. She wasn't a person who hated easily, if at all, but she hated Karim Al-Ahmad with every cell in her body. She hated him.

CHAPTER SIX

'WAIT for me in the car.'

Prue gritted her teeth at his peremptory tone, but her companion did not seem to take umbrage. It must be easy, Prue reflected sympathetically, to fall back into a pattern of behaviour established over a lifetime of unthinking subservience.

Karim waited until the women had left the room before turning to the younger man. He did not think Ian was a threat but, conscious that the star-crossed lovers scenario could be very attractive to the romantically inclined, he felt he should make sure there were no misunderstandings.

Before he had a chance to speak the younger man said, with an apologetic grimace, 'I know that Prue can come across as a bit…erm…self-righteous sometimes. But she means well. She just tends to rush in without thinking when she's in full moral crusader mode. The problem with our Prue is she had never quite caught on to the fact that one person can't make a difference.'

Karim's expression went blank. 'You are apologising to me for your sister?' At some level he realised that the anger building inside him was totally out of proportion with what he was hearing. On another more visceral level he had the compelling and shameful urge to shake the ungrateful little rat until his teeth rattled.

'I suppose so,' Ian said a little uneasily.

A muscle in Karim's cheek began to clench and unclench spasmodically. In his opinion people made far too many allowances for genius. 'And if I said to you that your sister is the most obstinate, ill-mannered and headstrong woman—if I suggested that she has exerted an undesirable influence on my sister—what then would you say?'

'Well, I suppose you have a point. She can be awfully stubborn.'

Karim inhaled wrathfully, his lip curling contemptuously as he fixed Prue's brother with a contemptuous glare. 'Any man worth the title would not stand there and permit me to abuse his sister.'

Ian blinked, recoiling from the blaze of fury in the tall man's blazing blue eyes.

'Prudence Smith may be stubborn, but she would defend you with her dying breath.'

Ian regarded the quivering brown finger levelled at his chest with some alarm.

'Your sister may have her faults, but disloyalty is not one of them. I think that she deserves a better brother than you are.' With this cutting observation he swept from the room.

Ian was so unsettled by the incident it was ten minutes before he returned to his earlier computations. Two minutes later, however, he was happily submerged in a world of his own.

* * *

'The Prince requests that you cover your head.'

Prue looked from the man with the scarred face and respectful manner to the piece of silky fabric he held in his hand. Across from her, sound asleep, Suzan was still wearing a tee-shirt and jeans.

'I appreciate your diplomacy, but the Prince has never *requested* anything in his life.'

A flicker of something that looked suspiciously like amusement flickered across the older man's leathery face.

'And why should I adopt traditional dress when Suzan isn't?' She bit her lip, wondering if she could have sounded any more childish if she had tried.

'There is no question of traditional dress—simply a headscarf. I believe, Miss Smith, that the Prince feels that you might attract unwanted attention.' His dark eyes touched the silky golden skeins spread out across her shoulders. 'He wishes to protect you from prying eyes.'

'Smuggle me out of the country without anyone being any the wiser, more like. I don't need his protection.'

'Of course, if you have no problem with people assuming that you are his mistress…'

'Mistress?' Prue yelped, in an accent of horrified revulsion, while in her head she saw an image of herself, reclining in an attitude of wanton abandon, on a bed covered with opulent silken coverings. She was wearing very little in this imagined scene.

If the shudder that chased a quivering path up her spine had had anything to do with illicit excitement she would have been seriously concerned.

'I admire your attitude,' Rashid complimented her quietly.

Prue, her thoughts still enmeshed in the silken drapes, and with anticipation curling low in her belly, shot him a startled stare. 'You do?'

'Why should you care what lies people print in these worthless papers? You know the truth and that is what is important.'

'Hold on,' Prue called after his retreating back. 'Tell him I'll wear it, but not because he told me to.' The addition sounded incredibly childish too, but that was what the awful man and his equally awful servant had reduced her to.

Rashid inclined his head solemnly and promised he would pass on her message.

Hearing Rashid enter, Karim put aside his pen and rested his steepled fingers on the tabletop. 'Tell her if she doesn't put it on I will personally tie her up in a sack.'

'That will not be necessary. The young English lady is only too happy to oblige you in this matter.'

Karim's eyes narrowed. 'The thing about lies, old friend, is that you have to keep them halfway believable. Once you wander into the realms of fantasy you lose credibility. I'm curious,' he admitted. 'How did you make her do it?'

'I think she found the idea of covering her hair preferable to being mistaken for your mistress.'

'My mistress!'

'I had the impression that she would have done almost anything to avoid it—including jumping out of the plane without a parachute.' A rumble of laughter was drawn from deep in his barrel chest as Rashid recalled her expression.

Karim's cerulean glaze swept over the face over the older man. 'Did she say that?'

'She didn't need to. She has a very expressive face, don't you think?'

'Her face is—' Karim stopped, an image of the heart-shaped face under discussion materialising in his head. Belatedly aware that Rashid was awaiting his response, he added abruptly, 'I think she is a little too eager to express herself, full-stop.'

'You must admit that it is a refreshing change from women throwing themselves at you.'

Karim felt no immediate urge to admit anything of the sort. Neither could he share his compatriot's amusement. His ego did not demand the adoration of every woman he met, and if Prudence Smith had thrown herself at him he would have rejected her advances. Maybe they were all good actresses, but so far he hadn't met a woman who had reacted with horror at the prospect of being suspected of sharing his bed.

'You seem to forget that this woman you appear to have so much admiration for is responsible for my sister running away.'

'I thought you had decided that she had no direct hand in the disappearance.'

'Without her influence such an idea would not have occurred to Suzan,' Karim insisted.

'No doubt you are right. Though I am slightly surprised that as you feel she is an unhealthy influence on the Princess you have brought Miss Smith with us.' He paused as the Prince opened his mouth, presumably to explain the sound reasoning behind his decision, before hurriedly closing it again.

'No doubt, sir, you are thinking of the old adage that it is wise to keep your friends close and your enemies even closer?'

'Exactly,' said Karim, thinking of how soft and warm she had felt in his arms. He remembered, too, the fractured little husky gasp she had given low in her throat as she felt his tongue slide into her mouth—it was not a sound he would forget anytime soon. Neither did he think it likely he would forget how sweet she had tasted. 'Closer,' he repeated.

If he hadn't had more pressing concerns Karim might have been tempted to keep Miss Prudence Smith very close. But his decision had been purely practical. His sister's compliant attitude was not down to any change of heart—it was simply a reaction to their father's illness. Once he was no longer in danger, Suzan wouldn't be so accommodating. That was when Prudence Smith's influence would become very useful.

Since leaving the plane, Prue hadn't seen either Suzan or her brother. The limousine from the airport had taken her straight to Zafsid's consulate in Geneva. Once there she had been shown to a luxurious suite of rooms, and while she hadn't been locked in after she had opened the door, there were two men standing outside who resembled large concrete outbuildings.

They had looked at Prue in polite enquiry until she had muttered something inarticulate and quickly closed the door. Polite—oh, yes, everyone here was polite—but underneath all the smiles it was quite clear to Prue that her status was less than that of a privileged guest.

She was no more than a cliché—a prisoner in a gilded cage.

She tried not to let panic take hold by reminding herself that this was only a temporary situation—that next term she would be back at school and all this would be a disturbing memory. The worst that could happen would be that nobody would water her pot plants. Her concerns should be reserved for Suzan. This was her life. And a very luxurious life it could be, if this place was any indication, she thought, her brows lifting as she walked into the most decadent bathroom—complete with sunken marble bath—she had ever seen in her life.

'Wow.'

As she walked around the enormous room, pressing a button which flooded the room with music, lifting lids off ornate glass jars and sniffing the fragrant contents, Prue actually started to feel almost calm—until she made the fatal error of letting her thoughts drift back to that kiss.

Never in her life had she felt so totally and utterly defenceless. Not because she couldn't have put up some sort of resistance, but because she hadn't wanted to.

Admittedly she wasn't likely to find herself in that situation again—the man probably travelled with a portable harem—but what if she did? Left alone to contemplate her plight, it was hard not to let her imagination run riot. What had she done? She was completely at that appalling man's mercy. She could vanish and nobody would be any the wiser. He could kiss her and she would regress to some pre-female emancipation mindless sex-slave.

But of course he wasn't going to kiss her again—a fact which she was grateful for.

Nonetheless a short time later, when a knock heralded the arrival of a young woman wearing a white apron over a navy shirt-dress, she was feeling physically sick with apprehension. She nodded her thanks as the girl laid down a silver tray on which was arranged a mouthwatering selection of sandwiches and sticky sweet cakes. For a split second she fancifully considered begging the girl to smuggle out a message to the outside world—until she recalled the attitude of the staff who had greeted them at the airport. Karim Al-Ahmad's word was probably law to these people.

By the time Suzan appeared, a couple of hours later, she had her imagination under control. Letting it run riot was doing her no favours at all. The chances were she would probably never even be alone with Karim Al-Ahmad again.

'How is your father?'

'Much better, apparently, though he looks terribly frail. But Karim says he's turned the corner and he'll be fine.'

The younger girl's total acceptance of her brother's word was not lost on Prue. Rather than being oppressed, Suzan seemed more the spoilt, indulged sister.

'He'll be well enough to be flown home next week. Karim will fly back with him.'

Settling into a chair, she reached for the untouched sandwiches.

'You know, Miss Smith, I'm really sorry about this—involving you and everything. I don't know how Karim persuaded you to come with us,' she confided with a smile, 'but I'm really glad you decided to come.

It'll be great having you around, and maybe you'll be able to talk sense to him.'

Prue blinked. She could hardly explain to the girl that she had not exactly come along willingly. What reason could she give? He blackmailed me and kissed me into it? God, the more she tried not to think of it the larger that kiss loomed in her consciousness.

It was obviously some sort of guilt thing. She had discovered that, given the right set of circumstances, you could respond sexually to a man even if he symbolised everything you disliked most. If she wanted to get things back into perspective she was going to have to cut herself a little slack. She had never been judgemental about her friends' weaknesses—why did she find it so much harder to forgive herself for a momentary lapse?

'I really don't think I have any influence over your brother, Suzan.' Prue needed to get that clear from the outset.

'But why did you come?'

'I've always wanted to travel,' Prue said truthfully. 'And anyway, aren't I living every woman's fantasy? Whisked away by a handsome desert sheikh?' Actually, it was one fantasy she had never bought into—never mind the reality she was living.

Suzan dutifully laughed at the joke, though she wondered a little about the strained expression on her teacher's face. 'I'd like to travel too one day. Perhaps when I'm married.'

Prue reached out and squeezed the younger girl's arm. She was obviously trying to put a brave face on it. 'Is the wedding soon?'

'Soon?' Suzan shook her head, causing the earrings she wore to jangle musically.

Prue's eyes widened as a horrible possibility occurred to her. Was it possible that Suzan was being married off to someone she hadn't even met? 'You mean he's a total stranger? You haven't even met him?'

'Met who?'

'The man—the one you're—' She stopped as she read the complete bewilderment in the other girl's face. There was no marriage. The utterly appalling man had been winding her up. 'You're not getting married, are you?'

'No.' Suzan looked baffled, and slightly amused. 'Whatever gave you that impression?'

'I must have got the wrong end of the stick.' As he'd intended, she thought grimly. 'It's just that I thought from something your brother said that a marriage had been arranged.'

Suzan's musical laughter rang out. 'You definitely got the wrong end of the stick. Karim is not an advocate of arranged marriages. Well, he wouldn't be, would he?'

'He wouldn't?' Prue echoed, not failing to notice the note of affection in the girl's voice every time she mentioned her brother.

'Hardly—not after falling in love with the woman promised to his brother.'

Karim Al-Ahmad had been in love? There was another Royal Prince?

'Not that he ever said so, but everybody knew it. Even I remember the way Saffa looked at Karim—all that hopeless yearning and stuff—and I was only little at the time.' Chattering away, Suzan seemed oblivious to the fact that she was revealing anything Prue didn't already know.

'But she married his brother?' It was totally incomprehensible to Prue.

'Saffa is very traditional—though I'm sure she would have preferred it if Karim had been the elder, but he wasn't.'

'So they forced her to marry his brother?'

'No—not forced, exactly. Saffa was brought up knowing that one day she'd be Queen, and she quite liked the idea.'

'That sounds very pragmatic.' Prue didn't consider herself wildly romantic, but in her opinion if you were going to choose a crown over a man you had no right to go around looking at him with hopeless yearning.

'I didn't even know you had another brother.' And Karim had stood by and watched the woman he loved marry that brother. She tried and failed utterly to picture the Karim Al-Ahmad she knew in the throes of hopeless passion. The furrow between her brows deepened. 'But I thought that Karim was going to succeed your father…?'

'Hassan was the oldest, but he died four years ago.'

'I'm sorry.' Prue, her thoughts still thrown into chaos by all the personal information she had received, didn't know what else to say.

'So Karim wasn't always—?'

'Crown Prince?' Suzan shook her head. 'No—though he always took his responsibilities more seriously than Hassan. I didn't get to hear all the really juicy stuff, but Hassan created all sorts of scandals. He was a bit of a playboy, I'd suppose you'd say.'

'Being married must have curtailed that lifestyle.'

'I think that was the idea. But…' Her shrug was

philosophical. 'Some men are like that. Still, I expect that Saffa and Karim will marry now.'

Prue was startled by the cheerful prediction. 'So Karim will marry his brother's widow?'

'People are surprised he hasn't already. But sometimes I think Karim avoids doing what people expect of him. Though in this case I'm sure he will, eventually.'

'She might say no,' Prue suggested, thinking of this woman he had always loved and wondering what she looked like. This woman he was so sure of that they had waited four years. Karim Al-Ahmad had not struck her as a patient sort of man. Though perhaps there was some etiquette involved of which she was unaware.

'Can you imagine anyone saying no if Karim asked her to marry him?'

Yes, Prue wanted to retort scornfully. But innate honesty stopped her. Part of the problem was that nobody had ever said no to Karim. But they had, she reminded herself. This Saffa woman who'd thought she'd look better in a crown than with him. Prue's expression grew contemptuous. She wasn't sure that even Karim, for all his faults, deserved someone that shallow.

She was feeling sorry for the man who had blackmailed and virtually kidnapped her—what a fool. 'Maybe he's met someone else?'

'I'm sure Karim's met a lot of *someone elses*—he's no saint. But there's only ever been Saffa for him, and he is expected to provide an heir. Hassan and Saffa only had girls—twins—and they adore Karim.'

Prue could tell by Suzan's attitude that the thing was a done deal as far as she was concerned.

She changed the subject. After all, it was nothing to her who Karim Al-Ahmad married...or kissed...

CHAPTER SEVEN

'MY STAFF tell me you have not eaten anything.'

Prue, sitting in a chair rubbing her wet hair with a towel, shot upright. She looked from him to the closed door and back again. 'What? Did you just come out of the bedroom?'

'There is an interconnecting passage between that room and my bedroom.'

'H…how convenient,' she choked, outraged.

He looked mildly surprised by her reaction. 'I'm sure it has been in the past.'

'I can imagine,' she gritted, trying very hard not to do just that. She lifted a wet strand of hair from her cheek and blinked away an image of waking to find a tall man with eyes like blue fire and a body your average Greek god would covet sliding between the silken sheets. 'I want another room,' she said, fixing him with a look of cold disdain.

'That won't be necessary.'

'I'll be the judge of that. Do you really think I could sleep in that bed knowing anybody could barge in?'

'Not anyone—just me.'

'That makes me feel so much better.'

The retort drew a grin of the wildly attractive variety. Prue felt her insides tighten and lowered her gaze hurriedly.

'You won't be sleeping in that bed.'

This drawled observation brought Prue's attention back to his face. She found herself holding her breath. If he had the gall to suggest she would be sleeping in his she'd soon put him straight.

'Because you and Suzan are flying out in two hours' time. Before then I expect you to eat a sensible meal.'

'I'm not hungry.' The sense of anticlimax she felt was ludicrous. Anyone would think she *wanted* to be invited into his bed.

'I have met women who live on lettuce leaves and strange milkshakes, but you do not have the body of a woman who deprives herself in this way.'

'Are you calling me fat?'

His electric eyes slid with slow, studied insolence over her feminine curves. By the time his eyes had made the return trip to her face her cheeks were burning with mortification and her chin was up.

'No, not fat…more lush. But, semantics aside, you will not starve yourself while you are in my care.'

'Your *care*?' she cried, throwing up her hands in a gesture of incredulity. 'Yeah, right—because kidnap and blackmail are such *caring* qualities.'

'Save the histrionics,' he advised, 'for someone who will fall for the broken voice and the heaving bosom.' Despite his sneer, Karim was uncomfortably aware that he was far from immune to either. Which probably made his response correspondingly harsher as he advised her coldly, 'Do not dramatise, Prudence Smith.

If you have any notion of staging a hunger strike, discard it. You will eat if I have to force-feed you myself. And do not imagine that you may behave in such a foolish fashion while I am here and you are in Zafsid. I will have reports.'

The belligerence faded abruptly from her face. 'You're not coming with us?' She was conscious at some level that this information should be affording her relief—only it wasn't. It was hard to put a name to what she was feeling, but one thing it definitely wasn't was relief. Aware that he was looking at her strangely, she tried to retrieve the situation by adding brightly, 'Of course you're not. Suzan did say something.'

'I will remain here until my father is able to travel next week.'

Prue lowered her eyes and swallowed. She struggled to rationalise her response. She was being plunged into a totally foreign environment—it was only natural that she wanted to have a familiar face close by. Only she was to know exactly how close she found herself picturing it.

'You will miss me?'

She opened her mouth to rubbish the totally ludicrous contention, and closed it again.

'I will send Rashid. If you have any problems just tell him. You will find there are very few problems he is not more than equal to.'

'I get the impression he thinks a lot of you, too.' She doubted even the redoubtable Rashid could sort out the problem she was barely able to admit even to herself. 'If Rashid is so marvellous, why can't *he* make sure Suzan doesn't bolt? In fact this whole thing seems totally unnecessary to me—unless this is more about punishing me. You want someone to blame for Suzan slipping the silken chains and you've decided that I'm it. Better that than face the truth and blame yourself.'

'My sister was perfectly happy with her life until you put ideas into her head. You made her reject the values—'

'I encouraged her to *think*,' Prue cut in. 'I happen to consider it my job. But actually I think you're making a fuss about nothing. Suzan has changed because that's what teenage girls do.'

'Are you suggesting I take joint responsibility?'

'I was thinking more of you taking *all* the responsibility—and for the record I don't want joint anything with you including interconnecting bedrooms.'

'When I join you in Zafsid we will continue this discussion of bedrooms,' he promised smoothly. 'In the meantime, eat the food I send or I will be back.'

Prue did eat the food—but only because she was afraid that if she didn't he would think she wanted him to come back. Which of course was a ludicrous idea.

Prue had anticipated that she would feel isolated and confined in the Royal Palace, but this didn't happen. She had previously had a vague idea of the geographical position of Zafsid, and an even vaguer grasp of its social and political make-up. But even had she been a world-acknowledged expert no book could have prepared her for the reality of the place.

Her determination not to be impressed or interested in anything, to indicate to all who cared to notice that she was not a willing visitor, had vanished the moment the plane had landed and she had inhaled her first breath of warm, fragrant air.

She'd defy anyone not to be enchanted by the place. After only a week she felt as if her senses had been permanently heightened by exposure to the intense colours and evocative spicy scents of the country.

She had thousands of images preserved in her memory: the blue of the sky against the deep russet of the desert sands, the dazzling reflection off the white buildings that lined the wide traffic-clogged avenues in the capital, and the cinnamon-spiced scents in the noisy narrow alleys that heaved with people. The unexpected emerald-green of the irrigated area that surrounded the palace, and the constantly shifting shadows of the desert beyond illuminated in the evening by incredible sunsets.

She was standing enjoying one such mind-numbingly glorious sunset when Rashid approached.

'Do you ever get used to this?' she wondered, lifting her face to the cooling breeze that blew in from the mountains which stood out as blue shadows framed by flame-coloured sky in the distance.

'One does take it for granted,' he admitted. 'And some people find our landscape daunting—the expanses of open space frighten them. But not you, I think?' He angled a questioning look at her profile.

Prue shook her head. 'It's fascinating. It'll be strange to go back to school when this is over.' And when would that be? she asked herself.

'You are, I think, a person who likes a challenge.'

'I don't think I like the sound of that.'

'I have a favour to ask,' Rashid admitted.

'I'm listening.' After a week in Zafsid Prue had grown to appreciate that within the Royal Palace Rashid was considered an influential person of some importance. He did not ask favours, he gave instructions—and they were followed. One of those instructions, she was pretty sure, was the reason she was treated with respect by everyone she came across.

However, when she heard what he had to say Prue was fairly certain that one of them was losing their mind.

'*Me?* You want me to stand in for Prince Karim at the official opening of a school?'

'Not just a kindergarten—there is a baby clinic attached. It is a project that is very close to Prince Karim's heart.'

'All the more reason for me to have nothing to do with it.' She could just imagine Karim's response if he found out *she* had been guest of honour at one of his pet projects.

Rashid responded to her protest with an indulgent smile. 'He has been most energetic in promoting free education and health care to all. In his absence the Princess was to deputise…'

'But she has a sore throat.'

The doctor had confined the teenager to her room until the antibiotics kicked in, which had surprised Prue until Rashid had explained that the Princess had contracted scarlet fever as a child. She had fully recovered, but her heart had been very slightly weakened. The information did go some way to explain her brother's over-protective attitude—although him being a control freak was a much more likely explanation.

'So cancel.'

'The community has been planning this day for weeks. They would be most disappointed if the planned celebrations could not go ahead.'

And why should that make her feel guilty?

The school, the clinic, Karim Al-Ahmad's plans for this country—none of them had anything to do with her. Though it was not hard to see why he was considered something of a champion to the people here. It would seem that he had used his influence as Crown Prince to instigate a series of social reforms in the country over the past few years.

'Look, there must be someone more appropriate who can deputise for Suzan—and I think we're talking just about *anyone* here. You could snap your fingers and get some minor Royal to do their duty, Rashid.'

'You mistake my position, Miss Smith. I do not snap my fingers at members of the Royal family.'

'No, you're much too subtle for that,' she retorted, not for a second convinced by his meek act. 'I appreciate that you're in a hole, and I'd help if I could—really I would—but I wouldn't be an appropriate person.'

'I disagree. You would be a most appropriate person. You are an educator. You taught the Princess. You are a friend and honoured guest of the Royal family. It is most appropriate.'

Prue started to shake her head. 'But I'm *not* a friend of the Royal family. He…the Prince…he….'

'In his absence the Prince has put you in personal charge of his sister. That suggests he trusts you.'

'He doesn't trust me!' Prue exclaimed in frustration. 'And you know it. I don't know why you're twisting things. He doesn't even need me here. Your Prince just likes making people do what he says. Likes showing he's the one in control.' The moment the words were out of her mouth she realised that this man who would lay down his life for his master without a second thought might not be the ideal person to disparage Prince Al-Ahmad to.

'I think the Prince has more on his mind at the moment than petty punishment, and when you know him a little better you will realise that he generally doesn't do anything without a reason. Even though,' he conceded somewhat cryptically, 'he might not always know what that reason is.'

'Don't look at me like that, Rashid, there is no way I could do it. You're wasting your breath.'

Rashid smiled.

CHAPTER EIGHT

'I AM so glad that is over.' Prue sighed as she headed the small procession that retraced its route through the complex. 'My knees were shaking. I thought I was going to throw up. I can't imagine how I allowed you to persuade me to do it.'

'It was not difficult. You have a strong sense of duty—a rare quality.'

'I suppose roughly translated that means I'm a total push-over?'

The grumbled aside caused a quiver in the Sphinx-like demeanour of the man beside her.

'You didn't tell me this was an all-day thing.' The tour of the facilities had taken several hours, and that had been before the opening ceremony and speeches.

'You did an excellent job,' Rashid approved, watching as she knelt down to play with the cherubic-faced tot who tugged at the long skirt she had considered suitable for the occasion. 'Your French is extremely good.'

She tipped her head in acknowledgement of the compliment. 'My roommate at college was French.'

'Male or female?'

At the sound of the deep, unmistakable voice Prue lost her balance and tipped forward, almost landing on the booted feet of the man who had apparently materialised out of nowhere. In her chest her heart began to beat, the sound so loud that it blocked out every other sound in the room. Palms flat on the floor, she lifted her head. It seemed to take for ever for her eyes to reach his face. There was a faint sheen of moisture over the golden skin drawn tight across the chiselled contours of his patrician face. She registered for the first time that he was dressed for riding—the boots, the thigh-hugging breeches and open-necked shirt topped by a traditional white headdress giving him the look of a desert sheikh.

Which, of course, was how he was supposed to look. A desert sheikh destined to be king one day, who had clearly leapt on a horse the moment he learned some jumped-up little teacher had seen fit to deputise for a member of the Royal family. She'd probably committed treason, or something, and the only reason he hadn't demanded she be thrown in a dungeon was because people were watching.

'I'm sure you look terrific on a horse, but an air-conditioned car would have been faster.'

'I enjoy riding, and it is not far from the palace. My flight got in an hour ago.'

She drew a deep shuddering breath as shimmering blue eyes locked onto her own, sending an electric jolt of sheer lustful longing through her body. She felt rather than heard his sudden sharp intake of breath, and her insides dissolved. No man had ever looked at her with such undisguised earthy sexual hunger. Her skin prickled with a rash of shivery sexual awareness she had never experienced in another man's presence. But then Karim was hardly just any man.

She stared, trying to fight her way out of the sexual stupor that held her in its thrall. When she finally did re-animate her vocal cords the voice they produced was weak and breathy.

'This isn't what it looks like—' She stopped. She could hardly tell him it was all Rashid's fault. He was going to be furious when he realised what she had done, but she couldn't lay the blame on someone else.

'You are not kneeling at my feet?'

'Not that—oh God!' Realising that she was literally doing just that, and that there were at least fifty people looking at her, she held the clinging toddler against her hip and tried to scramble to her feet.

Karim bent down and took the toddler from her arms, and handed him to Rashid before turning back to Prue.

She looked at the brown hand extended to her, and after a pause took it. The cool fingers closed over her own and hauled her to her feet, but they didn't drop away. Instead they stayed visibly entwined in her own. He continued to stare at her with that fixed hypnotic intensity.

'Sir?' Stepping forward, Rashid cleared his throat to attract Karim's attention. 'If I could just introduce...'

Karim nodded. It wasn't until he let go of her hand and said, 'We will speak presently,' that Prue realised that the appearance in their midst of their Prince had produced an excitement in the room that bordered on hysteria.

It was half an hour before Karim managed to extricate himself from the adoring crowd. It gave Prue time to prepare herself for the reprimand she was sure to receive and work out some sort of defence. It also gave her ample opportunity to observe how well Karim worked the crowd—but then that was his job, or at least part of it. While his brother might have taken his role as Crown Prince somewhat casually, Karim obviously did not.

As they emerged from the new school building Karim turned to Rashid and the men exchanged a few sentences in rapid Arabic. Prue had begun to feel they had forgotten her when Karim switched to English and said, 'I will take Miss Smith back to the palace. There is a car?'

Of course there was a car. If Karim had requested a hot air balloon Prue was pretty sure one would be procured without fuss. The car that was produced was a four-wheel drive Jeep-type affair. Before he got in Karim removed the covering from his head and angled a questioning look at Prue.

'What are you waiting for? An invitation?'

Prue, who had been staring at his silky dark hair, blinked and swallowed. 'More like an order,' she retorted, the sharpness of her tone only thinly disguising her extreme reluctance to get in beside him. 'Look, I appreciate you not screaming abuse at me in front of everyone, but is this really necessary?'

'Does everything have to be a matter of debate with you?' He slammed the door before she had time to respond.

'Where,' she asked as they drew away in a cloud of dust, 'is everyone?'

'"Everyone" as in…?'

'Everyone as in your bodyguards and whatever.'

'Actually, in my own country I get to move around pretty much as I please.'

'I suppose that roughly translates as you ignore what Rashid and everyone else advises?' she retorted tartly. 'I really feel sorry for that man—he has a lot to put up with.'

'One cannot live in fear. I do not take rash or reckless risks.'

A pity the same couldn't be said for me, Prue thought, wondering why she had got into the Jeep with him so willingly. As they drove over what seemed little more than a dusty track that seemed to stretch into the distance Prue began to think that his take on rash and reckless danger might not be the same as her own.

'Look, you're angry, so why don't you just get this over with? If it makes it any easier I'll admit I had no right to be there today. But the doctor wouldn't hear of Suzan leaving her room, let alone the palace. I just thought...and Rashid...not that it was his idea at all...well, I...'

'Rashid told me he asked you to deputise. Thank you.'

Prue stared at his cut-glass profile, not quite believing what she had heard. *'Thank you?'*

'Yes—thank you. I am not unappreciative of your assistance.'

'I thought you'd be furious.'

'Why?'

'Past experience, I suppose.'

His mobile mouth spasmed, but he did not respond directly to her jibe. 'We are taking a detour. If you don't have any objection?'

The time-lag before the addition made Prue smile to herself. He was making an effort and she kind of appreciated it. As she looked at him through the mesh of her lashes she noticed for the first time the signs of strain in his face. The darkness under his eyes that made them even more dramatic, the grooves between his mouth and nose etched deeper in his dark skin, the erratic twitching of a nerve in his eyelid as he concentrated on the road ahead. She found herself wondering when he had last slept.

'I had sort of figured the detour part. Where to?'

'I thought you might like to visit a real desert oasis. It is somewhere I go when I need to recharge my batteries and be alone.'

'Alone?'

His eyes flickered briefly to hers, the message in their blue depths making her stomach lurch. 'Not on this occasion. I seem to make a habit of kidnapping you. Speaking of which, I heard from your brother last night. He is well, and he sends his best wishes.'

'Does he?' That did not sound like Ian, who had a very slender grasp of social responses.

'Not actually. But if he had been able to tear himself away from his calculations he might have.'

Her hackles rose at the implied criticism. 'He's young.'

'He's older than you were when you became his guardian. I have lost a parent. I can't imagine how painful it must have been to lose both at so young an age.'

This empathy coming from the last person in the world she would have expected momentarily robbed her of speech. 'How on earth do you know that?'

Karim did not respond to her question. Instead, he demanded, 'Does he actually realise, this genius brother of yours, the sacrifices you have made for him? Why do you protect him from reality? He is a grown man, not a child.'

Prue shifted uneasily in her seat. 'What sacrifices? And how do you know these things about me?'

'The file that was missing the first time we met was located. I have read it from cover to cover. But I did not need a file to tell me that your brother is about the most self-obsessed person I have ever met.'

'A file on *me*?' Prue was horrified that he could be so casual about such a gross invasion of privacy. 'That's totally out of order—'

There was no hint of apology in his manner as he cut across her. 'You came into contact with my sister. It was necessary. It was not comprehensive. For instance, I know you go to the ballet when you can afford it, but I don't know if you like country music. I know there is no man in your life at the present, but I do not know the names of your previous lovers.' He moved down the gears as the Jeep struggled to reach the brow of a sharp incline. 'These details were not considered vital to Suzan's security, but I'd like to know.'

'I like Johnny Cash, and as for the other that's none of your damned— Oh, my goodness.' She stared in dazzled bemusement at the scene spread below. 'Is that real or a mirage?'

'Real,' said Karim, stopping the four-wheel drive on the crest of the hill and swivelling in his seat to look at her, rather than at the swathe of green and shimmering blue that stood like a bright jewel in the ochre-coloured landscape.

'It's an oasis!' she exclaimed excitedly. 'Exactly like in the films, only real, not a film set. Palm trees, water…that is totally incredible,' she enthused.

Belatedly realising that Karim's eyes were trained on her face, and that he was no doubt comparing her bubbling childish enthusiasm unfavourably with the sophisticated manners of the women he knew, like the elegant Saffa, she added with a shrug, 'It's really quite pretty.' The dignified Saffa would never bounce in her seat. She would be languid and witty and charming in a subtly sexy way.

'You sound very blasé.'

The comment brought her up short. He was right. What was she doing? What the hell did it matter what he thought of her? Why should she pretend to be something she wasn't just to impress him?

Angling a defiant look at his lean face, which clearly bewildered him, she wound down the window. Immediately the interior of the Jeep was filled with the energy-sapping heat of the desert. It hit Prue like a solid wall, drying the air in her throat and nose.

'It isn't quite pretty,' she refuted, sticking her head through the open window and letting the light breeze lift her hair from her scalp. 'It is stunning—the most incredible thing I have ever seen,' she cried, ducking back inside, her cheeks pink and her skin lightly slicked with beads of perspiration. 'I'll never forget it.' *Or you.* 'It's one of those images that will stay with me for ever.'

She knew the memory would always be tinged with pain—the pain of knowing she would never be able to explore the feelings this man incited in her. Feelings she had yet to experience with any other man, might never feel again. Because now, in this moment, she suddenly realised she spent much of her waking and sleeping hours thinking of him. She was fascinated by him, obsessed with him, hopelessly, helplessly, irrevocably fascinated…with a royal prince. A fascination that stood about as much chance of a happy ending as an ice cream did in the desert.

Every time she looked at Karim she knew exactly what that doomed ice cream felt like.

'And I don't care if that makes me sound like a tourist.'

'Not a tourist, but not blasé, which does not suit you. I don't think I have ever been in the company of a woman before who doesn't even attempt to say what she imagines I want to hear. Actually, I think you try and say what you think I *don't* want to hear, just for the hell of it. If you were trying to make me notice you, it worked.'

'I wasn't,' she retorted, her cheeks flushed by more than the heat. 'And frankly, I can't imagine anything I'd like *less* than being noticed by you,' she hissed.

'Oh, I think, *ma belle*, you enjoy me noticing you.' His blue eyes captured hers as he expanded on the theme in a low, huskily suggestive voice barely above a whisper—a voice that made every nerve-ending in her body quiver. 'I think it makes your heart quicken in anticipation.' His eyes slid to where the organ in question was hammering against her ribcage, and for a moment she thought he meant to cover it with his hand.

In her head she could see his brown hand cupping her pale flesh, stroking the straining pink bud with his finger, no barrier of fabric between them. The actual barrier that was there, outside her fevered imagination, did a very poor job of disguising how aroused she was, and under the light silk of her loose shirt her breasts tightened and swelled in anticipation of his imagined touch.

His eyes lifted. 'Your face is an open book, *ma belle*. Your body, too, is expressively responsive.'

She could hardly claim her body was reacting to the cold.

'You can't read my mind,' she protested, thinking that if he could he would not be very much wiser. Her attraction to this man had thrown her thoughts into total chaos. He belonged to someone else—a fact Prue knew she was in danger of forgetting.

'Perhaps not, but you just read mine.' Her anguished groan drew a raw grin. 'You should not regret your honesty or your transparency. When a man wants to please a woman it is useful if he can see what she is thinking.'

Prue started, but she didn't attempt to pull away as he took her chin in his hand and tilted her face, first a little that way, then the other. His normally crisp enunciation was slurred as he said slowly, 'It is a beautiful face.'

'I have freckles.' She struggled to resist the seduction in his voice, but knew that if he carried on this way her surrender was not a matter of if, but when.

The sense of anticlimax was intense when his hand dropped away and he leaned back in his seat. 'I like them,' he said, starting up the engine.

CHAPTER NINE

'THERE are people!' she exclaimed, surprised, as they came closer to the oasis.

'Certainly there are people. Generations ago my people were nomadic. Here in the south a few still maintain that old lifestyle. My mother's father was one of those people.'

'He was a sheikh. And now you are.'

'Suzan has been boring you with our family history, I see. Yes, the title passed to my brother on his death and then to me. My grandfather had no sons. There was just my mother, and her sister who died childless.'

'Isn't that unusual? I thought...'

He pulled the Jeep to a halt and slewed around in his seat to look at her. 'You thought what?'

'I thought that a man in his position would have been expected to take another wife if the one he had didn't supply a son.'

'That was what was expected of him,' Karim agreed. 'But my grandfather loved his wife very much. He would not put her aside even though she begged him to—as did the elders of the tribe.'

'He must have been a remarkable man.'

'He would have liked you, too. He had a weakness for blondes, though his was French.'

'Your grandmother?'

Karim nodded.

As they walked through the swaying palms the people there bowed low to Karim, but to Prue's surprise did not react as though his presence amongst them was unusual. She watched as he swung a child who had run up to him above his head, saying something that made the little boy laugh. It all struck her as a stark contrast to the formality of the palace. Karim seemed more relaxed here than she had ever seen him.

Inside a silken-swagged tent—lit, even though it was still light outside, by numerous flickering lanterns—it was amazingly cool.

Karim sat down cross-legged on the pile of cushions on a low divan which was set beside a low table. Prue ran a finger along the table's intricately carved beaten metal before hesitantly following suit.

'This is very decadent.'

Karim arched a brow and looked amused as she folded her arms primly across her chest. 'You disapprove?'

She shook her head. 'I just feel a bit out of place.' This was the sort of setting where a painted houri intent on pleasing her master would feel at home.

'You look like a spinsterish English schoolmistress,' he teased.

The more relaxed he looked, the more tension she felt creeping into her spine. Which might not be a bad thing, she told herself. Tension equated with caution, and she hadn't been showing much of that so far.

'That could be because that's exactly what I am.' And now might be a good time, Prue Smith, to remind *yourself* of the fact. 'I wanted to ask you when you can arrange for me to fly home. I mean, there's no actual point in my being here now, is there?'

'We will discuss that tomorrow.'

A lot of things, she thought, dragging her straying gaze from the sliver of golden flesh revealed where the top buttons of his shirt had parted, could happen before tomorrow. 'Why not now?'

He looked irritated by her persistence. 'Because I do not wish to discuss it.'

'Don't speak to me as though I was a child.'

'I do not think of you as a child. Are you not going to ask me what I *do* think of you as?'

Prue declined to meet the open challenge glittering in his deep-set eyes.

The coffee, when it came, was a very welcome distraction. It was served in tiny cups by a veiled young woman who bowed low to Karim and looked curiously at Prue through sloe-dark eyes huge within rings of decorative kohl.

The numerous bangles around her wrists jangled as she moved, and her long fingers decorated with elaborate hennaed patterns were covered in silver rings.

'Would you prefer some chocolate? This coffee can be something of an acquired taste.'

'A cold drink would be nice.'

He said something to the waiting woman, and a moment later a tray with glasses and a pitcher of iced lemonade appeared, along with a plate of sweet sticky cakes covered in nuts and honey. After drinking her lemonade Prue placed the glass down on the low table.

'I want to go home,' she said, sounding very much like the child she had claimed not to be.

'You are unhappy here?'

'No,' she admitted. 'But I'm surplus to requirements. I have no place here.'

'You had a place today,' he said, watching her nibble at her lower lip.

Her glance flickered upwards, but immediately fled the intensity of his blazing blue regard. 'That was nothing.'

'Actually, I can think of several members of our family who would have found the task much more daunting than you did. And they would have performed it with less grace.'

'How do you know I performed it with grace?'

His blue gaze shimmied over her shapely figure. 'You do everything with grace. As for being surplus—you are not. If you were not here I have no doubt that by now my sister would be planning another misadventure. Although I admit that there was some element of anger involved in my decision to ask you to accompany Suzan.'

'An *element*? *Ask*?' she echoed incredulously. 'You blackmailed me.' Glaring at him she picked up a cake and bit into it hard.

'I needed you.'

In the short, shocking silence that followed his explosive and angry-sounding statement their eyes clung. On this occasion it was Karim who lowered his gaze.

'Suzan could not stay in Switzerland. Our mother's illness was prolonged; it left her with a dislike of hospitals. Alone in the palace she would have fretted. She needed something to take her mind off what was happening. Being your guide around our country has done that. And you must know her compliance is temporary. She listens to you.'

Prue conceded this with a shrug. 'But what if I say the wrong thing? And anyhow, now you're here.' She looked at the cake in her hand, wondering how it had got there, and placed it on the tray.

'I have my hands full stopping my father doing what the heart attack failed to do.'

Prue's brow creased in concern. 'I thought he was better. I understand why you might want to protect Suzan from the truth, but if he isn't well she has a right to know.'

'I have not lied to Suzan,' he rebutted. 'My father is a resilient man, but I think this incident has made him aware of his mortality for the first time. He does not fear death, but he does fear being weak and incapacitated. I am afraid there is a very real danger of him pushing himself too far to prove that he is still the man he once was.'

'But I have my own life.'

'I am asking a great deal of you, but I am *asking* this time.'

Prue lifted a frustrated hand to her face and groaned. 'Has anyone ever said no to you?'

Karim, a gleam of satisfaction in his eyes, leaned across and removed her hand from her face before folding it within his. 'I wish I had unlimited time, but I don't. I will be missed at the palace. I have responsibilities—responsibilities I am neglecting.'

'Of course.' She started to get up, but he placed a hand on her shoulder and pulled her back down beside him.

'Shouldn't we go?'

'Not yet, *ma belle.*' The caressing endearment made her heart-rate quicken. Feeling suddenly incredibly shy, she let her head fall forward. He reached out and pulled a concealing lock of blonde hair from her cheek. Where his fingertips lightly grazed her skin it tingled and burned.

'I feel I may speak freely with you. There is an attraction between us. We have both felt it. And I think we have both been fighting it.'

Heart thudding, she lowered her gaze and muttered, 'This has no future.'

He did not deny her assessment. 'The future is not here and now, and the present could be pleasant, I think, if we stopped fighting it. I know that we would not under normal circumstances have met, but we have, and you have been on my mind.' He placed a finger under her chin and tilted her face up to his. 'At the palace there are too many eyes and ears. It would not be possible for us to be together without it reaching the ears of my father. It would distress him and he—'

'Wants you to marry Saffa,' she finished. His concern for his father's feelings did him credit; it just seemed a great pity to Prue that he didn't seem to have the faintest inkling that admitting he was ashamed to be seen in public with her might ever so slightly bruise her own feelings.

Clearly he supposed she would be so flattered by his attention that she would accept it on whatever terms he suggested—and why wouldn't he? She ruefully assessed her shamefully obvious behaviour from the moment he had appeared. She felt more alive when he was near than she could ever recall feeling before.

He looked surprised, but made no attempt to deny it.

'Saffa—you have met? I thought she was going back to Paris once she left Geneva.'

'Not met. She was getting into a limousine when Suzan and I were returning from the bazaar the other day.' It hadn't required a big leap to see the elegant couture-clad figure with diamonds shining around her slim neck being Queen—Karim's Queen. 'Suzan bought me these,' she said, fingering the string of semi-precious stones that she wore around her neck.

'Beautiful,' Karim said, looking at the neck and not the stones.

'It must have been nice for you to have company in Geneva.' Prue concealed her irrational spurt of jealousy behind a bright smile. Something in his expression as he looked at her made her wonder how successful she had been on the concealment front.

'Company?' He shook his head. 'Saffa only dropped in for an hour. She doesn't care for sickbeds. Even when Hassan was ill she couldn't bear to visit him. My brother...' Her dark lashes came sweeping down.

'I know—Suzan explained the situation.'

'What exactly did Suzan explain?'

'That you're going to marry Saffa one day. Are you?' She bit her tongue, but the question hung in the air between them.

'I did not bring you here to speak of Saffa.'

Prue's eyes lifted, resentment and hurt in the swimming depths. 'No, you brought me here to seduce me.'

'Are you telling me you do not wish to be seduced? Are you telling me that you have not been conscious of the chemistry between us?'

Prue found the growing humidity a lot easier to cope with than the sexual tension that was growing within the silken canopy. She struggled to introduce an overdue touch of reality into the highly charged atmosphere.

'If another man came out with stuff like that I'd laugh in his face,' she told him truthfully. 'Just because of an accident of birth you think I'll fall into your arms like a ripe peach.'

'Your analogy is not inappropriate. Your skin does remind me of a firm peach, and I don't deny that with a certain type of woman my birthright is part of my attraction, but with you I feel that this is something I must work hard to overcome.'

Prue attempted to hide the laughter that escaped her lips.

'Why,' he demanded, looping a hand casually in a strand of her long hair and drawing her face to his, 'are you laughing?'

'I'm laughing at you,' she whispered, breathless because his mouth was so close she could feel his warm, fragrant breath on her face. 'Because you think that women are attracted to you because of your royal blood.' Another gurgle of laughter escaped her parted lips. 'Women would be attracted to you if you worked on the checkout in a supermarket, because what you have has nothing whatever to do with money or prestige and everything to do with raw sex. It oozes out of your ridiculously perfect pores. Oh, my God,' she groaned. 'Tell me I didn't say that out loud.'

CHAPTER TEN

'You didn't say out loud that I oozed raw sex,' he said co-operatively.

'I hate you.' If that were true, how much simpler life would be.

'Come hate me some more,' he invited huskily, and he gently pushed her backwards into the mound of soft, satiny silk cushions.

Prue lay there, her heart thudding heavy and hard in anticipation against her breastbone. One arm braced above her head, the other stroking the curve of her thigh, he leaned over her.

'Your mouth—it is driving me crazy. It has been driving me crazy, *ma belle*,' he confided in a slurred, sinfully sexy voice, 'since the very first moment we met.'

Looking into his cerulean eyes made Prue dizzy, so she let her eyelids close. They felt very heavy as her pro-tected eyes burned with unshed tears of a nameless emotion—the same emotion that made her throat thick and dry.

She moaned as he caught her full lower lip gently in his teeth and tugged softly, taking a series of soft nibbling bites and then sliding his tongue very softly along the sensitive moist skin of her inner lips.

'You taste of honey.'

She sucked in a shaky breath through flared nostrils as heat pooled deep in her belly. His hand moved under the silk of her skirts, sliding up along the curve of her bare thigh.

'That's the cake.'

'I have been dreaming of you tasting of me when I kiss you.' His dark lashes brushed the flushed angles of his chiselled cheekbones as he slid his tongue sinuously between her parted lips. 'I would like that... Would you like that?' he purred throatily against her mouth.

'I think... I don't know...' The sheer depth of her inexperience suddenly came crashing down on her. It had very much the same effect as a cold shower. She stiffened and turned her head.

What was she doing?

Karim was an expert lover, and he thought he was dealing with someone of similar experience. She would be a massive disappointment.

'What is wrong?' he said, raising himself up on one hand.

'I'm not actually very good at this—seduction, sex, all that sort of thing.'

His expression cleared, his frown replaced by a smile. 'In that case I will lower the bar,' he told her obligingly.

She gasped, indignant.

Laughing, he caught the hand she aimed at his head. 'You are so ridiculous, *ma belle*,' he said, pressing her small palm to his lips before moving her hand to the floor above her head and pinioning it there. Their eyes meshed, and he wasn't laughing any longer. His expression was taut and needy as he gazed at her with a raw, barely restrained hunger that drew a low, keening whimper from her throat.

'Karim, I…I really do…you…'

The raw emotion he felt as he looked into her golden eyes was like nothing he had ever experienced. He shook his head, his eyes smouldering as he raised himself up to fight his way out of his shirt.

Prue sighed and flung her other hand above her head. She ran her tongue over her dry lips, marvelling at the sight of his marvellous, sleek, streamlined torso, gleaming bronze in the light from the lanterns. The aching emptiness low in her pelvis intensified as she stared at him. He was totally and completely perfect, a classical statue made of flesh and blood.

Her throat ached with the emotion locked in there as he joined her, arranging his long, lean length beside her and turning her onto her side so that they lay touching, her thigh curved across his hip.

'You are so beautiful,' she said, running her fingers over the taut muscles of his belly and feeling the sharp contraction as he sucked in a painful breath. She kissed his shoulder, running her tongue over his satiny skin and tasting the salt. 'And so hard,' she whispered as his nose nudged against her own. Her breath snagged on a tortured gasp and she moaned as she felt the iron-hard imprint of his erection graze against the softness of her belly. 'I didn't mean that…but that too,' she whispered into his mouth.

Both breathing hard, their hot breath mingled. He cupped her bottom and pulled her up against him, so that they were sealed at hip level and she could fully feel the strength of his need for her.

'This will be good,' he whispered against her ear. The heat of his mouth made her shiver. His promise made her shiver a lot more. And his kiss—a slow, languid exploration—left her breathless and aching, and wanting more, much more. 'I will make you forget any other man you have known, *ma jolie fille.*'

Of course if she had been in her right mind she would have explained then—told him straight that it really wouldn't be so difficult because she hadn't known *any* other man, not in the sense he meant. But she didn't, because she wasn't in her right mind. She wasn't sure if she had a mind at all.

She just had a desperate, driving need. A need to feel his naked skin slide against her own, to feel him heavy against her, hard inside her.

She didn't know she had expressed those needs out loud until he said thickly, 'You shall—you shall, *ma belle.*'

He was kissing her with a wild, erotic ferocity that drove any coherent thought from her head. She clung to him, sinking her fingers into his silky hair, pressing her aching breasts against him.

'I want to look at you.'

She closed her eyes as she felt warm air brush her overheated skin, and then, as he pulled the fabric of her silk shirt back to reveal the satiny camisole she wore next to her skin, she held her breath.

Karim caught his own breath. Her skin was pale and flawless, her rosy-tipped breasts full and luscious. He pressed his lips to the soft curve of her belly and her body arched. She grabbed his head as he trailed the kiss upwards to the valley between her breasts.

'So soft, so lovely…' He nuzzled her throat before

angling her face and covering her mouth with his. She gave a shocked gasp as he took the twin mounds of her straining breasts in his hands, drawing them together, burying his face in the softness before he lashed each turgid peak with his tongue.

He lifted himself off her to remove his pants. She lay there, staring up at him through passion-glazed golden eyes, her rapid and shallow respirations making her breasts quiver in a way that made it hard for him to perform the basic task. Hard for him to do anything but think of satisfying the primal need that roared like an out-of-control fire inside him. The need to plunge into her and lose himself.

The sight of him naked and magnificently aroused made things twist low and deep inside her. Prue gave a whimper and lifted her hips as he slid her pants down over her thighs with shaking hands. When he parted her legs and touched her she was washed away on a tidal wave of sheer sensation.

Shaking in every cell of her body, Prue raised herself up, her body curving towards him, and grabbed his head in both her hands as she fell back onto the soft pillows.

'Please,' she said, as he looked into her eyes.

He carried on looking into her eyes as he parted her legs and settled between them. He was still looking at her as he thrust into her and felt the resistance of her body. She saw the shock chase across his lean face.

At that point Prue became too engrossed it what she was feeling to think about that look on his face. She was just aware of the amazing sensation of being filled by Karim. Of him stroking her slowly—measured, rhythmic strokes that made everything burn and tingle, tighten and clench inside her. When the ripples began she gave a lost cry and called his name. She called it again and again as the full force of the climax hit her, the wave of sensation spreading all the way to her toes as she felt him shudder above her and then roll away.

Prue lay there, shaking and quivering, her mind still in a state of blissful disbelief. He rolled back to her.

'You were a virgin.' He had been totally out of control. He could have hurt her. The idea cut Karim like a knife-blade. The more he thought about it the sicker he felt. 'You preach sexual liberation and mock traditional values and you are a virgin.'

'Will you stop saying that?'

'How is this possible?'

'Well, I would have said I was choosy, but obviously I'm not. You know, I'm not in the mood for some sort of post mortem about my shortcomings.'

'Shortcomings? You're deliberately misunderstanding me.'

'Not much to misunderstand, is there? I was meant to know what I was doing and I don't. What do you want me to do, Karim, apologise?'

'You should have told me. It should have... I should have....' He dragged a hand across his eyes and fell onto his back.

'You're not what I thought you were,' he said heavily. 'It shouldn't have been like that.' The first time should have been gentle and tender. He had checked his passion as best he could when he had realised, but it had been too little too late. No wonder she'd acted as though it was a new experience when he had touched her—it had been.

'What's wrong? Ah—in your world you marry virgins and designate the ones who aren't as mistress material only.' Tears in her eyes, she started to grab her clothes. 'Well, don't worry, Karim. I'm not eager to be either.'

'You are talking nonsense,' he said, levering himself into a sitting position.

'Am I? Well, tell me this, Karim: if I had told you, would you still have taken me to bed?'

Their eyes meshed—tear-filled amber with grave blue.

'The truth is I don't know.'

'The truth is you wanted a cheap one-night stand.' And she had been stupid enough to think that he might have wanted something else. It was shocking to realise that she had thought it could be more—that a part of her still wanted more.

'Prudence—'

Deaf to the agonised emotion in his voice, she slapped away his hand and turned her back on him. 'You can take me back now. I think I've had enough of this detour.' She moved quickly, and winced as muscles she had never used before made their presence felt.

The colour drained from Karim's face as he saw her wince of pain, and the hand he had extended towards her fell away.

By the time they reached the palace darkness had fallen. Several times during the journey Karim had started to speak, and on each occasion Prue had shaken her head and begged him not to. She was deeply ashamed that she had succumbed so easily to temptation and slept with a man she knew was promised to another woman—a woman he wanted to spend the rest of his life with.

When they arrived he caught her arm and pulled her towards him. 'Look, this is ridiculous—we can't leave it like this.'

'Sir?' Rashid, looking apologetic, appeared. 'I thought you might like to know that the King has summoned several government ministers to his apartments.'

Karim released a long, frustrated sigh and rolled his eyes. 'I will be there. Prudence—'

Prue shook her head and gave a bright smile as she pulled clear of his grasp. 'Thank you for the tour, Prince Karim,' she said formally. 'It was most educational. Goodnight, Rashid.'

Watching her walk away, Karim swore softly under his breath before turning back to Rashid. 'My father,' he told the older man, 'is an idiot. And so, I begin to see, is his son.'

CHAPTER ELEVEN

PRUE had been so lost in her own thoughts that she didn't realise, until she walked through an arch and found herself standing in an unfamiliar large paved courtyard, that she had strayed into an area of the palace where she had never ventured before. This was not in itself surprising—the palace compound covered a vast area. For the first day or so in Zafsid Prue had struggled to get her head around the sheer vastness of what amounted to a walled city.

Now she felt almost wistful for that time, when she had had nothing more testing to struggle to comprehend. She was even wistful for the time when she had been worried about her growing obsession with Karim Al-Ahmad.

How could she have been so blind? How could she not have seen then that she was in love with him? Of course realising this now explained the ease with which she had been able to forget all the moral halt signs and sleep with him.

Falling in love with Karim Al-Ahmad was something she would never really be able to explain, no matter how hard she tried to rationalise or dissect her feelings. It was one of those things she just had to live with, and she had been doing that since the moment the realisation had hit her two days earlier. It had been the strangest thing—like looking at an out-of-focus picture that suddenly and without warning slipped into dazzling focus. She was living with her secret, but it was not easy.

And Karim... Sometimes—like now, when she was alone—she said his name out loud. Well, he was one of those things she was going to have to learn to live without. And she was getting some practice in. For the past week she had seen very little of him, and always in the company of others. He hadn't once made any attempt to seek her out, which pretty much said it all. He regretted what had happened and wanted to avoid a repeat of the emotional drama.

As she walked inside the courtyard, drawn by the soothing, musical sound of flowing water, she immediately recognised from the ancient stone of the walls and the priceless mosaic underfoot that she was standing in an original part of the building. A part that, according to the reading she had done on the subject in the palace library, had already been ancient in the days of the Crusades.

It was also, the princess had explained to her, the part that housed her father's apartments and a private art collection to which experts travelled from all over the world to view. The King frequently loaned out sections to museums all over the world. Suzan, who at that time had been keeping up with her father's progress from the twice-daily reports she had from Karim in Switzerland, had promised that one day when her father was better she would arrange for Prue to see the collection.

Prue now knew that by the time Suzan recalled her promise she wouldn't be there. The situation was becoming positively masochistic. There was no reason—if there ever had been—for her to be there beyond her reluctance to sever all links with Karim.

Trespassing in the most off-limits section of the palace, she mused, smiling a little to herself as she looked curiously around. And I thought the day couldn't get any worse. People probably got thrown into dark dungeons for being where she was, uninvited. Actually, she felt so wretched a dark dungeon might actually be a step up from where she was just now.

Though where she really was just now was incredibly beautiful—and, more than that, it had an air of tranquillity. As she gazed around her Prue felt some of that tranquillity seep into her. The air in the enclosed space was redolent with the strong scent of jasmine. Overlooked by a dazzling white tower on one side, and enclosed by high walls on the other, the sweet-smelling sanctuary was lush with greenery and splashes of colour supplied by exotic-looking blooms. The soothing sound of running water was supplied by a cascade spurting from the mouth of an ancient-looking mythological beast set into the stone wall to her right. It fell into a deep aquamarine pool lined with intricate mosaic that fed a series of slow-flowing canals.

She had turned, her intention to leave, when a movement in the periphery of her vision made her realise that she wasn't alone. She hung back, unsure whether to just vanish or to reveal herself to the man who was almost concealed by a group of lemon trees.

She was still hovering indecisively when a door set in the wall of the tower opened and a robed figure, leaning heavily on a cane, walked out.

She instinctively drew back into the concealing greenery. At the same moment there was a rustle of movement that came from where the concealed man stood. Prue turned her head and saw him, dressed all in black, his face hidden behind a hood, move forward. He raised his hand, she assumed to hail the elderly man, who was unaware of him. She saw no sinister significance in his actions—until she saw the glitter as the blade in his hand caught the sun.

He wasn't trying to attract the old man's attention. He was going to attack him!

Without thinking she began to run, waving her hands and yelling at the top of her lungs. The elderly robed figure was staring at her, oblivious to the man coming from the opposite direction. They were both within a few feet of the elderly figure when, with a final burst of speed, she managed to interpose herself between the running figure and the old man. The masked man was running too fast to stop and cannoned straight into her, sending her sprawling back onto the ground.

There couldn't have been a delay of more than a few seconds before the man was hauled off her. As two men in uniform restrained their prisoner, who was yelling and screaming abuse, the elderly man stepped forward. He was tall, his dark hair was streaked with silver, and his black eyes gleamed with intelligence in his lined face. But it was not the similarity of features which rang bells with Prue. It was the hauteur with which he carried himself she immediately recognised.

'You're Karim's father,' she said, before the blackness rolled in.

When she woke she was lying in a bed. There were blinds on the window through which slivers of sun fell, forming a striped pattern on the wall opposite. 'Where am I?' She smelt jasmine set in a crystal bowl and it all came flooding back. 'Did I hit my head? Did I knock myself out?' She could remember being crushed, and the hateful smell of the would-be assassin's hot body on top of her before they hauled him off.

'Lie still.' Karim, his expression stern, stepped forward and tugged up the sheet she had pulled back. 'Do not think about what happened,' he commanded. 'You must rest. I will call a doctor.'

Despite the statement he showed no signs of doing so. He just carried on staring at her with an unnerving intensity.

'Is your father…? It *was* your father…?'

'Yes, it was my father.'

'He's all right?'

'He'll be fine—not a scratch.' He swallowed, his eyes going to the heavily bandaged area of her shoulder.

'It really happened, then?' The unusual pallor of Karim's normally vibrant skin and the dark shadow covering his normally meticulously clean-shaven jaw and lower face made Prue suspect he was not telling her the whole truth. 'I thought maybe it was some sort of bad dream. Why did he do that…the man?'

Karim looked paler and sterner and a lot more tired

than she remembered. But she supposed that having someone try to kill your father would do that to a man. He gave the cover another twitch and shrugged, his eyelashes coming down in a protective shield over his electric-blue eyes.

'I imagine there were a number of contributory factors. Apparently he has a history of mental illness.' No matter how deep he dug Karim could feel no vestige of sympathy or compassion for the man who had nearly robbed him of what he held most dear in his life.

Recalling the wild, almost feral light in the man's eyes as he had borne her to the ground made Prue shudder.

Karim's hand came up to cover hers. 'We will not speak of it,' he said roughly.

Prue looked at his brown fingers curled over hers, and the fear that had tightened her stomach into knots receded. She shook her head and lifted her eyes to his. 'No, I want to know.'

After studying her face for a moment Karim sighed, and nodded his head in reluctant assent. 'They think what finally sent him over the edge was his daughter being accepted as part of the first intake of women at our medical school.'

Prue was bemused. 'I don't follow.'

'She plans to take up the place despite his strong opposition. He thinks she has brought shame on his family. He is one of a happily small minority who object to the change—who object to women having any life outside the confines of a family. He needed someone to blame, and my father is known to support the admission of women. Ironic, really. He had his doubts, but I persuaded him.'

Prue read the self-recrimination in his face and felt the craziest urge to comfort him, to tell him that everything would be fine and even if it wasn't she would be there for him. Only he didn't want her there—unless *there* was his bed, and even then he was ashamed of anyone discovering their brief affair.

'Beat yourself up if it makes you feel better, but if he's anything at all like you I can't imagine anyone persuading your father to do anything he doesn't want to.' Pleased to see a responsive flicker of amusement in his blue eyes, she tried to raise herself up on one elbow and collapsed, wincing. 'I've hurt my arm.'

Karim slung her a look of sheer exasperation and dragged a hand through his glossy dark hair. By the tousled condition of it she suspected that it wasn't the first time he had done so. 'Hurt your arm?' he echoed. 'Hurt your arm!' He closed his eyes and lapsed into angry-sounding Arabic.

'Why are you shouting at me? If it's about me trespassing in your father's private apartments, then it wasn't intentional, and—'

'Trespassing!' he exclaimed, burying his face in his hands and groaning. 'Do you do this to me deliberately, or are you totally insane?'

Insane sounded a pretty good adjective to describe a girl who loved someone who considered her nothing more than a little light relief. Loved him so much that it hurt, with the sort of hurt that, unlike the one in her arm, wasn't going to go away any time soon.

'You took the knife that was intended for my father,' he said, in a voice that was not quite steady. 'It severed an artery. You lost a lot of blood and you almost died.'

'Now I *know* you're exaggerating.'

Karim pointed, and her eyes widened as she saw the bags—one of blood, along with one of clear fluid—that were dripping slowly into her arm.

'I feel fine.'

'Lucky you,' snarled Karim, who had never felt less fine in his life. 'You realise that since the moment I saw you I have not known a moment's peace? First my sister falls under your spell, and now my father.'

'Your father?' she echoed, mystified by his uncharacteristic outburst.

'Yes, my father. You saved his life—you are a national hero.'

Prue gave a nervous little laugh, almost sure he was joking. 'I can't be a hero—I didn't do anything. I didn't even think.'

'Well, that would be right,' he raged, unable to contain his feelings after enduring a painful interview with his father and then twelve hours of sitting at her bedside with doctors telling him that she would wake 'presently'—just what sort of word was *presently* for supposed men of science to use? 'The same way you didn't think to tell me that you were giving me your virginity.'

A gift, as his expression made clear to Prue, that had been unwanted. She already knew this, but it hurt anyway. She closed her eyes and felt warm moisture leak from her sealed eyelids and spill down her face.

'You're crying,' Karim accused, a break in his deep voice. 'What am I thinking of? You've been ill, and I start yelling at you like a madman.'

Sensing he had moved closer, Prue, her eyes still tight shut, waved her hand. 'Leave me alone, Karim. I'm fine.'

Karim touched the single tear that glittered on her

smooth cheek. 'My father was right,' he said thickly. 'My actions have made me a man he should be ashamed to acknowledge as his son.'

Prue's eyelids lifted. Sniffing, she wiped the moisture from her cheeks with the back of her hand. 'Your father said that?'

Karim stopped pacing and tilted his head in confirmation.

'I love my father, and I respect him, but I will not allow him to dictate to me who I will marry,' he said, fighting the compulsion he felt to drag her into his arms and kiss her senseless. It was only the fact that she looked so painfully fragile that stopped him. 'A doctor should be here. I'll go.'

Prue caught his arm.

'I thought he wanted you to marry Saffa?' She struggled to sit up, causing the white shapeless hospital gown she wore to slip over her uninjured shoulder. Distracted by the smooth pale curve of her shoulder, this time Karim did not attempt to stop her.

He shook his head and looked impatient. 'Oh, it's not Saffa he wants. No, it's not Saffa he's insisting I marry now.'

My God! There were others waiting in the wings? Just how many prospective brides *were* there?

'Then who does he want you to marry now?'

'You.'

Prue's hand lifted from his arm. She shook her head and said in a small voice, 'That isn't very funny.'

'I didn't think so either,' he said, folding his long length into the chair beside her bed. He planted his elbows on the arms as he levelled a brooding gaze on her pale face.

The last residual vestiges of colour fled her already parchment-pale face, and she lifted a hand in a fluttery gesture to her mouth. 'You're serious. But why? I'm just…'

'You stopped being *just* anything in this country the moment you saved his life at the risk of your own. My father, not unnaturally, feels responsible towards you, and he does not feel…erm…well disposed towards the man who seduced you. This is especially true as you were an innocent at the time. He naturally insists that man marry you.'

'How did he find out?' she asked in a stricken voice. The idea of her sex-life being the subject of gossip made Prue feel physically sick.

'I told him.'

'You did *what*?' She lowered herself gingerly back down. The pain medication—and she now realised that she had been pumped full of the stuff when she woke—was beginning to wear off.

His eyes slid from hers as he got to his feet and began to move restlessly around the bright room—which might not have felt so claustrophobically small if Karim hadn't been in it.

'Someone came directly to tell me that my father had been attacked.' A nerve ticked away like a time bomb in his lean cheek as he recalled the sequence of events in a flat voice devoid of all expression. 'Fearing the worst, I ran. When I got there I found my father had taken charge—he was ordering people around, not dying.'

'That must have been a relief,' she said, her face soft with sympathy for his scare.

He stared at her. Into the stretching silence he

released a strange strangled laugh. 'Oh, yes—it was one of those occasions when a man counts his blessings,' he ground out.

She watched in confusion as he pressed his clenched fist into his forehead and said something low and passionate in Arabic.

Then, capturing her eyes with his own, he stalked across to the bed. His eyes were suffused by an incandescent, almost febrile glow as he leaned across and lifted a strand of her pale hair from the pillow. Very slowly he let it slide through his fingers. As his hand fell to his side a slow sigh shuddered through his lean body, before he collapsed back down into the chair.

'You were lying on the floor in a pool of blood, *ma belle*.' He closed his eyes for a moment and shuddered. 'So much blood, it seemed,' he murmured, swallowing. *Moderate blood loss*, the doctors had calmly pronounced when they reached the hospital—which had not given him a very high opinion of their competence. 'I thought you were dying.' He raised his eyes to hers, struggling with the memory of a horror that would haunt him for the rest of his days. 'I was not…you understand…' He cleared his throat and lowered his gaze from hers. 'I was not in control at that point. I said and did things…'

'Things like…?' she probed tentatively.

'Things like trying to throttle the life from the creature who did this to you.' His darkened glance slid once more to the heavy dressing on her shoulder and upper chest. 'Unfortunately the guards pulled me off.'

'Nobody would blame you for that,' she protested. It would take her some time to feel very turn-the-other-cheek about him herself.

'Things like telling my father that none of this would have happened if I hadn't brought you here.'

'It wasn't your fault—it was just a freak set of circumstances.'

'My father suggested much the same. Until I told him that I had blackmailed and bullied you, then acted without honour and stolen your virginity.'

'You said that? Oh, that really wasn't a good idea, Karim.'

'My hands were red with your blood,' he said holding them up and staring at them as though they were still stained. 'I was holding you and—' He stopped and passed a hand across his face, as if to block the images that were etched into his mind. 'I was not at that moment conscious of good ideas. Later, when we knew that you would live, he took me to one side and told me that the only thing that would make him look at me with anything less than total disgust would be if I made you my bride.' A ghost of a smile flickered across his pale face.

'My father is a pragmatist. He thinks you are good breeding stock—a tigress, a woman who would make children as fierce and strong as you are. That is a slightly edited version. My father's conversation when it comes to such matters can be a little earthy, as you will no doubt discover.'

'And you told him to go to hell? Not tactful, but,' she admitted with a teary gulp, 'I don't really blame you. I shouldn't worry too much, though. He'll come around when he realises how much more suitable Saffa is.' She stopped, an arrested expression stealing across her face. 'I've had the *best* idea.'

'You have an idea?' he asked, watching her with an expression of unwilling fascination.

'Well, what if your father could see for himself what a truly awful wife I would make for you?'

'And you would assist this how? What does your great plan involve? Using the wrong fork at the dinner table, perhaps? You really do over-estimate your powers of artifice, *ma belle.*'

Which was presumably Karim's way of telling her that he knew exactly how she felt about him. 'Well, I could tell him that you're the last man in the world I would marry,' she flung, fighting the tears of humiliation she was struggling to contain. 'Which, for the record, is true. There's not a lot the King could do about that, is there?'

'Are you suggesting that the idea of marriage to me repels you?'

Unable to speak past the great knot of misery and longing in her throat, she shook her head. Marriage to Karim was a dream, and the temptation was there to take what he was offering. In her weakened condition she was seriously tempted to let herself believe that he might grow to love her. But deep down she knew that was nonsense.

'Repels is a bit strong,' she conceded. 'But marriage is certainly not now and never has been on my agenda. So you can relax, Karim. I will never marry you,' she promised, injecting a note of amusement into her voice. 'Your father might be able to bully you, but me—well, I'm a heroine. He has to be nice to me.'

Karim sucked in a deep breath, his blue eyes darkening to navy as he advanced towards her. But before he reached her side a man in a white coat walked in. He politely pretended not to hear Karim when he swore fluently in several languages.

'So, our patient is awake.' His frowning regard fixed on Prue's face, he walked to the bed, interposing himself between the glowering prince and his patient and pressing his cool fingers to her wrist. What he felt made his brows lift. 'I think, Prince Karim, that our patient needs some rest. It might be better if you left.'

When Karim did not respond he walked to the door and held it open in pointed invitation.

Karim tore his eyes from Prue's face and flashed him a scowl that would have made lesser men back down. But the medic, who was made of sterner stuff, held his ground, though he did look shaken and visibly relieved when the Crown Prince moved towards the door.

When Karim turned back at the door and looked at her, every cell in Prue's body silently screamed, *Don't leave me.* Their eyes meshed. 'Go away,' she said, before the doctor injected something into her arm that made everything go black.

CHAPTER TWELVE

THREE days she had spent in the hospital bed, making—according to the doctors and nurses—excellent progress. During that time Suzan had visited, bringing with her books, flowers and bright, breezy and totally inconsequential conversation. Of Karim there had been no sign at all.

She had told him to go away and he had. This was, she told herself, something to be glad of. She worried sometimes about the soured relationship between him and his father, but mostly she wondered if she would ever feel any less wretched. She felt so apathetic she hadn't even questioned the presence of the two large men stationed outside her door who challenged everyone, including all the nurses and doctors who entered.

Then, on the third day, someone came to call whom they didn't question.

The King of Zafsid entered alone.

'Prudence Smith,' he declared, after looking her up and down, 'you look a great deal better than the last time I saw you.'

'So do you,' she said, glad that she was not faced

with the vexatious problem of bowing or curtseying and whether she, as the daughter of parents who had considered royalty an anachronism, should or shouldn't, because she was in bed.

She spoke nothing but the truth. The man before her bore little resemblance to the frail bent figure she recalled leaning on a cane. He was upright and proud, and his gaze was uncomfortably piercing. But, knowing his son, this did not surprise her.

'You look a man in the eye. I like that. And for your bravery—I have not the words to express my thanks.' Emotion overtook him and the fierce man's black eyes filled with tears. 'You have my undying gratitude.

Embarrassed, Prue lowered her eyes. She shook her head. 'I was just there.'

'I have been speaking with my son. His role in this is something which it pains me to discuss. I have told him where his duty lies, but he still refuses to listen. It shames me,' he said heavily. 'But I can only apologise to you for Karim's callous and obdurate behaviour.'

Unable to bear hearing his father speak this way of Karim, Prue held up her hand. 'Please,' she pleaded, keeping a note of appropriate respect in her voice, 'don't say those things about Karim. I can't bear it. He loves you, and he's an honourable son, but you can't *make* a person love someone—you just can't.'

'You defend the man who seduced you?'

'Seduced me?' she scoffed, her composure tipping over into anger as she heard him speak of Karim with such cold contempt. 'If we're talking seduction you might as well say *I* seduced *him*. He didn't know I hadn't had any other lover, and I promise you that situation doesn't reflect any great moral purity on my part. I wasn't saving myself—at least not consciously. The only reason I was a virgin was I'd never met your son. If I'd met him when I was Suzan's age I'd have done everything and anything I could to end up in his bed. I wasn't an innocent. I knew that if I'd admitted I was a virgin he wouldn't have slept with me. I didn't because I wanted that more than anything. If anyone did the seducing,' she finished on a note of breathlessness, 'it was me. I'm sorry if that shocks you,' she said earnestly, 'but it's the truth.'

'So my son is an innocent victim of your feminine wiles? I'm sorry, but I find that hard to believe.'

'That's because you don't realise what a truly remarkable man he is,' she told him sternly. 'You should know better than anyone what a hard job he will have one day. Don't you think he would do that job better if he had the woman he loves beside him?'

'You have certainly helped me. You are a very forthright young woman.'

'I'm wringing every last drop of currency from the fact you think I saved your life.'

The wry confession drew a laugh from Tair Al-Ahmad.

'And if you really are grateful to me you would let Karim marry who he pleases.'

'You must love my son a great deal.'

'Far too much to marry him when he doesn't love me,' she said thickly.

'I think... Well, actually,' Tair Al-Ahmad said, walking towards the door, 'I think I should let my son speak for himself.'

Prue's jaw dropped as the door opened and Karim, dressed in jeans and a white open-necked shirt, strolled in.

'How much did you hear?' his father asked him, nothing in his manner suggesting he was surprised to see his son.

Surprised—of course he's not surprised, you idiot, she told herself. They planned it this way. God knew what either of them imagined this subterfuge would achieve beyond humiliating her, but she was past caring. She just knew that she had had enough of being manipulated by anyone called Al-Ahmad.

'Enough,' Karim said, his eyes on Prue's face.

'I trust you can manage the rest of this without my intervention?'

Karim responded to the paternal sarcasm with a smile. 'You have my gratitude.' He inclined his head respectfully as the older man left the room. When he was gone he said something abrupt to the men standing outside and closed it. 'We will not be disturbed.'

Prue felt like saying, *Speak for yourself*, because she was feeling very disturbed. If she had still been attached to the monitors they would have been bleeping like crazy.

'*Ma belle,*' Karim said, pulling a chair across to the bed. 'You seem uncharacteristically silent.'

He regarded her, his head a little to one side, and straddled the chair, his hands resting lightly across its back.

Prue bounced to her knees on the bed. 'That was a set-up,' she accused wrathfully. 'You were outside the door, listening to everything I said. What a total and absolute snake you are.'

'But a very loveable snake, apparently,' he drawled. The colour that lent prominence to his chiselled cheek-bones deepened and he said, very slowly, almost gloatingly, 'You're in love with me.' He angled her a look that challenged her to deny it.

It was a challenge that Prue, her skin burning with mortification, had no intention of accepting. 'You stay right there,' she quavered, stabbing a finger in his direction as he showed signs of getting to his feet. 'If you come near me I'll scream.'

'You will find that the guards can be selectively deaf.' Deep-set eyes glittering, skin pulled taut across the bones of his incredible face... She could and probably should have felt threatened. She didn't, because she figured there was nothing he could do that would make her feel any worse than she did at that moment.

He knew she loved him, so she didn't even have the shreds of her dignity to pull protectively around her.

Of course fear would have been a lot healthier than what she did feel when their eyes locked and her hormones surged in reaction to his raw, rampant masculinity, the sheer danger he exuded. She knew that some women responded to danger in a man, but she wasn't one of them—and so she would keep telling herself.

'That I can well believe,' she retorted into the lengthening silence. He was dangerous, yet she had felt safe in his arms—safe enough to be able to lower her defences when they made love in a way she had never imagined being able to do with a man.

'You look more like yourself.'

'Well, it has been three days.' She bit her lip, hearing the resentment that had slipped into her voice, knowing that he must have heard it too.

'The doctors said I could not come if I was going to upset you. I gave you a fever.'

He'd been doing that from the moment they met. 'You're upsetting me now.'

'You're on the road to recovery now, and unlike the doctors I know you're a lot tougher than you look.'

Serve him right if she dropped dead at his feet, she thought resentfully.

'And that is also a much prettier nightgown than the one you were wearing last time.' His eyes darkened as they slid to the shadowy cleft between her heaving breasts, revealed by the deep vee of her thin flower-sprigged nightdress.

'You are totally disgusting.'

'And yet despite these flaws you still love me?'

'Will you stop saying that?' she screeched. 'My God, I give up trying to work out the way your twisted mind works, but your great plan—whatever it was—has certainly backfired this time. I was just getting through to your father—I really think he was ready to agree to let you marry who you want. I was about to remind him that you put duty ahead of your personal happiness once before, and that it was very wrong of him and unfair to expect you to do the same thing again.'

'I would,' he admitted, 'have liked to be a fly on the wall when you gave that lecture.' He shook his head, giving her a look of amusement. 'You don't have the faintest idea, do you? It is pretty well accepted—certainly by my father—that he is infallible. I can see that you think that is absurd, but you must remember that he came to the throne when he was barely twenty. He has been a feudal ruler with total power since that moment. People do not tell him he is wrong.'

'Well, he *is* wrong. And I don't want him to be angry with you because of me.'

'And you love me, so you want me to be happy even if that happiness does not include you?'

Cheeks flushed with mortification, Prue lowered her eyes. She had no idea why he was going out of his way to be cruel.

'I suppose you expect me to be lost in admiration for such noble sacrifice?'

Her eyes flew upwards.

'Of course not,' she grunted, brushing the stray tears from her cheeks.

'Good—because I'm not.' He fixed her with a fierce, steely-eyed glare that made it easy to believe him when he said, 'If the woman I did not feel whole without did not love me back I would not wish her well, *ma belle.*' White-knuckled fists clenched, he leaned forward and declared in a softly deadly purr, 'I would do anything within my power to take her away from the man she preferred to me, and I would hope that she would spend every moment of the rest of her life suffering as I surely would.'

Prue's stomach churned with a misery she knew would get a lot worse later, when she had time to replay this conversation in her head. Did he really imagine she wanted his love for Saffa spelt out? Did he really imagine she wanted to know that he felt incomplete without the other woman?

'Does there always have to be another man? Couldn't a woman just prefer to be alone?' Not that she could imagine Karim's chosen bride making that choice.

'With some women maybe that is true. But not you, *ma belle*. You were not designed to live alone. Or, for that matter, to love any man but me.'

This silky addition Prue ignored as she replied, though she had a depressing suspicion it was true. 'Well, I've been looking after myself for twenty-four years, and anyway we're not talking about me.'

'I am.'

She shook her head and looked at him warily. Not a muscle in his face moved. His unblinking stare remained trained fierce and compelling on her face. 'I don't understand.'

'That much is obvious,' he retorted drily. 'Though I think perhaps I too needed a shove towards understanding myself. Holding the woman you love in your arms when you think she is dying is quite a shove.'

She looked at him, seeing the shadow of dark memories surface in his incredible blue eyes. A little sliver of hope took root, but she wouldn't let herself quite believe. 'You don't love me—you said so.'

'I have never said that.'

'You said that you wouldn't marry me just because your father told you to.'

His head lifted, and the hauteur bred into his bones was very apparent as he smiled thinly and announced proudly, 'And I won't.'

'You want to marry Saffa. Everyone knows that.'

He disposed of *everyone* with a contemptuous click of his long fingers. 'I did imagine that I loved her when we were both young,' he admitted. 'But it was nothing more than a flirtation, really. As a young man

I was inclined towards intensity. Saffa gave me just enough encouragement, but kept me at arm's length. I think she enjoyed seeing me struggle to contain my feelings,' he observed dispassionately.

Prue could no longer contain her own feelings. 'Well, I think she sounds callous and heartless. And how she can leave those two lovely little girls here while she spends all her time in Paris or wherever, I don't know.'

'Well, you'd better marry me—or who knows? I might end up in the evil woman's clutches.'

'Don't make fun of me, Karim,' she begged, her heart quickening as he rose to his feet and walked purposefully towards the hospital bed. He lowered himself onto the edge and, reaching across, ran a finger down her cheek. The tender glow in his eyes made her own eyes fill with emotional tears.

'Saffa is not important. If I ever harboured any romantic feelings towards her they died the night she turned up at my apartment in Paris. She and Hassan had been married for about eighteen months at the time. She suggested there was no reason we could not conduct a discreet liaison.'

'You had an affair?'

For a moment a spasm of fastidious distaste distorted the sensually sculpted line of his firm lips. 'I did not,' he retorted, his face taut with anger. 'She was my brother's wife—what do you think I am? Hassan was no saint, but he did not deserve that.'

'Sorry—I shouldn't have assumed. It's just that she's very beautiful…' And when it came to Karim she was so jealous she couldn't think straight.

The anger faded from his face as abruptly as it had

appeared. 'I have not displayed much moral restraint around you, *ma belle*,' he admitted with a self-recriminatory grimace. 'So it is hardly surprising that you doubt me. But, no, you are the only woman I have no control around, *cherie*.'

This throaty admission made Prue's head spin dizzily. 'I did have some say in what happened between us,' she reminded him. 'I was not exactly an unwilling victim.'

'No, you were so sweet, so warm and loving, you took my breath away,' he confided huskily. 'In fact you have been taking my breath away on a regular basis from the first moment we met,' he admitted gravely. 'You gave so much of yourself and you asked nothing in return. I only wish I could have received the gift you gave me with the same grace you gave it.'

The expression in his eyes swept away the last of Prue's doubts. The joy that exploded inside her found release in tears, which spilled unchecked from her eyes.

'You're crying—what have I done?'

Smiling a watery smile, she lifted a loving finger to his lips. 'These are tears of happiness.'

'*Dieu*, I can't tell you what it did to me to discover that I was your first lover. I felt as if I'd violated your innocence.'

Prue couldn't let that pass. 'I was pretty damned happy to be violated, Karim.'

'I could have hurt you.'

'You didn't. You were—you *are*—perfect. When you didn't come near me I thought that you…'

'I couldn't come near you. I was ashamed that I had hurt you, shown no finesse or tenderness. And when we spoke last I did not articulate my feelings well.'

'You were angry,' she recalled, wishing that he would articulate them now. Until he did she couldn't quite allow herself to believe this was happening.

'I was distraught,' he corrected grimly. 'I had sat all night beside your bed, knowing that my actions had placed you in danger. I kept reliving the moment when I thought I had lost you. I had a speech all prepared—the things I would say to you. I planned on sharing the irony of my father commanding me to marry you when that was the one thing that I wanted to do more than anything.'

'You wanted to marry me?'

He nodded. 'But I didn't want you to imagine even for one second that my proposal had anything to do with his edict, or guilt, or anything but the knowledge that you are the other half of my soul.' He expelled a shuddering sigh as his hands came up to frame her face.

'Oh, I know that you will say a person cannot fall in love so quickly, and I might once have agreed with you. But I think I fell in love with you that very first moment. I might not have admitted it to myself,' he conceded, 'but my every action since has been designed to keep you close. All the time I spent at my father's bedside I couldn't get you out of my head. I kept seeing your face—when I was awake and when I was asleep.'

'No.'

He stilled, wariness sliding into his eyes as he scanned the soft contours of her tear-stained face. 'No?'

'No, I would *not* say that a person cannot fall in love that quickly. They can. I know, because I did.'

With a cry Karim gathered her in his arms and, drawing her face up to his, kissed her with a tenderness that brought a fresh rush of tears to her eyes. He touched her shoulder. It was the first day her wound had not been hidden behind a bulky dressing.

Prue peeled her nightdress back. 'The scar is not very pretty,' she said apologetically.

'It is your badge of courage. Wear it with pride and when it is healed I will kiss it, in fact I will kiss every inch of you.'

'That's a lot of kisses. Perhaps,' she suggested, flashing him a flirtatious smile, 'you should start now?'

'If I forget where I left off I might have to start again.'

'I can live with that,' she said, trailing a loving finger down his lean cheek.

As he bent his head to kiss her Karim paused. 'Are you sure, *ma belle*, that you know what you are taking on with me?'

Prue knew what he was saying. 'I know you come as a package—the man, the country. But the thing is, Karim, I can't live without the man, and actually I rather love this country. I have only one condition.'

'Name it.'

'I want to spend my honeymoon in a Bedouin tent.'

His wolfish grin flashed out. 'That I think I can arrange. I will even wait on you myself.'

'I suppose you're a brilliant cook too?' she teased.

'I am brilliant at most things,' he said modestly.

Prue grabbed his shirt-front. 'But now,' she admitted, 'there's only one thing you're brilliant at that I'm interested in.'

His husky laughter rang out as he slid a hand behind her head and tilted her face up to him. 'Tell me more.'

Prue did—but only after he had stopped kissing her.

Mediterranean Brides

**Two billionaires, one Greek, one Spanish—
will they claim their unwilling brides?**

Meet Sandor and Miguel, men who've taken all the prizes
when it comes to looks, power, wealth and arrogance.
Now they want marriage with two beautiful women.
But this time, for the first time, both Mediterranean
billionaires have met their matches and it will take more
than money or cool to tame their unwilling mistresses—
try seduction, passion and possession!

Eleanor Wentworth has always been unloved and
unwanted. Greek tycoon Sandor Christofides has wealth
and acclaim—all he needs is Eleanor as his bride.
But is Ellie just a pawn in the billionaire's game?

BOUGHT:
THE GREEK'S BRIDE
by Lucy Monroe

On sale June 2007.

www.eHarlequin.com   HP12636

REQUEST YOUR FREE BOOKS!

2 FREE NOVELS FROM THE ROMANCE/SUSPENSE COLLECTION PLUS 2 FREE GIFTS!

BOB07